KR JUN 2013

D0462142

*"And you are lovea* ........sly open, Sean spoke into her mind. *"I will always love you and keep you. Now, go to sleep."*

In the stillness that followed, he grinned. She had bewitched him but not broken his will. Not that he wouldn't like to let her break it.

A moment later, he felt the caress.

From his neck, over his chest, into the dip at his navel, down the slender line of dark hair below, the wickedly magical fingers progressed like a hot sigh in the night.

Sean held still. Since she wasn't physically with him, he couldn't do a thing to either stop or assist her. *"I think you should go to sleep, Elin."* His mind didn't pant so she wouldn't know he could hardly breathe, that his body was damp all over, that while he spoke like a schoolmaster to a difficult child he was dying for want of her finishing this long, exquisite torture.

КЯ JUN 2013

# ACCLAIM FOR *DARKNESS BOUND*

"Welcome to a thrilling new world where suspense runs *wild* (literally)! I devoured this book, I drooled over the hero, and now I'm panting for the next one in the series. Sexy, spooky, and suspenseful! Read this inside with the doors locked!"

**—Kerrelyn Sparks, *New York Times*
bestselling author**

"4½ stars! No matter what the genre, you can always count on the gifted Cameron to deliver an exciting tale filled with passion and thrills. Cameron launches her sizzling Chimney Rock series featuring werehounds and other supernatural creatures. Dark things are stirring on Whidbey Island, which means that for lucky readers, chills and thrills aren't far behind!"

**—*RT Book Reviews***

"*Darkness Bound* is filled with interesting characters, and a multitude of paranormal creatures...The writing is crisp, and the dialogue often amusing...I look forward to reading the next book in the series."

**—RomRevToday.com**

"Take one mysterious and sexy man combined with one woman looking for a new beginning, stir in some paranormal forces, and you have *Darkness Bound*...Full of suspense, passion, and discovery that had me fully engaged until the end."

**—JoyfullyReviewed.com**

# *darkness* BRED

# ALSO BY STELLA CAMERON

*Darkness Bound*

# *darkness* BRED

A Chimney Rock Novel

## STELLA CAMERON

FOREVER

NEW YORK    BOSTON

This book is a work of fiction. Names, characters, places, and incidents are the product of the author's imagination or are used fictitiously. Any resemblance to actual events, locales, or persons, living or dead, is coincidental.

Copyright © 2013 by Stella Cameron

All rights reserved. In accordance with the U.S. Copyright Act of 1976, the scanning, uploading, and electronic sharing of any part of this book without the permission of the publisher is unlawful piracy and theft of the author's intellectual property. If you would like to use material from the book (other than for review purposes), prior written permission must be obtained by contacting the publisher at permissions@hbgusa.com. Thank you for your support of the author's rights.

Forever
Hachette Book Group
237 Park Avenue
New York, NY 10017

www.HachetteBookGroup.com

Printed in the United States of America

First Edition: May 2013
10 9 8 7 6 5 4 3 2 1

OPM

Forever is an imprint of Grand Central Publishing.
The Forever name and logo are trademarks of Hachette Book Group, Inc.

The Hachette Speakers Bureau provides a wide range of authors for speaking events. To find out more, go to www.hachettespeakersbureau.com or call (866) 376-6591.

The publisher is not responsible for websites (or their content) that are not owned by the publisher.

**ATTENTION CORPORATIONS AND ORGANIZATIONS:**

Most Hachette Book Group books are available at quantity discounts with bulk purchase for educational, business, or sales promotional use. For information, please call or write:

**Special Markets Department, Hachette Book Group**
**237 Park Avenue, New York, NY 10017**
**Telephone: 1-800-222-6747 Fax: 1-800-477-5925**

# *darkness* BRED

# *prologue*

*5 years ago*
*Chinatown, San Francisco*

It was already too late.

Before the bouncer let him into the club, before the doors closed behind him, before he walked through a crowded hallway toward silver lights pulsing in time to mind-pounding music and a wildly spinning stream of shining reflections around magenta walls—it was too late.

A man hustling a woman up the stairs from the sidewalk outside had looked back at Sean Black and stood still for the beat of one long, triumphant stare. Then they had gone inside.

And Sean had followed like a jumper to the edge of a cliff.

He could never forget that face, the sharp, predatory features, the sneer creased across his almost lipless mouth. In the back room of a saloon in Creed, Colorado, Sean saved the man's life, and in thanks, the man had as good as taken his.

"Why, Jacob O'Cleary as I live and breathe," a smoke-stained voice ground into Sean's ear. "What a surprise to see you. Small world, as they say." The man had waited for him to follow, known he would. Holding the elbow of a young brunette whose eyes were too big for her face and scoured a puffy purple underneath, he walked ahead into the surging crowd.

Hearing his birth name for the first time in far more than a century jolted Sean. *Jacob O'Cleary*, and that was the only name this ancient werehound knew him by.

*Walk the other way, Sean.*

Only he couldn't because it was already too late.

Trolling San Francisco's Chinatown late on a Saturday night didn't happen by accident, not to Sean Black. Whispers through his own hidden world that a bad news character known only as Aldo had been sighted in the area and was asking about him had brought Sean to the city. He expected to spend days, maybe even weeks, tracking Aldo—not to all but fall over the guy.

But of course, Aldo had planned it that way. He needed to taste the power of dominating a superior intellect again, and that could only mean that Aldo had started to deteriorate.

Once through the entry hall, the place was bigger than it looked from the outside, with rocking, rubbing bodies mashed together on a central dance floor and tables all around the edge. There were booths for those who wanted privacy for whatever reason, and plenty of stools along a big bar for parties less concerned about their conspicuousness.

Sean looked around and quickly identified a number

of vampires and a shapeshifter in drag. What the shapeshifter might be without the curly red wig and four-inch heels would take Sean longer to figure out. The vamp groupies, male and female, were impossible to miss. Their fawning advances on those they desired were sickening, but the often degrading looks, touches, and even painfully administered physical rebuffs didn't stop them from pleading again to be used.

With the exhausted and scared-looking woman balanced on a stool, Aldo stood at the far right end of the bar. A tall, thickset man with oiled black hair that made a heavy blunt-ended helmet curving to his earlobes, he would be hard to miss.

Other patrons, most of them high almost to insanity, gaped but still had enough sense left to give Aldo plenty of space.

Aldo leaned back, bracing his elbows on the bar—staring straight at Sean. And his look as good as ordered Sean to go to him. They hadn't seen each other in over a century, but the look in Aldo's hooded red-brown eyes said he didn't doubt his power over the one he thought of as his escaped slave. Aldo expanded his chest and flexed muscle inside a skin-hugging green T-shirt.

Only he was not as massive as Sean became in his dense blue-black coat, and neither did Aldo share—nor was he aware of—the rare twist that helped bind Sean and the rest of his Team together.

Like his alpha, Niles, and those they regarded as brothers, Sean had even deadlier strength as a human than as a hound.

Sean braced his feet apart and crossed his arms. With

his eyes he dared the other one to try proving his superiority.

Aldo pulled the woman off her stool and she winced. Sean had no doubt that her tight-fitting sleeves hid bruising—or that when she was naked, her voluptuous body would be covered with marks of domination.

Tears shone in her eyes, eyes that Sean realized didn't focus. He took a step toward the couple. Aldo held his companion up. From the way she started to slump, Sean figured she would fall without support.

"How've you been?" Aldo said, his nostrils flaring despite the wider grin on his mouth—only on his mouth. He came closer, shuffling the girl along with him. "Let's see. Where was it we last met?" With one pointed forefinger, he tapped his chin.

"Do you need help, ma'am?" Sean asked the woman quietly. "Just say the word and I'll get you out of here."

"He always was an interfering fool," Aldo said, leaning down to put his head close to hers. "Don't worry, Lily. I'll make sure he doesn't take you from me." He tutted. "Still trying to pick off other men's women, Jacob? I would have expected you to be more mature by now."

Sean saw it then, what he had feared, the oblivious stare some drugs brought. Lily blinked slowly at Aldo and leaned, her face turned up to his.

"What's your game this time?" Sean said. "She needs to go home."

"She belongs to me," Also said through his teeth, his lips barely moving. "What I want, I own. You know that."

"Why are you here now?" Sean asked.

"I came for you."

Sean laughed. "Generous of you, but no thanks. I've got all the friends I need."

"Friends? I need no friends. You and I have unfinished business. I want you and you belong to me."

Sean forced down the urge to take this vermin by the throat. He ought to get out before he lost any of his control, yet he could not leave this helpless girl with Aldo, and neither could he go without attempting to turn the vicious animal into a toothless joke.

With his fingers sticking into Lily's thin arm, Aldo made to pass Sean.

"Leaving so soon?" Sean said. "Why did you come at all?"

Aldo's awful grin split his face again. "Did I say I was leaving?" he whispered hoarsely. "The fun has only just begun. Look around you. Everyone shares here and I must share Lily." He swept one arm wide. "My entertainment first, then theirs."

"Let her go," Sean said. He made sure that although his body might seem relaxed, every muscle and nerve was ready to spring.

Whatever Aldo had given or done to her was making Lily increasingly disoriented and helpless.

"Enough," Sean said, keeping his voice low but penetrating enough to get to Aldo. "If you want to push someone around, try me." He beckoned with both hands.

"Who could ask for anything more?" Aldo said and his red-brown eyes turned hot. "But sometimes a man wants to be chased. You come and get me this time."

The breath Sean drew in took long enough for Aldo to

slash a claw down the front of Lily's body. Sean reacted instantly.

He sliced the side of his right hand into the narrow space beneath Aldo's nose, and drove hard.

Aldo shook his head, blood flying from his nose, and bared his teeth. "Defending a whore's honor," he said. "How touching. She's here because she wants to be. Do you think I looked for something like her? She wants me and what only I can give her."

He threw Lily into the arms of a gawking, spotty kid who looked underage. This one held her up and gazed, fascinated. When he parted his lips, a double row of sharply pointed teeth showed and his ears began to elongate. He was some sort of fae.

Sean made a move to grab the woman away, but he felt as much as saw Aldo swing something through the air and whirled around in time to block a bottle heading for his own face.

The powerful hand that held the bottle connected with Sean's shoulder and glass shattered, hung in the air in a net of glittering shards, then sprayed over the nearest patrons.

Only in the farthest reaches of the club did people continue to dance and laugh, and ply themselves with whatever made them feel invincible.

Scuffles broke out, and shrieks. People bled from glass-inflicted wounds, most of them small, unlike the one on Sean's shoulder that soaked his shirt.

Sean's arm would heal soon enough. No time for giving in to pain. He hauled the woman away. Aldo was using her because he knew Sean would intervene to help her. Regardless of why she was here, or what choices she might have made, now she was suffering because of him and she was his responsibility.

The music stopped, but the screaming and panic raging around him rose like a shifting wall of sound. Weight on his back, pressing him down on Lily, infuriated him but he dared not show the full extent of his strength. To do so would mean that too many questions would circulate and an advantage could be lost to his Team forever.

"Two choices," a familiar, gravelly voice hissed into his ear. Aldo lifted Sean's head by the hair and slammed it down on Lily's. Then, under the cover of a confusing scuffle, he landed a kick to the vulnerable spot at her temple.

Sean managed to make enough room to stare at her face, at her glazed, staring eyes. They were the eyes of death now. "You've killed her," he shouted, breathing in blood from his own nose. "You've goddamn killed her."

"How can an upstanding man like you make up such lies?" Aldo ground out. "You attacked her and I'm trying to pull you off. And that's what the police will believe if you don't do what I want."

"Get out of my way." Sean heaved upward but Aldo clung to him, his face stretched into its foul, lipless grin.

"Too bad about that," he said, jerking his head toward Lily's corpse. "A little collateral damage. All I want is you. We only have seconds. Join me and you'll never be attached to any of this. Refuse and they'll get you for murder—if the crowd doesn't tear you apart first. There are enough of our kind here to do it."

"I'm not your kind," Sean spat out. "The answer's no. I'll take my chances."

"Change your mind—now," Aldo said, his smile gone. "You won't want for anything, ever."

"Never."

"I'll hunt you, Jacob. No matter what kind of noble little life you think you've created, I'll always be there to take it away. You'll never be free of me."

Sean stared into Aldo's cold eyes. Sirens wailed faintly in the distance. "I'll die before I give in."

Seen in San Francisco newspapers the following day:

Last night Jacob O'Cleary was arrested at a club in Chinatown and later charged with murder. During the night O'Cleary escaped custody. A full-scale manhunt is in progress.

Reported six months later:

Local authorities admit that there has been no progress in the search for accused murderer Jacob O'Cleary. No useful leads have been brought forward, but the police vow to keep the case open.

## *chapter* ONE

*The present*
*Whidbey Island, Washington State*

Elin was the supposed daughter of Tarhazian, Queen of the Fae. In fact, Tarhazian had stolen Elin as a baby. Tarhazian's excuse was that even then it was obvious Elin was uniquely talented and she needed the best of training to reach her potential. That was all Elin knew of her beginnings—all she had to tie her to who she had been, other than the few anonymous mementos Tarhazian passed off as evidence of her wish for Elin to know everything about herself.

But after asking only once for information about where she came from and who she had been with, Elin had known better than to ask a second time. Tarhazian had muttered, "You are *my* ungrateful child. You were in the hands of a demon and you'll return there if you question me again."

She wanted to know who she was, and living Tarhazian's imaginary perfect life, perpetually kept like a bright plaything to be displayed from time to time, was over. She was a woman, a passionate, independent woman.

For many months, since Elin had made Tarhazian angry enough to so-called banish her from the kingdom, Elin had lived with Sally, also a banned member of the fae community. Elin knew Tarhazian had not expected her co-opted child to actually leave her and the Queen made frequent overtures to get her back. That couldn't happen, or not willingly on Elin's part. She was moving on.

Sometimes that thought was exciting, sometimes frightening.

In Sally's magic shop on the outskirts of the pretty town of Langley, Elin slept among purple-lighted trees, buckets of wands, masks, shoes that promised to make you go far or keep you where you were, spells and costumes, books humans didn't know existed, and secrets in every tiny nook and cranny.

Whenever Elin considered the human community, she felt conflicted and confused. The kinship she felt with them didn't make sense but it was there nevertheless and grew stronger since Sally had tentatively suggested Elin might be more human than she knew.

She took a deep breath and grabbed the floral silk messenger bag Sally had made for her. The bag had been Sally's seal-of-approval gift before she left Elin earlier that evening.

Tonight Elin was to start a new life. She was certain she loved the man, the werehound Sean Black, and they intended to find out if they were destined to be mates.

Elin's and Sean's fascination with each other had been

what angered Tarhazian so much to begin with. "You must choose between that hound and me," she had threatened. Elin had chosen not to risk turning her back on Sean and regretting it forever.

The horrible threats Tarhazian had since added were constantly at the back of Elin's mind, but she couldn't give up now.

Loud purring stopped her for a moment. She had expected this but that didn't make it easier that Pokey, her very small pet guinea pig, was furious that her buddy Elin was up to something different. Or perhaps frightened by it. Pokey hated bags—she had traveled in one from the fae reservation, but she preferred to be safe in Elin's pocket.

"You're right," Elin said, "I'm leaving and I'm not sure where I'm going. I won't be until I've seen Sean. We don't know what comes next. Just hang with me, kid. I'll look after you."

The purr only got louder.

"I don't have time to cuddle you," Elin said, even though she couldn't see Pokey in whatever bed she had already chosen for the night.

Elin packed a little cloth doll, and her tattered blanket went into the bottom of her bag. The doll she had always had, or for as long as she remembered.

Pulling the floppy little creature out again, she kissed her faded, embroidered face and felt stupid at the tears that started. She never cried—Tarhazian didn't like it if her little darling cried.

She cried now; silly sobbing choked into hiccups. A few items of clothing went in on top of the doll. Sally had promised to get more things to her once she knew where she would be.

Another forever possession was the carved bamboo bird that burbled when you filled the bowl beneath the beak with water and blew through the stem. Just looking at its frayed little head made her smile again. She had taught herself to make the bamboo warblers but her old one was precious.

A car passed on the street outside, its tires grinding on gravel, and Elin held her breath for fear someone would come to the door. The car paused, as they often did when passing Sally's shop, but then the engine took off once more.

In a blue velvet bag lay a fine gold bracelet too small for any adult wrist. She only had it because as a child she had seen Tarhazian looking at it and begged to try it on.

"I thought I had shown it to you," Tarhazian said, feigning surprise. "You can have anything you want, my dear. Here, let's put it on."

The bracelet, adorned with a single circular disk, fitted snugly. "Well, wear it for a little while," Tarhazian said. "Then we'll put it away again. It's not really big enough for you."

But Elin never gave it back although she doubted it was forgotten. One word was engraved on the disk: Wise. She held it in her palm now and felt the familiar tingling it brought every time. Without any chance of finding out the truth, Elin was convinced this bracelet had been on her arm when Tarhazian first took her. She replaced it in its blue velvet pouch and pushed it deep into her bag.

Already late, if she didn't go now, Sean might think

she'd changed her mind and leave without her. He must have heard how uncertain she was about a total break with her past.

What sounded a lot like "whee," but was actually Pokey squealing, preceded the animal's plop on top of Elin's possessions in the bag. Curly whiskers wiggled and red eyes glowed up at her before Pokey worked her stiff orange and white fur between the clothes.

Elin let herself out and ran around to the back of Sally's house to a hidden garden where she would never be seen taking off to fly south.

She held the bag in her arms and left on her journey.

The expected rush of wind beat around her, tossed the many points at the hem of her silk dress, and wrapped them around her legs. Her long hair blew straight back. Elin had come this way many times before and needed only to think of the path to take it.

*Humans can't fly.* Of course they couldn't, and whenever she entertained the idea that she could perhaps be human, she soon remembered how foolish it was. *They also don't shapeshift.*

\* \* \*

Sean Black waited for her in a forest on the south shores of Washington's Whidbey Island. He offered her the hope of her own future—with him—even though they were still strangers in so many ways.

She quickly reached the place they had agreed on and hovered far above the small clearing in dense trees.

Sean was there, waiting for her. She felt more than

saw him and concentrated on the changes he'd made in her.

With her ebony hair streaming across her face, Elin settled where a limb joined the massive trunk of a towering Douglas fir and watched him, wondering what he was thinking. Sean's thoughts were closed to her but she felt his turmoil. Smiling, she reached out with her senses to touch him, and closed her eyes at his tensed reaction.

Tonight she was glad she could fly, and even shapeshift into the little cat, Skillywidden. The combination allowed her freedoms she would miss if they were taken from her.

When they first met while Sean's alpha werehound, Niles, had been pursuing a mate and Elin became the go-between for all parties, she had appeared as the small, gray, violet-eyed Skillywidden. Sean was in his very large, very intimidating werehound form, Blue, a huge, blue-black animal with golden eyes, the same color as his human eyes. As Skillywidden and Blue, they had become the go-between for all parties.

Even then the unlikely pair seemed compatible. In the following months the hound and the exotic cat met only as humans. They were not lovers, although Elin longed to join with Sean. He would only say that he could not lie with her unless they were to become mates.

And tonight they had come to tell each other what decisions they had made about the future—to go their separate ways, or risk suffering Tarhazian's threats by beginning a life together.

The woman she had called her mother had made the ultimate threat. She could bind herself to Sean if she must, but unless she wanted them both to live in the pain of separation forever, separation from the worlds they knew and separation from each other, Elin must become Tarhazian's spy on the Werehound Team.

The Queen, her delving eyes seeking Elin's innermost thoughts, left not a shred of hope for reprieve. "Fail me and you shall still never truly have him. You will see him and he will see you, but your skin will not touch his, your flesh will never join with his, and when your voices cry out, begging for solace, the words will be like dust falling on snow."

*  *  *

Sean Black felt the beat of his heart.

He heard it. And the shallow in, out, of his own breaths.

Awareness tightened the muscles in his shoulders. Not for the first time, his skin registered a light stroking, as of fingertips brushing across him.

Night had fallen, but from the forest clearing where he waited for Elin, he could see the moon's sheen on a blue-gray sky far above his head where the swaying crowns of giant firs seemed to prick the heavens.

Sean drew in the scent of those firs, the scent of their sap, of the thick carpet of fallen needles beneath his feet.

Heaven or hell.

If he defied the orders of his alpha werehound, Niles, and the wishes of the rest of their Team, and failed to break with Elin, he could be cast away from his own kind.

For the first time in the five years since the horror of being used as a killing weapon in San Francisco, Sean had true hope. In the black hours when sleep wouldn't come, he imagined Aldo appearing on Whidbey and trying to destroy what Sean had built with the Werehound Team. He wasn't foolish enough to feel too safe from the werewolf who had promised never to give up hunting for Sean.

To turn from Elin would mean the loss of the only woman he could love, the woman the other werehounds said had enchanted him, cast a spell on him. She would, they insisted, use him to spy on the hounds for their werewolf enemies, or for the local vampire scourge, who could sell the information to the wolves for blood. Almost worse, Elin could become the ultimate tool of the seething fae community bent on outwitting all of them.

Tonight he must make his choice.

\* \* \*

Without a sound, they touched. Sean shuddered and closed his eyes. She could do that, arrive silently and set him afire with nothing more than a fleeting caress with her fingertips. Sometimes all he had to do to feel her was to think about them being together.

Then he heard her.

Elin cried softly and he reached for her dark shape in the gloom. She evaded his hands and slipped from his sight. She slipped away only to layer herself against his back, her floating silk gown no barrier between his naked skin and her soft breasts.

He could not move. Since they met, their meetings had been stolen moments to talk, haltingly in whispers, while something deep wound them more and more tightly together until this time for decisions came.

No commitment had been made. There was so much they didn't know about each other yet, but the fusion of their hearts had become a thing of beauty and pain, and a point where Sean feared that to break away forever would be like death.

Her body, from her cheek, to the pressure of her hips, her slender thighs, and her toes against his heels, inflamed him until he was so tense he gritted his teeth to remain still.

Sean found her arms and wrapped them around him, trapped them to hold her tight against him, and looked up at the sky again.

When they met alone, it must be in darkness and he came in his hound form, with the excuse that he needed to make sure of his ability to shift. Before he saw Elin, he always changed into a man who could not help being aware of his size and power when he was with her diminutive form.

And as a man, he had no choice but to be naked after he shifted. Another reason to meet in the darkness and keep himself mostly hidden from her. She seemed so young to him, young and unworldly, yet more unconsciously seductive than he could have imagined in any female, no matter how experienced. And so often she spoke with a wisdom that surprised and pleased him— and puzzled him. Her mystery, the dichotomy between innocent girl and wise woman, intoxicated him.

Her tears were wet on his back but she dropped kiss after kiss along his spine.

"Come here," he said, keeping his voice soft but steady. "Let me see you."

Effortlessly, he pulled her around him until he could gaze down into her face. The bag she carried pleased him. He could hope it meant that she would agree to come with him.

She looked at the ground, stepped back a little, and stared at him through the shield of darkness as if she saw him clearly. He believed she did and smiled a little.

When she reached for him again, she stroked his chest, his sides, his belly, before she popped up to her toes and passed her lips fleetingly over his.

Seeking to capture her mouth and deepen the kiss, Sean reached for her. Elin evaded him and sank rapidly lower to play the satiny tips of her fingers over his pulsing flesh as lightly as a feather made of burning breeze.

While he could still think, Sean caught her hand. "Not yet," he said. "Perhaps never. The decision will be ours eventually, and it will be forever."

"But the punishment may be inevitable," Elin said. "Whatever we decide, they intend to sentence us to a living death."

## *chapter* TWO

Gabriel's Place, a Whidbey Island eatery and bar near the town of Langley, had a thriving base of regular customers—but not at three in the morning.

The most neutral and safest place the hounds could use for a meeting, Gabriel's didn't attract the local werewolves, who had no interest in fraternizing with humans, and other than Dr. Saul VanDoren, vampires did not venture there since they could not enter without invitation. They had never been invited. Saul was the exception because among the humans he was known as an eccentric doctor, not as a vampire.

Apart from Sally, assistant cook at Gabriel's, and now Elin, both of whom were banished by their Queen, visits from the fae world that was invisible to humans were rare. Occasionally fae disguised themselves so that they could move among the mortal community and there were always those fae, like Elin and Sally, who could pass as humans in their normal states.

Wind roared in the chimney, whipping up flames and crackling sparks from the fire. The log building was tight, cozy, and fragrant with the scent of cedar, but sounds of a storm outside had started in the past hour and scatterings of debris hit the dark window glass.

Only Niles Latimer, alpha werehound, and his sealed mate, Leigh, sat at a large, round table not far from the fireplace. Sally, also included in the early morning gathering, had hidden herself in the kitchen, away from Niles's mounting irritation. The owner of the place, Gabriel Jones, had left Leigh to lock up. She worked there and pretty much ran the business anyway.

"They should have been here two hours ago," Niles said, jerking out of his chair and plunking his fists on top of the table to brace his weight.

He stared at the front doors as if he could will Sean and Elin to materialize.

Leigh wasn't certain he couldn't actually do that but Niles was not one to interfere with his Team if it could be avoided.

*Change the subject.* Say anything, Leigh thought to herself. "At least we managed to talk Gabriel out of painting the inside of this place green," she said with a hopeful smile. "I love the peeled logs. They smell wonderful."

Niles stared at her, a bemused look on his face.

"Remember the last time Molly got in a big snit?" Molly was Gabriel's on-again, off-again girlfriend. "Gabriel bought all that paint because she said she wanted that place green.

"Now he wants to call this a bistro. That would mean changing the beautiful sign Sally had made." The neon sign was, in Gabriel's words, a flashing, neon monstrosity.

"What are you talking about?" Niles said.

"Forget it," Leigh said. "Have patience with Sean and Elin. They have so little time together. A romantic like you should sympathize."

"I'm not a romantic," he said gruffly, but he looked at Leigh and sucked in the corners of his mouth. "Except around you."

She pulled a chair close beside her and patted the seat. "Come here." If she had her way, they would never be parted, not for an hour. "I need you near me."

Niles's wavy black hair reached his collar, more than reached it, and his striking face mesmerized Leigh as much in this early morning as it had when they first met.

He sighed like a harassed man and loped to drop into the chair. Big, huge beside Leigh, Niles was all muscle. At the moment beard stubble darkened his jaw and accentuated the electric blue of his eyes.

"It won't work for them," he said, lacing the fingers of his right hand into those of Leigh's left. He took her hand to his lips and kissed the back softly. "What you think and what you want are more important to me than anyone else will ever know. But you will have to trust me to do what's right for the Team. It isn't safe for Sean and Elin to be together."

"Why?" She already knew his reasons, but perhaps if he had to talk about them aloud enough times, he'd realize they could be overcome.

"It's too dangerous," he said.

"That's what they said about us."

"We were different, we still are. You aren't attached to an entire nation of unpredictable whack jobs ruled by a woman who wants to control everyone on Whidbey."

"There are lots of really good fae. And Elin isn't attached to their community anymore. She's been cast out before, but now that it's gotten around that she and Sean are seeing each other, her separation from Tarhazian is permanent. Why would you want to push Elin out, too? Niles, you're kind and good, you can't want her to be alone. And she would be alone. I know she'll never love anyone else."

Niles looked sideways at her. "How do you know that? She could meet one of her own kind, the right one, and be just as happy."

"Really?" Leigh intended to sound sarcastic and Niles met her eyes steadily. "I know you're wrong because I've seen how they feel about each other. They're like you and me. We couldn't have lived without each other, and neither can they. Once they are sealed—once their flesh is joined—they will overcome anything that tries to come between them." She held up the palm of her right hand to show the small, circular purple mark that matched one on Niles's palm and signified that they were joined for all time.

His lips parted and she got ready for some angry retort, but he closed his mouth and breathed deeply.

She must stay focused and not think too deeply of what they were together, how they could close everything out. He was an amazing lover, who took her away from the world as she knew it. Their climaxes were mind eclipsing, and just to think of how she felt then was to wipe out all reason.

"Niles," she said tentatively. "Have you forgotten how Elin helped us when we needed it so much?"

He pressed his lips together but the crease between his brows gave him away. He knew that Elin, Skillywidden as she was then, the beautiful and strange cat with violet eyes, had carried desperate news to fae Sally, who helped them outwit their enemies.

"Niles?" Leigh prodded him.

"I haven't forgotten," he said, and pushed a hand beneath her hair to caress her neck. "My concern is as much for Elin as for any of us. Tarhazian will be merciless when she wants something from her."

"Sean is a very strong man. In both mind and body. If I didn't have you, he would be the first one I'd turn to for help."

Niles snorted. "I haven't forgotten how you let him rest his head on your thigh."

"When he sat beside me as Blue the hound, you mean?" Leigh laughed. "But now I remember, you got mad at him for being too near me."

"I'm told he's too damned attractive in any form," Niles said, but he laughed, too.

With a deep breath, Leigh forged ahead. "There's something I've wanted to talk about but I'm afraid you won't want to believe there's anything in it."

He raised his upward-slashing black brows. "Now you've got my attention. Come on, let's have it." Niles reminded her of a warrior who had ridden down from distant slopes, the wind tearing at his hair and fire in his eyes. Her desire for him never faded.

She gathered her wits. "Would you still have wanted me if I were all human?"

He looked puzzled. "Of course. You're Deseran but that means you're essentially human, human with paranormal powers and blood like none other. What does that have to do with this?"

Sally, who had connections to a secret society in New Orleans, had figured out that Leigh was a member of this rare group known as Deserans. They were considered by their supernatural parents to have no useful talents and, therefore, abandoned into foster care in New Orleans. Their numbers had become fewer and fewer until it was thought, wrongly, that there were none of them left.

"It could be the answer to everything," Leigh said. "I just don't know if you will listen to me with an open mind, or believe a word I say."

She didn't like his guarded stare.

Leigh and her twin sister, Jan—who had yet to exhibit any signs of the Deseran and knew nothing about them—had been two of those abandoned children.

Sally had found Leigh for Niles, who longed, together with the other members of the Team, to be accepted as humans. They were extraordinary warriors who fought on the side of good. For some years they had answered when the call came for contract special operations forces overseas.

The steady loss of both the females of their species and the offspring, who usually caused those deaths when they were born—also dead—threatened the extinction of Niles's

Team and the rare strain of hounds they came from, unless fresh female blood came into the picture. Preferably human blood that would tolerate that of the werehounds. Not all types were thought to be suitable.

It had been Sally who knew that in the realm of the unknown, the Deseran were the closest thing to universal blood donors in existence and might survive mating with this line of werehounds.

Leigh gave him a sideways glance. Some things were in the hands of fate, and she put all her faith in fate being kind.

His features darkened and heat entered his eyes. He leaned to kiss her thoroughly, and nuzzle beneath her jaw. "It's been too long," he murmured. "I want you."

"It's only been a few hours," she said, smiling and rubbing her hand over his belly. Instantly, an erection strained against his zipper.

Niles held her wrist. "Later," he said, grimacing. "And not much later. I've got to have a clear head for now. So stop trying to distract me."

With an innocent expression, Leigh walked her fingers down his thigh and pretended not to see him jump. "*You* stop distracting me. I believe Elin may be completely human. Tarhazian stole her as an infant—from a demon who must also have stolen her—and trained her to perfect the skills she has. But look at her. She could be all human."

Niles shook his head in disbelief. "How long did it take you to come up with that? Elin is fae and she's a shapeshifter. Square that with being human."

"I will. I doubt Tarhazian had any idea Elin might be human. And she still doesn't know. Many of the fae look human. Second, Elin doesn't really miss being in the fae community. She fits in with humans perfectly and she's comfortable with them. I tried to suggest she might be human but she thought I was making a joke."

"So do I," Niles said, but he gave her a slight smile to take out the sting.

"But she seems more human than fae."

"Is that why she hangs out with a werehound?" Niles said. Then he added, "Forget I said that."

"She loves our house," Leigh said, getting desperate to find her way past Niles's resistance to Elin. "And the cottage. She didn't grow up in a house but she's so comfortable in them."

They lived in Niles's house built on concrete bulkheads immediately above the waters of Saratoga Passage—part of Puget Sound between Whidbey and Camano Islands. But there was a cottage on top of the bluff behind Niles and Leigh's place, Two Chimneys, which had been left to Leigh by her dead husband.

"I don't know where you're going with this," Niles said.

"Do you know a case where a woman who was all human died after becoming pregnant by a werehound?"

"No." He didn't look amused.

"You don't know of a werehound who mated with a human, do you?"

"No."

"Then how do you know a human wouldn't be a perfect mate for Sean? They could probably have babies together successfully and that would help us increase our number and become more integrated with the humans."

Niles's sigh was becoming too familiar. He was afraid she would mention having a child again. Since their joining, he had become increasingly protective of her, and without hearing it from his own lips, she knew she feared that a pregnancy with him might hurt her—kill her.

Leigh understood but she would not, could not let him make this decision for both of them.

He cleared his voice. "If you expect me to swallow all this, you've lost your mind. What would Tarhazian want with a human? How could she train one to do what Elin does?"

"I've told you, more than once now, I don't think she knew what she'd stolen when she took Elin," Leigh said, jutting her chin at Niles. "But Tarhazian is an incredible paranormal talent and she could probably teach Jazzy to bend iron if she wanted to."

Jazzy was Leigh's blond, black-eyed part sheepdog, currently asleep in front of the fire.

"She got Elin exactly the way she wanted her to be, and now all she wants is to stop Elin from being with Sean because Tarhazian hates the hounds. She hates everyone but her own kind. If she can't stop them, she will do her best to use them. But you are not without defenses."

"You are really reaching," Niles said.

"And you are a stubborn man."

"Have you mentioned this to Sally at all yet?"

Leigh felt herself blush and knew her freckles would stand out on top of white patches against the rest of her scarlet skin. "Well, um—"

"I just bet you haven't." Niles smirked. "You know she'd laugh you out of town. What's more, that's just plain dangerous subterfuge, sweetheart. We've got to protect Elin—mostly from herself—not give her more excuses to keep going after Sean."

Leigh brought her fists down on the table. "She is not going after Sean any more than he's going after her. But think about this: Why would Sally go out of her way to introduce Elin to Sean if she didn't think Elin could mate with him? She wouldn't."

"Then why didn't Sally tell us?"

"She doesn't have to tell *us* anything. Perhaps she wanted to have them find out if they're a match all by themselves. She did with us."

"Sean and Elin are off their heads," Niles muttered.

"This is as good a time as any to tell you I'm loaning Two Chimneys to Elin. She has no place of her own. Sally loves having her, but unless she shifts into Skillywidden every night, there is nowhere but a cat bed for her to sleep."

"You what?" Niles looked amazed. "Why didn't you talk to me about it? She wouldn't be safe there on her own."

"I'll tell her you don't like the idea if you want," she said with a sniff. She had actually asked Sean to tell Elin she could use the cottage and by now she would know. "And Sean, too. He intends to be there to watch her, the way he watched me before you and I were sealed."

"So it's okay for him to sleep on the porch as a hound, but it's not—"

"Please don't be angry." She should have talked to him first. "Of course Elin can't sleep on the porch as Skillysidden, if that's what you were going to say."

"It's your porch. Who sleeps on it is your business. In the cottage, too."

"Niles, it was okay for Sean to sleep on the porch and watch over me." She did feel sheepish. "But you think what Sean does is something you get to decide. Sorry. We'll work it out."

"Dammit all, great. You know I won't stop them."

One of the front doors opened and Elin walked in with Sean behind her. Sean carried a floral silk bag over his shoulder.

Leigh leaned against Niles's shoulder and said, "Hi, you two," as if getting together at such an hour were routine. "Come and join us. Are you hungry?" She could feel knife-edged tension in the air.

Neither of the newcomers said a word or gave a hint of a smile. Without a glance at each other, they sat with Niles and Leigh.

Leigh didn't know what to say and evidently Niles didn't either. She stole a look and recoiled a little from the grim set of his face. He had already said he expected nothing but trouble from "this impossible infatuation" but he knew as well as she did that there was no simple solution.

"I thought I heard you come in." Sally's hoarse voice broke the silence. Her smile forced, she bustled toward them with her uneven, swinging gait that suggested arthritic hips. "I've got something in the oven. It's almost ready." A flour-dusted apron didn't come close to covering her green and yellow muumuu.

As always, her white blond hair was tightly curled all the way to dark roots, and liberally applied makeup made it impossible to guess her age—or the age she might appear to be without the makeup. With the fae, their years were unimportant.

She arrived at the table, all her attention on Elin. Sally had hidden Elin since she escaped from Queen Tarhazian more than a year earlier, hidden her in shapeshifted form as the small, silvery cat, Skillywidden. They both insisted Tarhazian didn't know Elin could shapeshift and that it was a gift she'd been born with. No doubt Niles would eventually use that as an argument against Elin being human.

Elin's eyes were that same vivid violet shade now as they were when she shifted into a cat. Her mass of shining black hair, scattered with glistening raindrops, swept back from a heart-shaped face and fell to her waist. Her frame was small but she was feminine and perfect, except for bruises that still marred one side of her lovely face and one arm where Tarhazian had beaten her the night she caught her visiting the fae kingdom. Elin had gone to see a friend but one of the Queen's many spies had reported the visit before Elin could shift back into her cat form.

Sally had rescued her by diverting Tarhazian and now Elin's banishment from the fae kingdom really was permanent and Sally was blamed for encouraging Elin's disobedience, making her own separation from her own kind just as irreversible—not that banishment meant they were safe from sly punishment if they were careless and let their guards down. Leigh believed, as did Elin, that Tarhazian was a long way from severing the strings to her "child," and there would be many more subtle, and not-so-subtle, attempts to control her again.

"You're healing?" Sally said to Elin.

"That woman had best stay far away from me," Sean said, his face rigid. "How could she hurt someone so gentle?"

"I am healed," Elin said in a small voice. "And I'm not helpless, Sean. I can protect myself." She looked at her hands, folded in her lap.

Leigh felt a special bond with the girl since she had spent a great deal of time with Leigh and Jazzy when they first came to Whidbey.

At this moment Jazzy was nosing at the bag Sean had put on the floor and she figured Elin's Pokey must be inside.

"Okay," Leigh said to Sean and Elin, "that's all I can take of this. What's the matter with you two? Are you mad at each other?"

"Mad?" Sean said. "As in angry? Only a woman would come up with something as ridiculous as that."

Leigh said, "In other words there's something serious going on."

"I'll get those pies," Sally said and retraced her awkward steps with Jazzy rushing along to keep up. Jazzy never missed the chance of a treat and followed Sally to the kitchen behind the bar.

"You wanted us here," Sean said. He had thick, dark blond hair tied at his nape and brilliant light brown eyes that could skewer whomever he chose to give his full attention with tiger-like intensity. "I...we didn't want to come. There's nothing to be gained." Sean was a man few people looked at only once. His sleek, Nordic features and lithe body were hard to ignore.

Elin's hand, stealing into Leigh's, worried her. The mysterious girl was frightened.

"What do you think you should be doing instead of making decisions with me?" Niles said, his voice even but pitiless. "Fleeing together perhaps? Don't try it. You'd better think long and hard about what you're doing. Tarhazian hates you for being with her little darling. She could decide to punish you both."

"What do you want of us?" Sean demanded, muscles working in his hard, angular jaw. "We're here because of your order. I would not have come otherwise."

"You must give each other up," Niles said, and Leigh could not bring herself to look at him.

"Never," Sean and Elin said in unison.

"Cast me out," Sean said. "If that will make you feel safer, tell me to be gone forever. But I will not be parted from Elin. We are not ready to be sealed but we believe we will be."

"Don't you understand what's happening?" Niles said. "You are becoming a conduit between us and the Fae Queen. She will use Elin as her spy. You know what Tarhazian has admitted. She will never accept this match, but then she wavers, and I know enough to read her mind. She will allow the match if Elin tells her our secrets."

"I would never do that," Elin said softly. "I want only to be with Sean."

Leigh gave Sean all of her attention and she didn't like what she saw. He was torn. Torn between his allegiance to his Team and his need for Elin.

Sally came from the kitchens, pushing a cart with

loudly wobbling wheels. "This will warm your hearts," she said, but her face showed nothing but deep concern. "Hot cider. Meat pies. Fruit pies. Mulled wine—"

She pushed the cart beside the table and sat down. "Help yourselves," she said, sounding grimmer than Leigh had ever heard before. "I will not allow this girl to be hurt. Not for the sake of foolish quarrels between you hounds and the fae, or the wolves—or whomever."

Sally usually deferred to others and this announcement caused silence.

She pinched her lips together and poured cider. This she passed around to each of them. "Warm yourselves. Settle down. Between us we have a good deal of power and we are not helpless. Even before the likes of Tarhazian."

Elin covered her eyes.

"The Queen wants to use Elin as a spy," Sally said.

"Just as I have said," Niles said explosively. "And there will be no way to stop information from being passed— even innocently—if Elin is in our midst." He paused and looked at Sean. "With the best intentions, my friend, ours is a great passion to share with our chosen mates and something might be said—in certain moments—that could damn your own kind."

Slashes of red burned Sean's high cheekbones.

"You have not had her yet," Niles said. "But when—"

"Enough," Sean said. "This is not the time nor the place to discuss such matters. I will see you outside."

"No," Leigh shouted. She glared at Niles. "Stop it. We must work together. This isn't a time for saber rattling between testosterone junkies."

"Testosterone junkies?" Niles's jaw dropped, then both he and Sean laughed.

"I think we just got put in our places," Sean said. He looked at Elin's sad face and held out his arms to her. "Come here." He took her onto his lap and kept a firm hold on her waist. She put her head on his shoulder and kissed his neck, softly, repeatedly. Sean said, "Leigh's right. We should listen to these women more. We will work together."

"You mean fight together," Niles said, but quietly. "Never think we aren't entering a battle or that it might not be violent."

"We know the risks," Sean said.

Niles gave Elin all of his attention. "If you were convinced Tarhazian would accept you back into the only world you've known—in return for having you spy on us—what then?"

"She has already given her answer," Sean said. "Elin would never—"

Elin's hand on his arm stopped him. "No matter what I say, you will doubt me," she told Niles. "But I hope you will come to trust me."

## *chapter* THREE

Niles stared at Elin for a long time and she stared back. Sean felt the battle of wills to his core and he admired his small love for showing no fear in front of the alpha.

"Trust," Niles said at last. "Time will tell but the stakes are high, Elin. I respect you but I cannot yet trust you."

She turned away.

"Forgive me for joining the party uninvited," a deep, even, male voice said.

Sean looked over his shoulder. Dr. Saul VanDoren lounged carelessly at a nearby table. "I didn't see you arrive," Sean said, knowing well that the vampire could come and go as he wished, where he wished.

"You were all so involved in your discussion," Saul said, resting his elbows on the table so that his full white sleeves draped elegantly. He laced his long, slender fingers together. "You hounds do have some interesting rituals. I wonder you don't find them onerous with so much waiting and watching—and wanting—attached to your mating habits."

"Damn it." Sean paused, trying to control his flaring temper. He smiled at Elin. "Our *habits*, as you call them, have their own benefits. But they won't interest you."

"We are having a private meeting here," Niles said.

Sean sensed his alpha's annoyance at the vampire's interruption. They had formed a tenuous friendship with him, or should that be tolerance, during a previous battle with Whidbey's werehound pack.

"Very private," Saul said. His dark eyes could appear black, as they did now.

"Should we put the rest of our discussion off?" Sean said. "It's very late."

"And you want to take Elin to Two Chimneys," Saul said, tilting his head to one side. His long, dark hair slid forward, framing his pale, saturnine face. "How kind of Leigh to insist you use it. But then, Leigh was always kind."

A subtle warning raised every hackle for Sean. This man's words might be innocuous enough but the threat behind them was unmistakable. Unmistakable and strange. What was he trying to say, or not to say?

The pulse beating in Elin's neck was very visible, and fast. Sean stared at it as he raised a hand toward her and she grasped it, hard.

"How long have you been here, Saul?" Niles said. "You must have heard our conversation earlier." His mild tone didn't fool Sean.

"Not long," Saul said. "Introduce me to your lady, Sean. You have good taste. She is very beautiful—very *delicate*."

"I am Elin," she said before Sean could respond. Her grip on him grew even tighter. "I am of the fae."

"I know," Saul said. "You must be the one cast out by that aberration, Tarhazian. How lucky you are to be free of that."

The man knew too much. "We are glad to have Elin with us permanently," Sean said. "She's where she belongs."

"I do hope so." Saul rose fluidly, his long, dark coat spreading behind him as he approached. When he was close enough, he pointed at Elin, brought a forefinger near, but not quite near enough, to touch her jaw.

The slightest gesture with that finger and Elin raised her chin. She looked steadily and directly into his eyes.

"There is a lot they assume about you," Saul said. He smiled, "But how could they not, when they haven't learned the rest."

Sean surged to his feet and pulled her against him. "What do you want, VanDoren?"

The smile Saul directed at him would have chilled a lesser man. "I am a friend, Sean. But you should already know that. A friend who cares about threats against you. Bear that in mind."

Saul walked away, the heels of his boots hitting the wooden floors, sharp, precise. His hair swung slightly from side to side and the coat flew behind him. "If you wish, I'd be glad to talk with you outside, alone."

Sean didn't see the door open, but he heard it close. Immediately he got up, guided Elin to sit in his chair, and followed the vampire.

In the forecourt of the business, Sean couldn't see Saul

at first. He almost turned on his heel and returned inside.

"I'm here," came Saul's voice.

To his right, by a clump of bushes, Saul's shadow moved forward and became obvious.

"I hadn't intended to confront you like this—here," he said. "But the presence of the woman who appears to be in your care, or perhaps control, means I must speak now."

Sean frowned, more confused than angry in that moment. "Save the riddles. Speak plainly."

"Your given name was not Sean Black," Saul said and added very quietly, "Jacob O'Cleary."

Instantly cold, Sean straightened his shoulders and set his jaw. Whatever was coming, he would meet it and not bend. "Say what's on your mind," he said.

"I had reason to cross the path of one who says he knows you. He wants to find you again. Since I have never doubted you, I didn't tell him I had met you or had any idea where you are. But if what he says is true, I can't stand by while you're allowed to be alone with a vulnerable woman. She couldn't defend herself against you. I think you know what I'm saying."

And Sean wouldn't defend himself against the lie Saul had been told. He braced his feet apart and crossed his arms.

"Do you know this man who approached me?" Saul said. "He was in the area looking for you. To bring you to justice, he said."

"Here?" Sean asked. "On Whidbey?"

"So you don't deny any of this?" Saul said.

The turning of his heart, the way his stomach dropped,

shocked Sean. He had convinced himself the horrors of San Francisco were behind him but they were rearing again, he could feel them. "I thought it was over," he told Saul honestly. "I was set up in a San Francisco club. By the man who made me what I am, a werehound. Believe me or not. I won't beg you."

"A man with black hair," Saul said. "Strangely cut to his ears. And his mouth is wide, a mere slit, but wide."

"Aldo," Sean whispered. "I should have hunted him down and killed him."

Saul gave a short laugh. "I think you may get your chance. But I also think I am inclined to accept that you are not the kind of man he accused—"

"He killed that woman," Sean broke in, disgusted by the memory. "He abused and killed her and managed to get me arrested for it." He shook his head. He had pleaded his case and the other man could believe or not. "I escaped easily enough but I've lived expecting him to find me one day."

"Very well," Saul said. "But I would be remiss if I didn't consider Elin's safety. It is my nature. You understand?"

Sean understood that part of him wanted to take Saul by the throat and warn him never to interfere in his and Elin's affairs again. Another part almost accepted that the vampire was on the side of good over evil.

He must keep his wits about him. "Where did you see Aldo?"

Saul made a vague gesture. "Not here, but I am not ready to discuss exactly where. Be cautious, Sean Black."

*chapter* **FOUR**

This is a strange toy for a man like you," Elin yelled over the wind tearing past Sean's Ducati motorcycle. She had not seen it before they left Gabriel's Place and he had retrieved the bike from an outbuilding. "Sean?" She tightened her grip on him.

Despite the speakers in their helmets, he pretended not to hear her shout to him.

"Why do you want to ride this when we can travel so fast without it?"

The bike covered ground with gathering speed, turning everything they passed into one long blur.

Sean was angry. Elin felt fury coursing through his body and longed to soothe him. But she didn't know enough about him yet to be certain how to please him, or calm him.

She intended to learn.

The Ducati was black with thin, red stripes. Elin decided they must be all but invisible streaking along the highway in the darkness.

She leaned against Sean's back and held as much of him as she could. He wore black leather and had made sure she had a coat even though she constantly assured him she didn't feel the cold.

Abruptly, he clamped an elbow over one of her hands to hold her tightly against him, and covered her other hand with his own. They leaned sharply and shot down the cut between trees at Leigh's Two Chimneys Cottage.

He stopped a short distance from the cottage, and helped her off the bike. Instantly Elin whipped off the helmet and jacket, reveling in the snap of breeze that lifted her hair and played in the clothes that skimmed her body.

"You hate restraint, don't you?" Sean said, his own helmet already off and hooked on his handlebars. He ducked his head to look into her face. "I wonder if there are any bonds you wouldn't fight."

"None," she said, laughing and shaking her head.

Sean didn't laugh. "We all have a few bonds to deal with. Bonds of blood or honor. Bonds we choose."

First he wheeled the bike into the cover of some dense trees, then he took her by the elbow and led her to the front porch of the cottage. Leigh had given him the key and he let them in.

"You'll be comfortable and safe here," he said. "Please wait while I check all the locks and windows, though."

"You're so stiff with me." She watched him shut and lock the door then move on to the windows. He drew the drapes. "Have I done something to hurt you?"

"The sleeping loft is up there." He nodded to steps

leading to an area beneath an apex roof. "Leigh said the bed is made up for you. If you get nervous, I'll be just outside the front door."

Of course Elin already knew where the loft and the bed were, having slept there as Skillywidden while Leigh still lived in the cottage.

Without breaking stride, he went from the cozy living room with its two fireplaces, one on either side, to the kitchen. Sounds of windows opening and closing and locks being shot back and forth came again.

Males could be so difficult. They thought they were superior, and if Sean didn't change his ways—quickly—she would tell him what she thought of this behavior.

He came back to the sitting room. "That's the bathroom," he said, pointing at the only other door in the room. "Do not unlock any doors or windows. If you want me, knock the inside of the front door and wait until I come to you."

"As if locked doors would keep some people out," she said—she couldn't help it.

"Apart from your own fae types, I'm not aware of much that doesn't at least pause outside buildings. Vampires can't enter unless invited—if that's what they call it."

She let his reference to *fae types* pass.

Without so much as a glance in her direction, he lit first one, then the second fire. She would roast but now wasn't the time to be critical.

"Right." Sean brushed his hands together. "I won't shift immediately in case you need anything in here but I'd appreciate having a chance to get a few hours' sleep."

In other words, he wanted to leave.

He was so much bigger than she. Elin was accustomed to being aware of his size, but with currents of agitation bouncing from him, he seemed to fill the room.

"You take the bed," she said softly. "I'll be comfortable on the couch."

"I wouldn't do that," he said.

"Sean, something happened with Saul, didn't it? You were already on edge—we both were—but there's something else."

He stared at the front door. "Let me deal with what's on my mind in my own way. It's for the best. We'll have breakfast together if you want to."

"What's your problem?" Elin said.

He slowly raised his eyebrows. There, she thought, don't think I can't be as tough as you?

"Speak to me," she demanded.

"Okay." Slowly, he took off his leather jacket. He wore a navy blue sweater and blue jeans—and black boots. "You want to push this, fine. But I don't like this kind of conversation. In fact, I'm not a man who talks a whole lot at any time."

"You think I don't know that?" she said softly. "I am not a woman who can live with unexplained anger—or any anger."

Too bad he looked so good that all she wanted was to curl up with him in one of the comfortable chairs or couches and sink into the heavy checked tapestry that covered them.

Sally told her never to back away from someone who thought they had the upper hand. Elin walked close to Sean and stared into his clear, gold eyes.

"Do I ever frighten you?" Sean said.

Whatever she had imagined, in even a wild flight of fantasy, that he might say, *that* would not have been it. She couldn't think of an answer.

"Nothing to say? Perhaps that tells me everything."

"What do you mean?" Elin made fists at her sides. "Don't you understand anything?"

He held his tongue but his eyes narrowed.

"Do you think I'm one of those women who get a kick out of being with...with a man who scares her?" She heard her voice get higher and felt furious. Always soft, when she got mad, it sounded as if she was breathless. "Why did you ask me that?"

"Calm down," he said, trying to move her to a chair. "Please calm down. This isn't good for you."

The instant she started to shrug him off, Sean let her go.

"I'm okay." She wasn't but she would be. "You could never frighten me."

His immediate, wide smile made him a different man. "It was something Saul said. I'm not even sure what it was."

"He probably didn't mean anything," Elin said. "He was a bit different tonight. You didn't tell me why he wanted you outside."

Sean's expression closed and he looked away from her again. "I think he was warning me about the danger of a rift within the Team. I'll talk to Niles and see if he noticed anything different about Saul. But not tonight."

"Not tonight," Elin said, momentarily distracted. "I believe they wanted to enjoy their privacy tonight."

The darkening in Sean's eyes caused her pleasurable

sensitivity all over her body. He was becoming increasingly anxious for them to have their own private interludes.

"Do you know what Saul might have been suggesting when he talked about not even you knowing everything about yourself?" Sean asked Elin.

She piled her hair on top of her head to cool her neck. "Perhaps he was trying to be mysterious. I know who I am and where I came from."

Sean scanned her body, then spread his fingers around her waist. "Do you? Do you really? Everything?" He slowly passed his hands up her ribs until he stopped with his thumbs on the sides of her breasts.

She shivered, but with delight, and kept her hands in her hair.

The faintest smile tilted the corners of his mouth. "You are a sensuous creature."

"Does it matter if I don't know everything about myself? I was abandoned, and I don't know who my birth parents were, but that doesn't mean I haven't proved my character."

"No," he said, using his thumbnails to make small circles on erogenous flesh.

Still Elin stopped herself from touching him, not an easy task for one whose every instinct cried out to show him more ways to please them both.

"You are practiced in seduction," Sean said. "I'm not sure I understand why." He kissed the side of her neck, nudged up her chin, and licked his way down and between her breasts. At last the pads of his thumbs settled on her nipples and he rubbed firmly.

She opened her mouth to breathe. They would become a perfect match, a perfect melding of their sexes—that was her eventual job.

"Do you think the clothes I wear are too flamboyant?" she panted. "For a human, that is? You and I intend to become part of this world we've chosen. I want to fit in."

He kissed her lips, tilting his head, nibbling her mouth, and opening it with his own. He passed his tongue along the edges of her teeth, before he licked the smooth, wet skin inside.

For an instant he paused. She had released her hair and held his shoulders. "You are yourself," he said. "I like what you wear. Your clothes suit you. But you will have to find a way to wear a coat in cold weather or there's bound to be talk. And when we are bonded, I don't want the locals suggesting I can't afford to clothe you."

She smiled. "I should like to unclothe you, Sean. Now. We could both lie together in the loft bed."

"You give me too much credit for control, my love. I am only a man, or mostly only a man."

"I would argue about the *only* part." Softly at first, and then more insistently, she leaned her body into his. "You are so much more than an ordinary man." As she could feel very well.

Stepping away from him, she slid her long skirts up, revealing her slender calves, then her smooth thighs.

Mesmerized, Sean stared at her legs. His breathing speeded and he knelt in front of her, kissing her belly through her dress, slipping his hands up the backs of her legs and holding her hard against him.

He nipped her mound through thin silk. "I should definitely leave."

"What would be wrong with our being together now? We have promised our bond."

"There is a great deal you don't understand," he said through clenched teeth and stood up. "When it's time, I'll explain, and I can only hope what I tell you will make us both happy."

"Sean?" Elin had tried to put her own questions aside. "Saul threatened you, didn't he?"

He looked away abruptly.

"He asked you to go outside and talk to him. What was all that about how you should remember he's your friend?"

Elin knew indecision when she saw it. Sean couldn't decide how to respond. "Do you doubt anything about me?" Sean said, turning back to her. "Anything that matters?"

Perhaps there were secrets between them. "You aren't ready to trust me with all your secrets," she said awkwardly. "I'll try to understand. Pokey's in my bag. He must have hated riding on the bike. I'd better get him out."

"You'll have plenty of time to decide what you think," Sean said, but he looked disappointed. "I'll be outside. Lock the door behind me."

*chapter* **FIVE**

With each shift Sean made, he was less comfortable becoming fully hound. But he couldn't hang around outside the cottage otherwise. People in the area were familiar with Blue, the huge, blue-black dog they thought of as an overgrown wolfhound. The locals assumed he belonged to Niles, and now Leigh as well, and they wouldn't think anything of him snoozing on the porch at Two Chimneys. No one was likely to come but he couldn't risk questions.

It was not that he hated the part of him that was hound, but he resented having to leave the body of the man he had been born to be.

He resented it most of all when the choice was taken from him.

Where he wanted to be was inside the cottage with Elin, who would be turning over what he had said to her.

*He* was turning it over. And the actual news Saul had brought.

At the moment, one question mattered more to Sean: Where was Aldo? For Saul to have encountered him, it had to mean the old werehound had been in the area, although he believed the vampire that they hadn't met on Whidbey.

Sean had felt more or less safe, even if he couldn't get that night in San Francisco out of his mind. He had made a clean getaway and Aldo didn't move outside the area he had made his home. Or so the story had gone until now.

Niles and the rest of his hound brothers knew everything that had happened and would protect Sean to the death from any threat. What kind of threat did Saul present? Would he use what he had found out against Sean?

Sean put his head on his paws and half closed his eyes. How long would it be before he dared to really rest again? Fortunately he needed very little sleep.

Elin was more than sensual, more than practiced in seduction. She had a magical affinity for reaching his male senses. A touch, a look, an angling of her body.

How could that be when everything Sally had told him about her convinced him she was an innocent? Her past experience made no difference to him yet there was this contradiction between her sexuality and everything else about her.

He had encountered Skillywidden when she ran interference for Sean and Leigh. It hadn't been until after Leigh and Niles were sealed that Sally introduced Sean to Elin, but she was oddly secretive about the girl. If they were to fall in love, they must be compatible in every way, the fae woman had insisted. But she had hinted that if their spirits meshed and they had a child, it should not kill Elin.

*Should not* were odds Sean didn't like.

*"Should I be really worried about something?"* Niles's voice broke into his thoughts. If Sean hadn't already opened his mind to hearing his alpha, Niles could not have entered. *"Are you outside the cottage?"*

*"Where else would I be?"*

*"I won't state the obvious,"* Niles said and he didn't sound amused. *"Can you communicate with Elin yet? Other than as—"*

*"No. But I'm still hoping. I need to work on it."*

*"What was going on with Saul? I don't know what you thought, but he didn't seem happy to me,"* Niles said.

*"He's not happy and he doesn't trust me. I think he wants to but—sheesh, it hurts to say this about a vamp— I believe he's principled. He won't stand by and watch someone get into trouble if they don't deserve it."* Sooner or later he had to break the real truth. *"Saul knows about Aldo."*

That stopped Niles.

*"How could he?"* he said finally. *"You said Aldo never—"*

*"Leaves San Francisco? That's been the word for years but he must have left recently because Saul said he met him in the area and I don't think Saul lies unless he needs to."*

*"Is he here on Whidbey?"* Niles said.

*"Saul said no, but he wouldn't say exactly where Aldo was when he saw him."*

*"There was something about the way he spoke to Elin. Does that mean anything to you?"*

*"Yes."* Agreeing made his head pound. *"He was deciding how much of a danger I am to her."*

*"Good God."*

*"He came right out and asked me. Then he let me know he'll be watching."*

*"Hell."* Niles's voice wasn't serious enough. *"I guess I'm going to need eyes in the back of my head or you and Saul will be scrapping."*

*"Scrapping? You can be insulting, Niles. Have I told you that?"*

*"Not recently. I figured it was about time, though."*

*"Are we done?"* Sean asked.

*"Not quite. I wanted to wait for you to tell me yourself but I guess I've run out of time. Have you told Elin about San Francisco—and the rest?"*

If he didn't think he'd disturb Elin, Sean thought he would howl. *"No. And it would be better if you didn't ask again."*

*"With all that openness, how can love fail?"* Niles chuckled.

*"I'm going to kill you,"* Sean told him. *"After I find a stake for that interfering rat, Saul's heart. That'll be before I do the other necessities to finish him off."*

Something small gently sliding against him, crawling and leaning on him at the same time, grabbed all of his attention. He held quite still.

*"You didn't just threaten your alpha, did you?"* Niles asked, still chuckling.

Sean ignored him. Elin, or Skillywidden as she was

at the moment, had gone against all of his instructions and come creeping, sneaking to the porch to curl up with him.

What had happened to knocking the inside of the front door if she thought she needed him? Did she honestly think he wouldn't respond with some of that anger she hated?

Damn, he hated it, too.

He kept his eyes closed and didn't react to the feel of the tiny cat.

*"Sean?"*

*"I'm busy."* The last thing he wanted was to be a big, lovable dog who cuddled up to an adorable little cat, damn it.

And she had left the cottage by some route other than the front door when he had expressly told her not to do that.

He sighed. Elin might not look it, but she was a strong-minded woman.

She started to purr. Softly, but purr nevertheless. Hearing her explain this should be interesting.

*"What's happening?"* Niles said.

*"I need to concentrate here."* He must consider how best to make Elin understand that his main concern was for her safety. *"Later, Niles."*

With the faintest growl under his breath, Sean stood and shook himself. He lowered his head to stare into those violet eyes, and he made sure Elin—Skillywidden or whoever—didn't mistake the look for other than a warning.

She drew back, blinking rapidly, whiskers twitching,

and Sean gave her a light bat on the rear, pushing her toward the back of the cottage.

The elegant cat made a wide circle around him, looking back, probably hoping for a change of heart. He gave another low growl and made a deliberately poor attempt at chasing her around the building.

A few inches wide crack in the kitchen door had been all she needed to escape, and if she thought he would follow her inside now, she was—unfortunately—mistaken.

The little manipulator had opened that door before she shifted. Did she do anything spontaneously?

He stood outside listening to the cat's rapid breathing.

The door slammed shut and the lock shot home. She had shifted back but she was letting him know he'd missed his chance to be with her.

Sean stood for a while before loping slowly back to the front of the cottage.

Lying on the chilly porch, he thought about Elin getting back into that bed, mad, and alone. Being strong for both of them shouldn't feel so lousy.

## *chapter* SIX

Another sleet shower threw ice pellets at the windows before Elin's eyelids grew heavy.

She snuggled into the soft bed…and turned this way and that searching for a comfortable spot.

He had chased her. As if she were nothing more than a pesky cat to be disposed of by a big, strong hound. It made her mad.

More giant handfuls of frozen rain hit glass. She was wide awake again. Wild weather excited her. If big, bad Blue wasn't staked out on the front porch, she would open the front drapes, make some tea, and watch the storm.

No man would tell her what she couldn't do.

With a quick shift back to Skillywidden, she bounded down the loft ladder and out to the kitchen door. With one paw lifted and her whiskers pointing forward, she listened.

A wonderful thought came to her. She would be amazed if Sean wasn't making the rounds outside the cottage from time to time. If he found her on the back step, he would be furious, could be furious enough to follow her inside and then they would see what happened.

Standing on the old, scrubbed wood draining board, she could easily reach her body out and rest her paws on the door handle. Shifting back to Elin might be the natural course, but this would be quicker. Several hooks from the very strong claws on a paw and the bolt inched open.

She hung from the doorknob until she got it turned enough and swung backward until a blast of air shot through.

Skillywidden smirked.

Dragging a blue and white checked pillow from the seat of a kitchen chair, she worked her way outside and set herself up comfortably in the corner nearest the door. She curled up, watching wind bend the bushes and trees, and rain and ice pass horizontally through the beam of light that shone from above the window.

She was so awake she couldn't imagine feeling tired again.

The sound of swishing made her smile. Her protector was getting ready to make his next round of the cottage. He would be so angry when he found her on a comfy pillow, enjoying the wet night air.

Or he would be even more furious than before. This wasn't a particularly brilliant move. With her heart pounding, she whipped back inside but couldn't resist making a quick change back into Elin and calling, very sweetly, "Come in and get warm. Come on in now."

Wind screeched through the trees, suddenly whipping branches low enough to scrape the roof.

Screeching turned into a gathering hum and into the light beam a long, black, flying creature like an oversized dragonfly made of shadows shot past the windows.

Elin didn't wait to see what happened next. She lunged for the lock on the door . . . but not fast enough to shoot the bolt home.

Elin backed away. Long curved nails protruding from the cutoff fingers of black gloves curled around the edge of the door and it crashed open.

One of those leather-clad fingers went to a full, dark red male mouth from which long incisors appeared. A vampire, and his smile sickened her.

"So kind of you to invite me in," the blood eater said. "Not a sound now. Come to me like a good girl. I promise you'll be glad you did."

"Sean!" Elin shouted. She dashed back into the sitting room and headed for the front door.

In a flash, the vampire inserted himself in front of her and reached out with both hands.

Where was Sean? Either fast asleep or making that tour around the cottage she'd been waiting for.

Elin whirled away and scrambled up the loft ladder while the creature laughed, a gurgling laugh.

She could scarcely breathe. Silvery hair flowed over the vampire's shoulders all the way to his waist. So white it appeared transparent, his slender face fixed in a menacing leer and his red eyes glowed.

He came toward her slowly, levitating, spreading his arms, his cape swinging away from a body suit that clung to every inch of him.

There was no way she could fight this thing.

Elin opened her mouth wide to scream and squeezed her eyes shut. The scream died in her throat. A flapping sound, as of many wings, slapped around her, like bats swarming. She waved her arms but they were quickly clamped to her sides by a sickeningly sweet-smelling sack that descended over her head and shoulders.

Instinctively, she shifted again, dropped down to Skillywidden's diminutive size, and escaped.

The vampire grinned with delight. "No wonder you are such a prize," he said. "What intriguing hidden talents. He who sent me has far more need of you than that dog of yours. You need not expect him to save you. I have lured him off into the trees in search of a moving shadow that isn't really there."

He leaned against the loft railing and watched her, clearly amused by what he saw as her helplessness.

The front door splintered under Sean's shoulder and he smashed through. Skillywidden could see how he took in the whole scene and she wanted to beg him to shift at once. Even as a hound, he would be outmatched by the vampire, but as a man, he had no chance.

"Come on, Vampire," Sean said, his voice shockingly soft. "Let's deal with this down here."

Skillywidden leaped her way to the exposed beams overhead and crouched there, hissing.

The vampire flew from the loft to the sitting room, set down without a sound, and began circling Sean, who pointed to Skillywidden without looking at her. "You stay right there," he told her.

She shivered at the threat in his voice.

"It's time we met," the vampire said, continuing around Sean, who turned on his heel to keep the other one in his sight. "Colin. No doubt you've heard of me. I don't normally engage in these little scuffles but I wanted to see you more closely. I wanted to find out what makes you so important to . . . to important people."

He threw off his cape and crouched, ready to attack.

There was nothing she could think of to do. Skillywidden edged forward along the beam until she almost looked directly down on the vampire and Sean.

Why didn't he shift?

Sean gave a thin smile, directed his narrowed tiger stare on Colin, and raised both hands. With beckoning fingers he urged the vampire to carry out his unspoken threat.

The creeping creature hissed, a soft sound more menacing than any shout. "If you insist," he whispered.

When he went for Sean, it was so fast, Skillywidden couldn't see anything but an uncoiling streak of black that connected with its target and wound without pause into the shape of Colin again.

The vampire bounced!

Skillywidden opened her eyes wide and stared down. Colin had bounced off Sean.

The vampire's rage turned him into a whirling mass of talons and bared teeth. "I came to capture, not to kill." The voice echoed through the little cottage. "You should have let me take her. At least you would have stayed in one piece longer. No matter, I'll take you both. Save time."

He lunged at Sean, who stepped smoothly aside.

Locked hands, slamming into the back of the vampire's head, sent him sprawling on the floor.

He rolled away and crouched near a wall, shaking his head. Blood drizzled down his chin where his fangs had sunk into his face.

Slowly he freed his teeth from his flesh and they made a sucking sound as they popped free. Fury turned his eyes black and he flattened to the wall, sliding slowly along, getting closer to Sean.

"Now you'll die," Colin said. "The one who sent me can take what's left of you if that's what he wants."

He threw himself forward, arms outstretched, bent on grabbing Sean, who welcomed him with a headlock.

While the vampire fought, Sean hefted him through the shattered front door and down to the frozen lawn.

Skillywidden scrambled from the loft, spitting as she went. Vampire, hooey, if Sean could risk everything for her, then she could gouge out that monster Colin's evil black eyes. That was exactly what she would do.

Yowling, she threw herself outside, turning herself into a whirling ball.

"For crying out loud, Elin," Sean said, catching her and clamping her against him until she stopped struggling. "Look." He held her in front of him.

Sailing away above the trees was the unmistakable form of Colin. Head over heels in arcs, he went until she couldn't see him anymore.

With a slam, a door landed on the lawn, only feet away.

Niles came into view with a grinning Innes behind him. "What the hell are you up to," Niles said, frowning at Skillywidden. "Don't you hurt that cat. She's very important to Leigh—and to me. And Jazzy would take a lump out of you if a hair on her body gets harmed."

Feeling smug, but amazed by what she'd witnessed, Skillywidden slithered free and scuttled into the cottage. She shifted even faster than usual and prepared to defend her actions.

Minutes passed and Sean didn't appear.

Eventually all three men assembled to tear off what was left of the old door.

"How did you know about that?" Elin said.

Innes looked away. Niles scowled at her and said, "We communicate and do what we say we'll do. Saves all kinds of trouble. I'm not happy with you, Elin. But that's up to Sean to take care of."

In half an hour, far too quickly for Elin, the door was replaced and Innes hauled off the broken pieces. "The new one will need oiling," Niles said. He glanced at Sean, who stood with his hands deep in his pockets. "But not today."

Niles and Innes met up and headed for the bank to go back to Niles's house.

There was no place to hide but she did wish she dared slip away.

With several logs under each arm, Sean came inside, pushed the door shut, and deposed wood on each hearth.

He didn't look directly at her until he'd made up one of the fires and fresh flames danced.

"Now," he said, facing her and brushing his hands together. "Do you still think what you did was a good idea? He could so easily have killed you."

She frowned and sat on a straight-backed wooden chair.

"Would it have been so hard to do what I asked you to do?"

"I don't like being told what to do."

"That's not what I asked. You could have been who knows where by now. Or dead."

She sniffed. "That creep wasn't going to kill me. He wanted me for something else."

A quiet pause made her fidget until she looked right at him. "That's right," he said. "And I'm sure you'd have loved what he wanted you for."

"No," she said quietly. "You didn't shift to fight him."

He returned her look then. "I needed everything I had to deal with Colin."

"But—"

"I'm stronger as a human, but that's not something I want generally known."

She nodded miserably. "Why didn't you tell me that before? Do you know how scared I was?"

"Do you know how desperate *I* was? I expected you to be gone or dead by the time I came through that door."

"I'm not helpless."

His laugh wasn't pleasant. "You're gutsy, Elin, but you have limits and you know what they are."

Exhausted, she didn't want to argue anymore. "Could we go to bed and talk about this tomorrow?"

Without answering, Sean started another examination of windows and locks around the cottage.

Back at the front door he paused. "While you're in bed, please think about what almost happened. I'll be out front again—also thinking.

"Being with me carries its own dangers for you. I've asked you to consider risking that because I can look after you—unless you won't let me when it's necessary."

"I'm trying to learn," Elin said but she couldn't meet his eyes because she really hadn't tried very hard. "I'll do much better the next time."

He drove both hands through his hair and said, "*Much better?* That's about the same as saying, 'almost saved.' People who are almost saved are dead. Think, Elin. From here on out, wherever you go, someone goes with you. And we watch you—for your own sake as well as mine."

Sean closed his eyes for a moment and covered them with a hand, then he stared deep into Elin's eyes. His gaze was heavy, and for a moment, he seemed to be struggling with what to say next. When he finally spoke, his tone was brisk. "Please, for my peace, do what I ask you to do. We don't have any choices, at least now. Good night."

Elin thought she caught a look of pain flash across Sean's face, but it happened so quickly she couldn't be sure if it was real or imagined. He studied her again and seemed about to say something else. Instead he nodded and walked out the door.

Slumped on the chair, Elin stared at the closed front door. Her eyes prickled and she sniffed. She had to be stronger than this. Stronger, smarter, and less compulsive.

Around the edges of the windows, a faint, foggy medium gathered.

Elin stood up, praying Sean wouldn't change his mind

and join her. This was one of the things over which she had no control.

Gathering density, taking on a spectrum of glittering colors, the vapor spread like a series of rainbows, surrounding Elin and growing more intense.

Listening for any movement from Sean, she watched and waited—and from the green part of the mass there was a spill, an overflow that came toward her. "The green," as Sally had explained, "has incredible power you can mold into something as small as a marble and use as a weapon to immobilize an enemy."

Quickly, she plunged a hand into the glitter and took a small handful. She squeezed it in her palm and dropped the ball into her pocket.

Sean didn't know that, like Leigh, she was Deseran. Elin wanted to be sure he could want her for herself rather than as a potential bearer of his children.

This was a visit from The Veil that invisibly separated the human from the metaphysical on Whidbey. Humans could not see past The Veil or know what lay beyond. Only the Deseran could use The Veil's power. Excitement shuddered through her. This was a secret she must keep, at least for now.

But then, she wasn't the only one keeping secrets. Sean could have told her that although he was strong as a hound, he was many degrees stronger as a man. But he hadn't wanted her to know. Because he didn't trust her? She needed to know the answer to that.

## *chapter* SEVEN

Exhausted but determined, Elin arrived at Gabriel's in the morning when the place was awake and busy again. She had slept very little and couldn't get the image of Sean's furious face out of her head. Obeying his orders might be what he wanted her to do, it might even be a good idea, but she didn't like feeling she had no choices.

Elin would not turn into a helpless female in need of protection from a big, strong male. She wouldn't be foolish, of course. When going it alone was dangerous, she would gladly accept help. But she would not be ordered around or have her life taken over without asking questions. She had escaped Tarhazian to get away from being treated as if she should accept a submissive role. There would be no going back.

Freshly determined, Elin walked through Gabriel's Place, heading for Leigh's office.

She didn't have to look behind her to know one of the

hounds was following, or to check outside to know there was at least one backup. Sean would have been there if he had not been called to a fire. Only when Elin pushed him had Sean told her he was also the medic for the contract special operations force he belonged to with the rest of the Team.

"Hey, Elin," Gabriel said with a wave and a grin. His tightly curled close-cropped hair was graying faster but his face didn't change. The ex-NFL running back was a big, handsome man with dark skin that made even more of his disarming smile.

She waved in return. "Hey yourself. Is Leigh in her office or out back?"

"Office," Gabriel said. "But Niles is out back working on the extension."

The local can-do-anything man, Niles was adding several rooms to the back of the building, including a larger office for Leigh.

She nodded and threaded her way through tables where customers talked and laughed over their food. Cliff Ames, Gabriel's chef, was famous for his ways with dishes that were ordinary in anyone else's hands. And people came for miles to eat his pies and pastries.

"Innes," Elin said, turning and meeting her bodyguard face-on as soon as they were both out of sight of the restaurant patrons. "I'm going to talk to Leigh. I don't need to be watched in broad daylight when I'm with friends."

A pair of very green eyes looked down into her face and she would have known he was laughing at her even without the grin on his very nice mouth. "You're quite safe today," he said. "I agree with you there."

Innes's dark brown hair was cut short, not usual among the hounds, and always looked as if he used his fingers as a comb. Elin had seen him ignore admiring female glances. She didn't know what made him so aloof, but she understood the glances.

"So you don't have to follow me around anymore, do you?" Elin said. "I'm grateful, of course, but from the way—I don't think my nasty visitor from last night is likely to be back soon."

He studied her. Lean, muscular, with an angular, hard-boned face, she knew what he was capable of as a man or a hound but she did allow herself to wonder, just a little, what he might be like if he was with a woman who interested him.

"Colin will be back, in his own time." Innes shifted his weight. "Would you like to see me beaten to a pulp—then tortured?" he said.

Elin frowned.

"If I left you, that's what Sean would do to me and the others would hold me while he did it. Once you're in the office, I'll wait out here, but I'll let Niles and Campion know where you are."

She puffed up her cheeks and shook her head before raising a hand to knock on Leigh's door. Campion, another of the hounds, must have been the other hound assigned to today's Elin Watch.

Leigh opened the door wide. "I knew you were here," she said, throwing her arms around Elin. "I heard what happened yesterday. You and I have to talk, really talk."

*She did know I was here before I knocked on the door.* Elin went in and closed it behind them. She wanted to try communicating with Leigh telepathically, but wouldn't without permission.

"Niles told me about that horrible Colin. One day I'll share my own brush with him. Are you okay?"

"I'm fine, even if I am in Sean's black book for setting myself up."

Leigh's blond, tufted dog, Jazzy, his fur popping up and drooping over his black eyes, came to Elin at once and waited to be picked up. The dog was not of the other-world, but he sensed that she liked him.

"We'd better get on with it," Leigh said, all business now. "I never know when that overbearing mate of mine will come in and demand that I look at this or that."

"I think he makes excuses to come." Elin laughed. "He just wants to look at you. Sometimes I think he's always worried something has happened to you. These men are possessive, not that I mind—most of the time."

Leigh's expression became faraway and she frowned.

"Did I say something wrong?" Elin said.

"No," Leigh told her emphatically. "I wish he wouldn't worry, that's all. Elin, I've never mentioned this to anyone since, but we swam together in Saratoga Passage and I should have asked you something then but I thought you might think I'm pushy—or nosy."

"I sensed there was something on your mind," Elin said. They might have to feel their way toward under-standing the paranormal talents each of them had, but they should get started. "Come on. Just say it?" They could help each other.

"You do know how few people could go into that wa-ter, particularly at this time of year, don't you?"

"I'm sure," Elin said. She didn't feel the cold, but Sally had said most Deseran didn't—most of the time. It could change under some circumstances but Sally didn't know what they were.

"Did you see anything you thought was unusual when I showed you the crater in Chimney Rock—under the water?"

Nuzzling Jazzy's head with her nose, Elin smiled to herself. They were fencing. "Not that I thought was unusual, no."

Leigh looked disappointed. She pressed her lips together and looked around the crowded little office with the football posters left over from when Gabriel had used the room.

"I didn't say I didn't see anything," Elin said softly. "Only that it wasn't unusual to me."

That got her Leigh's full attention. She tucked pieces of her shiny strawberry blond hair behind her ears and watched Elin intently. "What wasn't?" she asked when Elin didn't continue.

*Why play a game of "you first"? If she told Leigh something she didn't relate to—without being too detailed—there would be nothing lost.*

"Colors," she said, watching the other's piercing eyes. "The most beautiful colors streaming from Chimney Rock."

Dark flecks in Leigh's eyes stood out among the gold. "In ribbons?" Elin said. "Scarves of sparkling colors drifting from Chimney Rock. And I see them elsewhere, usually when I need strength."

"Most can't see them," Leigh said. "They are part of

the substance that makes The Veil between the human and the paranormal worlds. The Veil hides the other-world from humans, but the otherworld sees everything. Do you know what we can take from The Veil and use for protection?"

Elin looked confused.

"Strength that becomes solid in our hands. You will have to use it one day, I think. Just scoop a handful from the color green. Hold it in your hand to give you strength. Or wield it as a weapon and it will be very hard and sharp."

"I had no idea," Elin whispered, glancing around as if she feared being overheard.

"It remains invisible except to a few," Leigh said. "But be very careful not to rely on it always being available just as you want it. I believe someone has interfered with The Veil and twisted some of its powers."

Elin's eyes had grown very wide.

"Niles knows about The Veil but he doesn't see the colors," Leigh said. "Only the Deseran, like you and me, do, and fae with no evil intent toward humans," Leigh explained. "Very few in all."

"You really are Deseran, too," Elin whispered.

"I have the blood," Leigh said. "Sally knows, and now you, but that's all, although..."

Her stomach twisted. "I do wonder if Dr. Saul VanDoren knows about me."

"You know Saul is a vampire?" Elin said.

"Yes, but he puzzles me," Leigh said.

Pondering that, Elin put Jazzy on the floor. "Is he different from other vampires?"

"Niles says Saul is a man caught between two worlds and trying to work for good. That means he must constantly overcome his own nature. Niles told me Saul is separate from other vampires and that they fear him. But he could be hurt if there were several of them together and they wanted to harm him."

"Sean doesn't seem to like him much."

Leigh didn't quite manage to hide a smile. "Sean is cautious, that's all."

"You can't blame him for that," Elin said, feeling defensive for her Sean. "I thought Saul was a bit high-handed with Sean, and with me last night when we were here."

"So it's 'we' now. Is that a sign you and Sean are getting very close?"

"Not as close as I'd like," Elin said and grew hot all over.

"You're blushing," Leigh told her. "Have patience. There are many ways to pleasure a man and for him to pleasure you without—being sealed. After that it'll be time for—the other." The expression on Leigh's face could only be described as filled with knowing and desire.

Elin had a little smile of her own. "I know the ways of pleasuring," she said quietly. "I have hardly begun to use them on him but already my man grows angry with controlling his need to make love with me."

Leigh cleared her throat and Elin thought she looked at her with great interest. Leigh coughed this time and seemed to set her jaw, then she said, "How do you know these things about bringing men pleasure?"

Elin hid a smile. Sally had warned her that it would be an unusual woman who wouldn't be intrigued at the thought of special sexual powers.

"That is one of my talents," Elin told her. "According to Sally, I was abandoned in New Orleans as an infant because my parents thought I could not exist in their paranormal world. They didn't know I had this gift, or the others I can use. Then I was stolen by a demon and Tarhazian stole me from him, but she never knew what I could do. She trained me to develop silly faery tricks to please her and flatter her. I was never supposed to be anything else but her plaything."

"How did you . . . how did you find out about this particular power, the pleasure power?"

Elin did smile this time, and Leigh smiled with her. They giggled together and Leigh turned pink.

"I knew I had it, that's all, and being with Sean proved me right. I can drive him mad. You should see what happens to him." Elin sighed. "Such a waste."

## *chapter* EIGHT

If you needed information on the habits of vampires, why not go to your friendly local vampire?

As prickly as their last parting had been, when Sean called Elin, she had agreed the two of them should try to arrange a talk with Saul today.

Prying her loose from her closeted visit with Leigh hadn't been easy, but Sean had pulled an advantage and asked Niles to communicate with his mate telepathically. Niles had wheedled Leigh into breaking up the tête-à-tête.

Not asking Elin what the two women had talked about took a lot of restraint, but Sean figured he would get it out of Niles later.

With Elin on the back of his bike, Sean had left Gabriel's.

When he turned onto Gulliver Lane, he slowed his Ducati to ride past Read It Again, and Wear It Again, two favorite local destination shops. Elin's grip on him tightened as they reached a cul-de-sac at the far end of the lane and came to a halt in the driveway of Dr. Saul VanDoren's house.

From the front of the house only two floors showed but Sean had been in Saul's basement living quarters, virtually below ground level at the back.

Elin tapped his shoulder and Sean took off his helmet when he looked at her. "I am sorry about being so foolish last night. I didn't think anything like that could happen."

How could he not hug her? "We came through okay—this time."

"Are you sure this is a good idea?" she said, indicating the house. "I don't want you and Saul to fight."

There was an innocence, a trust in her eyes. "We won't," Sean said, hoping he wasn't fooling himself into such confidence. "We asked to come because we want information and advice, remember."

"You're annoyed with him. You could say something you don't mean. Let's get home. Maybe one of the others will stand guard for me so you can go get some sleep tonight."

That discussion would come later. When they were alone—together. Their situation wouldn't do the way it was. He felt ridiculous. Their positions were almost reversed. He had to be the one to tell this woman he wanted so badly, that they must take more time before they came together totally. He struggled with awkwardness, and a simmering anger. Whatever he did, he would not hurt Elin. If the Team would not bend, he would give up his promises to them, take her away, and make a life, just the two of them, if that's what it took. He would remain the strong-minded man he was, had always been, and keep her at his side.

"Sean?" Elin had taken off her own helmet and she brought her face close to his. "Please kiss me and tell me you aren't angry with me. You look so...so..." She bowed her head.

"How can I be angry with you?" Gently, he took her face in his hands. "You know what I feel about you. You know what I want. But you don't accept that there are things I must be sure about before we are sealed."

Her mouth, soft and full, trembled. Sean touched his lips to hers, first lightly, then with more intensity. He drew back for an instant. "You are everything to me. Do you understand why I have to be strong—for both of us?"

Resentment flared in her eyes. "Don't assume that I'm not strong, Sean."

"I wouldn't want you other than what you are," he said. His possessiveness toward her could be unnerving, but he welcomed it nevertheless. "You're determined. Look at me and listen. I have to be certain that I won't be the death of you, do you understand?"

For moments she didn't move. Her incredible violet eyes deepened to purple and she shook her head slowly. "No," she whispered. "I understand that if we don't hold on to each other today, there may not be a tomorrow. I'm not talking about death. We don't know what will come, Sean, but we do know what we feel—what we have now."

She touched him as he had never expected to be touched by another human being. But he did have to think about tomorrow and he didn't want to explain all of it to her here. "Then you have to trust me to do what's best for both of us."

Elin stood, a shoe on either footrest, and planted her hands on his shoulders. She kissed him until his head spun. With her lips, her tongue, her teeth, the winding of her body about his, she demolished his resolve. If she demanded, he would do whatever she asked.

"I am yours," she said at last. "If you insist we must wait, you have a reason and I'll wait for you to explain what that is." She gave a sudden, impish smile. "As long as you don't get too bossy. But you'll have to forgive me if I tease you a little. It's one of my weaknesses."

Relief started to flood him, until he studied the curve of her lips, the mischief in her eyes. "Tease away," he said, while conviction grew that this creature could be his nemesis, in ways he had never imagined.

"Hah," she said. "You'd like me to tease you, but you insist we've got more important things to do...first. Do we have to see Saul tonight? Are you sure we do?" Elin was wheedling and she wasn't even trying to be subtle.

"You thought it was a good idea to call him and he's expecting us." He glanced at the darkening sky. From what he'd seen, light meant little to the vampires in the area but Saul seemed to avoid broad daylight. Something else he needed to understand. "I think Saul would prefer us to visit now." Sean watched for some reaction, but Elin only nodded and looked unhappy.

She was used to vampires who walked by day as well as by night. But did she know there was another way elsewhere?

Elin went toward the front door, reaching her hand toward him as she went, and Sean held on, entwining their fingers. "Does he have fangs?" she whispered, hesitating on the front step. "I've never seen them. That Colin creature is horrible. I hope you threw him so far he never comes back."

He wanted her to remember what happened because it would make her more careful, but he didn't intend to dwell on the details of the previous night. "There is a lot about Saul that I don't understand. He's not like other vampires. He seems…evolved?" That wasn't what he had intended to say but it was true.

She turned her face up to his, a frown wrinkling her brows. "Leigh said that's what Niles thinks, too."

"But you find him ugly and unappealing?" he asked, knowing he was pushing his luck.

She took hold of his collar and pulled his face down closer to hers. "Saul is very, very handsome. He doesn't appeal to me…not so far." Her grin was wicked.

He rang the bell and listened to its echo deep inside the house.

No footsteps warned that Saul was coming before he threw open the door and stood there, arms crossed, unsmiling. "Welcome. I hope I can be of help," he said. His dark eyes stared into Sean's. Neither of them had forgotten what had passed between them.

"I don't like inconveniencing you," Elin said, keeping her eyes averted from Sean. "But Sean and I both want to know more about…" Her voice trailed off.

"About vampires?" Saul finished for her with a vague smile. "You came to the right place."

"Perhaps we've offended you," Elin said. She drew in a big breath. "We should probably leave."

Saul smiled and opened his door wider. "Why don't

you come in? The Team and I have an understanding. We may not always like each other, but we have respect, we have supported one another."

Sean supposed Elin was right, the man was very handsome, dammit. And mysterious and...well, who knew what a woman saw in a particular man?

"Thanks," Sean said but Elin's grip on his hand tightened. She wasn't comfortable here—Saul made her nervous.

He led them past the clinic portion of the building and downstairs to an art deco basement that favored lime green velvet, odd, fringed lampshades, and cabinets that looked more like pieces of art than furniture.

The light was subdued, but dusk was hitting outside and Saul showed no sign of having just climbed out of his coffin or whatever he slept in.

"What frightens you?" Elin said suddenly. "There's got to be something that isn't obvious. I was always told you vampires don't like silver, but what else? Is the garlic thing true?"

Hiding a smile, Sean looked around. "Is it okay if we sit?" he asked. This woman who fascinated him so, and who held his heart in her hands, never failed to come up with another surprise.

"Take that couch," Saul said, indicating a lime green piece with fat, roll arms. "It's more comfortable than it looks—or so I'm told."

Sean decided not to question what that meant and led Elin to the couch.

"Silver can be a nuisance," Saul said. "It burns. Are you planning an attack on me, Elin?"

"Of course not." She sounded amused. "I'm curious. I am curious about everything. I'm also not violent. Can you be violent?"

*This is one way to get to the heart of things.* Sean decided to leave the two of them to spar their way through whatever this meeting ritual was.

"I can be," Saul said frankly. "If I must." He wasn't smiling.

"Do you know a vampire called Colin?" Elin said, looking the man directly in the face. "He's disgusting and he tried to kidnap me last night. Hateful. He got into the cottage, and if Sean hadn't come, that thing might have succeeded."

"Indeed?" Saul inclined his head. "You don't know about our local scourge, our vampire group intent on making their reputation true? Colin, his sister, and the rest of their blood-hungry crew? Do you know where they *live*, where they . . . do what such creatures do?"

Elin shook her head, no.

"They are not far from here," Saul said with a vague gesture. He raised his face. "I can smell them by the essence of their acts." His disgust was obvious.

Sean certainly knew of the scourge. Niles and Leigh had encountered them once.

"Why aren't you like them?" Elin said, and Sean began to wish he had taken hold of the conversation. "Or are you like them and pretending not to be?"

"I can't make you trust me simply by saying anything," Saul said. "I will prove it to you, though. You will have to learn to curb your tongue if we are to win, Elin. Danger is ahead. It's everywhere, and it is beyond anything you may have imagined. We'll have to be subtle and very, very careful."

Undeterred, Elin said, "Show me your fangs. All vampires have fangs, don't they? And why can you go out in daylight? You're not supposed to be able to do that."

Saul raised his expressive brows. "You came to me for help," he said. "Because you have been attacked by a vampire and you need to understand them better to arm yourself against them. To explain such a long history would take longer than any of us have. Should anything else occur, contact me at once. Meanwhile, I am puzzled that Colin felt free to enter the cottage without an invitation."

"I think at least one of Elin's questions deserves an answer," Sean interrupted. "Why would we believe you're different from the rest of the scourge, from Colin and his sister, and all their kind? What could make us trust you?"

"You don't have a choice," Saul said. "You say, 'the rest of the scourge.' I am no part of the scourge. My people are few and far away and nothing like these *animals* who have allowed themselves to sink into the depths."

"That's a nice speech," Elin said. "Sooner or later we'll know if it's all true."

Saul sat in a bright magenta chair. "I have been a vampire a long time—I think you know what I mean by a long time. My contacts are many and my influence reaches very far. I have followed the progress of the werehounds with interest. You are not like the wolves, Sean. They have no interest in regaining humanity. As you will learn, they are largely responsible for what has gone so dangerously wrong on Whidbey and what must be stopped.

"What I know about the two of you I have learned from Sally. She is very wise. She is a friend, a good woman who has taught me a great deal, some of which has saved lives."

Sean wasn't sure how comfortable he was with all of Saul's "knowledge." "I don't understand your interest in any of this. Or your part."

"I'll show you soon enough. First"—he paused as if searching for his next word—"as I've already said, Aldo suspects you are here."

Sean frowned. His stomach contracted. "Who is Aldo and what is he to me?" Damn the man—the hound.

"You know that," Saul said. He threw back his dark hair and glanced at Elin. "He wouldn't have any idea where you are and I wouldn't know your connection to him if things were not going badly. There are rumors and they reach far beyond San Francisco—and your last encounter with him. But I do have reports from there and how this Aldo caused... you know what he caused. There are always those who are willing to hunt for a bounty. You were found, Sean. Aldo still wants you, but the situation has changed as you will find out in time. Probably sooner than we'd like. In other circumstances he would come himself. In his mind he thinks he needs something from you."

"What does he mean?" Elin asked Sean, her voice a little shaky. "Who is Aldo?"

"No one," Sean said quickly. He wasn't pleased with Saul bringing this up in front of her. "Well, yes, he is someone and I will explain in good time. Please let me decide when that is."

"My plan was to go to Niles with all this, but not until I had done more investigation," Saul said. "You forced my hand. Now I believe the fewer we involve, the better—for now. If you feel you must go directly to Niles, I won't attempt to stop you."

Sean didn't respond. No way would he tell a vampire that he, a hound, would take orders from him one way or another.

"Things have changed in our world, the paranormal world, and they will only go in a horrifying direction if we don't manage to stop the one who wants to own us all," Saul said. "The One on The Island."

"Where?" Elin said, her eyes huge. "What island? Who is he?"

Sean put a hand on her arm. "Don't be too quick to accept anything Saul says."

"I wasn't born a vampire, dammit," Saul said in the first show of temper Sean had ever seen from him. "I ended up here for two reasons. I was invited to The Island, and I don't mean Whidbey. There is another island out there." He waved a hand to the southwest. "And I discovered my host, known only as The One, although there is another name and I intend to learn what it is, The One was more dangerous than you can imagine. He *is* more dangerous than any you have encountered.

"He has already tried to alter all of us with his blood meddling. And he has altered many—most into twisted forms of what they already were. He has infected a vast number in our world with his failed experiments. Instead of bringing them to him as docile slaves happy to entertain him, he has caused them to stop reproducing. And this mad creature must be eliminated before he manages to unleash an army of mutant monsters on all of us, including the humans."

Sean stiffened. "But if you are right, that would mean hounds were invited to this island. And they went."

"The contagion is strong, deadly, it would only take one of you let loose on all the others. There must have been at least one, perhaps more."

Saul held up a hand for silence.

That silence went on and on and showed no sign of being broken by the vampire.

When Elin couldn't stand it any longer, she said, "Sean?" forgetting to keep her voice down.

"Hush," Sean said.

"I need to think," Saul said.

*"This is too weird."* Elin felt her thoughts reaching out for Sean's mind.

Sean looked startled. *"I'm hearing you telepathically,"* he said into her mind. *"We will practice, but we should wait until later. I dreamed this would happen for us."*

Elin couldn't help grinning. She wanted to hug him.

"Perhaps we should continue this later," Sean said to Saul, who might even have been asleep. "Elin has been through too much since yesterday."

Rather than argue, Elin bit her lip. She wanted to hear whatever Saul might reveal.

"You are so protective of her, which is a good thing." Saul wrapped his coat more tightly around him and glared at them. "The vampire attack will have shown you how serious your enemies are. Not that we know how many enemies you have or who they are. Haven't you questioned how Colin was able to enter the cottage? I take it you didn't invite him."

"No one did," Elin said.

"At some time he was invited in by someone other than a vampire. We need to find out who that was."

"I want to go home," Elin said. If Saul had something else to tell them, later would do.

Saul said, "I must ask you not to leave just yet. You are both aware that some of the local women have disappeared over the past few months."

"Of course," Sean said while Elin nodded. "Less and less is said about it. And there haven't been any more incidents lately."

"Not that anyone is aware of," Saul said. "They are fooling everyone into thinking it's all over. Most of the women who were taken have been returned, apparently with no memory of what happened to them. They have preferred to let the incidents drop. Without actual complaints, the authorities could do nothing—they could not have done anything regardless." Saul appeared tired. "I believe the victims were taken to The Island, the place I've already spoken of, and that's why their memories were wiped clean."

"Where is this island?" Elin whispered. "What is it called?"

"It is called The Island, that's all. It's volcanic and rises from the sea under cover of invisibility, except to those who are allowed to see it. Only The One, he who orders everything there, can make it visible—to anyone—except for the few vampires of my lineage who can also reveal the place, not that we would do so if there were an alternative.

"I was there because I was invited by The One. It sounded innocent enough, risky perhaps, but an opportunity for vampires to get together and discuss the progress of our world. Then I discovered he expected me to be one of his blood experiments before I went out to convince more vampires to come to him. He wanted all of us to serve him.

"I am of a Parisian strain and we are different, not easily used by anyone. Since The One is also Parisian, he should have known about us. I left and have been working to get rid of this madman."

Elin shivered and was glad when Sean put an arm around her. "Why hasn't this wizard, or whatever he is, come after you? I want to see him, and his island."

There was no mistaking the dangerous edge to what Sean said, or that he was letting Saul know he wanted proof of his accusations.

"Unfortunately I'd be a fool to imagine that I'm not marked for destruction. And this is no wizard, Sean. Sorcerer, perhaps. Possibly living sorcerer vampire."

Elin clutched at Sean. "No one can fight such a thing," she told him. "How does he stay alive? On what?" she asked Saul, terrified of his answer.

The vampire's eyes were black with no visible pupils. "I can't be completely certain but I don't think he needs to eat often. Perhaps even as rarely as every few weeks— unless he is ill and I think he may be." A thin red rim formed around the black of those eyes. "He eats human parts. Living human parts."

"Enough," Sean said through clenched teeth. "Save your speculation. How did he get those who disappeared?"

"He didn't get them. Your friends the werewolves decided to circumvent him by trying an experiment of their own. The infection enters the blood. They have suffered the same fate as so many. They were infected and their females died during pregnancy. But the wolves are undisciplined and think they can take control of anything. They took the victims they stole to The Island because they knew they would not be discovered. They have also speculated that the volcanic vein The One tends may have magical qualities that would help them."

Faintness started a buzzing in Elin's head.

"I don't believe any of this," Sean said, starting to pull Elin toward the stairs.

Saul cut them off. "If you don't believe, we'll all be lost. The wolves took women and transfused them with blood to match their own. It was their own blood they used. They think if they can change women who aren't part wolf, they will reproduce for them."

"Let's go," Elin said.

"What they did—if they did it—didn't work," Sean said. "The women are all back and involved in their former lives, just as they were."

"You know that's not true," Saul said. "Come with me." He walked to a corridor that led into darkness, and from the way he moved, he seemed to assume they would follow.

"What does he mean?" Elin asked. "We know it's not true that those women came back?"

Sean pulled her into an embrace. "Just go with this. If we need help, I can get it here in moments. But I don't believe he intends to harm either of us."

"Are you strong, Elin?" Saul asked. He didn't turn to look at them. "Let me know if you faint easily."

"Perhaps you should stay—"

"No," she cut Sean off. "I don't faint at my own shadow if that's what you mean, Saul. We're right behind you."

"Those other women show no sign of harm," Sean said.

Saul did glance over his shoulder then and his smile was more a grimace. "It's what we can't see that should worry us. Who knows what they are now, or what they are capable of becoming? Or if there are others we don't know about."

Elin's skin was clammy and cool. She was rarely aware of temperature and the sensation scared her.

Saul held a swinging door open for them. Bright, white light shone in a large room where stainless steel glittered from sinks and tables.

"I think you should wait here," Sean said under his breath.

Elin entered with him.

Along one short wall was what Elin recognized as a bank of refrigerated compartments. "This is a mortuary," she said, deliberately steady and clear. "I'd forgotten you're also the medical examiner when the usual one isn't available."

"I'm glad to do what I can for the people here," Saul said. "Every service is necessary and should be performed with respect. Sean, you will know the reasons for my concern soon enough."

He slid open a drawer in the refrigeration unit and Sean immediately moved in close.

Saul looked questioningly at Elin. "You don't need to do this," he said.

If she were honest, she would admit she didn't want to be there but she stood beside Sean and nodded.

When Saul peeled back the sheet covering a small adult body, he revealed a woman with pale, matted hair. Her discolored face was peaceful.

"Rose?" Sean sounded disbelieving. "She's still here? She died months ago. I understood..." He stopped and glanced at Elin, then shook his head.

"Yes, Rose," Saul said. "She is the only link I have. I know she was transfused. I know it did not go well, and as with a lot of The One's specimens, she was allergic to the blood she got from the wolves. But that isn't enough to kill in most cases. She had returned here and eventually might have done as well as the others—or as well as they seem to have done. Her body has already helped me immeasurably."

"She is so vulnerable," Elin said, wanting to cry for the sad, broken little body. "This can't be right to keep her here. She should be treated with respect."

"I have more respect for this body than you can know," Saul said. "It is our answer, if only we can find it. I have to be certain why she suddenly died when the others didn't."

"Certain?" Sean said. "You mean you think you know?"

Saul turned Rose's head to one side and lifted her hair away from her neck to reveal the base of her skull. "There," he said, pointing.

Elin's skin grew tight. It prickled, but she got closer.

Behind the left ear, on the bone, a mark shone. It almost glowed. A tiny, brilliant red O.

Shaking, Elin reached out and touched the mark.

"I think it is the mark of The One," Saul said. "His initial, perhaps. And I believe she died when that was put there. I'm searching for what makes the mark."

"A deadly poison?" Sean peered very closely. "Is it an O? Or a Q?"

Saul also bent to reexamine the patch. "There could be a tail," he said.

Elin couldn't stop her fingers from returning to the spot. She heard high-pitched wailing and felt herself begin to fade.

"He knows Whidbey well," Saul said. "The One. We don't know who he is, but he has an agent working for him here. I believe we look into his eyes, talk to him— too bad we don't know who he is when he comes."

## *chapter* NINE

So, what's the deal with barging in on Elin and me?" Leigh said, finding Niles at work in the addition to the back of Gabriel's. "You gave me a headache with all those orders. *Don't ignore me. I know you can hear. It's important for Elin to leave now.* No pressure, hm?" She was darned if she'd resort to mind talk when they were only feet apart.

Niles kept right on stapling wallboard in what was to become her enlarged office, making a noise like an assault weapon on steroids.

He wore an industrial headset and goggles.

Leigh made do with her fingers pushed in her ears and shouted, "Niles."

Niles didn't hear her and pretended he also didn't know she was there, which was dopey since there was no way to creep up on the man.

She wasn't a woman to waste an unfair advantage.

With both hands above his head, one holding the wall-board, the other aiming the staple gun, Niles was an irresistible target.

For a few wonderfully wicked moments, she took in the torn, paint-spattered T-shirt that didn't hide much of his tanned body and none of his taut, muscular midsection. Speaking of paint, his faded old jeans might have been applied with a brush. Surrounded by the scent of new cedar shavings, she closed her eyes, tried to steady her pounding heart and the rush of blood to her head and other places.

That was a wasted effort.

Leigh moved in, wrapped her arms around him, rested her face on his back, and wormed her fingers under the front of his shirt.

He jumped but at least he stopped stapling, even if she was glad she couldn't make out everything he muttered under his breath.

His belly sucked in tight and her little fingers slid so easily under the waistband of his jeans.

"I asked what was so important that I had to interrupt my visit with Elin?" she said.

"Sean needed her. Do you know how dangerous it is to attack a man who is using a staple gun?"

"Nope. Never did it before. And when did you start caring about Sean and Elin?"

"I try to be an understanding man."

She let that go. "Have I told you lately what your chest does to me? What every sexy inch of you does to me?"

"Remind me."

"Mmm." Leigh ran her fingers up, rib after rib, until

she reached his instantly tensed nipples. "Is it coming back to you?" Hugging him with all the strength she had, she clung to him.

"Not sure yet." But he sounded a little short of breath. He braced his arms against the wall and made no move to stop her. "Give it time, though."

"How come the rest of the guys left right after Sean and Elin? And how come Innes made a big deal of stopping by to let me know you gave them the rest of the day off?"

"They've been at it since early this morning."

"If they worked twenty-four out of every twenty-four, they wouldn't suffer too badly."

Niles's breathing got heavier with every stroke and probe of her fingers. "Maybe I wanted to be alone," he said, his voice taking on the low, husky quality she understood so well.

Leigh held still. "Should I go? I understand needing space sometimes."

"Don't you dare," he said with something close to a laugh.

It's hard to laugh when you're sucking in breaths at the same time.

"Okay," Niles said. "I'll fess up. I sent them all away because I just want to be with you. Is that a sin?"

She pulled his shirt up and kissed him between his shoulder blades. "Why don't you take this off," she murmured. "So much easier."

He did as he was told at once and gave her a speculative look over his shoulder. "I thought it was time we had some serious discussion that affects our lives."

His tone, the slight frown, made her stomach flip, but she kept a smile on her face and sidled over to lock the door. "A door that locks," she said, raising one brow. "In a room that isn't even finished and won't be for a while."

Looking smug, he leaned on it. "Finished the lock after the others left. Never say I don't plan ahead."

"I wouldn't," but she didn't entirely buy his playful words or approach. She was too in tune with him not to sense a darker undercurrent. "You do a lot of planning." Some of which made her suspicious of his motives.

"Maybe we should go home," Leigh said. That would buy her some preparation time and he might soften whatever was coming by dropping unintentional hints.

Niles faced her with his hands on his hips. She was confronted with his naked torso and powerful arms and she didn't need to know any more about anatomy to see that every muscle and sinew was tensed. The muscles in his jaw flicked and she could almost hear his teeth grinding.

"What is it?" she said. And her own temper thinned. "You look as if you'd like to have me for dinner."

His face relaxed a fraction. "I'd like you for every dinner. That's not the point."

"Niles, just spit it out. I can't stand seeing you upset—and don't argue, because you are upset."

He held out his arms and she flung herself at him. They held on to one another with the kind of ferocious desperation that excited Leigh while it frightened her. Something was very wrong.

She almost pulled away. This maelstrom of confusion and sexual tension that hung on the edge of something unknown was the last thing she could face when she was already so anxious.

Niles buried his face in her shoulder. "I love you more than I can explain," he told her indistinctly. "Without you I'd have nothing."

"The same goes for me. But we have each other. Are you afraid of something?" Leigh knew at least part of the answer and wished it weren't true. She had hoped he would relax the longer they were together. The reverse continued to happen.

He looked into her face and for an instant she thought he would let her into his deepest thoughts and allow her to share his fears. But then he crushed her against him again, found her mouth with his, and kissed her until she pushed on his shoulders and gasped for breath.

As quickly as she separated her mouth from his, Niles continued kissing her.

Leigh drove her fingers into his hair and squeezed her eyes shut. Cool air hit the overheated skin around her ribs. Niles pulled her sweater over her head and dropped it. His hands were all over her and with such desperate concentration that she could scarcely hold on to any part of him.

"There's nowhere," she managed to pant. "Can we go home?"

"Too late. I want you now. Any way I can have you."

Her legs turned to water and she almost sagged. Everything female in her burned until she longed to lie down and take him with her.

Niles's feverish, shocking blue eyes lost focus. He moved like a man obsessed, obsessed and separated from reason.

He didn't need her help to strip off the rest of her clothes, and his own. "Can't slow down," he panted, lifting her by the waist and kissing her breasts, the sides of her neck, her mouth, and returning to suck in a nipple.

Leigh gritted her teeth. All she could do was let him make love to her. She was no match for his strength or his mental and physical concentration on pleasuring her body.

Niles lifted her again, just enough to join them. Down onto him he guided her and she was lost to the searing, scalding penetration that was always their lovemaking. She held his slick shoulders through an explosive climax. Her cheeks were wet with her own tears.

Still embracing her as if he wanted to fuse their bodies, Niles slid down the wall, still inside her, until he could clamp her with his thighs and hold her where he could stare at her, his face still dark with passion but the tension drained away now.

The gently intense smile he gave expanded her with joy. She shook her hair back and laughed. "How did I get so lucky?" she said. "I can't help it, I just wonder why someone else hadn't snapped you up long before we had a chance to meet."

"We were meant to be," he said, and he was serious again. He leaned forward and kissed her face, kiss after kiss, drawing back from time to time to look at her.

Niles laced his hands loosely around her neck, stroked her shoulders, her arms, her breasts. Inclining his head, he looked at her breasts and spanned her ribs at the same time.

A very big man, every ounce of flesh was muscular.

The solid leanness of his belly and hips fascinated her. She started her own touching, testing trail.

Niles softly rubbed her hips, fanned his fingers forward and over her stomach. He framed her breasts again, supported them.

Leigh saw a subtle, gradual change in his expression and his gaze flew to meet hers. She tried to smile but bit her lip instead. Niles shook his head slowly. His mouth made a soundless "No."

The instant before he took her in his arms again, the instant before he shut his eyes, a sheen was there. A hard swallow jerked his throat.

"Are you?" he whispered.

She nodded on his shoulder, "Yes."

"But you're taking—" He broke off, running his fingers through her hair over and over again, his cheek pressed to hers.

"I was already pregnant. I think it happened the night we were sealed."

He shuddered. "My fault. All my fault."

Leigh held him tight. "This was how it all started, Niles. You wanted the hounds to start having children again and for the children to bring you closer to being human. You wanted this and now you have it. And I want it."

"I made assumptions," Niles said. "I chose to believe what seemed logical, that with human women we could not only reproduce again, but both woman and child would live and we could have what we've truly wanted— to become closer and closer to being the humans we were born to be."

Leigh made him look at her. She held his head with both of her hands. "I'm not surprised you're behaving like this. I don't know what's changed but you completely stopped talking about us having children. I was afraid to tell you. This should be the happiest moment in our lives but I'm afraid of your anger." She was close to tears but blinked them away.

"You will never be afraid of me," Niles said, at the same time struggling to keep his voice from rising. "Never, do you understand me?"

Leigh didn't answer.

"What changed for me is that all I care about is having you with me. If all the calculations were wrong and you can't carry this baby safely…and I lose you…" He turned her until he could hold her against him. "It's you I want. I don't care about anything else."

Gently taking hold of one of his hands, she pressed it to her belly. "Don't say you don't care about this little one. The baby needs your love, too, and your care and guidance when the time comes."

Stroking the little thickening at her middle, he rested his head against the wall. Leigh watched his expression go from confusion, to pain, to desperation.

"I want to hold our child, love it, care for it, but only with you beside me."

"I will be beside you."

"Leigh." He stared into her eyes. "If the child begins to sap you as the female werehounds were sapped. If I can tell you are fading, I—I will do whatever I have to do. If there is a choice to be made, I won't wait. I'll choose you."

## *chapter* TEN

Get your helmet on," Sean said to Elin. She stood beside the Ducati with her back to him and her arms crossed. "Are you okay?"

She shook her head, no.

"What is it?" He had been a fool to hope she hadn't really noticed what Saul said about Aldo.

"You're keeping things from me. I expect you to have your secrets—you must for your own safety. But Saul talked about this Aldo as if he expected me to know about him."

Sean went around the bike and took Elin by the arms. He sat on the seat of the bike and held her in front of him. "I should have told you by now. I've tried to put the whole thing behind me. Maybe I thought it would go away if I did that."

"But it didn't," she said. Her mouth was stiff. "Tell me, please."

He didn't want to. Stroking her upper arms, he looked away.

"We've talked about trusting each other, Sean. But you don't trust me with whatever this is. Okay." She shrugged. "Let it go."

"I can't," he said, facing her again. This feeling that he was joined to her was so good, but he was afraid of hurting her somehow. "Not anymore. I'm going to lay it out. If you know me at all, you'll believe in me—that's not fair. We all need time to take things in."

Elin never took her eyes from his.

"For five years the San Francisco police have believed I murdered a woman in a club there. There's no reason for me to think they've stopped looking for me."

Her features had frozen. He heard her shallow breathing.

"Aldo was the werehound who first turned me and he never stopped wanting to own me. He got me to that club and used me to kill a helpless woman."

Her lips parted. Sean waited for her to pull away, to run away from him, but she didn't move. "Used you to kill?" she said, very low. "How could that be?"

He didn't want to think about it, or remember the details. Explaining aloud would be hell.

Elin had started to tremble.

"Oh, my God," he muttered. "You've never been in a place like that and you'll never go. Drunkenness, drugs used in plain sight, debauchery—I can't describe it all. Madness all around me. That freak grabbed me and slammed my head into the woman's face." He felt sick. "Twice. It killed her and in all the chaos no one questioned that I was her murderer. Now Saul is saying Aldo has shown up—not here on Whidbey, but Saul has seen him."

He had the sensation that Elin could easily collapse but he was afraid to pull her closer in case she fought him.

"When Saul asked me to see him outside Gabriel's Place, that's what he wanted to tell me. I may not be crazy about that vamp but he was worried about you. He wanted to warn me not to do anything to hurt you."

"You didn't trust me enough to tell me," Elin said. She was very pale and she looked away repeatedly. "How do you have a lasting relationship with someone you don't trust?"

He shook his head, miserable, furious with his own stupidity. "I've always trusted you. But I was afraid you could be frightened of me. Who would find it easy to talk about something like that?"

"Look at me," Elin said. "Really look at me. Am I so scary? Didn't anyone ever tell you things just get worse when you lie about them?"

"I didn't lie."

He heard her swallow and her lashes got very shiny. She blinked rapidly. "In a way you did. When you kept it from me, you were lying. How many other things have you kept from me because you think I can't handle them?"

How could he blame her? "There may be things I haven't mentioned because they were no big deal," he said. "Elin, I've never felt close to anyone the way I do to you. You're my everything. If you won't stay with me...No, I'm not laying any threats on you."

"Finish what you started, Sean."

He let out breath on a whistle. "Hell, this is hard. I wouldn't ever have hurt you deliberately. If you won't stay with me, I don't know what I'll do, but the rest of my life will be about regretting what a fool I've been."

Getting up the courage to release her, he held his arms out, inviting her to let him hold her.

She hesitated, and came to him, rested her face on his shoulder.

"Are we okay?" He heard his own voice shake.

Elin nodded. "We will be. We have to be. Do you think I could let you go?"

"I hope not." The lump in his throat tightened. "I know you can't, any more than I can. Let me look at you, then we have to get out of here."

She pulled away a little, not smiling, but with love in her eyes.

"I've got you," he told her. "That's amazing. I never expected someone as wonderful as you to happen to me."

Elin looked at his mouth, traced his lips with a forefinger. "I feel too much to put into words." She put on her helmet. "Where are we going?" she asked and sounded as shaken as Sean figured she had to be.

He decided not to give her any choices. "Langley for something to eat. I don't want to run into anyone we know if I can help it." And since Saul's announcements had just rocked the world for all the people he cared about, he had to come up with a plan.

"That was a shock in there," Elin said. She glanced repeatedly at Saul's house. "Did you realize what happened when I touched the Q on Rose's neck?"

"Best not say that aloud," Sean told her, looking in all directions. Since Saul was probably right about this beast walking among them, it was incredibly important that he not know his cover was in the process of being blown.

She looked at him from beneath thick, shadowy eyelashes. "Right. Just think how bored you'd be if you didn't have to correct me constantly."

Women were so difficult to understand. "What happened when you touched the mark?" he said, deciding not to rise to the bait of her last remark.

"For a long time I couldn't take my hand away. It felt like the mark and my fingers were magnets—really strong magnets. I couldn't let go and I felt awful, like I would faint. I heard wailing."

He was stumped. "Yes, I noticed you were reacting but I don't know why. How do you feel now?"

"Scared. But okay."

"Mm," Sean said. "You're a tough cookie. I'm not sure I'll be able to keep up with you."

The sharp look she gave him suggested she didn't realize he was joking. With his right hand beneath her jaw, he stroked her cheek with his thumb. "You aren't a wimp, kiddo, and I like that. In fact, I might as well admit I'd rather be with you than anyone else."

She smiled at him.

The guinea pig that popped out of her jacket and ran around her neck until she could glance between them with her darting black eyes did seem to be smiling.

"Pokey!" Elin said.

"Nosey little pig. Put her wherever you keep her and let's go."

Promptly, the critter darted into Elin's jacket again.

Sean kissed her, long and lingeringly, before she moved her head slightly and whacked the bridge of his nose with her helmet.

"Ow."

"I'm sorry." She giggled. "That was awful. Completely spoiled the moment."

Smiling ruefully, Sean said, "Elin, we communicated in there." He indicated Saul's house. "Mindspeak. Do you know what that means?"

She shook her head, no. "Not really. It never happened to me before. Not like that. When I shift, I can carry and convey messages to certain sensitives, but I've never had conversations. Sally always tells me stuff aloud when I'm Skillywidden. I don't think about it. That's how it goes."

*"But you can hear me like this?"* He probed her mind again.

The expression in her violet eyes was almost funny. *"Yes, but I'd rather talk to you if we can."*

He hauled her off her feet and swung her around. "So would I, cat woman."

She rained blows on his shoulders, frowning furiously. "Put me down, dog man."

He grimaced and continued to hold her feet off the ground. "I get your point. I always thought cat woman sounded cool, is all. Dog man—"

"Not so much?" she asked, and tapped his mouth. "I like it that our minds can touch." Her gaze slid away. "What are we thinking about? We've got to talk to Niles and the others about what Saul told us. Now."

Slowly, Sean let her slide to stand on the road. "I

know," he said. "That's why Langley seemed a good idea. A chance to think through what Saul told us." And to prepare for whatever Niles's reaction was to Elin having heard everything.

"Niles will want to know about it quickly," she pointed out.

He nodded, yes, and narrowed his eyes to study her. "You're shivering. This isn't the first time you've looked so cold. I didn't think that happened to fae like you."

Elin shrugged. "It's probably because there's been a lot of tension. I don't know. It isn't important." He didn't miss the distance that came into her eyes. She might say it wasn't important that her body temperature had changed, but she wasn't sure about it.

He wrapped her close. Whatever was causing this chill in her, he would make sure she got warmer clothes. Darkness had begun to close in and the wind picked up. The uncertainty he felt himself was deep inside and sickening. He had stopped thinking the way he was expected to think—always with the good of the Team first.

The first thing he should have done when he left Saul's, without any question, was contact Niles.

"Can we go?" Elin said quietly.

Her leather jacket seemed useless. The wind had an icy edge and before long at least Elin would be at the mercy of whatever light came from a puny moon. "I want to put out a call for Niles," he said. "Bear with me."

He signaled his alpha and instantly flinched when waves of confusion came back. Sean's breath shortened. *What the hell's the matter with you, Niles? This is Sean. I need to talk to you. I just left Doc Saul's. He scared the hell out of me—or he will have if we don't figure out a plan.*"

"*Wait,*" was the one-word response, followed by the channel closing.

Elin was trying to see his expression but he didn't look at her.

The first needles of light sleet hit his exposed skin and he turned Elin's face to his jacket. "Shouldn't be long," he told her. "Niles will get right back to me." And, goddammit, if Niles messed him around much more, Sean wouldn't be available to be reached.

"*Are you still on Gulliver Lane?*"

No time for niceties, huh? "*Yeah.*"

"*Meet us at Read It Again.*"

"*The bookshop?*"

"*Last time I checked, that's what it was. On our way now.*"

Sean locked his jaw. Without a word, he lifted Elin onto the back of his bike and slid on in front of her. They had less than the distance of a couple of blocks to go; nevertheless, he drove too fast getting to the shop. Elin got off the instant he came to a stop in front of the lighted stained-glass windows of Read It Again.

She had to feel his simmering anger.

He cut the engine and kicked on the stand. "Sorry, Elin," he said, catching her hand. "I'm getting hell from Niles and I don't know why. I shouldn't take it out on you."

"You don't mean to," she said.

"He wants to meet here. Don't ask me why but it's weird."

"Could be he thinks it's safe," she pointed out. "We're friends with Phoebe."

The sleet set up a whirl like a tornado and Elin put her hands over her face.

Niles landed, Leigh clamped to his side, in a similar swirl of frozen rain. The alpha's expression reminded Sean of the way the man looked when he went into battle. Sean was glad Elin wasn't looking.

Leigh, her hands curled into fists against her mate's chest, exuded fury. "I didn't like that," she snapped at Niles.

Immediately Elin dropped her hands from her face and stared.

"It's okay, honey," Niles said, still holding her against him and stroking her back. "I know what I'm doing and I needed to get here fast."

"We'll talk about it later," Leigh said, and she was warning him. "In future I come by car. Or even on that mad Harley of yours."

Sean controlled a smile. "Up to some of your flying tricks again?" he said to Niles. They weren't supposed to fly as humans unless there was no choice.

"Get inside," Niles said. "Elin looks frozen."

They went toward the door and Phoebe threw it open before they reached it. "Come on in. You can have the upstairs to yourselves. You'll find anything you need up there." She must have been watching for them.

"Jan's not here?" Elin said. Jan was Leigh's twin sister.

"She doesn't work today," Phoebe and Leigh said together. Phoebe laughed and continued, "Business is pretty quiet at the moment."

With a hand at Leigh's back, Niles guided her upstairs and the other two went quickly behind.

"Just yell if you want me," Phoebe said, juggling books in one arm. "I've got a couple of hours of shelving to do."

A potbelly stove stood in the middle of the shop with hot chocolate and cider available on top. Book stacks stretched floor to ceiling and old but comfortable chairs were placed in convenient spots.

Upstairs was almost a mirror of downstairs except for a lot more disorder. Boxes and stacks of books yet to be shelved. Unsteady piles of magazines. And no stove. A dividing wall separated the open room from Phoebe's living quarters.

Chairs were arranged in a circle at the farthest point from the stairs, immediately beneath a skylight that showed only darkness beyond. Pots of coffee, a jug of cider, mugs, and cookies waited on a tray in the middle of a scarred cherry wood table.

It was Leigh who drew Sean's full attention. She huddled in one of the leather chairs, her arms crossed and her chin sunk on her chest. He had never seen her so colorless and pinched. But then, his alpha paced circles about the room in a manner not at all like his usual cool self. Sure, Niles had a temper, but there was something different about this.

The hard expression only softened when he looked at his mate. And then, soften it might but whatever lay beneath that expression was different, abnormally intent. His eyes, always impossible to ignore because they had the quality of blue flame, seemed to keep Leigh in their scope all the time.

"We met with Saul," Sean said, keeping his voice level and quiet.

"So you said."

Elin drew herself up and looked as if she would say something sharp to Niles but she caught the faint shake of Sean's head. "Why don't you sit down," he said and took off his jacket. "Put this over your legs, you look cold." She did look extremely cold and he could see her shivering. Perhaps she was getting sick.

Leigh looked at Elin with an expression Niles couldn't read. Suddenly she shifted and stood up, all determination. She dealt with the mugs, pouring cider without asking if someone would prefer coffee, and gave some to Elin. Next she put a plate of cookies into Sean's hands and said, "Make sure everyone eats some of those. A little sugar might help around here—carbs can raise the spirits." She looked into his face and said, "Have I told you lately that your eyes look like a tiger's when you've got a lot on your mind. They glow like you're on a hunt."

"Yeah?" This wasn't the time or place to get drawn into the confrontation he sensed was on Leigh's mind. She was angry, probably made angry by the tension all around her.

"You don't feel the cold, Elin," Leigh said thoughtfully. "The fae don't."

Absolute silence followed and lasted far too long.

"Elin's cold?" Niles said as if hearing part of the conversation for the first time. "Leigh feels the cold, too. Unless she's in the water." He turned up one corner of his mouth. "Would you mind waiting for us downstairs, Elin?"

"Yes, she damn well would mind," Sean blurted out. "So would I. Where I go, she goes."

Niles stopped in mid-pace and faced off with Sean

but Leigh interrupted him. "The fae don't feel cold," she repeated. She hadn't moved her gaze from Elin. "Why would you—"

"We'll take this up again later," Niles said to Sean.

"Why would a fae start feeling the cold?" Leigh repeated.

"I think it's Tarhazian at work," Elin said. "She helped me develop my talents because it suited her. I know what she's up to. She's changing things to see if I'll go running to her, begging to be forgiven. Some hope. So I get cold now. I'll get winter clothes when I get around to it."

"We'll get them immediately," Sean said. He stared at her and felt his scalp tighten. "If Tarhazian thinks to punish you by removing fae talents, what are we talking about? If she takes them all?"

"I don't want to discuss it," Elin said. "She may just be experimenting with my body temperature and nothing else. I prefer not to talk about other personal things."

"Like shapeshifting into an undersized cat?" Niles said. "Not much use in a fight, I'd say."

Rounding on him, Sean had to hold back from landing a punch. "You're in a foul mood. Save it. We've got enough problems here."

"You don't know half of it," Niles said. He threw himself into the chair closest to Leigh's.

Sean didn't want to say it but he had to. "Elin, don't shift again, okay?"

She picked a chocolate chip out of her soft cookie and paused with it on the way to her mouth. "I beg your pardon?"

"You know what he means," Leigh said.

"Maybe she'd prefer to get stuck as a cat," Niles said. "It might simplify her life."

"Shut up," Leigh said, and there was silence.

Niles shook a hand in front of his face. "I'm sorry. I take it back. I'm not myself."

"You're suggesting Tarhazian could take away my ability to shift," Elin said quietly. "Perhaps she could but I was born able to shift. And as long as I can remember, I could fly."

Niles looked a whole lot more interested in Elin. "I'm impressed—"

"I haven't finished," she said, cutting him off. "Skillywidden can also become invisible. There's more, but I don't choose to talk about it."

A knowing glance passed between Leigh and Elin and for an instant Sean thought they were going to chuckle. They both sobered and looked in opposite directions.

"What else?" Niles said.

"It's private," Elin said. "Let it go, please."

"I can't risk something happening that could be dangerous to the Team," Niles argued.

"Nothing about me could ever be dangerous to the Team."

Niles's glance at Sean suggested he thought Elin was being difficult. "You'd better let us know what else Tarhazian could do to you," he said.

"Please," Elin said. "There's nothing for you to worry about."

Niles shrugged but he didn't look convinced.

Neither was Sean. Later he would be getting any details out of her.

"Moving right along," he said. "Unless you want to waste more time on trivial crap, we'd better try to get our minds around Saul's announcement this afternoon."

"Do you think it would be quicker if we asked Saul to come over?" Elin said.

"If he'd spoken to the Team in the first place, it would have been quicker. Whatever *it* is."

"He, whoever *he* is." Elin was busy diving for chocolate chips again. "Saul doesn't know who this horrible person is when he's here on Whidbey. Maybe he's afraid he's one of the hounds. I suppose it could be. After all—"

"Elin," Sean said rapidly. "Niles needs the whole story, not just the end of what Saul said."

She frowned at him, but in question, not annoyance. "Yes, of course." Her head whipped in Leigh's direction and the frown cleared. "Of course. It took a moment but I see it now. Why didn't I know it as soon as you arrived. Niles has a lot on his mind and I bet he'd rather be alone with Leigh."

Niles cleared his throat.

"A baby," Elin said, grinning, her eyes filling with happy tears. "It's starting to happen, Sean. Our Team is going to have another generation."

## *chapter* ELEVEN

An hour and a lot of terse words later, nothing was much clearer, other than confirmation that Elin's uncanny ability to announce invisible pregnancies was accurate.

Leigh wasn't just upset by Niles's negative reaction to the baby, she was also afraid for all of them. Each time Sean relayed more of what he and Elin had been told by Saul, Niles's mood grew darker, and he interrupted every few sentences. Her own fear struck deeper as Saul's story emerged.

"Hey!" Phoebe called up the stairs. "Can I bring some fresh coffee?"

Niles tightened his lips. "In other words, she can hear every word we say up here. I didn't think it was a good idea to come here."

"It was my idea," Leigh said quietly. She raised her voice. "That would be great, Phoebe. Thanks."

"This is a good place," Elin said. She reached out and squeezed Leigh's hand. "But we have to be sure we aren't overheard."

"As far as I know, Phoebe can't hear us," Leigh said. "Not that I don't trust her completely so I wouldn't be worried if she did hear." Elin's cold hand worried her. She wondered if Tarhazian could do things they hadn't even thought of. "We're going to have to settle down, Niles. We're in some sort of trap and we don't know where the enemy is, or who he is when he's among us."

"Could just as well be a she," Sean said. "We can't be sure this sorcerer's spy is a man."

Niles looked thoughtful. "Sally has been a good friend but I wonder—"

"Sally has nothing to do with this," Leigh snapped. "If the fae do you a favor, you're going to owe something in return. I'm not saying anything we don't already know and so far she hasn't asked for a thing. But Sally has looked after Elin and we probably wouldn't have found each other without her, Niles."

"It's probably only because Elin is fae," Niles said. "One of her own kind. That's why she's so careful with her."

"No," Elin told him. "She's my friend. Do you want me to go away? If it'll make it easier on everyone else, I'll go back to Two Chimneys. You want to come, Leigh? You look tired out."

"Sally knows I'm not fae," Leigh said, becoming exhausted by Niles's antagonism. "She couldn't have done more for me if I were her daughter."

"If you and Leigh go, Elin, I'll have to go with you,"

Sean said. "We're going in circles. Niles, should we call in the rest of the Team?"

Niles turned his back and stood quite still for what seemed minutes. "Sean," he said. "We need to deal with some Team business. It won't take long."

On the way out the front door, Niles asked Phoebe to wait a bit before taking more coffee upstairs. Sean was grateful the other man made sure he sounded pleasant.

A few steps from the shop, Niles stopped and faced Sean. "We need to keep our voices down," he said. "Not that I can feel anything that shouldn't be around."

"Neither can I," Sean said, his face raised to the driving snow.

"I trust you like a brother," Niles said softly. "You are my brother."

Sean slapped his upper arm and held on. "The same goes for me. And the others would give their lives for us or for each other."

"I'm...I'm scared," Niles said, shaking his head. "Not for myself, for Leigh. Ah, hell, that means I'm scared for myself, too. I don't expect you to understand but I'd rather be dead than without her."

"Don't you?" Sean said.

Niles swiped snow from his face, staring at Sean. "Maybe you do," he said. "That's good news and bad news. We've got to deal with what's facing us right now. We're all going to need each other more than ever. I thought about getting all of us together, too, but I want to wait until there's some sort of plan. Then we'll just let it slip into place without drawing attention to any change in our behavior."

Sean felt watched. He glanced up at the building and through the windows saw the vague outlines of the two women at the top of the stairs.

"Until Leigh...until the baby comes, I want to be close to her. Does that make sense to you, Sean?"

"Couldn't make better sense."

"I need you to stand in for me, make decisions, more or less run things. Of course I want to be in the loop and I'll be second-guessing you all the way, but you'd be disappointed if I didn't."

Sean couldn't help smiling. "Yes, boss." Taking on a lot of the alpha's responsibility without actually being the alpha might be delicate.

"That's it, then," Niles said as if he intended to walk away at once.

"Hold it," Sean said. "I expect to discuss decisions with you. But it won't work if you always countermand any orders I give."

"I wouldn't do that." Niles sounded offended.

Sean laughed. "Wouldn't you?"

"No. That is—no, I won't, and if I do, you'll let me know I've stepped on your toes." He looked over his shoulder, then back at the shop. "It'll be my fault if Leigh...if something happens to her. I know this is what we all wanted, a chance to get closer to being human again, but I'm so damn disgusted Leigh has to be the experiment."

"She wants to be," Sean said quietly. "She's going to be okay. We've got to believe that."

"Yeah." Sean narrowed his eyes. "Let's get back."

*  *  *

"Here they come," Leigh said. "I didn't see any punches thrown, did you?"

"No. I wish they didn't feel they have to shut us out, though."

"They think they're protecting us," Leigh said although she was certain the private powwow had something to do with the baby. "These guys are big on protection."

Niles and Sean came upstairs side by side, wearing smiles that didn't look natural.

"Coming up," Phoebe called out, following the men. She brought another pot of coffee and switched it with the one on the table. She worked a big bag of M&Ms out of the waistband of her jeans.

The bag didn't make it as far as the table.

Instead of turning to leave, Phoebe slowly set the cold pot down again and shoved her hands into the pockets of her jeans. Her amazingly red hair escaped the bottom of a striped woolen hat she wore pulled over her ears and exploded in billowing curls.

Leigh waited for whatever Phoebe intended to say and it was obvious the other woman was organizing her words.

"What you talked about earlier—about me. I wasn't eavesdropping but I can't help hearing. I hear so much it's scary sometimes."

"Me, too," Leigh said automatically. She even heard small animals moving in the forest when they were far away.

"I don't hear like that," Elin said and she didn't look pleased about it.

"How do you expect to get anywhere if you can't trust a single person?" Phoebe asked Niles. "Suspicion makes you see things that aren't there. And imagine things that aren't true. I don't know what all this is about. But I do know it isn't good—it's very dangerous. You don't have to worry about me, though. If you think you do, lock me up or something—as long as you feed me." She gave a lopsided grin. "Any kind of chocolate will do."

Elin laughed and so did the others. And just as quickly they were all quiet again.

"Now you're thinking that as charming as Phoebe is, there's no reason for you to trust her," Doc Saul said, his voice calm but unexpected nevertheless.

He had made one of his silent and sudden arrivals, moving toward them from the top of the stairs, his long black coat swishing.

"If you're prepared to take my word about The One, then you should be prepared to take it for Phoebe. She has no connection to any malign forces."

"How do you know?" Niles asked brusquely.

Saul gave him a long, hard look. "There are things we will never understand about each other. But remember that you and I have fought side by side and we trusted each other. I trust you still. You must not forget that given her association with us, Phoebe isn't any safer than we are."

"Agreed," Niles said. "On both fronts. We will not abandon Phoebe." He took Leigh's mug and refilled it with cider. No one else accepted his offer of more. "Why didn't you come to me, Saul? I'm the one you should have told your fantastic story to."

"Perhaps I was wrong. Perhaps I should have come to you first. But you just showed why I may have chosen to speak with Sean first. You were wounded, Niles. The betrayal by one of your own—"

"Enough," Niles said, then shook his head. "I apologize. But that isn't a subject I want to talk about. It isn't what makes me so cautious. We are surrounded, Saul. With this new threat you talk about, there is no room for a single mistake. Too many need our protection. I expect attempts to eliminate any of us who get in their way—that's always been their preferred method."

They all stopped speaking and the only sound was the sharp rattle of hail on the skylight.

Leigh knew only too well how much Niles still suffered from having one of the hounds go over to the werewolves the previous year. And, as Saul suggested, the betrayal had deeply wounded Niles.

"Every step must be cautiously taken," Saul said. "Without wasting time on concerns about those who pose no threat." He looked significantly at Phoebe.

Did he, Leigh wondered, already know that Niles considered Elin a threat to the Team? And it only made sense that he would see Phoebe the same way. Not that she had the kind of closeness with a hound that Elin would soon have.

"We must start at the main root of the situation," Sean said.

"You've identified the main root and how to start there?" his alpha responded. "There will be a war, we both know that."

"We don't know any such thing," Sean said shortly,

and Leigh found it interesting to see how Elin looked at her future mate with admiration.

"You think we should wait until Saul has a whole row of dead women in his morgue?" Niles looked like a man already embattled. Leigh didn't regret her part in that. After all, he had looked for her as a mate because he wanted a living child. And he had found her and come to love her—they were fortunate, if only he would stop expecting disaster.

He met her eyes and, after a moment, smiled at her in that sweet, deep way that melted her. She kept the smile on her face while she turned inward, away from what he'd said about choosing her over their baby. Exactly what he meant wasn't clear, but she understood what the end result would be.

"I want to go to The Island," Sean said.

"No!" Elin was on her feet at once. "No, Sean."

"Can you get me there, Saul?" Sean said as if she hadn't spoken.

"I will be the one going," Niles said. "Once I know every detail Saul can give me. This person Saul calls The One is a risk as long as he survives."

Sean waited until his alpha gave him complete attention. "We should be alone to discuss this," he said. "But apparently we are not to be allowed that privilege. We have just discussed situations like this. For our arrangement to work, you must give me the power I need. Give me the power to lead." Sean's lean face took on a feral caste. The pupils of his eyes narrowed, and when he dropped his chin and looked up at them, Leigh's tiger comparison was even more apt.

"No one will go unless I take you there," Saul said. "You would not find The Island and you could not land there without The One's blessing. I already have that."

Both Niles and Sean folded their arms and averted their faces from Saul. Werehounds did not beg vampires.

A crash from below startled Leigh, and everyone else.

"The front door," Phoebe said, her pale skin pure white now. "It was locked."

Leigh noted that no mention was made of the ease with which Saul entered the building, locked door or not.

Phoebe leaped to her feet and rushed for the stairs but Sean, Niles, and Saul were faster. Saul moved her aside. "Do not come down yet."

"We'd only get in the way," Elin said, but Leigh made a run for it, slipped past both of the other women, and took the stairs downward two at a time. She might be pregnant but she was perfectly fit.

Elin and Phoebe weren't far behind.

The scene just inside the bookstore took Leigh's breath away. Cliff Ames, the cook from Gabriel's, and Sally held a sagging woman between them. When Cliff and Sally moved farther inside, the woman's feet dragged uselessly behind her and her head lolled forward.

Cliff picked her up and put her on a leather couch. He lifted up her legs and booted feet.

Dropping to his knees, Saul felt for a pulse in her neck, but Elin noted that he examined the skin beneath her hair all the way around. The negative shake of his head was almost imperceptible.

"It's Molly," Leigh said. Molly, Gabriel's flamboyant girlfriend, was supposedly taking a break from their relationship. He told them she was in Seattle taking "a time out."

"Where did you find her?" Elin said. She took off her coat and spread it over Molly's legs. "Was she at Gabriel's?"

"She called Cliff," Sally said. "Asked him to pick her up from outside the gas station and take her somewhere safe because she was in trouble. I was with Cliff and I came along. We knew Phoebe was here and we could get Saul to come and help."

Short and stocky, Cliff was a man of few words. He turned back to the door. "Got to get back to work. What do I tell Gabriel when he comes in?"

"Nothing," Saul told him. "We can't have an investigation now. The panic would get in our way. Just trust me on this, Cliff."

Molly's dark hair was plastered to her face and neck in wet clumps, a fake fur vest hung open over a torn black shirt and pants. The high heel of one boot was broken and hanging by a thin strip of leather.

Looking up at all of them, Saul said, "She's dead."

## *chapter* TWELVE

Sean's house nestled deep in the forest that melded with the mature trees covering a good deal of Leigh's land.

Numb inside and out, Elin was grateful to curl up in a blanket on a couch in front of the fire Sean built as soon as they got to the two-story building. There was also a basement, where he said Innes lived, but either Innes wasn't at home or he was sleeping. The place was silent.

"When Ethan and Campion want a place to rest up, they come here, too," Sean said. "Sometimes we must all go to Niles…" He screwed up his eyes at her. "You don't need to worry about that yet."

Elin nodded. She had nothing to add to the conversation. It was obvious that the Team was in charge. She decided to let Sean be the one to speak next, which might take time since he showed signs of having moved into another world at the moment.

"You do understand, don't you?" Sean said so abruptly, she jumped. "Why we made the decision we did about Molly?"

She breathed in deeply and pulled the blanket up around her ears. "No." She shook her head. "I don't know what the police could do to help, but they should be told. The same as they should be told about Rose. I was surprised when Sally didn't even seem particularly interested in the decision to let Saul do an autopsy on Molly, but Cliff amazed me. He looked unaffected, like he didn't care. He just wanted to get back to work."

"He's a loner, or so I've been told," Sean said. "He doesn't interfere in other people's business. I don't know his history but I think there's something there he doesn't talk about."

"If you're all so worried about me blabbing your secrets, why are you comfortable with Sally and Cliff?"

"I'm not worried about you. Sally's been involved in hound affairs for some time. So far she's proved trustworthy. The moment we think otherwise, things will change."

Elin didn't like the way that sounded. She didn't like the way a lot of what the Team said sounded. They spoke as if their decisions were beyond argument and often as if they wouldn't think a whole lot about doing away with anyone they considered a nuisance.

A tap sounded at the front door and Sean hurried to answer. He returned with Sally, who carried two floral duffel bags. "Supplies," she sang out to Elin, bustling into the spartan living room. "If I didn't still want to get back into the fae compound and spend time with some old friends, I'd use my favorite trick on Tarhazian. How dare she make you cold at this time of year."

Pokey chose that moment to wiggle into view and examine the bags. She grabbed a licorice pipe and stuck it in her mouth. But she chewed rapidly and quickly nibbled all the way to the bulb.

"I brought that for you, Elin," Sally said, frowning at the guinea pig. "She isn't getting any better behaved. Should I take her back with me and see if I can train her?"

"You won't be able to," Elin said, grinning. "She's impossible."

Sally pulled in the corners of her mouth. "And you like her that way."

"What do you mean by favorite trick?" Sean said, and Elin decided he could be very single-minded.

"Secret," Sally said. "But if you value your finger and toenails, don't get on the wrong side of me."

Pokey hummed all the way under a gap in the blanket, where she disappeared.

Sally didn't wait for more reaction but hefted the bags onto the couch beside Elin. "I think just about everything will be too big but at least it will keep you warm. You'll be fine for boots and shoes, though. I had some I'd made for the, er, smaller customers that come to the shop." She rummaged around in the bag and pulled out something made of heavy wool. "This coat looks like a blanket. It was Phoebe's but she's got a new one—or new to her. She found it at Wear It Again."

"That's going to be warm," Elin said, eyeing a plaid wool coat that zipped up the front and had a fur-lined hood.

Pokey popped her nose out and hovered, watching what Sally produced and humming excitedly over anything she thought resembled food.

By the time Sally got to the bottom of the bags, Elin couldn't imagine needing another piece of clothing—at least until summer.

"Saul gave me this for you," Sally said, handing a folded piece of paper to Sean. "He said Elin should see it, too. And he wants to know if there is some special weapon you could use in emergencies, Elin? Something unusual?"

Elin looked at her sharply. "What makes him ask that?" Surely the power of the green that Leigh had told her about wasn't common knowledge.

"Saul said he hoped you might be good at protecting yourself, that's all."

The idea appealed to her. She would go after some of the diamond-hard crystal from the green just as soon as she could.

Sean and Sally looked at her enquiringly, waiting, she knew, for her to reveal some magical defense. The gift of the green-born crystal was Deseran. Unless she could be sure those like her would want the information shared with anyone outside, she would keep it to herself. Her skin tightened. She should have told Sean she was Deseran a long time ago.

"What kind of defense, I wonder." Sean looked amused.

For the first time Elin really thought about being part of a singular group. They had been born to paranormal people who decided these children would not fit into the world of their parents. Who knew how many Deseran there were? Someone ought to. They all ought to—they had a bond. She glanced from Sally to Sean and smiled slightly.

She belonged to a special race. An odd happiness bubbled in her.

Sean shrugged, and without another word, he passed her the paper from Saul. "The mark is developing," was all it said.

Once Sally had left, Elin leaped off the couch and gripped Sean's arms. "That mark again," she said. "He can only mean—"

He put a finger to his lips. "Who knows what could give an intruder access to our conversation?" he said.

"I feel intruders," she told him, blushing. "Not always, but strong forces bring an awareness even if I can't identify them exactly. I felt it when Saul was coming into Phoebe's bookshop."

After giving her a very long look, he reached into the pile of clothes, took the first sweater he found, and pulled it over her head. Long, made of green mohair, it reached below her knees. Her thin dress bunched into an irregular frill that flopped all around.

Fluffy black socks reached under the dress to her knees. "I won't be cold now," she said, looking at Sean and daring him to make nasty comments about the awful outfit.

"Absolutely not," he said without a hint of a smile.

"You and Niles went outside to talk about getting the Team together," Elin said. "That can't wait long, can it?"

"It will all fall into place. We won't make obvious or

sudden changes but I prefer for him to initiate any discussions with all of us. When he says he thinks it's time, we'll go—if that's ever really necessary."

She didn't miss the "we." "Niles doesn't want me," she reminded him.

"I'm not leaving you behind," Sean said. He lifted her right hand to his mouth and kissed each finger, then her palm. Elin shivered.

"He is worried about Leigh and the pregnancy. I am to take primary control of the Team until Niles can give it his all. Now I vote we try to sleep for a few hours, then get to Gabriel's early," he told her. "If anything is being circulated about Molly, we'll hear about it."

Sean nodded to the hallway leading past the living room and away from the front door. "There are two bedrooms that way. Take your pick. They each have a bathroom."

Elin hadn't summoned up enough courage to say what she intended to say about that. "I'm worried about Gabriel. He loves—loved her. She was strange and we all knew it, but he would have done anything for her."

"She was used," Sean said. "Her death is a warning."

Elin considered that. "I think you're right. And they may kill again and again," Elin said. "Weakening everyone they hate—or discount—as they go. Fear paralyzes people and they stop doing anything to help themselves—that's what this could be intended to do. Make us all helpless so we can just be picked off."

"What do you think about the story Saul told us?" Sean took her by the shoulders and looked down into her face. "I want to know what The One needs so badly."

"We don't want to find out by becoming his victims," Elin said.

"A living sorcerer vampire who feeds on parts taken from the living." Sean scrubbed at his face. "If someone doesn't go after him and neutralize him, he'll spread horror everywhere. I think he's getting desperate. Why else would he start drawing attention to what he's capable of doing? I'm going to find out whatever I can and take him out."

Argument didn't make any points with Sean; that was already clear. Elin swallowed what she wanted to say. If he went to The Island, she would follow him and she still had ways of doing that.

"Sleep," Sean said, not meeting her eyes. He gave her a quick, hard hug, tipped up her chin, and kissed her. "Good night, sweetheart."

He guided her into the hallway, past the open door of a small study, to two side-by-side doors. Sean threw open both doors to reveal apparently identical bedrooms with big beds covered with old-fashioned quilts and very little other furniture.

"Just a minute," he said. "Let me get all those clothes. Choose a room."

Elin went through the first door, smiling to herself and crossing her arms as she considered her next move.

## *chapter* THIRTEEN

Sean closed the bedroom door behind him, pulled off his shirt, and did a belly flop across the bed.

Sainthood had never been his ambition. Only a saint or a sadist would wish Elin good night and walk away to another bedroom, especially when every signal from the woman in question was that she wanted him with her.

He thumped his fists on the bed in frustration. This room and the one Elin had chosen were only used when Team members stayed over. His own bedroom was upstairs but he wanted to be close to Elin.

Damn, he wanted to be close to her, and that didn't mean separated by a wall.

It was no accident that both rooms were built into the center of the house so neither had windows. He had stood outside Elin's door until she locked it with a key on her side. Rolling half onto his side, he worked a key from his jeans pocket and held it up to sparkle in the bedside lamplight. The duplicate key to her room, not that he would need it if he suddenly had to get in.

First he tossed down the key, then turned out the light.

He liked the darkness. It was always his advantage—over anyone or anything not in the circle of werehounds with perfect night-sight.

Sean thrashed in the bedcovers and shut his eyes tightly. Maybe if he didn't keep looking around the room while he listened for even the slightest sound that shouldn't be among the night sounds of the house, he would sleep. Or at least the hypersensitivity flaying his skin would stop.

In the morning after they went to Gabriel's to feel out any change in atmosphere there, he would have Sally, with Innes as muscle protection, make sure Elin didn't follow him when he left. Saul had to be persuaded to make a trip to The Island, taking Sean with him.

Niles wouldn't like it, but with luck they would learn something useful enough to shorten his furious reaction without Sean having to point out that, as acting Team leader, he could make up his own mind what to do—deferentially, of course.

The tension in his brow, so tight it hurt, began to soften and he breathed more easily. He wasn't sleepy but his face and neck, and his scalp, relaxed.

He must be falling asleep.

Throwing off the covers, he stretched out on the mattress. The faintest current of warm air stroked over his naked body and he smiled. This was what he needed, this release from vigilance, if only for a short while.

Sean drifted.

Like fingertips barely brushing the hairs on his legs, light touches passed from his ankles to his shins, grew infinitesimally firmer, and ran back and forth over his thighs, from knee to groin. Each time the touch flitted across his groin, he jumped, but then relaxed again.

Sean turned onto his stomach, pushed the pillows from the bed, and rested his brow on his forearms.

*You are loved.*

Startled, staring into the darkness at the table by the bed, the single white chair against a wall, he turned the thought over and over in his mind. It had come unbidden, like an emphatic voice telling him something he had never expected to hear.

Like Elin's voice but he had to be hearing what he wanted to hear. They hadn't progressed far enough, telepathically, for her to reach him like that.

Kneading at the base of his skull, down his neck, and along his shoulders made him sigh. He felt knots in his muscles dissolve.

A gentle vise clamping his sides brought another start. But the sensation, insistent, brushing to his spine, rubbing down to his buttocks, and exploring the hard flesh there, had him on total but willing alert.

This wasn't a dream.

This wasn't a trick of the air currents.

But this was most definitely a trick and Sean figured he'd already guessed the practitioner after all.

Breathing harder, wiping stinging sweat from his eyes, he flung over to his back again. He would swear his little angel had not known another man but she knew far more about how to please one than she should.

For what felt like hours, hands he could not see or touch caressed his body in almost every intimate way imaginable, and some he hadn't even imagined.

Sometimes, he told himself, this had nothing to do with Elin, that she couldn't possibly achieve such a thing and he was reacting to sexual deprivation. Then he rose to the tippy edge of climax again, only to be thwarted on the brink, and he could not believe this was not Elin's doing. She had touched him before, pressed herself to him before, and although never like this, he decided she had saved her full power for when she could have her way with him.

His smile faded quickly. There was no doubt that the imprint of her lips was on his. He knew her mouth now, would always know it, and she kissed him provocatively as if beckoning him to come to her.

*You are loved.*

"*And you are loved.*" Since the channel was obviously open, he spoke into her mind. "*I will always love you and keep you. Now, go to sleep.*"

In the stillness that followed, he grinned. She had bewitched him but not broken his will. Not that he wouldn't like to let her break it.

A moment later, the caress was back.

From his neck, over his chest, into the dip at his navel, down the slender line of dark hair below to the flare around what he longed for her to touch most, the wickedly magical fingers progressed like a hot sigh in the night.

Sean held still. Since she wasn't physically with him, he couldn't do a thing to either stop or assist her. "*I think you should go to sleep.*" His mind didn't pant so she shouldn't know he could hardly breathe, that his body was damp all over, that while he spoke like a schoolmaster to a difficult child, he was dying for want of her finishing this long, exquisite torture.

She wanted him to go to her and make love.

This deliberate teasing to the point where he wasn't sure his legs would bear his weight, and wasn't sure he could stay where he was, would only make sure he found a way to tantalize her even more.

The touch left him.

She might as well have put him in chains before she gave up her quest. There wouldn't be any peace for him tonight. When he had the energy, he'd shower. And he'd also see how much she liked being roused really early to go to Gabriel's. After all, she couldn't have been in a deep sleep while she took him into a sweet hell.

A silky veil settled over his face.

Over his body, inch by inch, The Veil slithered. He tried to capture it but found nothing.

The scent of the forest touched with lemon reached him. The scent of Elin's hair. Oh, help him, he couldn't resist much longer.

Pine, fir, cedar, lemon—they filled the room and her hair brushed over his belly, his hips, his penis.

She pulled him into a heated place, dragged his hips from the bed, again and again while he lay, not helpless, but strong and eagerly meeting her.

His senses cascaded, unstoppable and wrenching and so intense he only wanted to hold on to the feelings forever. But they slowed, receded, and he lay there, his heart pounding. How could it have stopped just when he needed it most?

Minutes passed before a small voice in his mind said, *"Was that right?"*

He covered his face with both hands. No one would believe this had happened to him. *"Perfect,"* he told her.

*"Good,"* she said.

*chapter* **FOURTEEN**

If Elin were the pouting kind, she would pout right now. Sean hadn't said one word about last night. Well, a few words at the time, finishing with, "Perfect," but nothing since he had hammered on her door just before five this morning telling her loudly that they had to leave for Gabriel's. They had business to attend to before the place started to get busy.

So much for her plot to lure him to her bed and let him have his way with her.

Bundled in Phoebe's coat, with Pokey deep in a pocket, and buffeted by wind and stinging sleet, Elin clung to Sean on the way to Gabriel's. She shot off the bike the moment it was parked, but snatched some pleasure out of being gathered against Sean's body under one viselike arm as they ran to get inside and out of the bitter weather.

At the door he pulled her to one side, under cover, and

said, "You understand not to mention anything that happened last night?"

She opened her mouth to ask if he thought she was an idiot, but gave a sly smile instead. "I would never embarrass you, Sean. Some things are absolutely private. Only you and I know."

His clear, gold eyes showed he knew exactly how funny she thought she was. "Good. What is it we're here to do?"

"You tell me." Now she was irritated.

"Elin—"

"You'd better be ready to learn absolutely nothing," she told him shortly. Her teeth chattered together—she was so cold. "We can only listen and watch. We already discussed this, remember? And you don't have to worry about Sally or Cliff. Sally will have warned him to pretend everything's fine. Our best bet is that someone saw Molly before she was picked up near the gas station last night."

"I'd give a lot to know how she got there," Sean said.

"Ears open, mouths closed," Elin said. She had never felt this cold.

"Right," he said, and the corners of his mouth turned up a little. "Too bad you don't have that incredible hearing like Leigh and Phoebe."

She dug him in the middle with an elbow and yanked open the door. "If I don't get close to the fireplace, my nose will fall off."

The warmth she craved blasted to meet her. She was surprised to see Gabriel there throwing more logs onto the already huge fire. Elin turned to catch Sean's eye.

He raised a brow and said quietly, "He gets in early but not usually this early. Something could be even more wrong than we already know."

"As in he's expecting Molly? Just don't say anything about her."

"No, ma'am," Sean said. "Morning, Gabriel."

The man stared at them and Elin realized they should have expected to be asked why they were there so early.

"Heat's on the fritz at my—at Two Chimneys," Sean said, and Elin noted that his ears turned pink. "I went over to try to fix it but Elin..." His voice trailed away. He was not a practiced liar.

"He needs parts and it was going to take too long for a fire to warm the place up enough, so we came here. Besides, my coffee is never as good as Sally's."

"Yeah," Gabriel said.

He didn't believe a word they'd said and knew perfectly well that two roaring fires would have kept the cottage warm enough.

Leigh and Niles came into the big bar from the back entrance with Leigh's dog, Jazzy, dragging along behind. The dog had clearly been woken up before she was ready. Niles's grim face didn't cheer Elin up, but Jazzy's excitement at seeing her did.

"Your heat gone out, too?" Gabriel said.

Leigh put a hand around Niles's elbow. "I'm always early," she said, too brightly.

"Not this early," Gabriel told her. "Not since you let this great animal sweep you off your feet."

Elin felt Sean stiffen and held her breath. She thought Gabriel had a good idea that the Team members were a lot more than they seemed to be, but the animal comment could annoy Niles.

"Sally's coffee is better than mine," Leigh said and looked askance at Gabriel, Elin, and Sean when they all started to laugh.

"I get it," Gabriel said. "Or I don't get it really. But you four want an early morning party here for some reason. I'll go tell Sally she's got customers."

Pokey slid from the pocket of Elin's coat and landed in front of Jazzy, who started to walk around her. The guinea pig would have none of it and all but glued herself to Jazzy's side all the way to the fireplace, where Jazzy lay down and the guinea pig snuggled onto her folded paws. The look Jazzy shot at Leigh begged for permission to bat the critter into the next century. Leigh said, "You're a good girl, Jazzy. You look after your little friend."

Gabriel could obviously hardly wait to ask, "Didn't happen to see a little green Fiat on your way, did you?"

Molly drove a green Fiat, but it hadn't been around for several weeks since she took off on her own.

"No," Elin said and felt inspired. "Are you talking about Molly's car?" She didn't check Sean's reaction.

"Yeah."

"We didn't see it either," Niles said.

Leigh cleared her throat. "Are you expecting her back, Gabriel?"

"Maybe." He carried on to the kitchens.

"So much for ears open, mouths closed," Sean muttered. "How come you didn't let me know you were coming here, Niles?"

"How come you didn't let me know you were coming?"

"You're being ridiculous," Leigh said. "Both of you. We all know why we're here and we've already found out one thing. Molly was on her way here—I think so, anyway."

"So why didn't she want to be brought here when she was in such trouble?" Elin asked.

"You thought you'd find something out and keep it to yourself," Niles said to Sean. "Did you think I'd be okay with that?"

"That's what you—"

"I've asked you to stand in for me in most things," Niles said. "That doesn't mean I want to be cut out of the loop."

"Something's eating the pair of you," Elin said. She couldn't sit mute any longer. "This isn't the place to talk about it. We'll have that coffee, see if there's anything else to find out here, then go where you can sort yourselves out in private."

"Niles remains my alpha, Elin, even when he needs me to take a more important role than usual," Sean said quietly.

She figured he had no intention of allowing Team pecking order to get in the way of his sneaking off to The Island, though.

Leigh took off her coat and tossed it over a chair. The rest followed suit, all except Elin, who kept on Phoebe's heavy coat and took a seat at a table close to the fire. Jazzy promptly leaped on her lap, leaving Pokey on the hearth.

"Ask Sally about the Fiat," Leigh said.

Trundling a loaded trolley, Sally came from the

kitchen. She crossed the floor with her stiff gait and waved them all to take their seats.

They joined Elin at the table, and Sally parked herself and her trolley between them and the bar. She started unloading mugs, jugs of coffee, and plates of fragrant pastries still steaming from the oven.

"When you found Molly, where was her Fiat?" Sean said quickly. "Where is it now? We need to get it out of the way until it's time to let Gabriel know what's happened."

"Oh, no." Leigh put her face in her hands. "Poor Gabriel."

"She was lying on the ground by the Dumpster," Sally told them. "No sign of her car."

"Did you know she'd contacted Gabriel?" Sean said.

"I didn't think she had. She didn't want to come here at all."

"So why is Gabriel asking about the car?" Niles checked each of their faces. "He wouldn't do that if he didn't expect Molly."

"We can't keep Gabriel in the dark," Elin said.

"Maybe he's not so in the dark," Niles said, then waved a hand as if to dismiss his comment.

"Keeping quiet is wrong," Elin went on. "What are you all thinking of? Sally, why were you so willing to let Saul take off with the body?"

"You're full of questions," Niles said, but he sounded thoughtful.

"We couldn't have a better ally than Saul," Sally said. She looked downward. "Some of you will fight that idea but I hope you don't fight it to the death—your own, or his."

"We made as good a peace as we can some months ago," Niles said. "I haven't forgotten."

Taking advantage of the coat, Elin pulled up the hood and made sure it shadowed her face. She didn't want anyone to see how terrified she was by this talk of the ones she loved destroying each other. Anything she said in argument would only make things worse. She gathered up Pokey and cuddled her close.

"Elin?" Sean said. "What's the matter?"

So much for hiding her feelings. "I'm trying to think a few things through. And with my newfound coldness I have to bundle up whenever I can. How much colder do you suppose Tarhazian can make me?" Wow, that had just popped out without her really thinking about the question before. "Oh, ignore me. I'm just waffling on."

Silence lasted too long.

When Elin made herself look up, four faces stared back with a variety of expressions ranging from thoughtful to horrified, with Sally taking the horrified prize.

"This is a change for you, that's the only problem," Sean said loudly, although his worried face didn't support his words. "You'll get used to feeling different temperatures."

"Her lips are blue," Sally said. "And her nose is so red it looks painful."

"Sounds lovely," Elin said with a weak laugh.

Sally poured coffee and said, without looking at anyone, "You can freeze to death."

## *chapter* FIFTEEN

Silverware rattled and slid around on the trolley. Sean grabbed a plate before it could flip off.

Sally slammed a hand on the side of the trolley and held on. "Is this an earthquake?" she said, her liberally powdered face puckering.

"I don't think so," Niles said.

Beside Sean, a figure gradually took form. Diminutive but with regal bearing, Tarhazian fully appeared.

She wore a circlet of black diamonds on top of the black satin turban that hid her hair. Everything she wore was black lace or satin. Her face, perfect in an unearthly way, bore a dusting of glitter.

Elin screwed up her eyes to peer at the familiar face. "Tarhazian?" she said, as if she didn't believe what she saw. "You said we would never meet again."

"A mother's love cannot be so easily extinguished."

Low and modulated, the Fae Queen's voice softened as she looked at Elin.

"What do you want?" Elin glanced at Sean, who attempted to adjust his scowl. Elin would be afraid of his antagonizing Tarhazian. He would never forgive her for what she had done to Elin but he wasn't reckless enough to forget that an attempt to punish the Queen could end in disaster.

"It has been brought to my attention that Colin tried to harm you, daughter."

Elin pressed her lips together.

"I wonder why that would have come to your attention," Sean said. "Perhaps it was you who sent him. You have done all you can to make Elin's life miserable. See how cold she is. If you know what's good for you, you'll reverse that."

Elin visibly held her breath and Sally made a frightened little sound.

Unbelievably, Tarhazian smiled at Sean. "You do love her, don't you? I assure you it was not I who sent Colin. Someone did but he won't share that information with me and it would be foolish to retaliate against him without knowing who he serves. He has information we all want, I think. Do you know of anyone who might have the power to make a vampire do his bidding, Sean?"

Sean detested Tarhazian's conversational tone with him. It was more ominous than reassuring.

Sean gave a slight shake of the head but she couldn't miss the subtle change in his face. The One was involved in all of this.

His back stiffened. Could it have been on The Island

that Saul encountered Aldo? It seemed unlikely but not impossible if the old werehound went there looking for a healing.

"No matter," Tarhazian said. "I shall find out—I always find out what I want to know. Colin is to apologize for his behavior. That should be an end of it. He won't make the same mistake again—regardless of who his true master is. I could make him very miserable."

"Best keep that blood eater away," Niles said. "We want nothing to do with him or his scourge."

Leigh said something about forgiveness under her breath and caught her mate's full attention. "Leigh's too soft." The moment he'd said it, he bowed over her and kissed her. Leigh put her arms around his neck.

Sally laughed and got a glare from Niles.

Leigh's face was comical. She hovered between amusement and annoyance. "Your Highness," she said, being careful not to meet any of her friends' eyes. "We have met before. You are a reasonable woman. We would be very grateful if you would restore Elin's usual body temperature."

The Queen's gaze settled on Elin. "I came with a message for you, my dear," she said. "I know I am not welcome here but, as you well know, where I go and when is almost entirely in my hands."

He would like to find out, Sean thought, what this creature couldn't control. He wondered why she was so bent on bragging about her dominance if she took it for granted, as she was supposed to. Could she feel the need to remind Elin? Was Elin's newfound independence making Tarhazian insecure?

Sally, who appeared to have lost the ability to move, suddenly shuddered, shaking the contents of her trolley.

"Will you make Elin as she was?" Leigh persisted.

"When she returns to me," Tarhazian said. "I know I am not welcome here, but I'm sure you know I only come because of Elin."

Pokey set up a sudden wild chirping and ran up Elin's coat to sit on her shoulder. If Sean didn't know better, he'd say the little animal glared at Tarhazian as if daring her to hurt Elin.

"At least this one seems to like me," Tarhazian said, her smile showing perfect teeth. "I think you should agree with her assessment, Elin."

When Elin didn't respond, Sean saw how Tarhazian's nostrils flared. "I regret my temper," she said. "I was hurt. I am hurt. But I'm sorry for any misunderstandings and I miss my beloved daughter. Forgiveness heals, my child. I'm here to forgive you."

Elin leaped up and stood beside Sean. "I am not a fool," she said. "We are not fools. That is my only answer—except that I am not your daughter."

Sighing, Sean caught her hand and jerked until she looked at him. *"Be careful."* While he watched, her face registered that she'd heard him.

"I know you don't mean that," Tarhazian said. "You are in love with this one, this Sean. We can come to accommodate that but we need to talk, alone."

He heard Leigh expel a hard breath and Sally mutter angrily. Niles was too controlled to allow his feelings to be obvious.

With Elin close to him, Sean smelled the scent of night jasmine that clung to her skin and his senses reeled. He must concentrate. Her violet eyes mesmerized him, and the soft, white skin of her neck took his breath away.

He had yet to see her completely naked. When he did, he was certain he wouldn't be able to hold back. Not that he had much control left after last night. If he didn't fear where the discussion would lead, he would already have questioned her about that very unusual skill of hers.

She kept looking at him. *"This is a trick. It backs up everything Niles, you, and the Team have said about Tarhazian planning to use me. She never forgives, Sean. Never."*

*"So we will play her game,"* Sean said, watching to see if she heard his mindspeak again. She smiled at him and he continued, *"Carefully and much more cleverly than she could even imagine. But we'll have to be prepared for whatever comes our way. Messing with your body temperature is bad enough."*

"Whatever you decide, I'll do," Elin responded, reveling in their closeness. *"Unless I'm convinced it would be dangerous—for you."*

"Look at the love birds," Tarhazian said, swaying her long, lace skirts. "How sweet they are."

*"Sally thinks the Queen's dominance over me may be fading,"* Elin told him. *"Even when she was showing me off like a pet monkey, she had to make sure everyone knew I would be nothing without her. It was as if she was jealous of me. It was some sort of competition."*

Clearing his throat, Niles speared Tarhazian with his blue eyes. "I would not sanction Elin returning to you," he said. "Any more than Sean would, or any of us. If Elin chooses a meeting with you at a more appropriate time, she will not be coming alone. She won't be coming at all if she doesn't want to."

Elin's fingers tightened on Sean's arm. She looked at Niles with gratitude. Sean needed to explain to her that whenever one of the Team, or someone important to them was threatened, they stood together.

"But—" Taking a step as if she might strike at someone, Tarhazian forgot she was being reasonable and all but snarled at Elin. "Only you need to be at the meeting. That's the way it has to be and you know the Queen must be obeyed. If you defy me, I'll, I'll..."

"You'll do more than strip away her warmth?" Sean said evenly.

Tarhazian managed to look bland again. Before their eyes, her face became a little rounder, her lips more bowed. She must think she looked more motherly. "We are friends. Friends don't argue, they accommodate. Come with me, Elin, there's a good girl. I promise you may return later—after our reunion."

Elin gave Sean a warning poke, which he ignored. "Elin has been through a good deal, including your beating," he said. "She needs a chance to get stronger again before she decides if she wants to discuss all of this with you."

"In the meantime," Elin said, standing straighter, "if you try to do me more harm, I won't have anything else to do with you. Ever. This meeting should be over now."

Sean felt Elin hold her breath as if she expected Tarhazian to call down awful retribution. Instead the woman bowed her head and said, "As you wish. I'll be waiting and I'm patient."

She faded more quickly than she had appeared.

"She has no patience," Sally said, her mouth pinched. "I'm sure Saul's told you about her alliance with the wolves and Colin's lot. She probably thinks she can bribe them into helping her get more power."

"How do you know about these things?" Niles asked baldly, propping his elbows on the table and lacing his fingers together. "You're a puzzle yourself, aren't you?"

Sally frowned at him but slowly the furrows smoothed. "Like you, I've known evil, and I've known what it's like to want something so badly you'd do anything to get it. I know what you want, but do you know what I want? You've made up your mind about me, but are you right? Have I done what I've done because I wanted to hold something over you? Will I ask for some awful favor in return for the little help I've given?"

Sean studied Niles. The man commanded attention wherever he went but he wasn't only a dynamic physical presence. Niles was deeply intelligent and introspective.

"Perhaps there is a great deal Sean and I should discuss," Niles said to Sally. "I admit that I've waited for the answer to at least one of your questions."

Unexpectedly, Sean felt calm settle on them. They gathered as equals, very different one from the other, but each with needs and desires. And by chance their lives had become entwined.

The fire crackled and spat. Sean breathed in the scent of wood smoke. He felt warmth and peace, but with the lingering threat of upheaval shivering in the wings.

They were all still, but the appearance of Gabriel, striding toward the entrance, broke the spell. He threw open the door and spoke to someone outside.

"Did someone knock?" Leigh asked.

"I think so," Sally murmured. "So quietly. How did Gabriel know they were there?"

Gabriel stood back and waved a man in. He wore his platinum hair in a long braid that reached his waist, and he walked with his head held high, looking in all directions, obviously expecting to be stared at. And he was.

"I don't believe this," Sean said. "Is he mad?"

"This is one of Tarhazian's tests," Elin muttered. "She wants to see if we attack him as she expects, as we probably should. Let's disappoint her."

Sean grinned a little and pulled her onto his lap. "I'll do my best, oh, Oracle."

The man halted when he saw them. Tall, leanly muscular and apparently sewn into his black leather vest and pants, he crossed his arms. A white silk shirt, open at the neck, flowed through its full sleeves. High cheekbones cast shadows and he had the mouth of a hungry sensualist.

Even Sean was fascinated, as much by the reactions he saw in the others as by the black-eyed man himself. They were all transfixed.

"Gabriel has some unexpected friends," Elin said.

Sally, Sean realized, shook from head to toe. She met his eyes and said, "We need to ignore that one. He couldn't come in here if Gabriel didn't invite him, but I don't know why he would."

Raising his head, Sean sniffed the air, and locked gazes

with Niles, who half rose but sank back into his chair when Sean shook his head. The scent of decay was hard to hide, even under expensive cologne.

Leigh gave a soft cry as if she was coming out of a trance. She stared at the tall, blond man who had begun to saunter in their direction.

## *chapter* SIXTEEN

How can I explain the depth of my self-disgust?" Colin said. He offered Elin his hand but withdrew it quickly. "No, no, of course not. I can't expect you to look at me with anything but loathing, especially so soon after my transgression. I treated you badly. My only excuse is that an enemy bewitched me and I was not myself. But I will prove how I've chastised myself. Now we can become friends." He smiled around. "All of us."

"Over my dead body," Sean said. He wanted to tear the vampire apart.

He waited for Niles to react. Colin had once captured Leigh, intending to molest her. He behaved as if he'd forgotten the event.

*"What do you think he really wants?"* Niles communicated without looking at Sean.

*"If he does have a master other than Tarhazian, and I'm sure he does, that's where the answers to all our questions may lie."*

*"Could this...Bear with me, Sean, but could this be a connection to Aldo? I don't like to mention—"*

*"You're only voicing what I'm thinking."*

Colin stood there, serene, remote, unfazed by the currents of revulsion flying his way. He sighed, smiled, although Sean noted he showed very little of his teeth and the fangs were suitably withdrawn.

"Charming ladies," Colin said, and Sean thought he must be hearing things. "Both of you." He gazed from Elin to Leigh and his gaze lingered on her. Spittle gathered in the corners of his mouth.

Sickened, Sean communicated with Niles, *"He is lusting after Leigh because she is Deseran. He knows he could drain her blood and she would recover quickly so he could drain her again."*

*"We would kill him if we didn't need to know why he's really here and what this is really about,"* Niles said. *"What's his connection to Gabriel and why would he show up now of all times?"*

Jazzy had been curled up almost on the hearth again. He stirred, sniffed the air, and slunk to Leigh, who picked him up.

*"Bad karma all around,"* Sean said. *"I can't think of a connection between Colin and Gabriel, but you can bet on it that Colin's tasted whatever The Island has to offer. I feel the strong connection."*

"I came to talk to Gabriel," Colin said, his eyelids heavy and half-lowered. "But I intended to look for you as well so this is doubly convenient." His eyes, which showed no pupils, concentrated on Sean.

Throughout the exchange, Gabriel had hovered near the bar. Sally hadn't moved a muscle.

"Molly's a good friend of mine, you see," Colin said. "I hadn't seen her in weeks when she showed up yesterday afternoon and now I understand Gabriel can't find her. Such a worry." He sounded anything but worried. Excited perhaps, but not worried.

The connection between Gabriel and Colin was made, although Sean would be surprised if they had ever met before.

"When did you last see Molly?" Elin asked. Sean increased his pressure at her waist but she took no notice. "Did she drive to your place?"

"Reg was out with his tow truck," Gabriel broke in, clicking off his cell phone as he came. "So the garage was locked up when you left her there." He narrowed his eyes at Colin.

Cliff chose that moment to hurry from the kitchens and throw more logs on the fire. He must have noticed that Gabriel wasn't paying attention to anything but Molly.

"Need you, Sally," Cliff said gruffly. "Anything else you want?" He addressed everyone at the table—except Colin, whom he pointedly ignored.

"Nothing else, thanks," Elin said.

Sally, who had yet to look at Colin since he arrived at the table, kept her face averted and followed Cliff back to the kitchens.

In a chatty way, as if he were with a bunch of friends, Colin said, "Molly came in her little green Fiat, but when she left, it was making very strange sounds. Well"—he shrugged eloquently—"of course I'm useless with such things. But I followed her to the gas station and left her there. They're good at that sort of thing, or so I'm told."

"Reg is the only one who works there," Gabriel said, and Sean could tell he was having difficulty holding his temper. "If you'd hung around long enough to make sure she tried the door, you'd have known he wasn't at the shop. He was out with his tow truck."

Colin shook his head sadly, "Darn it. How like a man like that not to be around when you need him."

"A man like that?" Sean said, unable to keep his mouth shut any longer. "He's a hardworking man running a business on his own. You'll have to excuse him for not living up to your expectations. So you drove off before making sure Molly was all right?"

"Why did Molly visit you?" Niles's cool voice cut through the babble. "Did you know this was one of Molly's friends, Gabriel?"

"No." Gabriel looked sick. He'd have to be blind not to know, or at least suspect, Colin was a vampire, especially when he had been around his kind before. "I'm going to call the police to help organize a search party."

Sean and Niles's eyes met. *"We can't stop him,"* Niles communicated.

*"I'll make sure Saul's warned,"* Sean came back. *"How do we get rid of this vermin, Colin? We may find we do need him, but he's been here too long. Nothing useful will come out of this. You do know there's only one reason Molly would be visiting him?"*

*"She's—was—a vamp whore."* Niles's mouth turned

down. *"I'd like to keep that from Gabriel but maybe he already knows. He loved that woman, no matter how she treated him."*

*"She didn't deserve to die like that,"* Sean said. *"I think this blood eater knows more than he's saying. It's dangerous for him to come here alone when he knows I can take him. He has to be desperate for something. Unless he's convinced himself that what I did to him was a fluke."*

*"Keep Elin close to you and Leigh—I'll find a place to contact Saul about the search."*

*"Elin?"* He attempted to connect with her.

*"Yes?"* Her startled reaction was almost funny.

*"I have to warn Saul about a search for Molly. Stay with Niles, please."*

Her silence made him expect her to pretend she hadn't heard this time, but after a while she gave him a slight nod and squeezed his arm.

"Excuse me, all," Sean said. "I'm going to bring the bike helmets inside." No need to get detailed.

He got up and went out into gusts of rain. At least it had warmed up enough to get rid of the sleet. Cold wasn't a problem for the hounds but he'd just as soon not have ice spicules peppering his face. Sean walked past the bike and crossed the gravel parking lot. Entering the dense trees that surrounded the place, he kept walking, dodging back and forth between thick trunks until he felt he was far enough away from Gabriel's.

Mind communication wasn't something he wanted with any vampire but at this moment it would be useful. He leaned on a tree and worked his cell phone from a back pocket of his jeans. Now he had to hope for decent reception.

He flinched at a sudden flapping in front of his face. A woodpecker made a show of flying away.

Sean called Saul, who gave him his usual monosyllables. Short translation: He wasn't worried about any search.

With a dramatic flourish, Colin appeared almost in front of Sean. "I hoped I'd find you easily enough."

Sean took his time putting the phone away.

"You're the reason I came here at all," Colin said. "You're all that interests me."

Instantly on alert, Sean said, "Aren't I lucky?"

"You're why I was at that cottage, too. I knew you would come to help the woman. I admit you surprised me with your trick of strength. In fact, you only become more of a curiosity. Could we be partners, do you think? What an alliance we could make."

The vampire never ran out of angles, Sean had to give him that. "Get lost," he said.

"You're typical of your kind, not that I've been unfortunate enough to meet many of you. Rude and arrogant. Detestable, in fact. I think it's time for you to understand your place and climb back into it. I am your superior."

Sean laughed. He couldn't help it. "Are there any more at home like you?" he said. "Or were your parents lucky enough to have only one son with delusions of grandeur? If you'll excuse me, I'll be getting back."

"You'll be coming with me," Colin said. "Much as I'd like to hang around and concoct an opportunity to steal the succulent Leigh, I'll have to make do with you. Duty demands it."

Until he knew what Colin had in mind, Sean didn't want to alert Niles. He needed him there with the women, not that he'd leave them with no protection.

"I'm intrigued," Sean told Colin. "Or I would be if I had the energy."

Colin quickly searched the area.

"Are we expecting company?" Sean asked.

"You tell me, but if you don't do as you're told, quietly, that female of yours will suffer. She obviously means a great deal to you. But you won't be able to keep her from me, and my kind, for the rest of her life anyway. That may be a short time given what I have in mind, but your disobedience will make sure her stay is even shorter than it might be."

"What do you want, blood eater?" Sean shrugged away from the tree and stood with his feet slightly braced. He had to hold himself back from taking this thing by the throat.

"You and I will leave quietly, now," Colin said. "We will attend a meeting, a momentous meeting and, for you, probably a very stimulating one. It will certainly be enlightening for me."

The other man's suggestive tone tensed Sean. "I have no business with you, or anyone you know."

"You're wrong," Colin said. "And you have been singled out for your interference in things that are nothing to do with you."

Sean decided to try a direct attack and hope he could shock this one. "Are you tight with Brande and his pack?"

Colin did pause, but only for a moment before he laughed loudly and shook his head. "You know better than that. I wouldn't be tight with Brande and his wolves any more than I would with you, dog."

When Sean didn't respond, Colin waved for him to follow and turned as if to make his way deeper into the forest. He stopped after a few steps and looked over his shoulder. "Come with me, unless you want me to *take* you, and you know I can. You're no match for me, Sean."

"Are you insane?" Sean asked. "Nothing has changed since I threw you away like a rag doll."

"A lucky accident," Colin said. "I was caught off guard."

Argument was wasted on this self-involved, self-indulgent creature. Sean stayed where he was, his head cocked and indicating his detached interest in whatever Colin might come up with.

"You're forcing my hand. Be logical. We have the same enemies and we could learn from each other."

"I've got to give you points for creative trying," Sean said.

Colin scowled. "Enough of this."

He moved as only a vampire can, so fast he became invisible but for velocity streaks marking his path. And then he was upon Sean, grabbing him by the throat and swinging him off his feet.

Sean's legs collided with a tree and he hooked them around the trunk. Grabbing Colin's body, Sean snapped him into the air and slammed him down on snags of fallen wood, rocks, and the wintry thicket, sharp where all leaves and berries had fallen from the pointed branches.

The vampire breathed like a train on an uphill path through a tunnel. Colin gasped loudly in the hollow way only vampires could achieve. He struggled out of the brittle underbrush that enmeshed him, faced Sean again, and tore at one of his ears before Sean realized his intention.

Sean heard the tissue rip, felt the pain, and slapped Colin's hand away. Since Colin had already encountered him in fully human form, there was no dilemma about shifting or not shifting.

Colin was on him again, trying to finish severing the ear, taking hold of Sean's right shoulder and moving violently to dislocate it and wrench the arm completely loose of its socket.

Using both feet, Sean landed a flying kick into Colin's throat. The sight of the vampire staggering, gasping, and rasping, if only for moments, allowed Sean to rush in and press his advantage.

Grimacing at what felt like thrusts with a burning sword, he jammed his arm back into place at the shoulder and rammed Colin backward.

How to disable him without taking him to the point where he was so disabled, the next act should naturally be to drive a stake into his heart and go on to kill him? Much as he wanted the other dead, he wanted the information Colin might have more.

The man's eyes were black with red rims around the irises. Hunger did that to these people. Sean smiled at him. "Can I offer you a snack? A few sips of something I think you'll like. I keep it in the refrigerator for surprise visitors. I do believe in hospitality."

Colin's tongue whipped, snakelike, over his red lips.

"Where did you get it? Do the Deseran, like Leigh, build up too much blood, is that it? Do they have to drain some away now and then?" He smiled, forgetting to keep his fangs retracted. "How luscious."

Sick to his stomach, Sean kept on smiling. "It usually goes for transfusions."

Colin threw up his hands. "Such a waste. Where is it? Quickly, while it's still there."

"You cannot know where... where it is. I shall have to blindfold you." And in the unlikely event that Colin did as Sean asked, he would then have to lead the vampire where he could contain him—whatever that would take.

"You think I'm a fool?" Colin sneered.

"No, that's why I didn't offer the blood immediately. Never mind. Perhaps another time."

"It is so sweet," Colin said, sounding dreamy. "I have heard about it. And your alpha doesn't even use it. Such a waste."

A movement behind Colin, at the base of a tree, then in the thicket, caught Sean's attention. He quickly averted his gaze. It could be nothing but a small animal making its way through familiar territory.

Or it could be a certain small animal up to no good and about to get them both in terrible trouble.

"I could keep my eyes closed while you take me," Colin said. "I am a man of my word and I won't look."

*Right.*

But why not try, and every moment bought was a gift. Sean took the man by the elbow and was immediately thrown off with enough force to toss him on the ground several yards away.

"Forget your little ploys," Colin said. "I only pretended to be interested. They are waiting for us, we have to go."

"They?" Sean said innocently.

Colin leaped on top of him, but immediately reared up to his knees and screamed.

Balanced on his shoulders, Skillywidden trailed a silver chain back and forth over the vampire's neck while he made disoriented swipes trying to dislodge her. Clamped in her teeth, the chain should have been too heavy for so tiny a creature, but she obviously had considerable strength.

Shaking his head, Sean gingerly took part of the chain and looped it around Colin's neck. He made a knot, then grabbed for Skillywidden, but she didn't intend to be caught.

She moved out of his reach, stood on her hind legs, and clawed at the air over her head as if catching a ball. With the pads of one paw spread, the claws extended, she bounded up Colin's back and drove the same paw into the side of his head.

His eyes closed instantly and he fell forward. Sean rolled out of the way just in time to let the man land, unconscious, on his face.

## *chapter* SEVENTEEN

The underbrush sucked at her paws. Slippery with rain that had slithered through the trees, the wet, mossy tangle made a treacherous course for Elin to use when she wanted to get up to speed.

Traveling as Skillywidden was an amazing advantage but there were places that could snare her small limbs.

Thank goodness Tarhazian couldn't reach Skillywidden with those cold fingers of hers. Elin leaped on, aware that regardless of how warm she was in her silvery fur coat, the temperature appeared to be dropping and there might be ice and snow to contend with later.

Yes, she was running from Sean. Wild as that seemed, she couldn't be sure how he would react to her interference in his fight with Colin and she wasn't ready to find out.

"Elin!"

A shiver rippled under her skin. He sounded furious,

which was an outrage considering how much she had helped him.

Suddenly stubborn, she whipped around, hid behind a tree trunk, and shifted to human. She stepped out, one finger held imperiously forward, and when Sean came into sight, she called, "Stay where you are."

He slowed down but didn't stop. Instead he crept toward her, his golden eyes narrowed to slits and a triumphant smile on his lips. His hair was free and swung forward, thick and casting menacing shadows over his face.

"If you come any closer, I won't tell you what you need to know, and I'll disappear at once," Elin said.

The smile became a grin. He paused and crossed his arms. "You terrify me."

"I just stopped Colin for you." She tried not to let him see her shiver.

The grin disappeared. "You did. Thank you for that although I might have managed by myself. I asked you to stay at Gabriel's—because I don't want you exposed to even more danger. How did you get out?"

"I went to the bathroom," she said smugly. "I wonder if Niles has broken the door down yet."

Sean smothered a laugh and took a step closer.

Elin stepped backward. "Stand still, or I'm gone and I mean it."

"I'll find you, and I mean it."

"You're really pushing things," she said, although she was beginning to feel both unsure of herself—and breathless with the prickle of sexual awareness. Everything about him excited her.

"How come you can shift and still be dressed?" Sean said, looking her over closely enough to bring a spasm of need between her legs.

"You want me to be naked?"

He considered her words. "Yeah, that's what I want. But this isn't the right time or place. How come you aren't—"

"Wearing only my skin," she finished for him. "Because my gift allows me to shift with my clothes. They just come back when I do. Don't you think that's a whole lot more civilized than your naked nonsense?" *Much as she enjoyed it.*

He smiled again and she felt herself blush. "The question is," he said, "how long Colin will stay the way he is and what should I do about it?"

"The silver will cause him a lot of pain," Elin said. "And there's another reason he isn't going anywhere fast, but... anyway, he could be unconscious for some time."

"You hit him with something I couldn't see," he said.

The pressure irritated her. "Perhaps I did." She still wasn't ready to share Deseran secrets, not until she asked Leigh, and not until she told Sean about herself. She felt panicky about how he would react when she did tell him. She would welcome the swirling drifts of glittering colors and their strange powers attracted her to them. She felt as if they kept her safe. But it wouldn't be fair to Sean to seek that comfort while she was with him.

"So you won't explain how you can knock out a vampire?"

"If I would explain it to anyone, it would be you,"

she told him quietly. "I trust you to do what you think is best, for you and for me. Can you say the same about me?"

"I trust you, Elin, but I fear that strong will of yours."

She had no answer.

Blood trailed from one ear and stained the side of his face. His clothes were torn. And he managed to look like the most desirable male she'd ever met—more desirable than that if it were possible.

"I think we should leave Colin where he is," Sean said. "He knows nothing about Skillywidden. You made sure he didn't see you. He'll be embarrassed that he couldn't subdue me and take me wherever he wants me to go. There'll be a pause in what he's up to, but not for long before he's back again. I'm going to Saul. I've got to get to The Island."

"No," she said. "I don't want you to go."

Sean shook his head. "You know I'll do what I think has to be done, Elin. First I have to get you to a place of safety and warmth."

He frowned and looked through rather than at her. She knew he was communicating with someone else. Quietly, she waited, watching him, battling the strangeness of being, at the same time, in extreme danger and so sexually aroused, she wanted to wind herself around him right here.

She must not practice her unusual skills of seduction, not now. But how she longed to stroke him with the essence of her body and watch him struggle. She could make him helpless in her hands, but that wasn't what she really wanted. Elin wanted Sean to take her in every meaning of the word. The decision about what happened with them was his to make now.

He looked at her and she saw he was no longer involved with another mind. "Niles isn't happy with what you did," he said, but a smirk was there. "Locking yourself in the bathroom and ducking out wasn't what he had in mind. Leaving Pokey in attack mode wasn't funny either."

"I didn't, exactly," she said, unable to meet his eyes. "All I said was for Pokey to..."

"Yes."

"I told her not to worry because I'd be back. She doesn't really understand."

"And she bit Niles's nose when he broke down the door," Sean said, but he couldn't help smiling.

"I must apologize to Niles," Elin said honestly and diplomatically. "He showed me he would be willing to accept me. I'll say I'm sorry for what I did."

"Wise woman," Sean said. "He thinks we're right to get out of here and leave Colin. That way it's just a skirmish between the vampire and me."

"And you told him you're going to get Saul to take you to The Island?" Elin said.

He looked at the ground, and started toward her again.

"You didn't tell Niles," she said, as she turned and fled once more.

She ran, growing colder and colder as the wind whipped through her thin dress. That iciness she had expected began to emerge and even her flying feet and swinging arms did nothing to warm her.

A fiery rim of copper from behind dark clouds showed

through the thinning trees, bringing in the dawn. She would not let Sean go to that place, Island or whatever, alone. The thought that he could die there terrified her.

"That's it." He reached her, whirled her around, and threw her, like a bundle of nothing, over his shoulder. "You have teased me, my love. I shouldn't let you goad me, but you have. I have a lot of business ahead of me. It's time to get some things clear between us."

*   *   *

He took her to Two Chimneys.

She said nothing when he carried her up the ladder to the loft and pushed her beneath the thick down quilt on the bed.

"Colin will be set free by his scourge but he won't come after me again too quickly. Niles will want to know what went down but he'll swallow his curiosity until a more appropriate time."

"More appropriate than what?"

In the darkness he saw her better than almost anyone else would. Cocooned in the bed with her head covered but her face exposed, she could not be more awake, or more aware of him.

"More appropriate than when people are exhausted and need to rest."

"I'm not exhausted."

He breathed deeply through his nose. "No, I don't think you are. But let's see."

Stripping rapidly, he kicked his clothes aside and slid into the bed with her. He gathered her close, hugging her, chafing chilled skin until her shivers subsided. And she clung to him, her face tucked into his neck, one leg hooked over his hip.

Her hands started to move over his body. Now stroking his face, her fingers fluttering along the outline of his mouth, now rubbing his chest, tangling with the hair there, slipping down his sides and around to his spine, back over his hips to his belly. Moving, moving, turning every inch of him white-hot.

He should not let this happen like this. It was not the way of his kind.

Under the covers she dived and delved, kissing a path behind her racing hands, sucking in the taught tissue on his abdomen while she squeezed his buttocks, ran her fingers between them, and pushed his upper leg back to make room for her mouth.

Elin licked him delicately. She had made this her time, she intended to complete her plan to seduce him, and he let himself sink into the seduction. When her mouth closed over his penis, she sucked softly, teasing until he didn't think he could hold back. Her fingers played to the base of his erection, weighing and pressing; so gentle, so firm—an exquisite pressure on a hair trigger.

Her silk dress wound about her body.

Now it was up to him. He raised her head, hardly able to bear the separation of her mouth from his flesh. Her dress came off so easily, and the filmy panties. She wore no bra, and in his hands her lithe, firm body slipped, twisted until she was once more wound about him.

From her thighs, to her hipbones, across her flat belly, over her small rib cage to her pointed breasts, Sean allowed himself to revel in the sexy, satin feel of her skin over tender flesh. She made small sounds, wanting sounds, and pushed herself harder into his hands.

Sean made circles around her breasts, trailing the backs of his fingers across her soft skin. He licked and kissed the sensitive places at the sides of her breasts and began to kiss the same circles he'd made with his fingers.

Flattening both hands on her pelvis, grazing over her mound, he stroked upward to cover those sweet breasts, to pinch her nipples between his fingers.

Elin convulsed, she jerked and folded, curled against him. And her teeth sank into his shoulder. She pulled his penis toward her, but he held her off, secured her arms to the bed, and slid down to tuck his tongue into the neat little cleft of her sex.

She struggled against him as if she could take charge again, which only made him smile even while his genitals pulsed.

Opening his mouth wide, he encircled the opening into her body and claimed the place that drove her mad. And within seconds she writhed against him, lifted her hips to meet his tongue, pushing as if to force him deeper.

He felt orgasmic tremors break over and through her and smiled again. Deliberately, he stretched his legs straight down, pressed himself into the bed to help him stay in charge of what was happening to him.

He must be the stronger one. She could be forgiven for giving in to appetite, he could not.

Elin panted. As Sean moved to lie, half over her with a thigh across her hips, she twisted to slide her arms around his neck and hold on tightly enough to make him protest.

She laughed. "Don't tell me I'm hurting you. I couldn't."

*There were many ways to hurt, many forms of pain, some of them irresistible.*

"Come to me," she whispered in his ear. "If you want to."

He nuzzled her neck. "I want to more than you'll ever know. Will you become my mate, Elin? Will you braid your life with mine so we're one?"

Silence made him frown, then he felt her tears on his face, their saltiness on his lips. "Don't cry, please don't cry." He wiped the tears away. "I want to make you happy."

"You already have. I want to be your mate."

He ran his fingers into her masses of black hair and combed it out across the pillows. "Then we are promised. We will become sealed and you will be my mate."

"And you will be mine," she said.

"First we must deal with the formalities of my people, and with the threats that have been made against all of us," he said.

"But you will make love to me now?"

Her small voice turned his heart.

"When I'm sure you are ready and I've done everything I must do to get rid of anything that could threaten you because you are my mate."

"Sean—"

He kissed her words away. "I'm going to hold you through the night, unless you tell me to leave."

"Never," she said, sounding cross. "I wouldn't let you leave."

"Then go to sleep. I don't believe we'll have long to wait, and I don't believe we'll have many moments to rest before then."

Suddenly, she nipped his bottom lip. "You'd better make sure it's not long or I may have to take drastic steps. And you never know when or where I'll take them. And you know I can do that."

*chapter* **EIGHTEEN**

Niles ran both hands through his black hair. "I expected Sean to get here three hours ago. What do I get? Not another word. I can't make a move as long as I think he'll show up, or if I think I could mess something up for him by barging in. Why not at least update me on his movements?"

Leigh figured he didn't expect any answers. She held Pokey in her arms, facing away from Niles so she couldn't see his glares. The little tooth marks on his nose had faded but his annoyance hadn't.

He had told her about transferring the primary decision making for the Team to Sean. Leigh knew him too well not to imagine how he chafed against sharing command in any way but she was touched by his love for her. The coming months, while they waited for the baby, wouldn't be easy but she had no doubt Niles would suffer the most.

\* \* \*

They had returned to Gabriel's after lunch because Leigh had to catch up in the office and Niles said he needed to make progress on the addition to the building—after he mended the bathroom door.

Innes had been working there when they arrived, together with two of the other hounds, Ethan and Campion, but one look at Niles and all three had found pressing duties elsewhere.

So far she'd gotten very little done between Niles's interruptions, and she doubted he had done anything at all.

"Can I hand you nails or something to help out?" she asked tentatively.

His expression suggested he didn't understand what she'd said.

"Maybe I can do something useful?" Leigh smiled and rubbed his arm.

Niles gave her all his attention. "How are you feeling?" he asked darkly.

"Great."

"Who is the doctor you've chosen? I want to interview him. I should make these decisions with you. We'll go into Seattle to see him."

"I've decided on a midwife." Why did he have to bring this up now? "There's a clinic in Coleville and it's really nice. That's where I'll go for regular checks, but the baby will be born at home."

"Are you mad?" He held both of her hands. "This could be a difficult pregnancy and birth. The next thing you'll tell me is you'll have Saul standing by in case there's trouble."

"Well, I did—"

"No." He sank to his haunches and put his face in his hands, all the time shaking his head. "You're going to make this so hard, Leigh. We can't take any more risks than we already are. And Saul? You can't be serious."

He was overreacting because he had too much on his mind. "First things first," she told him quietly. "Where was Sean when he contacted you? You didn't say."

After a slightly too long silence, Niles said, "Two Chimneys."

She smiled a little. "Inside or outside?"

"Inside, I think."

"Good, he needs to be where he can watch Elin closely."

Niles bounced to his feet. "Yeah, he'd better not let her use the bathroom alone."

Leigh knew better than to smile this time. Niles was still seething over Elin's neat little escape trick.

The distinctive sound of Sally's uneven footsteps came from the corridor. Leigh had never asked if the stiffness the woman suffered was because of something like arthritis, or the result of an injury.

"Can I have a few words?" Sally said from the doorway. She looked as if she hadn't had much sleep either. "I've got to. I should have come earlier."

"What is it?" Niles said. "Come in and shut the door."

Sally's plain, gray wool skirt and sweater were a complete departure from her usual flamboyant clothing.

"Have you talked to Saul about Molly's body?" she asked very quietly. "Do you know there's the same mark on her neck as on Rose's?"

"We heard the mark was forming."

"It's bright red now. I saw it today for the first time. The one on Rose, too."

"Their bodies should be dealt with properly," Leigh said. "This is awful."

"Awful but we don't have a choice but to wait and those bodies are all we've got as evidence—and for Saul to keep on working for an answer to what's happening," Sally said, her voice even huskier than usual. "But that's not why I've got to talk about it. I've been putting it off because I didn't want to believe what I was afraid of. I can't put it off any longer."

Leigh's heart thudded too hard.

"You do know what a living vampire sorcerer is?"

"Saul explained," Niles said. He looked worried and thunderous at the same time.

"Do you know what happens if they don't get what they need to feed on?"

Leigh had the feeling Niles might be trying to get her out of here if he weren't concentrating so hard on Sally. "They don't feed very often," he said.

"Unless they've interfered with their natural chemistry and they're sick, that's true." Sally crossed her arms. "We've got ourselves one messed-up living sorcerer vampire in our neck of the woods."

"You can't be sure of that."

"I can and I am. This one's taking risks. He's leaving his safe place and hunting. His kind is so powerful you don't even want to think about it. They don't normally hunt, they send a minion for what they want—kind of like take-out food."

Niles leaned against a Sheetrocked wall. "And you think this means, what?"

Sally hesitated. She went to Leigh and surprised her with a hug. "You okay, hon? The baby feeling good?"

"Yes, thank—"

"Say what you're trying to say, dammit," Niles demanded.

Sally let out a slow breath. "It isn't a good idea for Sean to go to The Island. He hasn't been invited. The risks are unspeakable. This sorcerer vampire is seriously twisted up, maybe mad or sick in some other way. And there's something else none of us counted on."

"Aren't they all twisted?" Leigh said hurriedly, hoping Niles might not pick up on the comment about Sean. "People like this vampire, I mean. They obviously control with fear."

"What do you mean by something else?" Niles said. "Sean isn't going to The Island. We already had that discussion."

"Did he say he wouldn't go?" Sally said. "You said you would. He said he would. You told each other not to go. It's over the edge dangerous for either of you but he's gone. He's on his way right now."

Niles started for the door, only to stop again. "Where is he going? Where is this place?" He held up a hand, raised his eyes, and stared at the window. Seconds later he swung around, frustration twisting his face. "He's closing me out."

"All of you mean so much to him," Sally said. "He thinks it's up to him to make everyone safe, the whole lot of us."

"And while I need to be here for Leigh, he is my surrogate," Niles said. "But he should not have left without my blessing."

"You asked him to share leadership with you at present," Leigh said quietly.

Niles put a fist to his brow. "Whatever has to be done should be planned. We should plan together. Where is Elin?"

The expression on Sally's face made Leigh's stomach plummet.

"I don't know where she is," the woman said. "I can't find her. She doesn't understand how vulnerable she is. She wouldn't try to follow Sean, would she? Niles, Aldo, the man who tried to implicate Sean in murder, could be involved. He could be on The Island."

Niles didn't respond.

"I don't know where The Island is—I've never been there," Sally said. "I've never been invited. I'm not useful enough to be invited."

"Sean wouldn't let Elin go somewhere so dangerous," Leigh said and met Sally's eyes. Understanding passed between them. They both knew Elin would do anything for Sean, with or without his blessing.

"How do you know he's gone there?" Niles asked through his teeth. "And how do you know about Aldo?"

Sally cleared her throat. "I was at Saul's when Sean came and said he wanted to be guided to The Island."

"And Saul told him how to find it? That means you must have heard what was said if you were there."

"Saul didn't give Sean directions," Sally said. "He told Sean he understood that he wanted to put Aldo to rest, as he put it. That's exactly what he said. Then Saul said he'd take him."

## *chapter* NINETEEN

The surreal, free flight from Whidbey to a fog-shrouded cove on an island Sean had never seen before took him over water, but he caught only glimpses of it through dense, dark clouds.

Seaweed, thick and slimy, spread over huge pebbles underfoot, and ahead jagged crags of lava rock rose, sheer and denuded, to disappear overhead in a crown of blue-black vapor.

Sean had traveled there with one hand on Saul's shoulder, entrusting his life to one who should be an untouchable enemy. To trust a vampire should be unthinkable for a werehound. With no other way to find his target, Sean's human necessities overtook instinct.

"This is The Island," Saul murmured. "It's a minefield. You can't know what you will see or experience next—and without warning."

"I should shift," Sean said and began to do just that.

He and Saul had already decided it was too dangerous for him to remain in human and possibly recognizable form. Before he was fully transformed, he said, "Will we stay together? Or am I on my own now? It's your choice but I can probably fit in better on my own. Do you think it's probable there are others of my kind here? You weren't sure."

"Not any that you would know. These will be different creatures. But enough of that for now. We will stay together. You'll be able to hear me talk so I'll make sure you know what we must do. You'll have to find your own way to communicate with me. Stop moving, touch me, whatever. First we have to negotiate our way past any coastal outlaws. They are the ones who have been banished from his court by The One. They live in gangs just waiting for fresh, unsuspecting victims to capture."

Sean completed his shift. He stretched his long, heavy limbs and shook his blue-black coat, settling into his hound.

"I have an advantage," Saul said. "I am a maverick vampire with a long history that strikes fear into anyone who knows about me. My roots stretch into an ancient and evil society. What they don't and won't know is that I am evolved enough to use my reputation without sinking back to what I once was."

Saul spoke in a low, soft voice but it was clear to Sean's enhanced hearing. It surprised him that Saul would share such personal details.

"We have to lose ourselves," Saul said. "Out here we're too obvious. We want to observe, not be observed. And we must find our way without attracting enough attention to cause a fight—or for The One to be alerted we're here."

Sean surveyed his surroundings and loped over the beach toward a sawtooth outcropping. And Saul moved with him as if they had silent understanding.

From the cover of that first ridge, they could see the entire cove, including an opening from the sea into a channel that led who knew where.

"Those who need conventional means of transportation enter through that channel, but only at the invitation of The One," Saul said. "It winds to the heart of this mountain. I was brought here with an escort apparently considered appropriate for me. But in truth, The One is extremely careful. He assesses each visitor individually. We could not risk going in by that route.

"The Island is a volcanic mountain rising from the water. I believe it's part of the same geological formation as Chimney Rock under the water of the cove near Leigh's cottage—in front of Niles's place. There is definitely another source of what so many call The Veil, erupting here." He raised his face to the dark, shifting vapor. "Up there alone, at the very top. From what I understand, The One lives alone there, in quarters near a crater that opens into the earth. As far as I can tell, he hasn't been able to use The Veil for any of the purposes he may have had in mind. You will have to be very watchful to see if there is some clue to his agenda."

Sean stared at Saul, who gave a thin smile. "We must find him and hope we can either shock him into revealing something of what he wants and what he intends to accomplish with all of his mischief, or discover what we need without being discovered. And then we must try to stay alive long enough to get out. Groups of beings without consciences have made their quarters in mostly hidden pockets in the cooled lava inside."

Sean met Saul's eyes in a moment of complete understanding.

Nearby a clump of seaweed abruptly tore loose from the stones and swung a few inches into the air.

Sean stiffened, staring at the spot. He took a step toward what was now a gluey, green glob of strings rising and falling, the movements wilder by the second.

"That's what makes us most vulnerable," Saul said, standing beside Sean. "What we can't see. At least, I can't see what's moving that, can you?"

As abruptly as it had started hopping, the weed fell inert again.

"I think we can assume we have company," Saul said. "Let's move. Our best hope is to be in and out fast. We can be grateful Niles has no way to follow—as far as we know. He could cause a short and unhappy war—for us."

Sean realized there were things he should have asked before allowing himself to go verbally dark. He sat down and stared at Saul. He had a sensation that there were elements here that would bother him much more than they would Saul.

The vampire pushed back his long, black coat and planted his hands on his hips. "You don't think I'm right?" he said.

Sean didn't move or even blink.

"You want to know exactly what I expect from this trip?"

Sean closed his eyes briefly.

"Very well," Saul said. "I expect, or hope, for some in-
dication about what's happening to The One to make him
behave as he is. I think that's what you want, too. If we
learn what he plans to do and why, and what kind of danger we're in on Whidbey, fantastic. If we only learn what
his next move is—or why he's taken the steps he already
has—also fine. I can't get past the conviction that he's
ill somehow, and deteriorating. After all, he is alive. You
agree?"

Sean closed his eyes in brief agreement.

Perhaps they would find The One was indeed failing,
perhaps close to his own death. That would make him
more desperate and more dangerous. It would also increase his vulnerability.

Sean stood and waited until Saul started forward again,
leaning into the incline that snaked from one craggy ridge
to another. At least the outcroppings offered cover in
places.

The silence, the stillness began to grate on Sean. He
heard only the subtle grind of their feet on shale and
searched in all directions for whatever might be traveling
with them.

A plop caused Sean to halt and look back. They had
wound around a turn and could no longer see where they
had started their trek.

Saul also glanced over his shoulder and they both
stood still. A trickle of tiny rocks showered from the air
a few inches above the ground to land and scatter among
dozens of others.

"Rocks in midair," Saul remarked. He came close to

Sean and whispered, "Our company behaves as if it wants us to know it's here. That, or it's very inept. Emptying the rocks from a shoe, perhaps." He raised his voice deliberately. "We'll fight if we have to. Whenever we have to."

On they climbed until Saul stopped suddenly and sat at the side of the trail. "There's something unnatural about all this," he said. "When I was here before, the place teemed with life—or it teemed with something. What I couldn't see, I could hear. Babbling conversation, shrieking, laughing. Arguments, fights, struggles . . . and an orgy here and there." His expression didn't change. "Where are they all? I believe something momentous is happening. That, or it's already happened."

*Or they were being set up.* A faint thrill, like that he always got before a fight, ruffled Sean's fur. He looked out through the rocky wall on his right, over the beach below and the sea that disappeared into the shroud of fog that protected The Island from prying eyes. Nothing moved.

"Stop!" As if to make a lie of Saul's theory that the place could be deserted, a misshapen and shriveled creature, little more than bone and transparent skin, landed on the path in front of them. He wore only a loincloth. "Who are you?" he said, his voice unexpectedly deep. "What do you want? What makes you think you can pass by my home without paying a toll?" Large, pointed ears twitched and doleful gray eyes filled with tears.

"Are you mad?" Saul said, sweeping a hand behind the fellow's knees. "Get lost while you still can."

With the force of that single light swipe from Saul, the creature rose in the air, turned over once, and landed on his large feet again. Shrieking, he scrambled away and disappeared into a hole so small he had to squeeze himself into an elongated, putty-colored sausage to pass inside.

Sean stood by the hole and stared from it, to Saul and back again. He started looking around, pawing rocks aside to look underneath.

"Your instincts are good," Saul said. "This pile of rubble is filled with tunnels and caves. Many of them are considered the private domains of certain groups. From inside the mountain I saw tunnels from out here, but I don't know where there's an opening big enough for us. I hope we find one higher up."

Without warning, lightning cleaved the clouds and hit the mountain, sent a shower of sparks accompanied by loud crackling. Thunder bellowed almost at once, deafening, shaking the earth.

Wind blew sheets of rain sideways and Sean was glad of his dense fur. Saul was quickly soaked. "Massive storms are frequent here," he said.

They moved on, but Saul stopped again, holding up a hand. He turned slowly to face Sean and put a finger to his lips while he watched something behind Sean.

Sean pushed back onto his haunches and stared back the way they had come. Not twenty feet away, a short, thick stick hung, horizontal, perhaps six or seven inches from the ground, a crooked stick, unremarkable except for its resistance to gravity and its lonely condition.

"Any ideas?" Saul asked.

Sean shook his head. If The Island was as mysterious as Saul had said, then this could be anything, including someone's silly effort to be annoying.

"It looks like a wand," Saul said. "I haven't seen many because I don't move with those who use them, but they can be powerful, and mischievous."

For an instant Sean saw a wavering shape, a ghost of a shape, something small and long and so faint he couldn't identify what kind of creature it was.

As quickly as it showed itself, it was gone, and the stick glided along to disappear around the next bend.

Saul gave Sean a long and serious look. "Sally has sticks that are wands. There are plenty able to make very efficient wands, they just aren't usually among those we're likely to come across."

Wind-driven rain beat against them. The scent of salt came heavy on the wet air and the sky disappeared behind lightning-ripped, dark cloud.

Both Saul and Sean held their heads high, staring ahead, watching for what they expected at any moment—an attack.

Thunder rushed at them in echoing, flesh-shaking blasts.

They trudged on.

And twice more Sean saw the floating stick.

The ghostly, transparent shadow came and went again.

He halted, and so did Saul. The vampire faced him, his long, black hair sodden and water dripping from his face. "I saw a phantom—I think it intended to be seen." Their eyes met and Saul said, "I believe you have your hands very full."

Sean took off, ran past Saul, but hesitated when the other zipped in front of him and held up a hand. "Did you know she could become invisible as that cat? She attached herself and followed us—came with us. Elin can be invisible, or should I say Skillywidden? She will only slow us down, or worse. Should we turn back?"

Pacing, Sean thought. He and Elin had only communicated telepathically as humans. He had no way of getting into her mind and telling her to come back to Whidbey with them.

Saul raised his hands and let them fall heavily to his sides. "Women were always spoilers. They could always make men weak. Damn, why do they have to be so irresistible?"

This piece of insight was something else unexpected coming from the vampire.

"There's no way to communicate with her?"

Sean shook his head.

"Then if we go, we won't be sure she's with us so there's no point. We go on and encourage her to stay with us—and do no harm."

Making his decision quickly, Sean shifted again. He stood, naked, in the raging storm. "I have to be able to talk to you," he said. "I need a disguise."

He accepted the coat Saul took off and offered without question. The thought seemed to have come to both of them instantaneously—a prospect Sean had no intention of examining too closely.

The coat had a hood and he pulled it far forward to shadow his face. Voluminous and heavy with an attached cape, the long coat slapped at his skin. Saul's white shirt stuck to his body. On any other man his skin would have shown through, but not on the pale vampire.

"Elin," Sean hissed, ignoring Saul's muttered protests.

"Elin, stay close and show yourself. I know you can hear me now so don't try to pretend you can't. I've seen you—stop hiding. Come to me. We'll go back to Whidbey."

A blast of rain hit like a wave crashing from the sea and Sean wiped his face to see. "You'll be fine as Skilly-widden. If someone sees you, they'll think nothing of it."

Seconds turned to minutes and no small, silver cat appeared.

"Damn," Sean said, throwing off the hood and shaking back his hair. "She won't show herself. She wants us to finish what we've come for so I won't return—or so she thinks."

"I doubt we'll return," Saul said evenly. "And who knows if we'll even leave."

Sean glared at him. "Pay him no heed, Elin. Just show yourself."

Nothing.

"Two choices," Saul said. "Go back and hope she's with us, or carry on and hope…Just hope."

Sean made up his mind. Anger thumped at his temples as he leaned once more to climb upward, this time without the benefit of shoes, or hardened pads on his feet.

"This has to be done," he said to Saul. "We'll never be free if we don't stop this thing. Stay with us, Elin," he said. "And don't try any heroics. If something happens, don't interfere. This is an evil place."

"You'd do well to be afraid, Elin," Saul said to the wind and rain and emptiness. "It isn't me you'll have to deal with when we get out of here but I doubt the experience will be pleasant nevertheless."

With Saul at his shoulder, Sean scrambled to the top of the next rise only to face a rough and muddy downhill stretch. Fortunately he was too surefooted to slip. "You've really made a mess of things this time," he told Elin—wherever she was and that couldn't be far. "Who gave you the silly stick? Sally? Did the pair of you think it would be any defense against what we're facing? Get behind us and stay there." It puzzled him that there was no sign of that stick at the moment.

"Look," Saul said suddenly and lowered his voice. "Just up ahead. That rock's moving. The wand. It's the wand doing it."

Quite a large rock heaved loose of the mountainside under the unlikely leverage of their familiar floating stick. The boulder tipped slowly forward, rolled sideways, and slid onto the pathway.

"Why did you do that, Elin?" Sean said. "I can tell it's you with the stick." *Which should have snapped off the instant she tried to use it.*

"Better not insult the wand," Saul said, laughing un-expectedly. "They have personalities, or so I understand. You could get yourself punished."

Less than amused, Sean stalked toward the fallen rock, and Elin, or where she must be, the wand held high.

"Get behind us," he told her, his jaws aching with the effort of not losing his temper. "Do it now. We've got—"

The wand disappeared—into the ground.

Squabbling voices wafted from the place where the boulder had been dislodged. The babble grew louder, the babble and argumentative yelling.

Saul hauled Sean behind a row of rocks and they threw

themselves to the ground. "Elin's probably down there," he said.

"We'll see," Saul responded although he didn't sound calm. "Be grateful she's invisible."

Like a flock of gray birds, figures resembling a retreating army clambered from the earth, falling over each other, climbing on those who fell to keep going, and yelling all the time. Most of them wore gray leggings and tunics and a head covering that looked like a medieval chain mail cowl with a fencing face mask.

Among these, and there were many of them, a ragtag melee of various creatures rushed along, some willingly, some dragged.

The whole streaming band scrambled and leaped their way toward the beach until they passed out of Sean and Saul's sight.

"I could feel something different going on here," Saul said. "Some change. I told you as much."

"Looks like rats abandoning the ship to me," Sean allowed. "I couldn't even tell what most of them were, other than the ones in uniform or whatever it was."

Falling silent, Sean stood and went to the spot where the wand had slipped from sight and the exodus erupted. He reached the hidden rim of a large hole.

Hardly daring to breathe, he knelt and looked over the edge. A few feet of rough-hewn lava rock angled away from him before he saw a step, and the shadow of a second. Beyond that, everything was dark.

He stood up and looked around. "I've changed my mind. We'll have to go back."

His eyes met Saul's.

The vampire gave an eloquent shrug, and raised his arms. "Nothing's changed, my friend. We don't know where she is. Leave and she might come with us. Leave and she might already be poking around inside that hole and on the way to hell—alone."

## chapter TWENTY

*A*t last the rushing horde of yelling riffraff were all gone, scuttling through the hole Elin had found. Little did they know they'd had invisible help getting out of the mountain.

She breathed more easily.

Unbelievable. Neither Sean nor Saul had considered that the wand might also be capable of invisibility. She felt it at her side, occasionally tapping against her. Bless Sally for her wonderful gift. Just its presence gave her confidence. Elin hoped the wand would be useful if she got into even more trouble—she also hoped Tarhazian wouldn't find out and punish Sally.

It would be a disaster for Tarhazian to know Elin and Sally were close conspirators.

Mmmm, she loved the feel of her sinuous Skillywidden body winding along. But then, her Elin body could be supple in all the right ways, too—if she wanted it to be.

Until Sean and Saul passed her, Elin huddled at the side of the long flight of rough, downward-sloping stairs she had uncovered. She wanted to throw herself at Sean and feel safe in his arms. But this was no time or place for wimps who couldn't stick to their plans.

Both men kept their voices very low but Elin heard them clearly. She was almost certain that even now she could communicate with Sean. But it suited her to have him think she was guilty only of hearing him and not doing what he wanted, rather than also deliberately not talking to him.

*Doing what he wanted? He did still have things to learn about her.*

She slunk along behind the men. Sean had to be uncomfortable in Saul's heavy, wet coat but he kept it on and the hood up. He looked so much better naked.

Later she could expect him to blame her for his discomfort because he'd shifted back to try and talk to her.

If she were talking to him, she'd say he should use his head not his heart and return to his hound. Conversation with him at present was out of the question. He would only spend valuable time trying to persuade her into something he decided was safer for her.

Saul stopped walking and held up a hand. "This looks like the first inhabited cavern." He edged forward and leaned into a space that had been invisible to Elin.

"Empty," Saul said, bracing his hands on either side of an opening he had to crouch to enter.

"Who's usually here?" Sean said, dropping to his haunches and staring past Saul. "Is that some sort of altar? On the far side. The top looks fluorescent."

Elin peeked inside. *Too bad there isn't a supply of The Veil hanging around with some extra green I can use. Who knows how many monsters I may need to get rid of in here?*

"Yes. An altar. The group that was here fashioned themselves after the original Templars." Saul went into the cavern. He called back, "They sacrifice whatever they can get their filthy hands on. Like deadly scavengers. They are a banished band of Austrian Verbols. They began as members of the renegade Embran tribe and continue to manifest in many forms as the Embran do, but they cannot return to the center of the earth, where the kingdom of their ancestors flourishes again now."

"And The One wanted all these creatures here? Nothing seems too low for him to gather in. He really is desperately searching for something," Sean said. "But even these have deserted his mountain."

"Or been sent away because he decided they weren't of any use to him." Saul peered into the semidarkness. "They haven't been gone long. They must have been in the middle of a sacrifice when they left. See, the blood on the altar and the floor? It still looks wet. And there's enough of it to float a boat. God knows how many deaths have happened here."

"Do you think they would just leave?" Sean said.

"Not all of them. Look over there, on the left."

"Rags," Sean said, following Sean inside.

Elin skittered in behind. At least she could feel Sean's aura, his strength, and be near him. *Please don't let him leave me after this.* Her stomach squeezed painfully at the thought.

Saul pulled the black rags aside, or tried to. They were attached to the neck of a colorless man with a completely bald head. Death had already filmed his wide open eyes and a gaping gash across his neck from ear to ear showed how he had died. Saul grunted. "They are more easily killed than either your kind or mine."

Werehounds and vampires did not usually die from a wound.

"He's not the only one here," Sean said. He stooped to peer through another opening. "There must be more than a dozen bodies in here." He entered this new cavern.

"We'd better get on with it," Saul said. "Let's see if we can find out what The One's up to and get the hell out of here."

"Yeah." Sean's voice echoed back. "Throats cut. Every one of them. But no blood. Can you explain that?"

"Verbols don't bleed," Saul said. "Neither do they breathe. It's air that can kill them if it enters their bodies. The wounds on their necks let air past their nose and mouth shields. It got inside them and they died."

"How do they survive at all?" Sean sounded increasingly curious. "Are we likely to encounter more of them?"

Saul appeared to be searching for something. "They suck out entrails," he said. "I told you they can assume many forms so we could encounter them anywhere here if some escaped this slaughter and disguised themselves. There must have been some of them with the bunch who ran out of the tunnel before we came in. What I'd really like to know is what or who they were sacrificing before so many of them went on their final trip."

The men backed out of the cavern and continued down

with the steps growing narrower before they got even rougher and began to climb steeply upward.

Elin stayed near and breathed a little faster when they turned a corner and the tunnel lightened.

The hacked-out walls glistened wet and fluorescent yellow. They gave off light that washed a dull glow over the tunnel. Elin swallowed harder. She didn't like it in here, and from the silence of the two men ahead, it didn't seem they were thrilled with their surroundings either.

Sean checked behind him repeatedly and she knew he was convinced she was there—and worried out of his mind because he might have no control over what happened to her.

"Stay with me," he whispered, looking past her, searching. "But don't... stay right here and wait."

They had arrived at another hollowed-out cave where more creatures were heaped up and very dead. These differed from the other group in that they had large feet and ears, but Saul told Sean they were simply more Verbols who took a slightly different form from the first batch.

Elin remained in Sean's footsteps on the way into the cave, and when he climbed out again.

"Saul." Sean pulled the vampire to face him. "We have no definite plans. We want to learn the reason why The One is causing us trouble on Whidbey and stop him. But we haven't discussed how we will fight him if it comes to that. Or how we will respond if we're attacked and seriously outnumbered."

"If you can think of a way to answer those questions, I'm all ears."

Sean shook his head slowly. "In other words we

keep going and hope we'll know what to do if we have to do it?"

"That's about how I see it," Saul said. He raised a hand. "There is more I know. Details I saw no point in mentioning unless we actually got here. We must be ready for the worst, Sean. That creature up there thinks he sees a way to get what he wants. He works on it day and night. But his body is alive and must be fed. It's worse than you can imagine."

"I doubt it," Sean said, stopping, obviously waiting for Saul to tell him everything.

Trembling, Elin crouched against the slimy wall again.

Saul stepped backward to stand beside Sean. "You can't persuade The One of anything or get any sense out of him. I'd say he was mad but I don't think he is. But he's vicious. With his bare hands he tears open living bodies and eats...He eats the organs."

"From any creature?" Sean asked.

"Humans," Saul said. "He was careful I didn't see any prisoners, but chains and manacles hung from the walls. I believe he chains his captives to the wall where they can watch when he feeds.

"The mountain spews thick vapor sometimes, not like an eruption, it just bubbles up from a hole inside the cave, and subsides again. He catches parts of it and works with it, screaming all the time that he's being tricked. And he talks about making his enemies suffer and about his Bloodstone. His Bloodstone is almost perfect, or so he says, and nothing will escape it when he's finished. His aim is to have the stone respond to his desires, to change the will of those he wants to serve him. It will, or so he believes, serve two purposes: to bring others under his control, or to kill them if they resist.

"He wants to have a big Bloodstone, but when he tries to form more than small amounts of what he takes from the crater, it crumbles once it's dry. Little metal pots of red, steaming vapor are stacked up and he keeps filling more from the vent. One at a time is what he keeps muttering and he says it's too slow. But he also says he'll get his island in the end. At first all I could think was that he'd already got it so I didn't understand."

Sean stared at Saul and said, "He means Whidbey, not this island. There's something there he wants or needs. I'd put my money on need." He looked upward, then around as if he was searching for Elin. "Why haven't you tried to interfere with his plans before?"

"I waited. That's my way. I prefer to see what develops and to be certain how I will deal with a problem. Until meeting Aldo, and then being involved with you, I was still collecting information and making decisions.

"Now is the time. You are the key I needed, and whatever you decide, I'll do," Saul said.

Elin could hardly believe she had just heard a vampire cede authority to another species.

"We find him," Sean said. "Before he finds a way to go after everyone on Whidbey."

They kept climbing. After three more caverns of the dead, Saul and Sean stopped checking. They went upward silently and swiftly. Elin paused every few steps and looked back nervously. A scream echoed and it wasn't far enough away for Elin's comfort.

The men halted.

"Is that The One in a rage?" Sean said. "Or is it one of his victims?"

The next scream rose to a roar, then a strangled gurgle. The sickening noise ended abruptly but loud and ragged breathing whirled around the tunnel like a tornado.

Sean carried on more slowly, looking past each bend before continuing. When he motioned for Saul to wait, Elin zipped around both of them. They might think she was useless, but sometimes the small and insignificant could accomplish amazing feats—like pushing crazy men into their own bubbling craters.

The man she loved might want to get to the bottom of a mystery, but if she could get rid of the cause of the mystery, the mystery would go away and they could get on with their lives.

Elin shuddered. A delicious, sensual shudder. She could just be with Sean and keep teaching him her wiles.

*Disgraceful, Elin. Behave yourself. This is life or death here.*

There it was, in the middle of a large cave, the steaming crater. But it was much smaller than she had expected, perhaps a foot and a half in diameter. She lifted her upper lip in a silent hiss. Quite big enough for a man to fall into. Including the stooped, man-shaped creature gasping against a wall where he tore at empty air. His frustration over his experiments must have swelled into his great screams.

Elin realized Sean and Saul were still hanging back, deciding on their next move. She needed to work quickly to have any hope of averting what could be a disaster for the three of them.

A sound stopped her. Every nerve on alert, she stepped backward. Two people slumped against the wall, pinned there by manacles. They were conscious and pulled against their restraints with ineffectual tugs that suggested they had all but given up hope. A man and a woman and both young. They looked alike and she wondered if they were brother and sister.

The One staggered to the center of the area around the small crater. The sounds he made resembled death rattles but Elin didn't fool herself she could be that lucky.

This monster railed aloud against what he considered injustice against him. He twisted his body and shook his fists heavenward, "They think they've got the best of me," he shouted suddenly and clearly, rearing up and bellowing. "All they've done is ensure their end will be horrific." He stared at his captives and Elin respected the stony expressions they kept on their faces.

He spun in her direction, cloaked in flowing scarlet that swung free from his shoulders in many layers. His head and face, completely exposed, lacked hair or distinct features.

Trying to be brave, Elin sat on her haunches and waited, and stared, looking for the means and opportunity to upset this crazed thing. As she watched, he continued to throw himself from rocky wall to rocky wall, but something changed.

His face melted into shapelessness and re-formed several times. He was a shapeshifter.

Back and forth he morphed.

And Elin continued to wait for her opportunity. She sensed movement behind her and had to hang on to her concentration.

Their unwilling host stopped moving. He stared at his captives from the one eye he possessed in that second and took a key from his robes.

A long, heavy swath of white hair appeared on his skull and he stroked it with one hand, the delicate fingers of which were encrusted with rings, each one set with a glittering gem.

"Leave them alone." Sean's voice cut through Elin and she felt her heart drop. "Move away."

The One grew still again before he turned slowly toward Sean, who stood where Elin could see him. He moved and she gasped. So fast Elin couldn't actually see the man, Sean wrenched the chains that held the captives free of the wall. "Go," he told the couple. "Run. You'll be given instructions."

That must have meant that Saul would tell them how to get out and probably to hide when they did.

"Stop," The One shouted. "I need them. Don't you understand, I have to..." His voice faded away. The scarlet robe lost some of its flamboyance and hung in subdued folds. All form left the man's face except for two holes that showed a dark gleaming deep inside. His eyes, Elin assumed.

The two young people dashed to the entrance and out of sight. The One didn't spare them a glance. Instead he concentrated on Sean and then, to Elin's horror, at the exact spot where she sat. He began to rock gently back and forth and made a soft, satisfied sound.

"I am saved," he said fatuously. "How kind for both of you to come to me. I know it couldn't have been an easy task to find me. Look at you. How sweet. I had heard you two were becoming very close. I didn't believe it. How could I be so fortunate. Everything I want in one place."

Sean looked sideways. He saw her, too. Elin bowed her head to curl up even smaller—and watched her waist-length black hair fall forward. "No," she whispered and stared at Sean. "This has to be Tarhazian. She's found a way to interfere even with—"

"Even with the fae powers she helped you develop?" The One's voice echoed as if he were hollow. "She has taken away your shapeshifting—and your invisibility. How delicious. I must find a way to thank the Fae Queen. We three will have everything. We will have everything you need and I will have everything I want. With you in my care I cannot fail.

"Did you know I can draw strength from your kind, werehound? We have a symbiosis more rare than you can know. And this little fae? Her heart grows again the moment the one she already has starts to leave her body. Her liver, her kidneys, her lungs, every part of her will grow back for me to enjoy again. I will have to be more delicate in my removal techniques but it will still be so much easier than all this time wasted on hunting food, or having my slaves hunt for food. They are so inept."

Elin rubbed her very real arms and felt sick. She had become visible in her human form. Skillywidden had been whipped away.

Softly; twisting, twisting, she felt something against

the palm of her right hand. The wand had not become visible and it was reminding her of its presence.

She could sense that Sean was about to attack. Trying to stop him was out of the question, but if he understood an unspoken message and acted on it, perhaps she could help him.

Quickly, she slid the wand against his fingers. Sean would feel but not see the stubby piece of wood. When he glanced at her, their eyes met and she saw understanding dawn.

His fingers closed on the wand and he prepared to rush The One.

So quickly, Elin thought she must be imagining it, the red-robed being changed shape. He swelled larger and black hair appeared that reached his ears in a curved, blunt helmet shape. His wide mouth was an almost lipless gash and he didn't take his dark eyes from Sean. "Finally," he said. "It has been a long time, but I have you now."

"Aldo," Sean said. "Damn you."

Saul burst into the cave. "What the hell's happening?" The sight of the other man stopped him.

Aldo laughed, delighted.

"I met him here on The Island," Saul said. "But I thought The One was up here."

"He was," Sean said. "Aldo is also The One."

Aldo shuddered, his features seemed to run downward, and in seconds The One appeared again.

"You absorbed Aldo?" Sean said with awe in his voice. "He's part of you."

"I needed his strength," The One said. "Such as it is.

He is of use to me. But he came here for my help, Sean. He was looking for you because you can renew him. How useful that would be to me. He told me that your touch and your approval can make him whole. So we know what must be done."

"I hope this thing has a mind of its own." As if it were a baton, Sean clutched the short, thick wand in his clenched fist. "Magic isn't my field." He rushed The One, raising his arm as he went, ready to strike.

Elin held her breath. She had been amazed when the wand responded to her wish that the big stone be moved from the mouth of the tunnel.

"You're gone, sick beast. Deviant." Sean took hold of the scarlet robes and beat the sorcerer vampire's head. "Go."

"What do you think you're doing?" Saul cried. "What good is that going to do against him?"

"Sean has the wand," Elin said, swallowing painfully. "It's still invisible."

Saul gaped. He took a step closer to Sean and stopped. "My God. It doesn't look as if invisibility takes anything away from its strength," Saul said. "Powerful ally to have—if you know how to use it, I suppose."

Sean clung to a handful of scarlet fabric that trailed, limp and empty, from his fingers. "Damn it to hell, I've lost him," he muttered. "He could be anywhere but he's gone from here, just gone."

"Just like you said you wanted him to be," Elin said quietly. "We need some wand lessons."

## *chapter* TWENTY-ONE

W here did she come from?" Saul said, nodding at Elin. "Does she look a bit blurry around the edges?"

"Tarhazian is still meddling with my talents," Elin told him. "But I think her power over me is growing weaker. That's what might make me look blurred."

Sean didn't bother to answer Saul's questions. His own mind raced, jumbling how badly he wanted to see her, to hold her, with disbelief that she'd taken such a risk in coming, a risk to all three of them.

Saul said, "You followed us—or came with us. We knew you were there. We couldn't risk going back in case you weren't with us. Do you know how much danger you put yourself in?"

Burying his face in Elin's hair, Sean held her against him and ignored Saul.

"Please take your time with this touching reunion," Saul said. "Disaster hovers in every corner, but don't let that interfere. Should I leave you alone here? Of course, if our creature returns, it could be a little uncomfortable for you. But what the hell, you're broad-minded. Enjoy yourselves. I'll see what I can do to get our survivors off The Island."

Elin rested her forehead on Sean's chest. "We'd better go," she whispered.

An abrupt wave of anger caught Sean by surprise. "You've got that right. Can we rely on you not to do anything else to put all of us in danger?" The words were out before he could temper them.

Pushing away, Elin looked first at Saul, then at Sean. "We don't know what might have happened if I *hadn't* been here," she said. Her voice shook. "I didn't come because I was sure it was the right thing to do, or because I was sure I could help. I couldn't bear to have you come here and never return—and then never know what happened to you, Sean."

She made to leave but he caught her by the arm and wouldn't let go even when she pulled against him.

"You could have put an end to our efforts," Saul said evenly.

"But I didn't. You didn't have a plan to deal with that, that *thing* and neither did I—until we were up here. We've lost him but only because we aren't practiced with the wand. And chances are we'll get out of here in one piece and live to fight again. All my life I've been told what I should and shouldn't do—when anyone bothered with me at all. I'm finished with that."

Saul withdrew behind his usual almost expressionless face. "Thank you for your efforts," he told Elin formally.

Moving his grip to her hand, Sean said, "You helped us, but you shouldn't have come and you know it. It could have ended differently and it was only an outlandish chance that saved us all."

She raised her chin. "An outlandish chance we wouldn't have had if I *hadn't come*." Tugging him, she led the way out of the cave and they sped ever faster until they reached the exit from the mountain.

All the way down Sean had wrestled with what it would take to mend the rift between Elin and himself. He still didn't know. And the nagging whisper that Tarhazian could have asked her to spy on the hounds kept bothering him. He didn't think she had wanted to become visible when she had. Would she ever have admitted being with them if that hadn't happened?

Why would he doubt her now when it was the wand Sally had given her that saved the day? Only after Elin discovered she was visible as herself again, though...

He collected himself. "Please let me look outside first."

Saul looked as if he would argue but turned his head aside instead.

The top of Sean's head barely cleared the rim of the hole before the former captives were upon him, watching him with hopeful eyes.

Sean searched in all directions but detected no other signs of life. "Have you seen anyone else?" he asked the man.

"Earlier," he said. He looked nervous. "There was fighting between them but boats came from the river entrance into the mountain and took them away. Then we saw him." His voice faded away.

"Him?"

"We thought you must be dead," the woman said. She and the man were olive-skinned and dark-haired. Both could be French or Italian although there was no accent. The woman took a deep breath. "But we could only wait and see if you escaped."

"The One," the woman said. "He appeared by the water. He was black-haired. Big and muscular. He looks like that when he's strong. When he's the white-haired creature, he seems weaker. He goes back and forth between the two appearances."

*Aldo was part of The One and the duo was alive. They would be back because he, Sean, had only gotten rid of them temporarily.* Sean recoiled from the memory of how The One's features had morphed into Aldo. *And that thing could show up anywhere, including Whidbey.*

The woman became agitated. "Huge wolves used to come to the cave—they could turn into men. They threatened him and said he owed them an equal share in whatever he found. Then one time he got mad. He touched one of them—just touched him—and he keeled over. The other ones dragged him away and they never came back."

"Brande's pack," Sean said quietly. "Sounds as if they got over their argument in time for a touching reunion today."

"The One told his servants—his army—they were useless and he sent them away." The man's voice got tighter and higher. "They didn't come back either. He started screaming for them, ordering them to get back but they were gone.

"He faints when he's really angry, or goes into a sort

of coma or something. But you can't trust that to last. He can come right back most of the time. He was usually the dark one when he returned. It was as if the dark one always came when the other one fainted or looked sick."

"That's who he was when the wolf men came," the woman said, pointing at the beach. Saul joined them, a hand on Elin's elbow. Sean wasn't surprised when the couple's attention settled on her. They had been too frightened to really see her in the crater cavern, but here with the prospect of safety ahead, they stared at her, open-mouthed.

"I'm Elin," she said.

"Cassie," the woman said. "This is my brother, David."

"We were all kidnapped," Cassie said. "We come from New Orleans. The One said we were marked to die now, no matter what happens."

Sean raised his brows at Saul, who inclined his head and studied the darkening sky, then looked into the eastern distance. "We'll be on Whidbey well before dark," Sean said.

"It's getting dark now," David said, an arm around his sister's shoulders.

"No problem," Saul said. "But there's a storm coming in so it'll be a bumpy ride. Hold Elin, Sean. She's light— we don't want any losses."

"I can travel alone," she said hotly. "I can travel as fast as you can. All I need is to know the direction."

"Hold her," Saul said, ignoring Elin's glare. "And put your hand on my shoulder. The rest of you, hand on the shoulder in front of you. Close your eyes against the wind."

"You never said you could travel," Sean said, studying her expression, watching for a reaction. "You haven't done it as far as I know."

She turned pink. "I do it all the time if I need to. I'm sure you've just forgotten."

"Are you sure Tarhazian hasn't interfered with that, too?"

He wondered what else Elin hadn't told him about her powers.

* * *

Buffeted by wind and rain, the journey was blessedly short. Sean was surprised when they glided in to touch down on the beach in front of Niles and Leigh's house—with the couple waiting for them.

"You have a lot of explaining to do," Niles said.

Sean blinked into his friend's all-seeing blue eyes and shook his head, gradually regaining his balance on the snow-covered beach in Chimney Rock Cove. "How did you know we were coming?" He turned to Saul. "Why did you decide to land us here?"

Saul shrugged but Niles said, "Sally called and told us to wait for you here."

*Because Saul had let her know they'd be there, unless it was Sally who was giving the orders and had told him where to land.*

"It's snowing again," Elin wailed. "I hate it."

"You'll have your turn to talk later," Niles snapped, turning to Sean. "How can I rely on you to share Team responsibilities when you don't really give a damn?"

Sean turned hot with anger. "Don't speak to Elin like that. I haven't done anything to threaten the Team and I'm the one making primary decisions, remember."

"I expect you to make sure we know where you are. You went silent on me. What if something had come up and I needed to leave Leigh at the same time as I needed to be with her? We can't take anything for granted with this pregnancy. If she needs me, I'll be with her, and you will stand in for me."

Sean held his voice down. "That's what I've been doing. It's what I'll continue to do. I went *because* this Team needed someone to go. I knew you wouldn't—and shouldn't—do that now."

Swathed in a fur-lined parka, Leigh gave her mate a push, and another one until he had little choice but to look at her.

"They're back and safe," she said. "They'll tell us what's happened in good time. You know they didn't go just to annoy you."

"I don't know why they went," Niles said. "That's the point."

"I'll make sure you understand what's at stake here," Sean said. "*When* I'm ready. Take the coat, Elin." He started to undo the buttons.

Elin stayed his hand. "I don't think that's a good idea but we should get out of this deathly cold before we freeze—or I do."

The completely unexpected smile on Saul's elegant face made Sean laugh.

"What's funny about any of this?" Niles said. "Who are these people?"

He meant Cassie and David, whom Saul introduced while Leigh led the way toward the house just above the beach where she and Niles lived. "Come on," she called. "It's too cold out here. They'll all get sick. They look as if they're fading away."

They followed her. Sean wanted to go to his own place but knew better than to question Leigh when she was in take-control mode.

"The One—he's—"

"I know who he is," Niles cut Sean off. "Sally told me."

Sean was losing patience with Niles's attitude. He wasn't sure who the man was himself so Niles surely didn't know. "He's a living vampire," Sean said. "He eats human organs. That's why he had these folks manacled to a wall."

"He was going to *eat* them, Niles," Leigh said, her face horrified as she glanced back. "If Sean and Saul hadn't gone, these people might be dead by now."

"And if Sean hadn't gotten mixed up with someone who has upset the delicate order we've managed to make here, we wouldn't be involved in any of this."

"Goddammit," Sean said, catching up with Niles. "You took Leigh as a mate because you want your humanity back and she can help. But you would have wanted her anyway. The fact that she's a Deseran—which means human as far as I'm concerned—and has blood that blends with yours and gives us hope of a living child at last is a good thing. I don't even want to talk about what would happen with Elin and me. Tarhazian stole her as a baby. She doesn't know who or what she really is and neither do I, but the decision about what we do is ours to make."

"This can wait," Niles said sharply. "I don't want to talk out here."

"Really? It wasn't bothering you when you were doing the talking."

Niles spun around and pulled Sean to a stop. "You got involved with this woman against my wishes. I told you her fae connections could bring us trouble."

"We're used to trouble," Sean said.

"We were starting to settle down," Niles responded. "Sure we had problems, but we didn't have a damn *living vampire* on our hands. I don't know exactly how, but she brought this on us and we don't want it—particularly now. That means…you know what it means. The Fae Queen would sell her soul to get more power, if she had a soul."

"What do you mean, *I* know what that means?" Sean said and heard his voice shake with frustration. "Without Elin, the rest of us wouldn't have come back safely from The Island. She has not passed on any information, dammit."

"I didn't," Elin said suddenly and loudly through chattering teeth. "I haven't and I never would. I would die rather than tell Tarhazian anything about any of you."

Leigh kept walking and the two they had rescued went with her. Elin stayed beside Sean.

"This monster you've found is hugely powerful, am I right?" Niles said.

"Yes," Sean said. "But he's already been among us. I think he's been here for some time."

"On Whidbey?" Niles's brow furrowed.

"Sometimes." How much could he say without jeopardizing his own credibility? "On The Island, that's what it's called, I saw someone I knew before. I didn't even realize who he was at first."

"Who?" Niles asked, but worry etched the lines of his face. "Not the man you were—"

"I think so," Sean said, cutting Niles off. He didn't want to hear himself referred to as running away.

"That would mean a rogue werehound could morph into a live vampire. I hope you were wrong."

"So do I." Sean decided not to mention that The One seemed to shift from himself into Aldo or that Aldo had supposedly been absorbed into the living vampire.

"The plan is for the living vampire to gain control of the paranormal world here and who knows where else, and as much of the human world as he thinks he needs?" Niles said.

"I think so."

"Which means he needs inside information about the structure of our worlds, lots of information, and Tarhazian will be only too happy to help him out if she thinks she can share the spoils."

"He won't share anything," Sean said. He saw how Elin shivered and grabbed her back into his arms.

"She's powerful enough to make things uncomfortable for him if he breaks promises to her. He has to know that. There would be a compromise between the two of them and we would suffer. What about Brande's pack? They've gone dark. We don't even think they had anything to do with what happened to Molly."

Sean drew a deep breath. He indicated Cassie and David. "From what those two said, it was wolf men who took The One away after he escaped from us. That had to be Brande's pack."

"Perfect." Niles bared his teeth and his hot-blue eyes narrowed. "So we are a tiny army against the battalions of the paranormal world. We don't know what allies we have, but even if there are some, they may get the hell out of this mess."

Elin twisted in Sean's arms. "He won't believe me, Sean. What can I do to help?"

"I think you know," was all Niles would say.

## *chapter* TWENTY-TWO

Sean and Leigh passed in her kitchen doorway. He started to speak but she looked away and pushed a box into his hand. Under her other arm she carried Elin's Pokey, who had been in a huff since their return.

Then Leigh whispered so that he had to strain to hear, "Just do what you have to do. Wait half an hour or so. Two Chimneys will be unlocked." He carried on into the hallway, sidestepped into the mudroom, and closed the door gently behind him.

There was no reason to turn on a light. Sean could see perfectly clearly in the dark and he examined what Leigh had given him. Not a plain box but a leather one shaped like a miniature trunk firmly closed with a strong gold hasp.

He knew what he held.

Beneath the lid in a cradle of velvet hollowed out to a perfect fit were the parts of the die and the seal used by the werehounds to seal a male to a female as permanent mates. This seal, when given by a woman to a man and a man to a woman, formed an indelible mark in their flesh, an unbreakable bond between them.

Even death did not break the seal.

Sean rested his back against the door and closed his eyes. Leigh had taken a bold step in getting and giving him the box. Her message was clear: Seal with Elin and prove to Niles that she was one of them. He closed the box without looking and held it in one fist. There was more to it than that. He didn't give a damn what Niles did or didn't think, did or didn't want for Sean and Elin.

This was their life.

He had come to respect Leigh's wisdom but this wasn't close to being as simple as she thought. If Elin agreed to be his sealed mate, she must fully understand what that meant, including the bonds that would be between them whether they were together or apart. She had to know everything about him including the ties that bound the hounds together and their ultimate goal to get closer to their human roots again.

But if she agreed after that, he would have the proof that she put him before all else.

The door handle moved behind his back. Sean wasn't ready to face anyone. He let whoever it was push. They would assume the door was stuck—or locked.

Moonlight penetrated the small window in the door to the outside, shimmered over icy crystals on the pane. All he could see clearly in his mind was Elin. He was convinced she was beautiful inside and out.

Leigh would have returned to the others by now. All

the hounds were there, gathered close together at the front of the house, discussing strategy. They accepted Sean's temporary leadership without question.

He heard the scrape of something pulled over frozen snow outside. The shadow of someone's head appeared at the window, hands cupped to frame a face, eyes staring hard to see if there was someone inside.

Sean reached back and very deliberately, very quietly locked the door. There could be no mistaking Elin's black hair shimmering around her head and shoulders, or her small, pointed face.

So perhaps his hand was being forced and he must make a decision.

He let in a stream of icy air and swept Elin inside. He bent and brought in the box she had stood on inside in case it raised anyone's curiosity.

Holding her at his side, he closed and locked that door, too. "What the hell do you think you're doing?" he whispered hoarsely, taking her in from head to foot. "At least you've got warm clothes. Are those Leigh's?"

"Sally sent for them because Leigh's wouldn't quite fit."

"Where do the others think you are?"

"Lying down trying to sleep," she said sheepishly. "Leigh told them you'd gone to check on Two Chimneys. She knows you're here. Sally does, too."

"A setup," he said, shaking his head. She resembled a balloon person, silvery parka and snow pants, reinforced ski gloves, puffy knee-high snow boots. "You, Leigh, and Sally hatched this up. How much did you talk about it? What did either of them tell you?"

"Sally left—well, she did make a suggestion. But

Leigh told me to come and find you as soon as the others thought I was really asleep. She talked about a safe room somewhere but then changed her mind. She said it could be problematic."

"Yeah," Sean said. "Particularly if we set off alarms. I haven't practiced turning them off fast. I should do that in case I ever need to know. There's a heavily fortified safe room behind the house, built into the cliffs. It's for emergencies." And other things, like a place to go when a hound wanted complete privacy with his mate.

"Sean, I would never do anything to hurt you." Elin's voice broke.

"I know." She struck him to the heart. He believed her absolutely but the truth was that Elin couldn't be certain what influence Tarhazian, the wolves, and other malevolent forces could exert through her.

He bent to kiss her, softly on the lips. Driving his fingers into her hair, he nuzzled her face and she kissed him back feverishly. "We have to talk," he said. "But we have to be careful we aren't overheard."

"Only Leigh knows we're here," Elin pointed out. "And probably Sally. We'd hear if there was someone coming."

He hoped she was right.

"The One. The guy in the crater cavern on The Island, I know now that I met him before—more than once."

She sat on the floor in a corner by the outer door and pulled him down beside her. "Hold me," she said. "Don't let me go."

He did as she asked. "Did you understand what I just told you?"

"I wish I didn't," Elin told him. "I'm afraid to know about it."

"You don't have a choice unless you want to leave me."

"Tell me," she said, looking up at him.

"I was human, you realize that?"

"Yes, of course, but I don't understand it all."

"It was a long time ago, in a little room behind a saloon in Creed, Colorado." He considered his next words. Either he trusted her absolutely or he gave this up. "My name was Jacob O'Cleary and I was barely twenty-two. My dad had been a sawbones and I learned a lot at his elbow—I had to. This man, Aldo is the only name I knew him by, he got badly wounded in a fight and I put him back together as best I could. It wasn't until his teeth were ripping through my coat and shirt and I was wrestling with a monstrous creature covered in thick fur that I knew my life was fading away.

"Aldo was a werehound and he turned me."

"After you helped him? After you saved his life?"

"He's a monster," Sean said. "He drew strength from me and left me close to death. I didn't recover for weeks and then I couldn't go back to my old life so I changed my name and struck out on my own. I didn't see Aldo again until five years ago in San Francisco. You already know this was the man who wanted to take me as his slave—and he got me accused of murder so I had to flee. Now I think he's closing in on me again, only he wants much more than me. He changed into something much more complex and he craves immense power in the paranormal world and he doesn't care what he does to get it."

"But—"

"Let me get through this. The One says he has absorbed Aldo, but I believe Aldo is the stronger and has chosen to meld into The One's form. They are an unholy duo in one body. He won't be happy with only the paranormal world scraping at his feet. He's looking at the human world and figuring he can get his fingers into that, too. It's going to be a deadly fight, unless we can get rid of him, or even get him on the run for long enough so that we can be more prepared.

"What we need are allies. We don't know whom we can count on. If we can give him more time, he'll make more enemies and we should be able to pick them up—but I'm not a politician so I can only go on what seems logical."

Elin's violet eyes caught the crystalline light. She lowered her lashes quickly but not before Sean saw tears hanging there. "Why won't Niles let go of this theory he has about me?" she said, so quietly Sean had to bend over her to hear.

"It's not that," he said, rubbing his jaw over her brow. "Niles will never be able to stop feeling responsible for the Team. He doubts—"

"He's suspicious of me," Elin cut in. "I don't even blame him, but I also don't know what I can do to change his mind. If you and I are together, it could be the end of me unless I spy for Tarhazian—maybe the end of both of us. And she knows we're together now, I'm sure of it. She has already interfered once when we were in the mountain. I can't think of any other reason why I would slip out of invisibility.

"But I did feel some hope. It took a long time for

my body to be stable and I think that's because she's finally wearing out her hold over me. I can see now that she always felt the two of us were in competition, even though it seems ridiculous, but maybe she's spent so much energy controlling me she's wearing it out. We have to hope she can't send us into that living death she threatened."

He gathered her into his arms. "Hush. I won't allow anything like that to happen to you."

"What do you know about magic? What do I know? Niles doesn't realize that I have been kept from learning the ways of the fae. Sally is trying to help me, but she must be careful, too."

Sean had put the box on the floor beside him. He knew what Leigh wanted him to do and what he wanted himself, but how could he figure out if Elin was ready?

"I will never hurt you," Elin said. "I'll settle for only being able to know how you are if that's all I can have. I'll...I'll leave you before I'll hurt you and the rest of the Team."

This wasn't the first time he'd considered leaving Whidbey and taking Elin with him. First he had to try and protect her—them—right here.

"Will you come up to Two Chimneys Cottage with me?" he asked her.

She looked puzzled. "Why?"

"Because I want to be with you without any chance of being interrupted. We have to make decisions and they aren't simple."

Elin scrambled to her feet. "We'll have to be quiet leaving. You need warm clothes."

"I've got a sweat jacket on. Werehounds don't feel the cold, remember?"

She sighed. "I miss being like that."

"I'll lead the way because I know it better than you do. Be careful not to slip. The door will be unlocked."

"How do you know?" She sounded bewildered.

"I was told it would be."

"By Leigh?"

"Of course. The steps will be icy. Don't say anything else until we're up on the bluff."

As soon as Elin turned to the door, Sean stuffed the little box in a pocket.

Once outside they held hands. Underfoot the crunch of the crisp snow seemed as loud as gunshots. They crept from the mudroom door to the corner of the house, across a terrace dotted with pots where the naked skeletons of plants cast ragged black shadows on the snow—to the steps leading up to the bluff in front of Two Chimneys Cottage.

Sean put Elin in front of him and made sure she used her hands as well as her feet to climb the treacherous, sheer face. Time and again one of them stumbled or slipped, scarcely breathing for fear of making too much noise.

They made it and at the top they stood hand in hand again before striking out for the cottage. Sean smelled wood smoke before he saw it unfurling faintly against the pewter sky.

"There's a fire alight," Elin whispered. "Leigh shouldn't do so much. You think she did it? Light a fire?"

He grinned in the darkness. "Leigh will do as she likes."

The front door opened as promised. Lamps had been turned on and the living room glowed. Only one of the fires had been lighted but warmth spread to meet them.

"Should we put off the lights?" Elin whispered.

"You can't see the cottage from Niles and Leigh's house," he told her. "You don't need to whisper anymore either."

She grinned and wrapped her arms around his waist. "Don't forget we have to get back before they miss us."

"This doesn't have to take long," he said, looking over her head and deep into the flames. "This time."

## *chapter* **TWENTY-THREE**

Elin's stomach flipped.

She felt a change in Sean and slowly withdrew her arms from around his waist although she made sure he would still feel the pressure of her body on his.

Predictably, when she moved away from him, his hand went to his middle and he frowned. At least Tarhazian hadn't been able to interfere with a power she didn't know about.

Sean gave a short laugh. "Now I think about it, I do feel a bit chilled." He inclined his head and his eyes turned the piercing tiger gold that made her tingle. "It's weird. Sometimes I think I can feel you touching me when you're not." His voice was even but the intense stare didn't change.

*It'll keep on being weird,* Elin thought. *We all have our little secrets.*

*Like bringing her up to the cottage in secret with only known-romantic Leigh's awareness.*

Sweat prickled between Elin's shoulder blades. Tension built until every breath she took was an effort.

"I'm too hot," she said, struggling out of her parka, snow pants, and boots.

Sean unzipped his brown sweat jacket and set it on a table beside the couch that faced the fire.

She pulled a high-necked sweater over her head and sat down on the couch, once more dressed in one of her thin, silky dresses, this one a dark green. She wore leggings the same color that left her feet bare.

"You're going to be cold again in that," Sean said.

Instead of breaking the almost painful connection with his gaze, she had made it more intense. Standing beside her, he looked down, giving the impression that she was in the sights of a predatory jungle cat making up his mind whether to spring.

"Elin?"

She jumped. "Yes?"

"You're close to Leigh."

That wasn't what she'd expected him to say. "Very." A big, soft quilt draped along the back of the couch slipped to the seat. Elin drove her fingers into the down and held on.

"You're edgy," Sean said.

"You're the edgy one," she said. "Edgy as a cat." She closed her mouth firmly and felt her eyes widen.

"Maybe we're almost even."

Sometimes holding your tongue was the best course. Elin didn't ask who he thought won that contest.

"How much has Leigh told you about our history? The werehounds? Why there are so few of us? There are small groups spread around, mostly in Europe, but we keep to ourselves and we haven't grown in number for a long time."

"Leigh hasn't talked about it." She sounded croaky. "She said you'd tell me anything else I needed to know about your world."

"So you did ask her."

"Would you have asked?"

"About you?" He gave a fleeting smile. "If there had been anyone to ask, I would have, but you seem to be one of a kind and I know better than to grill Sally. You're her chick, or kitten, or whatever."

Elin put her hands in her lap and smiled, bending her supple fingers back one at a time. "Are you going to tell me about the werehounds?"

"I have to."

Her chin snapped up. "Why would you say that?"

He sat beside her. "Because I've got to make sure you can't tell me later that I held something back." Resting one hand on her thigh, palm up, he waited for her to place her much smaller one on top and closed his fingers around it.

*He had something big on his mind and it wasn't the weather.* Elin almost laughed. She leaned against his hard bicep to hide her face. He thought she was edgy? Her insides were leaping like fireflies and any laughter would be hysterical.

The touch of his lips along the tendons on the back of her hand didn't help a thing—except her desire for him. She wanted to hold time exactly here. It would be enough.

"There are no female werehounds—that I know of."

She felt him watching for her reaction. "I never thought of that."

"Not for years. And no children."

He confused her. "I thought werehounds were made, not born."

"Made from humans? In a way, and our greatest wish is to be accepted by the human world again. We are not like werewolves, we don't enjoy being part wild animal."

She held up a finger. "Leigh and Niles are expecting a baby."

Silence fell between them and grew unbearably long before Sean said, "Yes, and that's why Niles isn't himself. Leigh is the center of his life and he's afraid this pregnancy will kill her. The way pregnancy eventually killed off all werehound women and the babies they were carrying. Either Leigh's baby, who will be mostly human, will be a step toward what we want most, or we will know it's never going to happen."

"If Leigh dies?" Elin's heart beat faster and faster. "She's not afraid. Leigh's happy. She wants this and now I know why she seems to want it almost more for Niles than for herself."

"She believes what we all hope, that her Deseran blood will keep her safe, and the infant safe. You don't have that blood. I have no idea if there could be a sympathetic match between us."

So he would say they could not seal, could not have children because it was too dangerous?

Elin pulled her hand away and rested her elbows on her knees. She hadn't wanted to tell Sean, now she wasn't sure. It was certain that it would be a mistake for Tarhazian to find out Elin was a valuable prize to offer the werewolves or vampires to get something she wanted.

"Sweetheart?" Sean's big hand settled on her back and he rubbed her slowly, his heat permeating her skin as if she were naked. "Tell me what you're thinking."

*I'm Deseran, too. Niles and Leigh took the chance, why shouldn't we?* If she told him that, he might think her an opportunist who only shared things closest to her heart when she wanted something in return.

"I'm not afraid."

The rhythm of his hand faltered. "You would accept me as I am, knowing what it could mean to you?"

If they bonded, then she would tell him what she knew of her beginnings and what she had discovered about the Deseran connection—once she was certain she knew all the truth. "You might as well get used to me, Sean. I'm not going anywhere without you. And if you try to leave me, I'll just follow." She meant it.

"If Tarhazian tries to hurt you—"

"Please," she said, fingers on his lips, "not now. We will manage and you've said you think that woman is weakening when it comes to me. Whatever happens, we won't give up."

His hand slid from her back to her neck, under the dress, and cupped her shoulder. "Will you be my mate, Elin?"

Her throat didn't want to work but she said, "Yes, please."

"You will seal with me?"

"Yes."

"It means that we would be joined forever whether we're together or apart—and even in death. We would be life and death mates."

Only children leaped around when they were excited. Elin settled for kneeling beside Sean on the couch and kissing his face until he held her head, laughing.

He couldn't hold her head and her hands at the same time. And he could never restrain the part of her that was only hers to use.

Sean's face froze. He looked shocked, and dazzled at the same time. When he glanced at his lap, she deliberately didn't do the same but slid her hands around his neck.

He closed his eyes and moaned.

Now she wished there had been someone to ask about the intricacies of her gift to excite a man by touching him in certain ways. She had felt before what she felt now, an aching need for complete closeness with Sean. She would never forget the night at his house when they had slept in separate rooms yet she had felt as if he were in the same bed.

When he took off his sweater, she couldn't make a word. His wide shoulders and chest narrowed to a flat belly, where a slim line of bronze hair disappeared under the waist of his jeans.

She slid so easily beneath him, his face supported on one hand while he studied her, keeping his weight off her by leaning on an elbow.

The slow stroke of his free hand up her body, from

thigh, to hip then waist and ribs, made her light-headed. She parted her lips and he kissed her, long and deep.

His hand remained, long fingers and thumb spread, beneath her right breast.

Elin let her head fall back on the couch. Never taking her eyes off his, she ran a single finger from the little dip between his collarbones, down the center of his chest, and on to his jeans. She unsnapped them and hooked the same finger inside to the base of his rigid penis.

So fast, she clung to him, Sean lifted her to her feet on the couch and stood before her. He caught the hem of her dress, pulled it over her head, and tossed it onto a chair.

Covering both breasts, he massaged them with his palms, making circles that rolled her burning nipples until they turned hard. He took one between his teeth, carefully, and sucked. Elin's knees started to buckle but he held her up. With a thumb he flipped back and forth over the other nipple and she heard her own incoherent voice.

His hair was loose of the band and swung forward to slip against her skin. Each kiss he planted on her lips grew more demanding.

"These are cute," he murmured with his fingertips working down her leggings and panties. He held her around the waist and pulled them over her feet.

She started touching him remotely again, skimming his buttocks, sliding beneath to cup his testicles and loving the absorbed amazement on his face.

Struggling, he tore off his jeans with the look of a man in pain and wrestling free of his bonds. She had not seen him naked and completely erect until now and she knew at once why he had seemed in pain. He belonged inside her and she recoiled slightly at the unlikelihood that it was possible.

Holding Elin by the hips, Sean lifted her high and shot his tongue between the most intimate folds of her body. He worked back and forth until her hands dropped away from his head and she arched helplessly backward. An exquisite spasm ripped through her, and another, and before it was done, Sean had brought her down and pushed himself into her wetness and the aching miracle leaped into full bloom again.

And when he started to move her, to move himself inside her, she clamped her feet onto his flexed thighs, holding in the cries that wanted to break free. With the beauty of it there was pain now, real pain that jarred her teeth together.

*He will never know about any pain.* She let her hair hide her face and buried it in his neck, glad for the waves she felt breaking within him, and his muffled shouts of triumph and release.

Slipping to his knees, keeping her in a crushing embrace, his breathing gradually slowed although she still felt the wild thump of his heart.

"Elin," he said, pushing back her hair. "My Elin."

Slowly the joy faded from his expression. He stretched her out on the couch, on top of the quilt, and sat beside her.

As if he were afraid to see, he looked down and winced. Gentle fingertips brushed the insides of her thighs and he raised his hand. "Too much blood," he murmured. "I've torn you."

"No," Elin insisted. The pain was subsiding although

she knew she would be sore. "I don't think you're like other men, are you? Don't say anything. I wouldn't change anything about you. In a little while it will be easier."

His frown puzzled her.

"A little while?" he said.

"Perhaps half an hour?"

He hugged her hard enough to wind her and she didn't get an answer. Instead he sat her against one of the couch pillows and wrapped her in the quilt. Quickly, he stepped into his jeans and fastened them.

Feeling her eyes on him, and seeing her amused smile, he said, "Someone has to preserve some decorum, my love. You said you would be sealed to me."

She nodded, yes, emphatically.

He took a small leather box with a curved top from the pocket of his sweat jacket. Sitting down, he placed it on the couch between them and opened the lid. Inside were several small parts he took out and assembled. A little black stone bowl was suspended in a frame over a shallow stone well, also black.

First he took a piece of purple material from a silk pouch, dropped it in the bowl, and lit a candle beneath. The piece of purple quickly turned liquid and shiny.

A stylus, like a slender pen, fitted into an indentation beside the burner. Sean took this, showed Elin the tiny, deeply etched gold seal sunk into one end, and dipped it into the bowl.

"This is the mark of our forever bond," he told her. "It will burn but only for a moment. Do you still want this, Elin?"

"You know I do."

He pressed the seal into the flesh just beneath her thumb, on the palm side of her right hand. She closed her eyes briefly, then smiled at him.

Elin took the seal when he offered it to her and gritted her teeth as she sent it into the same spot on his right hand.

The candle was blown out and the box set aside.

Their kiss was tender and seemingly endless. Sean found her right hand with his and laced their fingers together. The night wouldn't be long enough.

She owed him every truth about herself, had owed it for a long time. Gently, Elin shook him by the shoulder. "Sean, listen to me."

"Mm?"

"I have not told you because I wanted to be sure it—" This would not sound as she'd thought it would. "I believe I am Deseran. I was taken from New Orleans by some sort of creature Tarhazian would never speak about and she stole me a second time."

His body tensed beneath her. "And you didn't tell me, why?" he asked slowly.

"I didn't want to influence your decisions about me." She choked and cleared her throat. "I wanted you to want me for myself, not because I'm Deseran and have the right kind of blood."

He didn't answer for so long she began to cry. She felt her tears run between her fingers on his chest.

"Stop," he said, brushing a hand over her face. "Stop now. Am I happy you didn't trust my love for you—no. But I'd be a fool if I couldn't see why that was. You really do love me."

She burrowed into him and he held her still. "Don't do that," he said. "It's dangerous."

"I kept wanting to tell you but there didn't seem to be a right time and I kept doubting myself."

Sean raised her chin and found her mouth. He kissed her long and deep. "Later, I'll think of a way to punish you," he said, stroking the length of her spine. "We're going to need a long discussion about what it means to believe in someone—both of us—but we're going to rest for what little time we can."

She stretched out on him.

"I'm so glad you're Deseran," he whispered sleepily.

Sean slept before Elin and she lay on top of him beneath the quilt. This was how love completed felt.

A single knock sounded and the front door opened.

Hauling the quilt to cover her, Elin sat up and stared at Ethan. He remained on the threshold, his face averted. The big, blond man's wild appearance frightened her. "What is it?" she said.

Sean maneuvered himself up, wrapping both of them in the quilt. "Tell us, man," he shouted.

"Leigh sent me. She whispered to me when Niles was talking to Saul on the phone. Get back to the others, Sean. Elin—they think you're in bed down there. Please go back at once, but don't go near Leigh. Niles wants you to stay away from her.

"Niles thinks Leigh's losing the baby. He thinks they're both dying."

## *chapter* TWENTY-FOUR

Elin did not go with Sean.

At last he had given up trying to persuade her and left, making sure she locked herself in.

She had done nothing wrong yet Niles blamed her for Leigh being in danger. Much as she longed to be with Leigh, she would not upset Niles even more at a time like this.

Up in the loft, she sat cross-legged on the bed and watched the front door and window. Fear was something she could keep at bay but she had always been cautious. From where she was, she could see if anyone entered the house, not that she was equipped for a physical fight.

Elin didn't cry often but she cried now—for Leigh and her baby, and because she missed Sean. And she didn't know what to do next.

There was no knock, no opening door, no sound of any

kind, but a figure standing in the living room startled Elin
so badly she almost fell off the bed.

A cerise parka swollen to big proportions by its down
filling didn't cover the yellow skirt Sally wore underneath. Her snow boots matched her parka and fluffy ear-
muffs.

"Are you coming down, Elin, or should I come up?"
Sally sounded anything but happy. "Sean sent for me to
come and be with you until he gets back but I was looking for you anyway."

Elin climbed from the bed and down the ladder to the
living room. She wore her leggings again, a big sweater
that belonged to Leigh, and the parka.

Promptly, Sally took Elin's right hand, turned up the
palm, and kissed the seal. For a moment she looked ra-
diant, one big smile, but the happiness faded instantly.
"Silly girl," she said. "Sitting up there doing nothing. You
have to take this situation into your own hands. It's the
time for you to prove what you're made of and you're
made of the best stuff. Do you understand me?"

Elin didn't believe it, so she couldn't make herself
answer.

"Well you are. And now you have a mate who is wor-
thy of you."

"I have estranged him from the Team," Elin said. "He
has been as respected almost as Niles had been respected.
Now he'll be blamed because he is sealed to me and they
all think I've brought trouble on them. They think Tarhazian is trying to use me as a spy."

"They're right."

Elin frowned at Sally.

"But you haven't brought any trouble to the Team and you'll fight Tarhazian. So will I. It's time to stop being afraid of her and look for ways to stop these wicked plans of hers."

"Leigh may lose the baby," Elin said quietly. "And she may not live either."

"I know about it," Sally said. "I was there, remember. I was also sent away."

"Because you're my friend and you introduced me to Sean?"

Sally shrugged. She pointed a finger at nothing Elin could see until the crooked little wand appeared to hover in the air. "You probably won't need it but keep it around. I'll teach you some of the things it can do. Mainly make you feel safe and perform simple tasks if you ask nicely and don't use big words. Put it in the pocket of your parka."

The wand went to the pocket and tucked itself inside.

Sally said, "Hmm. Getting too smart for its own good. It can be useful that it throws flame. Big flame, if that's what you want. Remember that."

"I'm carrying a flame thrower," Elin said slowly. "In my pocket."

"Every girl should have one," Sally said with a big, forced smile.

Elin had no doubt Sally was trying to lift her spirits but felt no better. "I'm going away from here," she said.

"I expected that," Sally said, crossing her arms. "You're being called home, and by the time you get back here, we can hope our werehound friends will have decided you are not the enemy."

"I'm not coming back."

"You and Sean are sealed." A deep frown furrowed Sally's brow.

Elin put another log on the fire. She had started to shiver again. "We will always be sealed," she said with difficulty. "That can't change. But we can't be together now—maybe never if I cause him and his brothers pain."

"Does he know you are Deseran?"

"I told him tonight. At first he was sad that I'd kept it from him, but he understood. Then he was glad, probably because he thought it was safer for me. Now, Leigh..." Her words trailed away. "I won't force him to stay with me when it will worry him so much."

Sally snorted. "*Force* him? He can't stay away from you and now he doesn't have to. You're sealed."

"He has to stay away if he can't find me. I have to find out about myself, about all the ones like me. I want to prove I am not a creature who can be manipulated—by the Fae Queen or anyone."

Sally looked skeptical.

"You don't think I can do it," Elin said. "With your help, I can."

A thump came from the porch, and a cry that stopped abruptly.

Elin and Sally stared at each other. "I expected Sean to send one of the werehounds to check up on me," Elin said. "But—"

"But that was a cry of pain and it was from a woman." Sally snapped off the lights while Elin edged the door open.

Lying on her back, her face twisted toward them, lay Cassie, the woman they had rescued from The Island. Her eyes were dull with pain but she reached a hand toward the two women.

Sounds in the woods suggested someone was moving rapidly through the trees, away from them.

With Sally's help, Elin dragged Cassie inside. They got her onto the couch, where she writhed, tossing her entire body from side to side.

Her thin arms were purple from the cold and the marks where the manacles had been showed clearly. Her long, dark hair hung in wet, matted clumps.

Sally pulled the quilt around the woman and turned her onto her side. The circular red mark was on her neck, beneath the dark hair. It was also the faintest either of them had seen.

"He came for me," Elin said suddenly. "The One. He thought Cassie was me."

"He would have taken her if that were so."

"Not if all he was trying to do was make a chance to get Sean. He would expect Sean to come looking for me, then snatch him. If he still wanted me, he could come back later."

"You can't be sure of that," Sally said, still studying the mark while Cassie moaned.

"Yes, I can," Elin told her. And she could. She saw The One's plan clearly. "When I touched the mark on Molly, it felt as if it was drawn to me. As if I was a magnet and could pull it out, only I was too late and she was already dead."

She reached her hand past Sally and settled her fingertips on the red mark. "It looks more like a Q than an O," she said.

"An O would be for The One," Sally pointed out.

Elin's fingers fastened against Cassie's skin as if they were fused there. A soft current of air slipped around them and Elin saw, for the first time in too long, the sparkling colors of the phenomenon Sally and Leigh called The Veil. Like a surreal, glitter-painted rainbow, the colors swept in an arc over them, then curled around the whole room.

"It is here for you," Sally said. "Take handfuls from the green. Keep it with you. You'll know if you need it."

"I know about the green," Elin said. "I have used it before." Her fingers sprang free of Cassie's neck and the mark had dissipated. It didn't float away, or attach itself to Elin, but simply evaporated and Cassie stopped tossing.

"Take the green now," Sally said.

Elin swept both hands into pools of shifting green, felt the weightless substance harden into solid balls, and thrust them into another pocket in her parka.

"Cassie?" Elin said. "Why were you outside?"

Shivering, Cassie spoke through chattering teeth. "There was such anger at you and Sean. I didn't really understand but it made me sad because it's so wrong. I wanted to see if I could help you somehow. I saw Sean come into the house from outside and I followed his footsteps here. I don't know why I collapsed like that. There was a lot of pain."

"You'll sleep now," Sally said.

"If he'd intended to kill her, she'd be dead," Elin said dispassionately. "I'm dangerous as long as I'm here. The

One wants Sean and he'll use me to get at him. I will not put Sean in any more danger—I can't."

Sally straightened and looked into Elin's eyes. "Do you know where you're going?"

"Away from here. That's what Niles meant when he said I knew what I had to do. He didn't know why but he was right."

"But where? You do know, don't you?"

Elin took a long breath through her nose and checked Cassie, who had fallen into a deep sleep. "This is only for you and me to know—and Leigh if that's what you decide. If it's meant to be, I'll be able to come back one day. But now I must go to New Orleans."

Sally smiled a little. "And what will you ask the person you go to see?"

"You know it's a man," Elin said. "I do, too. I want to find out the story of the Deseran. Who we are. What we are. How we should live and fit into the world...and whether we are dangerous to others and should exile ourselves. Most of all, I hope he can tell me how to keep Sean safe from The One...and perhaps how to make all the danger go away."

"That's a lot to hope for." Sally shook her head but her expression was soft. "Perhaps you're right. You need an oracle. You said you can travel. How far?"

"I've never gone so very far," Elin admitted. "I've barely traveled a mile or so."

"Do you want to fly? On a plane, I mean?"

Elin's violet eyes widened in horror. "I don't have the time that would take." She hadn't tried since the episode on The Island but she had thought about it and decided it was probably the shapeshifting Tarhazian had interfered with, and the invisibility had been messed up when she made the involuntary change back into human form. Elin believed she could still fly. And when she could be sure of remaining alone long enough, she would attempt to revisit Skillywidden, but not now. "I'd rather fly by myself," she said firmly.

Sally smiled. "Good girl. But this time you're going a long way and you'll be glad of your light dress when you arrive, especially since you have to wear the parka for most of the journey. If you get tired or feel weak, rest. You'll know if you need to do that." She pulled a scarf from around her neck, retrieved the contents of Elin's pockets, and twisted them inside. This she tied around Elin's waist. "I don't think you will need this, but it knows its role and might be useful. When you get where you're going, you'll find a man who has seen too much. He understands needing answers and knows more than you or I ever shall."

"How will I know him?"

"He will know you. You'll arrive outside an antique shop called J. Clive Millet on Royal Street, and when you have gone inside and climbed all the way to the attic, you will find Jude Millet. He has seen a great deal and knows a great deal. He is the ancient oracle of the Millet family. He will expect you."

## *chapter* TWENTY-FIVE

Y ou're not an obstetrician," Niles told Saul. "I should never have agreed to let you look after Leigh."

"You didn't," Saul said calmly. "She made that decision. In a few days, if she's willing, take her to Seattle for another opinion. I expected this. You almost made me believe you trusted me after all we went through together. But old superstitions don't die easily."

"I regard you as...as a trusted acquaintance," Niles said. "That doesn't mean I want you responsible for this child Leigh and I are expecting."

Sean turned his back on the pair and on the rest of the hounds. Elin shouldn't be alone up at the cottage yet he couldn't talk to Niles about their sealing while Leigh and the baby were in danger, and neither could he send one of the other hounds to guard Elin.

He felt the seconds and minutes pass. It had already

been more than half an hour since he left her. And he'd caused her pain—she would be uncomfortable. Damn, he'd been so eager to accept Leigh's idea, so eager to be with Elin completely, he had rushed into a situation that was dangerous now.

He had to try to reach her telepathically. *"Elin are you all right?"* They hadn't had a lot of experience communicating but they had already discovered they could. *"Say something, Elin. I'll come back."*

Without looking at the others, he started toward the hall. *"How is Leigh?"*

*"We're not sure yet."* He wouldn't dwell on both women being Deseran and the new uncertainty that brought while they waited to see how Leigh fared.

*"Sally's with me. There's no need for you to come. Stay there and help."*

*"Good, I'm glad she arrived."* At the steadiness of Elin's voice, relief swamped him. *"Tell me if you need me."*

*"I will if I do. I won't. I'll always love you, Sean."*

*"Me, too,"* he said and he felt her mind move away. He could hardly summon the memory of how he felt before he loved Elin—he didn't want to.

Saul's still voice reached him. "You called me, Niles. Now you want someone else to see her. How will you manage that tonight? Take her through freezing skies to Seattle, not knowing where you're going and who you'll try to see? Go to Emergency at a hospital you don't know where you don't know if you'll get the best help for the job?"

"I wouldn't take her anywhere. Someone must come here."

Sean looked at Saul's pale, cold face and swallowed. He prayed the vampire wouldn't just leave.

Saul had already been with Niles when Sean entered the room. After they returned from The Island, the vampire had left for home. Now he was back again but he couldn't have arrived long ago.

"Let Saul go to Leigh," Sean snapped. Blood started to pound at his temples. "Are you going to let her die just because you can't let go of your prejudices long enough to help her? You know Saul is on our side."

Niles turned his attention to Sean and for an instant he visibly prepared to attack.

"Out of my way," Saul said, pushing past Niles. He headed for the corridor to Niles and Leigh's bedroom. "Better get on the phone and start looking for that second opinion," he said. "But keep it down out here and keep it calm—for Leigh's sake."

Ethan and Campion looked anxiously from Niles to Sean. Hovering at one side of the room, they both had their hands in the pockets of their jeans and repeatedly aimed their eyes at the floor. These two and Innes were part of the original Team that had worked together in Afghanistan. Innes had been the contract group's communications expert.

Starting to pace, Ethan glared at each of the others in turn. He stopped suddenly and pointed at Sean, who was afraid the other man was about to blurt out where he'd found Sean and Elin, and at the least appropriate moment.

"You've helped with deliveries," he said. "And miscarriages."

Sean heard Campion and Innes groan. Tact wasn't one of Ethan's strengths.

Sean was the Team medic. On Whidbey he worked with the volunteer fire department.

"Get in there," Ethan said. "You, too, Niles. Leigh needs to have you with her."

Sean went without hesitation. He should have offered help anyway but hadn't wanted to get in Saul's way unless asked. Niles arrived at the bedroom door a couple of seconds later.

With her eyes shut, Leigh lay flushed and motionless. Saul finished reading her temperature and said, "Get this thing off the bed," plucking at a thick down comforter.

Stumbling in his hurry, Niles hauled off the bedcover and threw it into a corner.

"How long have you felt like this?" Saul asked Leigh.

"It started when I woke up in the morning, but—"

"Why didn't you say something?" Niles said, sitting down on the bed with a thump and immediately leaping up again. "We could have got help hours and hours ago."

"I didn't feel really bad until early evening. Then you went off like a wild man and you wouldn't listen to a thing I said."

"But you went out in that freezing mess outside?" Sean said to Leigh. He couldn't help himself. "And you...you did too much, didn't you?"

She looked miserable and shrugged slightly. "I guess so, but this was going to happen and get worse."

"Now you're going to have to rest," Saul said. "You chose a bad time to overdo things. It's a good thing you're strong. Drink lots of fluids—and you'll drink them even though you won't want to. Niles will make sure of that. And sponge her with cool water to help keep her temperature down. If it gets too high, we'll rethink that."

Sean began to understand what Saul was suggesting; at least, he hoped he did.

"What's happened?" Niles said. "Tell me now. This was going to happen anyway, Leigh? And you never told me?"

"I didn't know," Leigh said. "Who knows they're going to get the flu and not just a cold?" She watched her mate's face grow incredulous and shook her head. "Good grief, you just jumped to the worst conclusion you could come up with, didn't you?"

"You didn't say anything about flu," Niles protested.

Leigh blinked feverish eyes. "You didn't tell me you thought I was losing the baby. I said I wasn't well, that's all."

## chapter TWENTY-SIX

Striding across snow that cracked like ice, Sean made for the steps and the bluff. It wasn't so funny that Niles had been terrified for Leigh. He knew nothing about pregnancies and anyone could have rushed to the wrong conclusion.

Sean grinned, remembering the expression on Niles's face when he realized the truth.

Poor Leigh looked as if she felt horrible and Niles didn't look much better. If he got the same thing as Leigh, he would be unbearable.

Sean's phone rang when he reached the bottom step.

Cliff Ames's voice surprised him. "We've got a big problem, Sean. I tried to reach Sally but I can't find her. Someone's going to have to scrape Gabriel off the rafters. He's got the police here and he's still ranting about Molly."

Elin had been right not to want to hide the truth about

the woman's death. Sean cleared his throat. "You can't blame him. This is—God, it's awful. I take it you haven't told Gabriel you helped Sally take Molly to Phoebe's?"

"If I did, it would kill him. He'd want the rest of the details. Then he'd think I betrayed him. Don't make me be the one to do that. The man took me on when no one else was interested. He's my best friend."

"What made Gabriel lose it tonight?"

Cliff took a while to answer. "The guy at the gas station came in to Gabriel's. He said he'd been questioned because someone told the police Molly was left at his place to get help with her car. He thinks they suspect him of doing something to Molly. Gabriel's mad at the cops, mad at everyone. He listens to you. I thought you'd want to come."

Sean wanted to go to Gabriel, but not until he'd talked to Sally, Saul, and the others.

And he couldn't do a thing about any of it until he had Elin safely at his side. "I'll come when I can," he told Cliff.

"But Gabriel trusts you. You'll be able to help him. Please come."

Cliff was a reserved man but his attachment to Gabriel was no secret. Sean wanted to go and help them but his hands were tied.

"Let the police do their thing, Cliff. I can't leave right now—"

"Sure you can. You have to." Cliff breathed heavily. "We need you, Sean. I told him I'd call you."

*Oh, great.* "Tell him we've got problems. Leigh's not well." He hated using her as an excuse but it was the best he had. "I'll call him. In the meantime, take care of things for me." He clicked off before Cliff could say anything else.

Slipping and sliding, he climbed the rest of the steps.

Smoke still rose from one of the chimneys at Two Chimneys, but in a much thinner and intermittent stream. Elin might have decided to go to bed. Sean hoped she had and intended to join her there.

He had the key to the cottage now and let himself in. "Hi, Elin," he called so she wouldn't be nervous. "It's Sean, sweetheart."

She wasn't upstairs. He could see her in a curled ball on the couch, the quilt wrapped around her.

"There you are, Sean. I've been expecting you." Sally came from the kitchen with a steaming mug in her hand. "Take this coffee. I'll get some more in a minute. Sit down. How's Leigh? Tell me she'll be okay."

"She's got the flu. A really bad case. Niles jumped to the wrong conclusion. He was out of his mind. But I think Leigh will be fine. She didn't tell him what she thought was going on and Niles didn't tell her. They're so busy protecting each other, they're only causing trouble."

Sally started to laugh but stopped abruptly. She stared at the coffee in her hand and held it out to Sean.

He took the mug and looked at Elin. "My girl's really sleeping," he said. And he'd be a liar if he didn't admit to himself that he was disappointed.

"Sit," Sally said and waited until he took one of the chairs. He noticed she remained standing.

"Get yourself some coffee," he said. "Come and sit with me."

She wiped the palms of her hands on her yellow skirt. Passing him, she raised a curtain to look outside. "A winter wonderland again. I thought we'd finished with the ice and snow for the year." Sally peered into the distance for a long time. "It's a clear night, though. That's a good thing."

Sean wasn't accustomed to feeling chilled, but cold goose bumps came out on his arms and legs, and the small hairs along his spine rose. Her distant tone, the way Sally wasn't answering any questions directly, unnerved him.

"It's crisp." He couldn't think of anything else to say.

They fell silent.

Sean picked at the worn, deep pile fabric on his chair. The room was a reminder of the cozy nest Leigh had made there with her first husband before he died.

Sally continued to stand at the window. "Is there something on your mind?" Sean said.

Elin moaned and turned over in her quilt. Her hair escaped and slid to trail off the edge of the couch. He frowned. It looked as if it had gotten very wet then dried without being combed.

"There's plenty on my mind," Sally said. "I'm trying to figure out how to explain it all. Sometimes you must accept what you can't change, Sean. Others make decisions we might not make, but as long as you know they only want the best for everyone—especially you—you have to try to understand. When someone takes painful steps, they need support, not anger—even if you don't agree with them."

He took a deep breath. "You're saying the same thing every way you can think of. You're afraid of how I'll react to whatever you want to tell me. I'm a reasonable man. Can't you just trust me until I give you a reason not to?"

"I trust you, Sean," Sally said. "Of course I do. I also know you're passionate and single-minded. Don't do anything foolish."

Sean shot to his feet. "About what?" he said, louder than he had intended. He set the mug down. "What is it?"

Sally turned to the couch and raised a corner of the quilt to show the sleeping face...of the woman they had brought back from The Island.

Sally took advantage of his shocked silence to pull him into the minute kitchen and close the door. "That's Cassie. She came up here after you went back earlier. She followed your footsteps. It was Elin she wanted to see. Obviously she trusts her and the anger down there at you was getting frightening. I think she was shut off in a bedroom and didn't know a thing about Leigh being ill. So she split."

"Is Elin in the loft?" Sean said, finally finding his voice.

"No." Sally took a pot of coffee off the old stove and set two striped mugs on a blue and white checked tablecloth. She poured coffee and replaced the pot on the stove. "Join me."

"Where's Elin?" Sean asked. "Something's happened, what?"

"Cassie was attacked on the porch. When we opened the door, she was just about unconscious. She had the red mark on her neck but Elin managed to draw it out. I don't know how—except that your mate is a very powerful talent, and she's also almost a complete mystery.

Cassie fell into a deep sleep afterwards. She's going to be okay."

Sally's mouth trembled before she bit her bottom lip to hold it steady.

"And Elin?" He felt rigid from head to foot. "Where is she?"

"Elin is certain she was supposed to be attacked, not Cassie. And Elin believes the idea was to snatch you while you were trying to help her."

"I didn't see anyone hanging around out there," Sean said. The slow, heavy beat of his heart sickened him. "Did you? When you brought Cassie inside?"

"No."

"So Elin isn't sure this attack was meant for her?"

"Yes, she is. She's gone, Sean. Elin won't risk putting you in danger so she's left the area."

"And gone where? Where is she?"

"I don't know where she is right now."

Sean thumped the table and the mugs jumped, slopping coffee. When Sally made a move to get up and clean the mess, Sean clamped a hand on top of her wrist on the table. "Tell me now. I've got to know where she is."

"I don't know the answer to that. Not for sure. Trust her to do the right thing and come back to you."

"It never struck me she might not come back to me—until you suggested it. Please, Sally, tell me where Elin is."

Sally, known for her stoicism, began to cry. She covered her face with big, work-worn hands and sniffled.

"You're frightened about something. Tell me."

She shook her head, no, and took a long, shuddering

breath. "I will stand by her," she said. "I always have since Tarhazian got so difficult about her. I am banished from my own people for refusing to do what Tarhazian wants. She keeps asking me to deliver Elin to her. I would never do it. But I'm afraid she could do more things to interfere with Elin's powers—at least the ones she knows about. Tarhazian must not know Elin's gone. On her own she's more vulnerable."

Sean shoved a hand into his hair. "Elin told me she thought it was Tarhazian who found her on The Island—remotely—and forced a shift from Skillywidden."

"I don't think she could have," Sally said. "How would she know where she was?"

"I don't care." Sean stood up, rested his knuckles on the table, and looked down at Sally. "Elin thinks Tarhazian's power over her is fading. I'm just hoping she's right. Tell me where Elin's gone."

The woman shook her head, no.

"Sally—"

"I will be sent to the Outer Reaches before I betray Elin," Sally said.

The Outer Reaches were spoken of as a place of confusion and pain used as a prison by the very powerful. Since no one ever returned, there were no firsthand descriptions.

Threatening Sally would get him nowhere. Sean felt ashamed for even thinking of trying. "Elin needs me," he said, softening his voice. "And I need her. Dammit, we belong to each other now. We're stronger together. We can fend off anything."

"No." Sally shook her head. "No, you can't. Do you know what I really think?"

He raised his brows.

Sally put a hand on one of his. "I think it was The One who shifted Elin out of Skillywidden on The Island. And I've decided it was him, or someone following his orders, who attacked Cassie. When he saw it wasn't Elin, he took off. She believes she can be used to lure you to that man and that's why she's gone."

"I don't want her to protect me. I don't need her to do that. She needs me." Frustration strangled his voice. "I'm the one who must protect *her*. She would be helpless against that monster on her own."

"If she makes it where she wants to go, she won't be on her own." Sally pressed her fingertips against her lips. "Sean, you're wrong to behave as if Elin is a weakling you have to protect constantly. She has already shown how strong she is."

Sean narrowed his eyes and pulled her hand away. "Who is she going to? Where is he or she?"

"A long way away," Sally whispered. "That's all I can tell you."

## *chapter* TWENTY-SEVEN

A basset hound wearing a tiara and pink tulle tutu rolled happily in a pile of dried horse droppings.

Elin closed her eyes and opened them again. Dogs everywhere, and every type of dog. All in costume.

She was still regaining her balance from the long trip to New Orleans and for an instant wondered if she was imagining things.

"Cute, darlin'," a man smothered in strings of shiny beads that jangled on his robust stomach shouted at her. He flapped his painted face back and forth in front of Elin, laughing and showing off large, perfect teeth. "You from the frozen land of the north or something, sweetness? You gonna be bar-be-cewed in that costume soon enough. You surely are." He whipped off several of his purple, gold, and green bead necklaces and draped them on Elin before dancing on, flanked by four Dalmatians in police uniforms, minus the pants and shoes.

He'd been right about the parka. Elin struggled to take it off while she worked her way between dogs in decorated buggies, dogs trying to bite their neighbors, and robed dogs on elevated, rolling thrones, to the other side of the narrow street.

It was early afternoon and she was tired and hungry. That she had the power to make such a trip seemed unreal.

A costumed jazz band pranced by, aiming polished instruments in all directions while the onlookers danced, waved their arms, gyrated, and laughed, all at the same time.

Elin started to laugh, too. Trailing the parka from one hand, she forced her way through two- and four-footed participants onto the opposite sidewalk. She was in the French Quarter, and it was Mardi Gras, or it soon would be if she remembered her dates properly.

Tarhazian had discouraged reading but Elin had made friends with the sprite of the Forbidden Library hidden away on the fae compound, and the wizened little creature had led her willing pupil through hundreds of books on many subjects. Elin's determination to educate herself had been just one more infraction on Tarhazian's long list.

A fresh cheer went up. Two women on stilts wearing feathered headdresses and very little else carried a fringed, gold satin banner that proclaimed, "MYSTIC KREWE OF BARKUS." The canine krewe was in full swing and this was Royal Street. Under a valiant sun, the tongue-in-cheek takeoff on the famed Krewe of Bacchus yipped and strutted its way. Elin recalled from her reading that the biggest Mardi Gras events wouldn't take place for two weeks.

Icy winds and snow-blown bluffs seemed far away from bubbling, balmy New Orleans. A woman could get drunk on the scents of jasmine and honeysuckle trailing from pots on black-painted iron balconies above the street level. And explosions of hot orange, purple, and pink bougainvillea from more pots could easily make her dizzy.

But Elin must not dally.

She was scared and she already missed Sean so much it hurt. Who could this person she was to see possibly be that he might supposedly help her with what was happening thousands of miles away on Whidbey? How did he know about the Deseran? If he told her to do something she didn't want to do, what then?

First she must find J. Clive Millet, the antique dealer's shop. Then the only thing she could do was follow Sally's instructions and trust her own instincts.

She faced the buildings that crowded together along the sidewalk. Furniture, glass, porcelain, and too much else to take in filled shop windows. Elin looked up. *J. Clive Millet*, painted in gold letters on a shiny black background, meant she was exactly where she needed to be.

At every step she took, Elin could sense stares and felt herself blush. It must be her floating, unusual dress. Not that anyone ought to notice amid such chaos.

She met a man's eyes and he smiled, and bowed. "You are so beautiful," he said, "Too beautiful to be real." He carried on as if saying such things to a stranger was normal on any day.

Elin looked at the ground and scurried into the set-back doorway of the shop. "Well, I'm very real," she muttered. She didn't find a suggestion that she might not be at all comforting.

A bell jangled over the door when she went inside. The skin around her waist turned very warm and she pressed her hands against her stomach. She felt the wand and the balls of green wound inside Sally's scarf. They were hot and she didn't want to let them go. The thought that the wand had the capacity to burst forth flame didn't comfort her. She didn't feel confident she could control such things.

A distinguished-looking man with visible muscles filling out the shoulders, chest, and sleeves of his green velvet jacket talked seriously with a woman examining a shiny game table set for chess. The woman didn't look Elin's way, but the man, his head shaved, settled startlingly green eyes on her and gave the slightest of smiles. For a moment he stared past her, then he nodded and returned to the woman and the table.

Elin looked over her shoulder to see what the man had stared at.

Just a staircase. A dark staircase with carved balusters and banisters that shone with age.

Sally had told her to climb the stairs in the shop and keep on going up until she got where she would know she was supposed to be.

She caught the man's green eyes once more and he nodded again, silently sending her on her way. Either the customer was too engrossed in the gaming table to notice Elin, or she couldn't see her.

It would have taken a lot less intuition than Elin had not to be sure the woman couldn't see her.

With her hands still on the scarf, Elin climbed the stairs to a landing, and took a second flight. At the top of this she saw a door with blazing insets of stained glass. But she didn't pause for a moment. This was not her destination.

To the top, Sally had said.

Elin climbed again and as she went, her spirits began to fall. This wouldn't be the place either, she was sure of it.

With a solid thump, a huge marmalade cat with eyes more orange than its coat landed at the top of this flight of steps. Elin hadn't seen where it came from.

The cat sat and stared at Elin. For an instant the animal lifted the sides of her mouth to expose sharp incisors and gave a muted hiss. The cat raised its nose and sniffed the air. Long whiskers twitched.

If a cat could look suspicious, this one did. As abruptly as it had sat down, it stood again and backed off a few inches—inviting Elin to join her?

Hoping she wasn't about to be attacked, Elin climbed to the next landing and faced her orange reception committee. The cat came closer, sniffing repeatedly, then, without warning, wound around her ankles, rubbed her silken head against Elin's legs. An odd, chirping little sound was familiar. The cat was meeting one of its own kind—it sensed the cat in Elin.

With purpose, the cat crossed to a narrow, dark passageway and batted a rough wooden door wide open. More steps rose inside and Elin followed to the top.

A door there opened without either knock or push.

Confronted by a very tall man whose white-streaked black hair fell past his shoulders, the next breath she took caught in her throat. He studied her so closely she bowed her head.

"Elin," he said in a deep voice. "Elin of Wise. Or Elin Wise as you now are. We've been expecting you."

She gaped at him. This was the first time she had heard herself given another name. She had always been, simply, Elin. Or when Tarhazian decided, Princess Elin. The man's thin features bore an aristocratic stamp. A firm mouth, clearly delineated, smiled a little, brightening eyes as blue as Niles Latimer's. That's where any similarity ended.

*Elin Wise. The disk on the tiny gold bracelet she still hadn't returned to Tarhazian had one word: Wise. It was her name.*

She felt jumpy with excitement but concentrated on Jude.

This lean, imposing figure wore the kind of black suit she had only seen in paintings and etchings from ages long gone by. His simple white linen showed lace at the neck and wrist but he exuded masculine strength.

He swept an arm wide, inviting her in, and she went, the cat at her side, without even a shred of fear about stepping into an attic with an anachronistic stranger.

The cat sashayed in front of the man in a way designed to capture attention. "Marigold," he said. His voice was deep but also whispery. "You did well. You may yet earn your outrageous comforts. Please close the door and sit if you like, Elin of Wise."

Elin closed the door in a room where there was nowhere to sit but the floor. Behind the man a softly undulating white curtain divided the room. She tried to look more closely but couldn't without being rude. But that curtain was different—it gave off a muted light, and when it made a subtle change of color to pink, then purple, Elin jumped. Her hands automatically went to her middle, where she encountered warmth that had become calming and soothed her now.

How could she not think of their own Deseran colors in The Veil?

"You can't," the man said. "I would be disappointed if you didn't think of The Veil."

Startled, Elin said, "You read me so easily."

"I've had hundreds of years to hone my telepathy," he responded.

"Who are you?" Elin said before she could stop herself.

He smiled once more. "Someone trusted by your friend, Sally, although we have never met. She and I have close allies in common. But this is not about me. You have a great deal to confront before you will have time to remember me at all. Just think of me as someone who wanted to repay a kindness done to my family long ago."

"Why should you do this for me, though?" Elin asked.

"Because I believe I can help you. My own journey isn't yet finished, but I've learned a great deal in my time of watching, waiting, and sometimes interfering." He smiled again. "You met—or rather saw—one of my descendents, Pascal, in the shop. I informed him you were coming and that he should give you a sign of welcome.

"Sally—the fae person—who contacted me told me a great deal about you. Let's hope she didn't put too much faith in my ability, and my contacts. We shall see."

Elin went to a dormer window so high above the street that the people looked small and the dogs, little more than the size of Pokey. Poor Pokey would wonder where she had gone but Leigh would take care of her.

"My only window on the contemporary world," the man said. "Not that I would choose to walk among those people. My name is Jude. May I call you Elin?"

"Of course," she said, swinging toward him. "I am in trouble, sir. But I believe my first job is to find out more about myself. I understand you know someone who would help me. Then perhaps it will be easier to go forward and make sure my mate is not destroyed just because he chose me."

Jude crossed his arms. "I know your situation. And I assure you that your mate doesn't regret his choice. Sally approves of him for you and I know the fae are very fussy about who gets close to their own."

Should she, Elin wondered, say that she wasn't fae?

"I know you are not fae," Jude said. "You are fortunate to have made good friends. The Deseran so often live an isolated existence, many not knowing what they are and believing they are an anomaly. It's a sad story but perhaps that is about to change."

He frowned and closed his eyes.

"Are you well?" Elin asked quietly.

"Your mate is an agitated man. I can connect with him. He is being very persistent about trying to find you. I hope he doesn't complicate what we have to do. He isn't patient. If he were, this might be simple. The one you need is Dora. If she does come, and soon, perhaps you'll be on your way back quickly. That will be a good thing."

"What do you mean about Sean?" she said.

He waved an airy hand. "He is determined to find you. But no need to worry about him unless we have to. Do you want to sleep while you wait for Dora?"

Elin regarded the bare room with its dusty wooden floor and said, "No, thank you," very politely. Would she ever have what humans considered a normal life? Even as normal as Leigh's seemed most of the time?

"Normal is many things," Jude said, causing Elin to start. "Depends upon who and what you are. I haven't forgotten the different types of normal I've encountered. As long as a person is comfortable with a situation, they consider it normal."

"You read my mind so easily," Elin said. "You do it as naturally as if everyone read minds."

He looked amused. "They probably could if they believed they could. You can."

"Only with Sean. My mate. And Tarhazian—she's—"

"The Supreme Queen of the Fae, the second one to steal you when you were a baby," Jude finished for her. "A dangerous and selfish woman, but do not fear her as you did. She is making her own lot with you."

"I can close her out of my mind and not hear her," Elin continued. "Then she can't hear me and she gets furious. When I shift to Skillywidden—that's—"

"The cat who is your altered self," Jude announced. "Soon you should revisit your Skillywidden. Confidence is everything and you must gain confidence with your gifts again. When Dora has time, and if I can persuade her to explain, I should like to know more about that. If such an opportunity ever arises."

"When I'm Skillywidden," Elin said, determined to finish what she had started, "then I can enter into any mind I need to enter—not on a whim, of course—but I hear and understand, and act. I can't speak."

Jude rolled onto the toes of his black boots and jiggled there. "Fascinating," he said. "It isn't my place to tell you about yourself but I will allow myself one indulgence. You have many more talents than you know, many strong talents. You are rare." He put a finger to his mouth. "That is between you and me until Dora explains, and she will."

Elin could only stare at him.

Marigold stood abruptly, her whiskers wiggling.

"Must be Dora," Jude said, and a slender woman about the same height as Elin materialized immediately. "Afternoon, Dora," Jude said.

"Is it?" Dora peered through the window. "Yes. And this must be Elin. I don't suppose you remember me. No, how could you? When you last saw me, you were a tiny baby. Hug me."

Without hesitation, Elin walked into Dora's arms and was squeezed much more tightly than she had expected.

She liked being squeezed, and the kiss Dora placed on her cheek—and the scent of bluebells that clung to the woman.

"Welcome home," Dora said. "You're one of the ones who was born here in New Orleans. Many have been, but not all."

"May I at least listen to all this?" Jude said, actually grinning as he asked.

Dora gave a short laugh. "We both know you can listen to whatever you please, Jude Millet. But I will be happy for you to be with us."

Neither of them asked Elin's opinion and Dora pulled forward a stack of cushions Elin would swear hadn't been there before, divided them into two piles, and sat on one. "You take those," Dora said.

Elin sat, and since Jude seemed comfortable standing, she didn't ask where he would sit.

From a pocket in her dress, a similar style of dress to the one Elin wore and made in shades of rose and pink, Dora brought out a flask. "Water," she said. "And here is an egg, and a croissant and a peach. You must be starving, Elin."

With the first bite of egg, Elin realized how hungry she was and devoured the food and water more quickly than she should have. "Sorry to gobble," she said, a little sheepish.

Dora smiled. She really didn't look older than Elin although she had to be by at least a generation—or much more. Elin thought about her own age. She recalled being a child, and growing into an adult, but could not think how long ago that had been. It seemed like forever.

Dora's dark gold hair curved under from a central part and she had the unexpected appearance of a healthy, blue-eyed all-American girl.

"I can help you," she told Elin. "You will know who you are—well, more or less. And why you became my foster child—and how Tarhazian came to have you. I

have been told about the troubles you and your mate—
and your friends—face on this Whidbey Island." She
gave a shudder. "How can anyone live where there is ice
and snow?"

"It never bothered me," Elin said, "until Tarhazian interfered with my body temperature. I was never too hot
or too cold until Tarhazian decided meddling with that
should be one of my punishments."

"That gift came to you as a Deseran although not all
of you have it unless you are in water." Dora threw up
her hands. "I gave myself away. I am not Deseran. You
thought I was, of course. I am fae, but like your friend,
Sally, I was separated from my own kind. In my case because I chose to mate with a vampire."

"A vampire?" Elin realized her mouth remained open
and closed it.

"There are vampires, and then there are vampires,"
Dora said, looking smug. "My vampire's what humans
would call one of a kind. But we aren't interested in my
story."

Elin certainly was.

"I have a vampire friend," she said quickly, embarrassed by her reaction to Dora's announcement. "Saul is
wonderful. He's a doctor and my mate thinks highly of
him." Not always quite true. "Did I tell you my mate is a
werehound?"

Dora said, "I already knew from Sally. She is an old
friend but I had lost touch with her. I'm glad you've
helped us find each other again. You and I have a lot of
work ahead of us, Elin."

Elin nodded, but kept quiet. Her anxiety only grew.

Sean would be angry with her for leaving and she didn't blame him. If he did the same to her, she would rush to find him. And if he had let her think he was something he wasn't for as long as she did, she would be devastated.

She tried to hide her growing misery behind a composed face. A glance at Jude's bland face suggested he wasn't following her thoughts, but a flicker of sympathy in his eyes made it obvious he knew what she was going through.

"Your problem," Dora said. "The problem the Werehound Team and so many on Whidbey Island are facing is The Bloodstone. The One as he has been called, wrongly, created the problem but he is weakening, and from my sources, I learned he could be dealt with. His meddling with The Veil has caused a great deal of misery and death. He believed he could separate The Veil and distill the red element, or the blood it represents, into The Bloodstone he discovered had been owned by those who live at the center of the earth, the Netherworld. They are called Embran, which need not concern you now.

"He saw only the respect certain of these creatures got from their underlings. Unfortunately for him, and many others, he didn't find out the whole story. He didn't find out about the disarray that fell on his heroes because they misused, and abused, power.

"What Quitus didn't and still doesn't know is that control of The Bloodstone was lost and has never been regained. It is a rogue element, usable only in small quantities—as it is being used on your island. What he has extracted from The Veil has become his own potential destruction. He has produced... you will not understand yet. And I, as the mate of a vampire, detest to mention the blood weakness, the only known vampire disease that kills vampires."

Elin's interests lay elsewhere. Hardly able to sit still, she said, "Quitus? Who is that?"

Dora shook her head. "The One is really Quitus, and... it is more complicated than that, but we must stay on track. Your mate can tell you more about that, I believe. If he hasn't already. Does he know about that Aldo and his alliance with Quitus?"

"I was with him when he saw Quitus turn into Aldo, and back again," Elin said. "It was horrible. No wonder Sean didn't want to remember the man or talk about the murder of that poor woman."

"No." Dora looked thoughtful. "But it should help you forgive yourself for not telling him you are Deseran. You both had secrets you kept for different, but understandable, reasons. From now on, your task will be to avoid repeating deception."

"I wouldn't lie to him again about anything," Elin said quickly.

Dora smiled. "You'll try and mostly you'll succeed. But don't forget that you are at least as much human as Deseran. Let me tell you more about what has already happened.

"The people who have died—on The Island, and on Whidbey—have been victims of Quitus's experiments. If the pieces of unstable Bloodstone he makes don't kill on touch—and they usually do—they weaken the victim or make the mind unstable. If the touch is very light for some reason, it can be reversed—but by very few. You are one of them."

"Cassie," Elin muttered.

"Yes, Sally reports that Cassie is recovering well."

"The mark is a Q, not an O," Elin said, almost to herself. "This Quitus has to be stopped."

"Not until he leads you to his surrogate on Whidbey."

A wave of sickness hit Elin. "But we must do it quickly. Who is this surrogate?"

Dora looked at her hands. "I don't know. I don't even know if it is a man or a woman."

## *chapter* TWENTY-EIGHT

Night had begun to fall on the rain-slick streets of New Orleans's French Quarter, where Sean had landed. Neon signs tossed bright wavering reflections across shiny pavements.

He was very close to her now.

Ignoring the looks he got from passersby, Sean pressed the heel of his right hand to his brow, stood still, and closed his eyes.

Of all people, it had been Niles who broke down and told his second-in-command the most secret facet of the werehound bond to a mate. Through their seal, they could make a connection the werehound could follow. Niles didn't know if the same went for the werehound's mate, and on his long journey, Sean had promised himself he would be unmerciful about Niles's chauvinism.

But perhaps he wouldn't do that in front of Leigh. The

wrath of a werehound's mate was something best not encouraged.

Niles would never have told Sean anything if Leigh, still struggling with a fever, hadn't said she thought Elin would go to New Orleans. After that Niles followed Sean when he blindly walked outside with thoughts of just going to New Orleans and combing the place until he found her. And thanks to Niles's revelation, Sean had gone on his way knowing he held a compass in his hand.

Fortunately he was a seasoned traveler, and since he knew how to find the Louisianan city, he made few wrong turns on his way. He traveled very fast.

Sean stood at the corner of Dauphine and St. Louis in the French Quarter. The people who passed, or came in and out of bars, did a lot of laughing, and he figured from the unsteady gait of many that booze fueled a good deal of the hilarity.

Thrumming zydeco rhythm beat into the seething air from a nearby gumbo shop. The smells were rich and spicy—and matched everything about the city.

This wasn't a place for Elin.

He did smile. Perhaps she would enjoy the danger of it all, at least if they were together. An ill-received thought came that his mate could be more complex than he had yet accepted. She clearly had courage.

The prickling in his seal started again. It was strong but confused. Nevertheless he followed his instincts and walked first southeast on St. Louis, so narrow he couldn't imagine two vehicles passing each other there, then he felt another pull and made a sharp turn to his left on Royal.

Shops lined both sides of the street but there weren't many people about. The lack of strip joints, bars, and restaurants could account for that.

The heel of his hand burned. But it burned with the same intensity wherever he stood, no matter which way he faced.

Half an hour later he leaned on the window of a tiny shop that sold only Limoges boxes highlighted by a single spotlight that covered all of them.

He cursed to himself. Elin was here. She was within feet or yards of him, but short of hammering on every door and asking, "Is Elin here?" he couldn't do a thing to find her.

Sean walked to the middle of the street and raised his face to the misting rain. "Is Elin here?" he yelled. "Is Elin here?" Lights showed in some apartment windows for several stories above the businesses. Not a soul answered his cry.

He didn't feel even a shred of embarrassment. The scattered people who passed showed no sign of noticing that a man was standing in the street, yelling.

High above his head a dormer window slammed open.

Hell, what did he have to lose? "Is Elin here?" he called again.

The window shut at once.

He was alone now. Not a soul in sight in either direction. And all he had for company was the sharp burning awareness he rubbed with the fingers of his left hand.

All he could do was use his hand like a divining rod, concentrate, and be sensitive to the slightest change in what he felt.

Slowly, Sean went, step by step, along the sidewalk. His hand throbbed but only at the same intensity. When he had passed the police precinct house, walked across the next narrow street, and focused on a fairly major crossroad ahead, the sensation lessened and fell into a dull, regular pulsing.

It was fading and he stood still.

On the opposite sidewalk, he began walking back in the direction from which he'd come, his right palm still turned up.

Bars covered the windows of most shops and the question came that always did in such places. Were the inhabitants keeping others out, or themselves in?

Weird what you thought about when your mind either wandered or was in distress. Sean's was distressed.

The next pulse shot into his palm, fierce and sharp.

Shops butted up against each other here as if they were guarding their territory.

Sweat joined the rain on Sean's face. While he wandered up and down in the French Quarter, Elin could be terrified somewhere. Kept against her wishes. Lost. He squinted, trying to close out the direction of his thoughts.

The next pulse made him miss a breath. He turned toward the street and the sensation eased but only slightly. Facing the shops, he felt as if a hot ice pick were being driven into his flesh.

He loved that pain. The shop windows in front of him were dark. A faint light showed deep inside but nothing moved. J. Clive Millet, Antiques, the shop was called.

A single bark surprised him. To his left, poking through the bars of a high, ornate gate that joined the corner wall of the shop to the next building, he could see the muzzle of a small, wiry dog.

Sean approached. If the dog set up a howling ruckus, so much the better. Maybe that would bring out someone who could help with finding Elin.

When he reached it, the dog's black nose shone wet amid sprouting coarse fur, and a pair of liquid eyes watched closely.

He didn't want to be bitten, but Sean risked reaching in and scratching the animal's head and the back of his neck.

The dog wriggled appreciatively and stretched to encourage more attention. This must be one of Jazzy's long-lost attention-mad relatives.

Playing with a dog wasn't helping a thing.

He noted the gate had a big circular inset with a fanciful griffon arranged so its claws gripped the metal ring.

Sean pressed his hand to his head once more and turned to walk on.

Chirping stopped him. Chirping and purring. He spun around, searching for any moving shapes in the darkness, expecting to see Skillywidden shoot from some small hiding place and leap into his arms.

The cat that appeared was huge—bigger than the rough-haired little dog although their color was similar. Both seemed red or orange.

Daintily for an animal that probably weighed twenty pounds, the cat stepped between two bars, wiggled a little to get her belly through, and rubbed against Sean's legs. He bent to touch her and the sensation in his hand went mad. "Elin?" he whispered. It was always possible she had morphed into a different cat, he supposed.

He didn't get the reaction he wanted. Instead, the cat passed back through the bars and looked at Sean over her shoulder. The dog gave what sounded like a sigh. Elin, Sean thought, might also have touched the cat and her scent was what made his seal react.

He must be losing it. Analyzing family pets when his own mate was missing in a city where lone women, lone beautiful women, should not be abroad in the night.

Both animals sat on the inside of the gate, staring at him.

Okay, stranger things had happened in his life than being accosted by a couple of domestic animals. He gripped the ring surrounding the metal griffon and almost howled. Like a white-hot knife, the pain stabbed at him.

And the gate opened under his hand, swung soundlessly inward on well-oiled hinges.

Sean stepped inside and pushed the gate shut behind him. When he walked carefully forward, his feet scrunched on gravel and he expected a furor to break out at any second.

Not a sound.

Past a row of apparent storerooms with big double doors and into a courtyard where a single blue-green glow showed through the satin-slick leaves of ferns, palms, and a jungle of tropical shrubs. Red ginger pierced through a space between foliage. He could smell gardenias.

This wasn't going to work, not walking around someone's private garden late at night and with no plan.

Sean jumped and took a backward step. A tall figure stood in his path. The cat sat beside this person in the familiar way of an animal with a long acquaintance. Sean started to say something but looked more closely. The figure was stone, a slender angel with folded wings and beautifully carved robes—and an unforgettable face.

He would go toward the light.

The cat, with the scruffy little dog close behind, trotted ahead, looking back from time to time with apparent approval.

Wall lights showed that doors and window frames were painted shiny green and metal stairs rose between floors of the surrounding buildings.

The light came from a fountain where a stone boy angel tipped luminous water from a shell into a much bigger shell. Bubbles frothed, ice white, at the surface. And suddenly the whole area seemed alive with figures. Stone angels sat, knelt, stood, and reclined among the shrubs. The shop and Royal Street were behind him and he saw he was in an enclosed courtyard with several stories of apartments on each side including above the shop.

And getting arrested for trespassing wouldn't be helpful, even if he could get out of that easily enough.

Elin was here, somewhere here.

The cat was a beautiful marmalade and the little dog wasn't scruffy, he just had coarse, reddish fur. Back and forth ran the cat, from Sean, toward the rear of the courtyard, and then retracing her steps.

It wouldn't be the first time he'd followed a cat. He smiled and it felt good. He went after the cat up two flights of metal stairs and a short way along a balcony to a front door flanked by windows. Light glowed through curtains in the room to the right.

*"Sean!"*

Elin's voice blasted in his brain. He staggered and braced himself on the wall.

Why hadn't he tried to connect with her before? "*Elin, I'm here. I'm in New Orleans. On Royal Street. On a balcony above a courtyard full of stone angels.*" He had just assumed they were too remote from each other.

Scrambled voices bounced around his mind and the door in front of him opened—just a crack.

Two faces, one above the other, peered out. Elin and a golden-haired stranger looked at him with disbelief.

"Is it him?" the stranger asked.

Before Elin could open the door all the way, Sean snatched her from behind the other woman and swung her into his arms. "I am so angry with you," he said, bringing his face close to hers. "Why would you run away from me like that?"

Elin's fine dark brows came down in what was supposed to be a ferocious frown. "I'm angry with you, too," she said, pushing against him and getting nowhere. "Put me down at once. *You're mad at me?* Do you have any idea what I went through to get here? Quitus is after you. I'm convinced of it now I've spoken with Jude and Dora. And he tried to get at you through me at the cottage, only it wasn't me who got hurt, it was Cassie. He'll keep on trying."

He had no idea who most of these people were that she was gabbling about. "Did you even consider discussing this with me?"

She trembled in his arms and he knew it wasn't from fear. "You're freezing again. You're going to get sick like Leigh."

"She shouldn't feel the cold," the other woman said. "That has to be fixed although she thinks it's starting to get better already. Bring her inside. I'm Dora. I was Elin's foster mother before a demon stole her from me before Tarhazian stole her from him."

He stared at this golden-haired young thing and checked around for other signs of Never-Never Land.

Walking into a little apartment furnished with pretty, comfortable antiques, Sean kept an eye on this Dora person. "Not one word of what you just said makes any sense," he said. "You might be about the right age to be Elin's sister, but you aren't old enough to be anything else. Elin, I hope you haven't fallen for any of this codswallop. She's probably in the white slave trade."

Elin snickered, "Talking of codswallop," she said, "not that anyone does that anymore as far as I know. What Dora says is true. She's fae and her mate is a vampire. And I just love her, don't you? She's the closest to a real mother I have."

Sean made a noncommittal noise and slowly set Elin down. She slid into the corner of a gold velvet couch.

"Jude—he's the man Sally sent me to—he's hundreds of years old, I think, and he's Dora's friend. He was able to get her to his attic. That's where we met. Then he told us we could rest and talk here in Willow and Ben's apartment—they're descendents of Jude and they're away right now. Other members of the present Millet generation use the other apartments—they're the people who own the antique shop. Jude said Ben and Willow won't mind if we use the place. Sean, I've found out so much about myself—and about The Island and Quitus—he's so bad. And I've learned a lot about the trouble on Whidbey. That's going to be our biggest challenge."

At last Elin took a breath. Dora gave Sean a frown he took to mean that he should go easy on Elin.

"Quitus?" The name had almost gotten lost in Elin's rapid outpouring.

"That's the real name of The One. And it's not an O the red stone makes—it's called The Bloodstone, by the way—it's a Q for Quitus. And there's so much more but we have to be quick and find Quitus's surrogate on Whidbey before he—or she—can kill anyone else and stir up more mayhem."

Sean put a finger on her lips and sat beside her. "What do you mean by surrogate?"

"Someone on Whidbey who does the killing and capturing for Quitus. A Trojan horse. This person has no conscience. He could be capable of any horrible behavior. We don't even know how many times he's killed already. There could easily be victims we don't know about."

"Elin—"

"It's almost certain the victims are supposed to be taken to Quitus for experiment—and so he can eat, er, parts of them." She turned decidedly green. "But we already knew he was eating people."

"Don't the fae on Whidbey know what's going on?" Sean said. "It would have been a lot less trouble for both of us to find all this out from one of them."

Elin jumped up. She lifted her arms and dropped them with a frustrated thump. "Not everyone knows these things just because they're fae," she said. "And Sally's banished, too, remember. She can't just walk among her own kind. They wouldn't tell her anything for me, and they wouldn't tell Sally unless she said who she wanted the information for."

"Why not for you? You're harmless enough—I take that back—you seem harmless."

She looked so startled by the question that Sean took both of her hands in his. Once again he wished Dora weren't there, but the fae had pulled a chair close and sat down where she could be sure not to miss any of the action.

"Elin," he said quietly. "What is it?"

"Have you forgotten I'm Deseran," she said and took a deep breath. "You're still angry with me for keeping that from you. I can feel it. But honestly, I decided if you thought I was fae and if you fell in love with me, I'd know it wasn't because I've got this universal blood and I might be able to carry your child."

He breathed deeply through his nose and said, "You lied to me." He felt more confusion than hurt. "Or you weren't honest. But neither was I with you."

"She's been abandoned once already," Dora interrupted, with tears in her eyes and voice. "You can't blame her for being afraid you might not want her for herself."

"Dora," Elin said, winding her fingers together. "Sean and I have to talk this through. Sean, I just didn't tell the truth."

"What is it when you don't tell the truth?"

"Doesn't it depend on the situation?" Elin asked, challenging him. "Like when you fall for someone the instant you set eyes on them and you know you're probably not at all what they're looking for."

"Go on," he said, feeling just a little bit guilty for wallowing in being loved by the only woman he wanted.

She settled her hands on his shoulders. "You are ... incredible. Not just the most gorgeous male imaginable, but you've got a good, kind heart. And you're so smart. For a long time I felt I wasn't the one you need. You need someone who matches you. A woman who's all woman. But I am meant for you. I am your match. I make you all you can be just as you make me all I can be."

"Uh-huh." He gave Dora a long look and she tiptoed out of the room. They heard the front door close. "We are perfect together, my love. Without you, I'd be lost. You are perfect to me—except for your shaky judgment about some things. You are my forever mate, ma'am, so we'll just have to work on it."

"Yep." Elin made a sad face. "I need work but I'm willing to learn—as long as you take a look at yourself, too."

He grinned at that. "Could be fun. You're going to want to spend time here figuring out what it means to be Deseran, aren't you?"

"I won't be the only one. I wonder how many of us there are. Sean, you know I'm as involved in what happens on Whidbey as you, don't you?"

"Yes. But I don't like it that you have to be."

"We have to go back and look for whoever does Quitus's dirty work."

The front door slammed very loudly and Dora entered after knocking on the sitting room door. For an instant she was silent, then she spread her arms as if she would burst into song. But she didn't.

"What is it?" Elin said.

"You'll have to go back to this nasty Whidbey place with him." She wrinkled her nose at Sean. "Since he's your mate. But that's not the only reason. Well, I suppose it is. You can really help him but you've got to promise me you'll come back to me sometimes."

"I will," Elin said.

Sean was edgy to get going but Dora came close and looked up, unblinking, into his eyes. "The story they tell about Deseran is false. They were never given up because they were thought to have no useful paranormal skills. They are the most versatile and superhumanly skilled of all. The combination, always of a superior human and a super talent, produces creatures like Elin. They have been abandoned because it was thought best—by some of the old ones who feared them—to try to hide the truth about them. She is more evolved than any I have seen but she has barely begun to develop. When I took her as a baby, it was my intention to bring her to her full capacity. Now that is your responsibility, Sean—or at least to help her when she asks you, but I will share it with you if you want me to."

"Who are my parents?" Elin asked softly.

Dora sighed. "I expected that. I don't know. There is always an intermediary who delivers the child and never returns. That's all I can tell you. You are more fortunate than your friend, Leigh. She lived for some years without knowing she was different from the humans around her. She will need help to realize her potential. Perhaps she will come here with you one day." She pressed her hands over her ears and her eyes widened. "It's Sally. Can you hear her, Elin?"

Sean watched his mate with amazement as she nodded. "We have to go now," she told him. "Right now. Sally's calling for us."

"Something terrible has happened," Dora said. "I think—" She covered her mouth.

Elin said, "She fears for her life. But her voice is garbled now—I can't make any more of it out."

She wrapped her arms around his waist, murmuring words that sounded senseless, and they spun until the room disappeared, until there was no form around them.

Sean held Elin tightly. They were as good as fused together. He felt their joint power propel them into flight.

## *chapter* TWENTY-NINE

$S$ean? Sean? Help me."

It was still dark.

He sprang out of calf-deep snow, onto the porch at Two Chimneys, following Elin into the cottage.

Elin knelt on the floor of the living room, holding Gabriel, rocking him. "This is meant to stop us," she said, looking up at him. "No one is safe. They want to frighten us into not fighting back."

"My God." He dropped down beside her. "They're not going to win. Sally and Cassie are gone?"

"Where can they be?" Elin massaged a bright red Q on the back of unconscious Gabriel's neck. "He's still alive. Do you think this just happened?"

"Maybe not. It could be that it's taking longer to work because he's strong," Sean pointed out. "He's big and athletic. He's got more to fight back with than the average woman."

"We haven't seen this done to another man," Elin said. She had torn off her parka and the skirt of her dress clung, sodden, to her legs. "It's happening. The mark is reacting to my touch. I can't get away from it now."

"When you drag off the mark, why doesn't it hurt you? You're small and light—you ought to be hurt by the thing. Maybe all the power goes out of it with the first strike."

Her smile wasn't what he expected. "Or perhaps it's because of what I am. I must be immune. Or I hope so. The one on Cassie disappeared once I pulled it off. I hope my luck doesn't change." Her smile disappeared. "We can be strong together, can't we?"

Sean nodded, yes, but he had doubts about fighting the forces of evil they confronted now. With one hand he pulled the quilt from the couch and threw it over Gabriel before going to close the door.

"Elin?" He searched around. "What time is it? What *day* is it? With two of us together we must have at least halved how long it took to get back here."

"And we were both sure of the way this time," she said, working on the red Q, starting to lift one side of it from Gabriel's neck. "We probably made the journey very fast."

Sean checked his watch. "You left yesterday. I left early last night. It's three in the morning. We're in the same twenty-four hours. When I left, Cassie was still in a deep sleep on the couch and Sally was here keeping the fire going."

"Contact Niles or one of the other hounds," she said. "Ask if Sally and Cassie are there."

Niles was already hammering at Sean's mind, demanding to know where he was. Sean had shut him out until now. *"Are Sally and Cassie down there?"* he said, prepared for Niles's wrath.

*"Where have you been, dammit? I wouldn't have tried to help you if I'd thought you'd decide this was any time to run off somewhere private with your mate. You know you're needed here. I need you here while I'm unsure about Leigh. I told you that."*

Sean winced. *"I wish I had been having a cozy time with Elin. Save it, Niles, and answer me. Are Sally and Cassie there?"*

*"No. Cassie's brother said she was up at the cottage with Sally and he went up to be with them."*

Where were the clues he needed? *"We're at the cottage and they aren't here—none of them. We just arrived and found Gabriel. He's been hit with that damn Bloodstone. That's what makes the red Q. I told you about it. Thank God these madmen haven't got the thing right yet. No...no more explanations now. It'll take too long."*

Elin tapped his arm. Her eyes were huge and horrified and she made a sign that she wanted to talk privately.

*"Stay where you are. All of you. I'll get back to you. It's important for you not to come until I tell you,"* he told Niles and shut down on his alpha. He knew Niles would do as he asked because only a dire crisis would make Sean assume the lead, and he was assuming the Team lead.

"Look," Elin said, pointing to one of Gabriel's clenched hands.

"Something he grabbed?" Niles looked closer. "Yellow fibers."

"Yellow silk fibers. Like the dress Sally was wearing. He must have tried to save her from something."

"Or to stop her from doing something," Sean said, looking away from Elin. "Like hitting him with that stone. She was here alone with Cassie—and probably David after he got up here. I know Gabriel wanted to see me and he could have decided I might be here with you. Could be Sally panicked and started taking them out."

"Killing them? How can you say that? Sally's my best friend—she's stuck with me through everything and Tarhazian makes sure she suffers for it. She couldn't kill anything."

"Then where is Sally—and the other two? Whoever did this to Gabriel expected him to die before anyone came."

Rumbling started at the front of the cottage, at the foundation. Elin kept massaging Gabriel's neck but she reached for Sean and he took her hand.

Neither of them spoke but they both looked around them and the rumbling continued, under the earth, gradually surrounding all of the little building. The lamps rocked. The crystal birds on the bookshelves clinked together. In the kitchen something fell to the floor and broke. The entire cottage shook.

"Is it an earthquake?" Elin asked. "It feels as if it is."

It wouldn't be the first Sean had lived through but this was no earthquake. He put a finger to his lips, slid his hand from Elin's, and bent low to work his way to the front window. He switched off the lights and stood where he could see through the side of the curtain.

And he swore under his breath. "Vampire attack," he

said. "I recognize Colin and his slaves, Fireze and Hubert, but I don't see any others I know. Brande's there, and all his pack, including some new candidates. Seven is with them, and Mark—and Booker. I didn't think he'd recover after the last fight. There are more of them, an army."

"Is the renegade hound who betrayed all of you there?"

"No. We won't speak of him."

Elin shook her head. "What do we do?"

Elin's calm made him proud. "I think I'll make sure Niles and the rest don't try to come up here. There's not enough of them to wage a fair fight—for the hounds."

"We need an edge," Elin said.

He didn't want to, but Sean pulled out his cell phone and called Saul, praying the vampire would answer. He did. And he listened to what Sean had to say without interruption.

"I don't know why they would send such a horde," Sean finished.

"Don't you?" Saul said. "Look at your mate and ask that question again. Her organs renew, just like her blood. The One—or Quitus as you probably know he is called by now—wants her at any price. I noticed Elin never mentioned being Deseran but you must know this too."

It galled Sean to ask but he said, "Any ideas about how to get out of this?" He refused to comment on Elin denying her roots.

"Make sure the rest of the Team stays where it is. If they come up the bank, they'll die."

"I know," Sean said.

"Does Elin have her wand?"

"Wand?" Sean said to Elin, raising his brows.

She nodded and touched a scarf wound about her waist.

"She has it."

"Very well. Tell Niles to stay where he is and not to make a move until he hears from you. I'll wait."

Sean contacted Niles and told him to keep everyone where they were. Niles was still cursing when Sean broke off the connection.

The door crashed inward and a werewolf Sean didn't know reared up on the threshold.

Elin screamed and the wolf lunged toward her, in time to fall over Sean's leg and smash his head against the rock fireplace. He fell unconscious but Sean didn't expect that to last for long.

These wolves had never discovered that the werehounds were even stronger in human form but that was a secret the hounds preferred to keep. Colin ought to believe it, but didn't seem to want to.

Sean wasn't ready to cut off his verbal communication so he would resort to diversionary tricks for as long as he could. He was determined to be accepted as a human and for him that meant that he would avoid taking on his werehound form whenever possible.

He shoved the phone to Elin, who picked it up and slammed it to her ear. "Saul, they're breaking in," she said, watching Sean take a long, curved knife from a sheath beneath one jeans' leg. "The werewolves are breaking in. The vampires can't come over the threshold. I hope not anyway."

She hesitated, listening, and covered the mouthpiece.

"I think he's laughing at me. I guess he'd already know about vampires and thresholds but he doesn't have to be so arrogant."

"Okay," she said and listened again. "He says he's on his way, Sean. He wants me to make fire with the wand and throw it at the wolves and vampires."

Sean stopped himself from groaning. Elin didn't know how to do these things.

"Perhaps it won't work," she said breathlessly into the phone, but she worked the wand free. "Why do you think it will just because I tell it to?" She gave Sean a helpless look and raised a hand.

Frustrated at being on the outside in this exchange, Sean longed to snatch the phone back.

"He says it'll throw fire if I want it to," Elin said.

Sean crouched, ready to spring from behind the open front door.

Elin peered into the darkness. "There are too many of them," she said, her voice failing her. "We can't fight them all."

But he crouched back, preparing for the next on-slaught.

"Right!" Saul appeared behind Sean and slammed the door shut. He bowed slightly and said, "I have a permanent welcome in the homes of my friends unless they say otherwise."

"Welcome," Elin said in a quavering tone. "They're going to kill all of us."

He went to examine Gabriel and said, "He'll pull through. Follow me, Elin, and stand by the front door."

"Just a damn minute," Sean said, leaping into Saul's

path. He remembered the knife and sheathed it. "She's not going anywhere near the door."

"She won't be alone," Saul said. "Break the logs into thinner pieces and get them ready to throw. Elin, point the wand to the fireplace and light those logs."

This was not a man to be argued with. With the wand held in a shaking hand, she pointed it at the fireplace, closed her eyes, and told it to burn. The immediate blow-back of heat shocked her. When she looked, logs in the fireplace shot flames up the chimney.

"Fire won't stop them forever," Sean said. "But we all know that." He began to shift and the change was fast. The thick, blue-black coat covered him and he felt his jaw cracking into its canine formation at the same time.

Another werewolf, one Sean knew by the hostile but familiar greeting he gave, appeared in the doorway. It only took one bound before Sean was upon it, great teeth flashing, his body twisting the other's this way and that, rolling over and snarling.

Twice the wolf went for Sean's throat, and twice Sean evaded the fangs. At the second attack he ducked his head and ripped open the belly of the other animal. Blood and entrails spurted and a glance showed Elin with her face buried in Gabriel's back.

Sean hauled the other wolf into the air and thumped him down in a senseless, bloody heap. He yelled a triumphant, "Done."

"We mustn't forget for an instant that even as they go down, they're already repairing themselves," Saul said. "So will the vampires if you burn them."

Sean gave a derisive grunt.

The rumbling in the earth continued and Sean saw the ring of creatures outside move a little closer to the porch. They seemed like one silent entity.

"Out of my way," Elin cried.

She dashed to the door and hurled out three flaming torches, one after the other.

That brought noises from the ones outside.

Back and forth, she ran, tossing out more sticks of fire, pausing momentarily to light another bunch with her wand when the supply got low.

"You cannot help her with that," Saul said, and a strange expression came over his face. "But she's giving us the diversion we need."

"Either we hold them off and get rid of them, or they'll finish us," Elin cried.

"You are about to learn more than any nonvampire has learned. You have to do what I tell you, Sean." Saul took a polished jug with a long neck and a stopper from a deep pocket inside his coat and held it by an ornate handle. "Enough fire and the werewolves will scatter. But this is the blood weakness—or so I believe. The only known disease a vampire can contract and very rare. If I can, I'll tell you how I got it one day, but not now. Its real name in Italian is *Sangue Debolezza*, but it means, simply, blood weakness."

Sean looked at Elin's slender arms and wrists, and her hands covered with black soot, and feared she couldn't keep up what she was doing.

"You call out those words very loudly and we'll hope all the vampires make a run for it. If they don't believe what they hear, hitting one vampire with some of this should prove we aren't lying. The rest of them will be gone before we can turn on them. And the ailing one will follow to infect the rest." Saul's eyes were like black holes. "I must ask you to shift again and throw some of the contents, Sean. I believe it may sicken the werewolves but they will recover in time. Any vampire who comes in..."

"How can you hold a silver jug?" Elin asked, pausing to breathe.

"It's pewter polished to look like silver. Keep the fire going. Will you do it, Sean?" Saul's jaw worked. "I can't be absolutely certain what will happen to you if the powder touches your skin. Perhaps... If I'm careful about the direction of the wind, I should be able to—"

"No," Elin shouted, intensifying her barrage of fire. "Neither of you can take that risk."

Already changing, Sean struggled to free himself completely of his hound form. He yelled and grabbed Saul as he would have gone out the door. "No! Give me that and stay back. Elin may need you."

He seized the jug and ran outside. "Blood weakness," he shouted, holding the shining silver thing high so it reflected fire. "Blood weakness. Who will be first to test the *Sangue Debolezza*?"

A mumble of voices among the vampires rose to a roar, then gradually sank away to sibilant whispers that passed between them in waves.

Sean pulled the stopper from the jug and moved forward. "Come on. Who's first?"

The wolves' howls rose, unearthly, terrified, but the vampires acted first. They levitated into the air, one after the other, jostling together in their haste. But Sean moved quickly; he shook a stream of liquid from the jug over the closest vampire.

The creature gave a terrible howl. He screamed and tore at his clothes, swung onto his back above the ground, and writhed in uncontrolled spasms.

Coughing, choking, he wrapped his cloak about him and flew slowly into the darkness, rolling over and over, making sounds only a dying thing would make.

The rest scrambled to get height in the sky and then they were gone like streaks of smoke through the sky and the wolves raced, yipping and howling, for the forest.

## *chapter* THIRTY

Before he had left, taking unconscious Gabriel with him to care for, Saul insisted the vessel disguised as silver, and its contents, be placed in the wide ring of light that shone from above the front door onto the porch. Its very presence would guard the little house, he told them. Neither he nor Sean thought their enemies would return soon, particularly since the night's hours were numbered.

The men seemed almost disinterested in Sally and the brother and sister who had disappeared.

When they were alone, Elin said, "You don't think we should look for Sally?"

"My guess is that she's with Tarhazian," Sean said. "This may be her opportunity to find favor with that woman. We have bigger problems to deal with."

"But they won't give up, will they?" Elin said, and

immediately regretted her words. "Quitus? And the ones who came here? At least, they might not give up."

Sean had retrieved his jeans but he remained bare-chested and barefoot. He moved restlessly around the perimeter of the room, glancing at her frequently, his jaw set and his eyes stark with rage.

"Let me get you something hot to drink," she said, wanting to comfort him.

"It's not cocoa I need," he said, barely moving his lips.

"Go up and sleep," she told him. "I'll keep watch."

Sean laughed and the sound raised goose bumps on Elin's arms.

"No need to watch now," he said. "Damn them. They won't come after you the same way twice. Right now they're with Quitus. When he stops punishing them for their failure, he'll plan the next move."

She swallowed and said in a small voice, "Then we should make a move first."

"What do you think I'm doing?" he asked, shoving a palm toward her. "I'm trying to decide the best course and I know we can't move too quickly. First we must be sure they're all together. Then we have to have a plan of attack. It will be a long day. The coming night will probably seem too short."

Elin could smell soot and smoke on herself. She combed her fingers through her hair and they came away even blacker.

"I'm going to shower," she told Sean. "Please call out if I need to come."

His laughter was humorless.

Elin ran up the ladder to the loft and gathered clean

clothes. There would be no comfortable sleep in comfortable nighties until this was all over—which meant she might never sleep in comfort again.

When she climbed back down the ladder and went swiftly to the bathroom, Sean didn't as much as look at her. Inside, with the door shut, she couldn't deny that she hoped he would come to her.

Through a small, pebbled glass skylight, she saw how the night weakened and cold, winter stars began to fade. Then steam from the hot water coated everything and she luxuriated in the heat.

She didn't know Sean had come in until she felt his presence. The bathroom door was already closed and he stood outside the shower doors, watching her.

Elin knew he saw her shadow, her face raised to allow water to splash, the way she shampooed her hair, winding it into heavy, lathered swirls on her head.

If he wanted to be excited, she would do her best. Sliding her hands up her slick thighs, she let her head drop back and turned to face away from the shower head. Over her belly and her ribs and up to cup her breasts, her hands moved naturally. This was how she always showered. But she didn't always pinch and tug on her own nipples while her hair fell in a long, heavy, wet sheath. And she didn't always slip a hand between her thighs and slide it into the folds of her sex to send a dart of pleasure through her, and buckle her own knees.

Elin smiled and eased open one of the shower doors. He would have to be unconscious not to see the invitation.

The man who joined her in the small shower stall, who

planted his fists on his hips and allowed his arousal to sway before her, was an intoxicating stranger.

Water plastered his hair back and spiked his eyelashes, but his eyes were the deepest gold and they skewered her.

Sean shot an arm around her waist and hauled her onto a raised thigh. He kissed her, open-mouthed, tonguing his way across the insides of her mouth to her throat, and Elin's body pulsed while she strained to get closer.

He slid fingers between her labia and rubbed with such force, she almost cried out. Just as quickly, he released and stood her on the tile again.

His next kiss was softer but just as deep. The fingers that pinched and rolled her nipples were gentle, but Elin just wanted more and more of him. She caught up the soap and lathered his back while their bodies slid together. His buttocks were hard beneath her hands and he jutted his hips toward her each time she swept arcs over the firm flesh.

"Sean," she said tentatively, "I want you all the time."

"You have changed me," he said. "I am a man who used to feel complete on his own. Not anymore. I need you."

"Is that a bad thing?" She took his penis in her hands and squeezed, stroked its length, and felt a burst of joy inside when his hips came toward her—helplessly.

"You like to control," he said, but he didn't sound angry. "You love the power you have over me."

"Only because I want you, Sean. And when I feel how much you want me, it's incredible."

She dropped to her knees and took him in her mouth, slid her teeth gently back and forth until he shoved against her.

The sound he made was like a stifled scream in his throat and he lifted her as if she were nothing, and wrapped her legs around his waist. "This is for the lust," he said. "Then we explore the love."

Lust meant she fell onto him and he penetrated her in a single stroke, with a single pulse of finding each other before the wild driving, the taking of both of them, carried their bodies over the edge. Elin's jaws ground together. She dug her fingernails into his back, meeting each of his thrusts with matching force. Sean squeezed the cheeks of her bottom and ran a finger up the cleft to spread his hand across her back and press her even closer.

They thundered together, lost, and never wanting to be found.

She smiled at the warm fluid spreading over her thighs, and mourned not being able to capture and keep it all.

She heard, "I love you," and whispered, "And I love you so much more."

"Not possible," Sean said.

They stood, breast to breast, belly to belly, thigh to thigh, and the evidence of their completion still pulsed, one against the other.

Elin held him beneath his penis and weighted him, and smiled when he drew in a sharp breath. Beneath her hand he started to reawaken—and his fingers slipping between her legs made the pulsing, thrumming begin all over again.

Pretending to growl, Sean pushed her under the cooling shower and sluiced off any soap. She did the same for him, slicking the soap from his hair and body, and laughing when he almost slipped and clutched at whatever he could find—her waist—which he quickly abandoned to sweep her up into his arms.

"Turn off the water," he ordered, his voice even lower than usual.

Elin complied.

"Are you ready for the loving, ma'am? Although I can hardly believe our recovery rate." He kissed her ear.

"I am ready, sir." Her very spirit bubbled. "Not too gentle, though, hmm?"

Sean smiled against her neck, and nipped a little skin between his teeth. "Be careful what you wish for."

By the time he climbed the ladder to the loft, he had Elin draped around his shoulders and she still felt too slippery for safety.

Soon she didn't care if she ever felt safe again.

*chapter* **THIRTY-ONE**

The fire roared into the chimney again. Sean doubted either Elin or he had slept more than an hour at a time in the loft bed. But she wouldn't let him leave her alone even to bank the fire.

Naked, swathed in a down blanket from the bed, they leaned against the base of an easy chair in the living room and watched the flames. Elin's head fitted into the hollow of his shoulder, and although her arms couldn't close around him, he engulfed her in his.

With a light hand, he stroked the side of her face and ran his thumb across her bottom lip. A small enough shift and he smoothed his fingers from her collarbone to her breast and covered it gently.

She breathed so regularly, he thought for a moment she had fallen asleep, but only until she looked up at him. "If we could remember to treasure even our shortest times together, we'd know what happiness really is," she said.

"I already know, and I'd stopped thinking it would ever happen for me." Longing for a life partner had turned into the hunt for a mate and somehow he had given up on finding what he had now. "You're not the other half of me. I...you're all of me. Where do I begin and you finish? It doesn't happen. We make one whole."

Elin rubbed his belly and he felt her smile when the muscles contracted. "I never expected you to be poetic," she said.

"Just honest, and struggling my clumsy way through the words to find some that work."

"Was there someone—a woman—before you were changed?"

He worked not to let her feel the wash of tension. "Not anyone serious. I was working my way across the country—following whatever they all said would be the next sure thing. There wasn't time to have relationships. I wanted to be where I could help people the way my father had, and still get by. Being paid in a chicken here and a jar of jam there made for a tough go."

"Then Aldo came along and you saved him."

"Mmm. I would have been happy with a chicken payment that night." He looked down on the top of her shining ebony hair. "But then I wouldn't have met you. We wouldn't have sealed and been together like this. Do you know what I mean when I say it's as if there's no beginning or ending between the two of us?"

She nodded. Her lashes were wet against his chest and tears slipped over his skin. "I'm so lucky."

Sean tightened his grip on her. "We won't argue about

who is or isn't lucky here. I feel you when you're not with me, have I told you that?"

He thought she smiled again. "Sort of."

"Is that something you do, Elin? In New Orleans, Dora talked about how powerful you are and how many talents you have."

Elin breathed in slowly, and he didn't know if she'd answer. Her teeth closed on one of his flat nipples and he jumped. "You're something," he said. "Wily."

"I do it," she said almost under her breath. "I don't know how or why, but after we met—after I loved you and was sure it would never stop—I just thought about you and felt your body against my hands."

Bending forward, he raised her chin and frowned at her. "How many men can you do this with?"

"Only you, silly. It will only ever be you. One day I'll find out more about who and what I am, and where these things came from. For now I'm going to accept the good stuff and not think too hard about it."

"We'll go back to New Orleans and find Dora again— and this Jude you talked about."

She sighed. "We'll find Dora. I know we will. But I think seeing Jude was something different. I don't believe he lives in this world."

Sean let that go. "We have a long journey ahead. I look forward to it with you. I don't think I could ever have loved anyone else, but I felt something different the day we met."

"Yes, you thought I was very different," she said with a sniff. "I bet that was it. The waif who was all hair and eyes. People have said that about me before."

"And you take it wrong. First, your body...darn it, Elin, you're making me hard again."

She laughed. "Such problems you have."

"You're beautiful and you know it. I don't mind you being beautiful, but I'd still love you if you looked like a troll."

"Hey. Watch it!"

"I mean, I love you for who you are and the gorgeous trimmings are a bonus."

"Same here," she said. "Although your gorgeous trimmings don't hurt."

They fell silent. Sean glanced toward the curtained window. Dawn pushed fingers of gray through a narrow gap at one side and stroked across the wall.

"I wish we could stop time," Elin said.

"If you figure that one out, count me in."

"We'll have to go to Niles and Leigh once it's light. Is Niles trying to reach you yet?"

Sean scooted down and nipped her shoulder. "No. I think he'll wait for me unless we're still not out of here by noon."

"Let's wait till noon then," Elin said. "I mean it."

"I'd like to mean it, but we need an edge today. Niles has to accept my help and he can't do it with strings attached. I want his input, but I'll have to lead the way to take out the wolves."

"What about the vampires?"

He kissed the dip between her breasts. "Maybe we should stay here until someone drags us out. Or maybe we should never leave."

"Vampires," she prodded.

"You were with Tarhazian most of your life. Didn't she tell you the pecking order where vampires are concerned?"

"All she said was that she didn't ever want me near them."

He thought about that. The Fae Queen might love her stolen child after all. "They are the strongest of us all— and the hardest to get rid of. You're never going to forget how it felt when Colin tried to snatch you away. You couldn't have fought him."

"But you did."

"We hounds are not understood by many. We are stronger than the wolves and more patient. We prefer to use more than the obvious when we're forced to fight." He didn't like talking to Elin about this.

"What would that be?" she asked, as he expected her to.

"You deserve to know everything about us, and about me, but could we wait until today is past? And maybe tomorrow and the next day if that's how long it takes to fight our way out of trouble." He wouldn't admit that he had doubts about how easy that would be, if it could be done at all.

"Sean, is this all because Quitus hopes to make a Bloodstone big enough, and powerful enough, to bring everyone and everything he wants under his control?"

"Yes. At least, that's what I believe. And his master plan has gotten bent so he's flailing and having to work on grabbing what he wants in little pieces. He doesn't want to subdue one victim at a time. He wants this whole island and that wouldn't be enough for him. Then he'd want more. But he's made a hash of whatever he's done to the elements of The Veil."

"Red," she said quietly. "Blood as he's decided it is."

"And something is making him sick and weak."

Elin shivered. "Which is why he wants us. Aldo is part of him and Aldo knows you can renew him. Now he believes my blood and organs are essential, too."

He would not make her frantic by admitting Aldo was still an unknown quantity to him, or that what he feared most was this unknown surrogate they spoke of. "He won't get you. But you will have to—"

"Follow your orders?" she broke in. "I will unless I don't agree with you."

"Elin!"

"Yes, I mean that. You want to carry the burden for everyone and absolutely for me, but you said you couldn't find where you ended and I began because we're one and the same. I don't have to tell you what that means. Please make love to me again."

He dragged her to sit on his lap, which did nothing to help his case when he said, "There isn't time, my love. We could easily be interrupted."

"Sean," she said, twisting to sit astride his thighs and teasing his penis against him. "This could be the last time. We don't have any guarantees."

Even if he was admitting she was right, he couldn't make himself deny her.

He let her guide him deep inside her body, and helped stretch them out, still joined, on top of the down blanket.

## chapter THIRTY-TWO

Rather than noon, Sean and Elin walked into Niles and Leigh's house at eleven o'clock. And still all of the icy atmosphere wasn't left outside.

Sean hardly dared to look at Elin. He had to keep a steady head if he was going to argue his points with Niles, but when he met Elin's eyes, he couldn't make himself care as much about what happened beyond their private world.

"Gabriel is with Saul?" Niles said.

The preliminaries were brief. Niles's narrowed eyes moved between Sean and Elin and probably saw everything, including the strength of their bond.

Good. So be it.

Squinting against a cold sun through the windows by the water, Sean set his jaw and his resolve. "I already told you he is. Saul will make sure Gabriel comes through this okay."

"But you don't know where Sally or Cassie and her brother are?"

"You know I don't."

"Aw, hell." Niles threw himself onto a couch beside Leigh and closed his eyes. "This is an unholy mess and it doesn't end here."

"No," Sean said, keeping his voice level. "It doesn't end here. But you asked me to be responsible for the Team until you feel you can be fully back in control and I agreed. Having you back where you belong can't come soon enough, but if I'm running things, let me run them, Niles. We can't have two leaders making so-called final decisions."

Niles watched him steadily.

"I would always try to involve you in any major calls—if there was time," Sean added. "But you have to trust me to make good calls. You've got to be behind me." He threw up his hands. "If you can't, I'm through."

His alpha shook his head slowly.

"Niles?" Sean said.

"Okay," Niles said, "Okay, okay, you're right. When I'm ready, I'll take over. Until then, I'm damn lucky to have you to step in for me." He nodded repeatedly.

"I have to know you would join me if things go badly," Sean said.

Niles put an arm around Leigh. "We'll work it out. I'll be there if I have to be. But this woman doesn't just hold my heart, she holds our future in her body." He smiled at Elin. "But she may not be the only one for long?"

He winced when his mate elbowed him in the ribs but Elin turned very pink.

"Give us time," Sean said.

"It didn't take us much time," Niles pointed out.

Sean rolled his eyes. "Okay. You're right. We'll let you know about that."

"We have to look for Sally," Elin said.

"If we don't stop Quitus, it won't matter whether or not we find Sally," Sean told her. He concentrated on Niles. "Do I have everyone with me? I'd like to have the guys who prefer their own territory with us, too. Piers, Renny, and Simon only need the word and they'll be here."

"Will it be enough?" Niles said.

"I hope so. It probably depends on how the pack reacts to what happened in the night. Do you think they'll lose wolves now?"

"Yeah," Niles said. "But we can't count on it. The real wild cards are the vamps. They're very self-protective. They won't open themselves up to this *Sangue Debolezza*. Just knowing it's in the area must have them retreating and regrouping."

"We can hope," Sean said. "I plan to hunt them down, whoever is with Quitus, and I expect to find him, then surround, and attack."

Niles gave no argument.

"Innes and Campion are already out scouting. They have their orders."

He avoided meeting Elin's stare as long as he could. Finally he had to look at her but he couldn't answer the questions on her mind. She wanted to know what the plans were. He shook his head slightly, smiling at her, but she averted her face.

"Where is Phoebe Harris?" Niles said.

In other words, were all the known Deseran safe? "Saul will watch over her," Elin said. "He regards her as a close friend and she trusts him."

Niles snorted. "She should choose her friends more carefully, but I suppose if anyone can look after her, he can."

Letting out a frustrated breath, Sean said, *"Niles."*

"Yeah," Niles said. "Right. A vampire saint. I forgot for a moment. Oh, come on, I'm sorry. He's the first one to talk about old habits being tough to get rid of."

"Leigh and Elin will stay with you," Sean said, letting the subject of Saul pass. "But we need a backup in case I have to send for you."

"I'm going with you," Elin said. She stepped backward away from him and toward the door. "Where you go, I go."

"Where I go, you'll be with me," Sean said. He couldn't even identify all of his feelings. "You'll be here, but with me, do you understand?"

She didn't answer.

"If you were physically there, I couldn't do what I've got to do," Sean told her and her mouth trembled.

"Bear with him," Niles said. "You won't like it, Elin, but it could be we need to pull in Tarhazian. Quitus double-crossed her. She has to want his blood now—and for what it's worth, I believe she loves you."

Elin covered her face, muffling her voice. "In her own way she does, but she loves herself a lot more."

## *chapter* THIRTY-THREE

When Sean had left, Elin felt as if her life were going with him. She couldn't beg him to stay, but she wanted to.

"Hush," Leigh said, putting an arm around her waist. "They have to be the ones who feel strong and in charge. They are the strong ones, but are they in charge?"

Elin saw Leigh's arched right brow and had to smile. "Just don't let either of them know what we think," she said. But the ache she felt was deep and mixed with horrible fear—for Sean, and because she couldn't face Niles's suggestion that they might have to go to Tarhazian.

She patted Leigh's back. "How do you feel?"

"I'll be okay," Leigh said. "It's just a bug. It was violent but I've come out of it fast and the baby seems just fine. Come into the kitchen. It's Niles's least favorite place."

Understanding the message, Elin followed to the kitchen at the back of the house. Niles seemed to have moved into his own world and she was fairly certain he was connecting with the Team.

Leigh closed the kitchen door behind them. "Notice there's no window and no external door in here," she said. "The only way in is through that door and that would mean coming through Niles or Ethan. Ethan's at the back entrance until he's called to join the others. Then we'll have to be where Niles can see us all the time."

"Yes," Elin said but she didn't feel better. "I don't want to go to Tarhazian. How can anyone understand how I feel? I care about her in a way, but she used me and she had no right to me in the first place. We could never be on equal terms and I wouldn't accept anything else—even if I didn't know how devious she is."

"I do understand," Leigh said. "But Niles won't contact her unless he doesn't have a choice and then he'll come up with a way to make sure she doesn't betray us."

Elin wished she could accept Leigh's assurance.

"You're really in love with Sean, aren't you?" Leigh said, smiling and rubbing Elin's arm.

She pressed her eyes. "You know how I feel. I can see it in you with Niles. We are so lucky, Leigh. How did we get this lucky?"

Leigh hugged her. "You and I have a special bond. We're the same kind. I still don't know about my sister, Jan, but she's my twin. I keep expecting her to contact me and say something, but . . ." She let the sentence trail off. "And there's Phoebe. We know so little about ourselves."

"Like how many of us there are," Elin said. "And all the other questions you and I already have. Sean knows

I have to go back to New Orleans." She told Leigh what had happened on her odd journey. "Dora wants me to take you with me."

"How do we cope with it all?" Leigh sat down hard on a kitchen chair. "For so many years I had no idea there was anything different about me. I will always thank Sally for helping me find Niles."

When Elin didn't respond, Leigh said, "What is it?"

"Sean doesn't seem to trust Sally anymore. Maybe he doesn't trust any of the fae."

"Not even one of them?" Leigh said. She frowned and shook her head. "Of course, all that's changed."

"Yes, he knows I'm not fae now," Elin told her. "I don't know how much damage I did by keeping that from him, but he's decided the fae shouldn't be trusted, none of them. He hates Tarhazian."

"Do you?"

"Most of the time. But she hasn't always been the way she is with me now."

"Not when she could make sure you did what she wanted?" Leigh said.

"I guess." Elin bit her lip. "But I haven't always been unhappy. She wouldn't let me grow up—or she didn't want me to grow up. I don't know which is really true."

Leigh looked thoughtful. "If she had a decision to make that could change your future, in a way that might break your heart, what do you think she'd do?"

"I don't know," Elin said promptly, but the thought lingered that perhaps she did.

"Just a minute," Leigh said. Her expression became distant.

She had to be communicating with Niles. Sean said they were really good at it and Elin wished he would say something to her now. If she tried to contact him, he would only worry more.

"Oh, boy," Leigh said. She stood up. "We've got company. Cliff Ames from Gabriel's. He's looking for Gabriel and Sally."

Elin sighed. "I hope I'll know the right things to say."

In the living room, Cliff sat on the edge of a chair but looked as if he could take flight at any moment. He wore a heavy gray wool coat that hung open over his batter-smeared apron and white pants.

"Leigh," he said when he saw her and jumped to his feet. His relief showed. "How're you doing? I wouldn't come only there's nowhere else. I closed up when I left— figured you and me could open again if we go back together. The twins are there, but that's all. The four of us can hold things together."

When Niles kept his eyes down instead of interrupting, Elin figured Leigh didn't like him talking for her.

"Sean said he couldn't come when Gabriel was taking it so bad about Molly," Cliff said, looking at Elin. "I called him. I thought he would come and help when he could."

Elin didn't know what to say.

"Let's go over this," Leigh said. "Sit down again, Cliff. Do you want anything? Coffee?"

"All I want is to find Gabriel and Sally," Cliff said, but he did resume his place at the edge of the chair. "I think it was the night before last when I called Sean. Gabriel was . . . he wasn't making any sense, just yelling and out of his mind about Molly being missing. I couldn't get hold of Sally so I tried Sean."

Elin found her voice. "When did Gabriel leave his place? Didn't he tell you where he was going?"

Shaking his head, no, Cliff laced his thick fingers tightly together.

Without a word, or making a sound in his bare feet, Niles got up and went to stare out of the window. He only made Elin edgier and Cliff jumped visibly when he saw the other man move.

Leigh said, "When did you last talk to Sally?"

"When she was leaving Gabriel's the day before yesterday. Her shop in Langley hasn't opened as far as anyone knows. There's no sign of her."

Shifting restlessly, Niles said, "We'll find her."

Cliff's hands unclenched on his thighs. "I knew you'd figure things out. I forgot, Phoebe said she'd come in and do what she can to help. She knows the cash register. Maybe Elin—"

"No," Niles broke in. "Either you stay closed or find another way."

Cliff hung his head. "We're still on the edge with the money," he said. "Leigh knows that. It's better since she came but it's still uphill. We can't afford to be closed."

"I'll be in," Leigh said, looking mutinous. "If Phoebe comes, Saul will be there. We'll be well looked after."

Niles muttered under his breath.

"Not in my kitchen," Cliff said. "No one would eat the food if they saw the vamp in there."

Leigh and Elin laughed. "Your prejudice is hanging out," Elin said.

Eventually she had to look at Niles and her stomach turned. There was no man like Sean, but Niles was a knockout, and with the light in his black hair and his electric blue eyes narrowed to slits, he made some picture.

He was furious.

"Give us a little time," Leigh said to Cliff and with a challenging stare at Niles. "Go back and whip up some goodies in that kitchen of yours. We'll be along when Niles can bring us."

## *chapter* THIRTY-FOUR

Hours seemed to have gone by since Sean, Innes, and Campion started their careful combing of the island, looking for Brande's pack and always keeping watch for signs of vampires.

Halfway across the island, still clinging to the cover of trees, they were joined by Renny, who lived on a small island by himself. Then came Piers from his retreat to the north and finally Simon, the quietest of the bunch but perhaps the one Sean considered the steadiest.

*"Gather on the beach at Slater Inlet,"* he told them all. *"Our wolf friends aren't fond of the open air. Stay under the bank."* He didn't need to tell them how imperative it was not to be seen or heard. He couldn't see any of the others from where he was. Each of them had spread out to reduce the chance of too much movement in one place being noticed.

Dusk approached by the time he reached the inlet.

They would probably need darkness to do what must be done, but Sean wished they had seen some sign of the enemy.

Nothing.

Renny, dark-haired with dark eyes and the muscular body of a weight-lifting athlete, was already there with slender Piers, a pianist who preferred to remain alone with his music than congregate with his brothers. But Piers never failed to come when needed. Gradually the others slid in and they closed into a circle, the better to hear each other without shouting.

"I've seen them." Simon arrived last. "They're dug in a couple of miles south of the abandoned water tower."

"Dug in?" Sean asked.

"I almost missed them. Seven pushed up a slab of grassy earth as if it was a trap door. I watched and saw one after the other come and go. There's an area above ground that's completely covered with brush. Looks like a mound. But they go in there, too."

"Brande's lodge, you think?" Sean said.

"No, Brande came from underground. There were two other...I'm not sure what they are. Short, bald, grayish creatures. Large ears. They scurry as if they're terrified."

"Austrian Verbols," Sean murmured, remembering what Saul had told them when they were inside Quitus's mountain. "They're creatures of the middle earth. No wonder they scurry in the daylight." He could only hope Quitus was with the Verbols—and that his assumptions about what would kill the living vampire sorcerer, as long as he was as weakened as he was supposed to be, held good.

"They seem to belong to the mound." Simon crossed his arms and fell silent. He'd finished what he had to say.

"How hard will it be for us to get there without being seen?" Innes asked.

"After dark, not hard."

Sean watched Simon's expression carefully. He tended to leave a lot unsaid. "Not easy, either?" he ventured.

"There's open ground before we get to the trees where their clearing is. We couldn't risk daylight. We could easily be seen."

"Darkness then," Sean said. "And we go as men."

A murmur broke out. "Are you serious?" Campion said. "Then they'll know the truth about us."

"That we're stronger in human form?" Sean nodded. "We'll need all the strength we have tonight, and the cunning. You all have your knives?"

A murmur of assent went up. Piers said, "There is a way to extract the short-term memory from a werewolf's mind. But only the fae know it and probably very few of them."

"We could make the wolves forget us," Sean said, smiling. "Great, only I don't have any fae friends, do you?"

"What about Elin?" Innes said, smiling from ear to ear. "Did you forget her?"

Sean's back teeth ground together. "Elin is Deseran, like Leigh." He looked from man to man, and they had to see he didn't intend to say more.

"Sally, then?" Campion said, looking away.

"Possibly," Sean said. Keeping your own counsel could be a good thing and he was not certain about Sally yet.

*   *   *

Little more than another hour passed before the light faded enough for them to start their journey. With the aid of a chart drawn in the sand, Sean had designed their approach and attack. They had traded ideas about how long to observe the wolves before closing in and how to prepare for any enemy fighters who turned up late to the event.

"We're ready then," Sean said. "Remember, the Verbols don't tolerate air inside their bodies."

"Which may make knives even more valuable," Renny said tonelessly.

*   *   *

The moon was high when Sean finally saw a break in the forest ahead. *"Water tower due north, forest to the south, and I already think I see where a clearing could be,"* he reported to the group, none of whom he could actually see. *"Do not attack until I give the word. Take them out as the opportunity presents. Surprise is on our side, twice over. They aren't expecting us, and they would never expect us as fully human. If Quitus is there, you'll know who he is. Leave him to me."*

He landed in the crown of a fir at the edge of the clearing and didn't have to check to know the others would be similarly placed but carefully hidden.

*"I see the mound but no movement,"* he said.

*"Ditto."* It was Simon who answered and silence from the others meant they concurred.

The silence continued, but werehounds were patient.

A breeze picked up, rocking the limbs around the one where Sean had settled.

And time clicked by—and by.

*"Dead center,"* Innes hissed. *"Damn, it's just Verbols."*

*"Don't take them lightly,"* Sean said. *"Saul said they're vicious, and they shift. And you don't know what they're shifting into next. I'm waiting for Brande and his bunch."*

Two Verbols crawled from underground and went to the mound, where they disappeared through an opening that instantly closed.

*"How about a decoy?"* Innes said. *"I shift, land, draw 'em out or not. If they don't come for me, they aren't there. But you can all start down to get closer."*

Sean didn't like it. *"Two Verbols might be able to take you before we could do anything. We can't be sure of their capabilities. We could land on your bloodied bones, brother.*

*"Good idea, though. Stay with the others this time. I've been close to these Verbols before. The rest of you, do as Innes suggests. Start down and watch. Blink for too long and that could make the difference. If something bad happens to me, ask Niles for orders."*

There were no arguments, and if there had been, Sean wasn't waiting for them. The only alteration he made in Innes's decoy plan was to remain purely a man.

He landed softly. From this angle he could see where the turf was flattened around an oblong area. The Verbols had come from beneath this. How many of them there were, he didn't know. Fleet, adrenalin pumping, he sprinted to the grassy trapdoor and threw it open.

Before he could see the entire rough hollow beneath, his knife was free of its sheath. *"I think I know how this is going to go,"* he told the rest of them. *"Brande's bunch can be relied on to duck out when the going gets too hairy for them. But keep coming. We still have the Verbols to deal with."*

To his other leg he had strapped a smooth, strong piece of wood he had sharpened at one end. Sean lifted his shirt and shoved the stake through his belt.

Without pausing, he approached the mound and stopped a few feet from the disguised entrance. *"I need you with me,"* he said shortly, feeling the other minds open to his.

There was no need to check that the Team was getting into position.

He felt around gently until he found the edge of the flap and threw it back.

Boldly, Sean walked in, surprised by how light it was inside the semicircular structure.

He counted quickly, accounting for the way the Verbols tried to hide, one behind the other. Only four of them. Their voices were squeaky and whatever they said made no sense.

"I thought you'd come." Cross-legged on the bare earth, his back against a wall, sat Quitus. Tonight his robes were not a flamboyant color. Light gray, shiny, and voluminous, they hung from thin shoulders. Predictably he wore a hood and it hid his face.

"What do you want?" Quitus said. "Are you tired of your miserable little life? How would you like me to put an end to all of your friends? You, I intend to keep, and if you will do as I ask, I may save the others."

"You're foolish," Sean said, looking into every shadowy corner.

Quitus gave an unpleasant chuckle. "Come out, my friends."

Sean held his ground but he reached out to the rest of the Team. *"Get close to the entrance. All of you. One shout from me and you rush this place."*

Three more Verbols emerged from beneath a table draped with a long, white cloth and covered with bottles and jars, burners, crucibles, pestles and mortars. It was a small but complete-looking laboratory. One flaming burner kept the contents of a vessel bubbling and Sean decided the acrid scents that reached him came from this. There was no doubt that those contents were a familiar dark red.

One of the creatures went close to Quitus and launched into a stream of noises, waving his big hands between pointing at Sean.

"Where is the pack?" Sean said. "Brande and his pack?"

"Don't know what you're talking about," Quitus said. He returned his attention to the Verbol. "This is a werehound. Like our werewolf friends, he is human when he wishes to be and we can assume he comes in peace since he chooses to be a weakling in front of us."

"Like your werewolf friends—the ones you know nothing about?" Sean sighed. "I repeat, where are the wolves?" He edged closer to the robed figure but stopped when all seven Verbols fell silent and watched him with their colorless eyes. They closed in around Quitus.

"Brande and I decided I am very capable of looking after myself. He took his pack elsewhere."

"You mean they had enough of a fright when they came for me at the cottage to make them run away when they discovered I was after them again," Sean said, curling his lip. "I'm hoping you and I can talk alone, Quitus. Perhaps we can help one another."

The stake was hard-edged against his belly. He still found it hard to believe the wolves had made a run for it, and he couldn't afford to believe it until he was sure.

A harsh ripping sound from behind him had to be the entrance to the mound being torn away. Sean kept his eyes on Quitus and the Verbols. Quitus remained in his hunched position but the Verbols edged apart, stretching open their wide mouths to reveal what must be the filter that excluded air.

He hadn't shouted for the rest and wanted to look behind him. But his turning around could be the opportunity they hoped for. If it was the wolves who came, or more Verbols, he was finished anyway, but he didn't believe the wolves could get past his Team.

The Verbols spread out in a semicircle. They hopped rapidly from foot to foot and raised their arms, revealing claws that curved from the ends of formless bunches of sinew.

"We're with you." It was Campion to his right and Innes had appeared on his left.

The Verbols set up a hollering shriek and began to spit. The thin moisture hit Innes's forearm and he sucked in a breath. "Their saliva burns," he said. "Be careful."

But the Team had no choice but to advance.

Sean felt his band fall in around him, knives drawn.

"Watch their weapons," Quitus cried. "Do not allow them to pierce you."

But pierce them they did, and with the first sinking of a knife into one of the Verbols' throats, there was a loud rattle, like a snake, and the creature folded over. He fell lifeless and the rest of his kind drew back, babbling to one another.

The fight seemed too easy. Quitus didn't move from his position on the floor but watched the scene with a smile.

Wherever one of the Verbols landed a stream of spittle, or a claw, burns spread over the werehounds' skin, but each man kept advancing and ignored the painful welts.

Three of the Verbols fell.

"Let's finish this," Sean shouted.

Before any of the werehounds could attack again, the remaining Verbols fled into crevices at the back of the cave and disappeared.

Sean stood in front of Quitus and worked the stake free of his belt. "Your time has come," he said. "You've already done more than enough harm." Using both of his hands, he raised the stake above his head and started to bring it down with all the force in his strong arms.

Laughter rang out. It rose and Quitus rolled forward over his knees, wracked with mirth. "This is too good," he managed to get out between gusts of chuckles. "Don't you see who has joined your band of warriors."

Frowning, Sean paused and glanced quickly around him. The Team was just as he was used to seeing them.

"The gang's all here," Quitus spat out and laughed some more. "Welcome, Niles and Ethan. Good of you to leave the lovely Deseran ladies alone."

"Niles?" Sean said, noticing him and Ethan for the first time. "You left Elin ... and Leigh?"

"You called for us," Niles said, his feet braced and the curved knife cocked and ready to slice off the living vampire's head.

"No," Sean said. "No, I didn't."

"Just a detail," Quitus chortled. "Someone called for them and they came. They left the women at that place, what is it? Gabriel's. But only I have the power to stop them all from dying. So drive in your stake, cut off my head, burn my bones, but be prepared to bury the lifeless bodies of the ones you so-called *love*. Pathetic."

*"My God,"* Niles said, moving into mindspeak. *"The message was clear. We didn't question it. We have to keep this thing alive in case we need him."*

Quitus shrieked with laughter. "I've won," he said. "I'll have everything I want."

He threw back his hood, revealing a bald skull from which sparse tufts of white hair sprouted. His eyes were so shrunken they showed only as pinpoints of light. The flesh on his face, yellowed and creviced, clung to protruding bone.

He bounced up and down but quickly grew short of breath. He panted. "I need to eat. We must go to that Gabriel's Place at once."

An abrupt swelling of his head and body shocked the

hounds into taking a step backward. All except Sean, who stood his ground and watched Aldo take shape, his dark hair clipped into its usual helmet shape, his lipless mouth stretched wide, showing pointed teeth. "First you and I must share an interlude," he said, pointing at Sean. "We can't take long. This one who has absorbed me weighs me down. The faster we get what he needs, the better. Niles is to remain but the others should go into the clearing. If they make a move to attack, all of you are finished. Most particularly, your women are history. They are being watched. One word from me and...Need I tell you more?"

*"Niles, I don't even know what it is he wants from me. Could be to bite me again. But I think we can use the weakness of the other one—Quitus—to put that off."*

*"By taking him to Gabriel's? He intends to start ripping organs out of someone."*

*"I know, we have to buy time but this will be dangerous. Let me talk this through,"* Sean said. *"Shall we send Innes and Campion ahead to Gabriel's? At least they could give Leigh and Elin some hope."*

*"I'm hoping Saul keeps his word,"* Niles said. *"He has told me he will keep watch, but in his own way—not that I ever know what that means. I don't feel confident about it. Go ahead and send Innes and Campion."*

Sean hoped he looked as relaxed as he intended. "We know when we don't have the upper hand. What happens if Quitus dies on you, Aldo? Trust us enough to tell us what we should expect. Will whatever is left of him slow us down? Will he affect your mind? Will you die with him?"

The pause that followed was more than Sean could have hoped for. Aldo shuddered and bowed his head for a moment. "We will do this my way," he said, bravado dripping from every word. "I've decided to feed Quitus before you and I deal with our business."

*chapter* **THIRTY-FIVE**

Elin and Leigh tried to behave as if they didn't suspect anything was seriously wrong. They had been assured by one of the twins—as soon as they were left alone by Niles—that they were being watched, and if they tried to leave, or contact anyone, it would be disastrous—for all of them.

Gabriel's Place was closed. No fire burned in the fireplace. Slumped in a chair in a dark corner, Gabriel himself had been a surprise when Elin noticed him. He had remained there, his eyes closed, and had yet to say a word.

When the twins had let Elin and Leigh in, they said Cliff was in the kitchen and Saul was on his way with Phoebe. Niles and Ethan were relieved and took off immediately.

Cliff wasn't there and Saul didn't come.

The twins, visibly shaken, had refused to answer any questions. They had gone to the kitchens and closed the door, apparently following orders. Whose orders, the women didn't know. They had both attempted, unsuccessfully, to communicate with their mates.

Pokey and Jazzy set about a methodical sniffing of every inch of the place and they kept at it. Neither Leigh nor Elin made any comment about the behavior.

"I should see what I can get done in the office," Leigh said, her face strained. "I hope Cliff and Sally get here before opening time."

In other words, Leigh was sure they were overheard by someone they couldn't see. The sniffing animals suggested the same thing.

"You should sit down and have a glass of juice or something," Elin said. She didn't want to be left alone or to have Leigh alone somewhere, either.

Leigh got the message. "I'll have apple juice," she said. "I should probably wake Gabriel up from his nap, too. It isn't like him to allow the fire to go out."

"He's had such a hard time worrying about Molly." Elin wanted to sound normal but she was frightened. "I'm worried about him. I'll get the fire going first."

She piled up kindling and set it alight before putting a couple of logs on top. And with every passing second she longed to hear Sean's voice. She kept her mind as open as she knew how in hopes that he would contact her that way.

Even the sight of flames curling up the chimney didn't make her feel better. She pulled a chair close and waved Leigh to sit down. Jazzy promptly jumped on her lap but she didn't settle down.

Hotter than was comfortable, Elin dragged off her parka, then her sweater. Her hands went to her waist.

"What is it?" Leigh said.

"I'm surprised to feel warm," she said, avoiding Leigh's real question. Sally's scarf with the wand and green inside was still at the cottage. Not that they were likely to be of much help if everything went sideways here and Elin didn't feel good about the atmosphere.

\* \* \*

But she did feel warm, even as she moved away from the fire. Or she felt normal, for her. She couldn't dwell on whether Tarhazian had relented on at least that element of her punishment or if the Queen's power over her was fading.

Every few moments Elin glanced at Gabriel, willing him to wake up and help dispel the growing sense of doom. Something awful was coming.

She knelt beside Leigh and could hardly hold back tears. "Will Sean and Niles be all right?" she whispered. "They didn't know it was like this here. I don't understand it. What if we left?"

Leigh put an arm around her. "Hang on. If we try to go, we may start an attack on us. What we can't see, we can't fight, but I have faith in our men. Don't forget we're probably being watched."

Pokey crawled up Elin's back and settled on her shoulder. She made bleating sounds as if sympathizing.

"Okay. Juice coming up, then I'll see what I can do for Gabriel."

Elin went behind the bar with Pokey still clinging to her neck.

Scuffling came from the corridor to the office and the new extension to the building.

Leigh shot to her feet. "Come here," she cried to Elin. "Stay with me."

Before Elin could move, Cassie and her brother, David, all but fell into sight.

They were both disheveled and drawn, their dark hair matted, as it had been the last time Elin saw either of them. She smiled. "Thank goodness you're okay. Who took you? We didn't know what had happened to you— or Sally."

The pair stood, back-to-back, keeping Elin and Leigh in sight.

Elin frowned. "What is it?"

Staring at her, Cassie's throat worked but she didn't say anything.

"There's a man over there," David cried, indicating Gabriel, still collapsed in his chair. "Who is he?"

"Hush," his sister said. "I think he's already dead."

Elin didn't like the *already dead* comment. She didn't think Gabriel was other than comatose at the most, but Cassie sounded as if she was expecting some sudden deaths.

The front doors swung wide. Freezing air, fir needles that crackled dry along the floor, and swirls of grit blew into the big room, accompanied by Innes and Campion.

Elin almost fainted with relief. "We don't know what's going on," she said.

Rather than offer comforting words, Innes and Campion smiled tightly but remained silent while Leigh ran to Elin and the two women huddled together.

The two werehounds searched the room visually. Both of them were obviously surprised to see Gabriel. They made no comment about him, or about Cassie and David.

"Can we leave?" Leigh asked.

Innes smiled at her again and said, "Be patient."

"I can't do this," Cassie said suddenly. "These people thought they were saving us and they took us off The Island for our sake, or so they thought. They didn't do it for themselves."

"Quiet, Cassie," David begged. "We can't fight Quitus and Aldo."

Elin felt the weight of hopelessness settle on her. They were all betrayed.

"What do you think they're going to do with us?" Cassie said.

"They'll send us back to the Embran just to make points," David said.

Elin could scarcely catch her breath. Who did they mean were controlling them? Jude had mentioned the Embran and how the Verbols were related to them. "Why would they send you to the Embran?"

"Because that's where we escaped from," Cassie said. "We were Embran slaves and we hated everything they stood for. We wanted to live on Earth again and leave the other world behind us. But Aldo captured us and he knew he could use us to get things he wanted from the Embran. They will always want to get us back and punish us."

David hung his head but nodded from time to time.

"I want to sit down," Leigh said quietly to Elin. "If

they stop me, they stop me, but I'm going over there."

With Elin holding tightly to her arm, Leigh made for a chair not far from Cassie and David. They didn't attempt to stop the two women and Leigh sat down. Elin pulled another chair beside Leigh and joined her.

She tried to reach Sean's mind again but met another wall of silence.

"We're going to take Leigh and Elin out of here," Innes said. "I don't see anyone who can try to stop us."

At the same moment as Elin started to hope, that hope was crushed.

Quitus, the hateful creature she had seen in the mountain cave, came through the door of Gabriel's. Tonight he was covered from head to foot in gray.

Elin hadn't forgotten the Verbols in Quitus's mountain. One of them stood at the left hand of the man in gray. Niles and Sean stood on his other side. She wanted to run to Sean but knew better.

*"Sean?"* She tried to reach him with her mind and figured Leigh would be doing the same with Niles.

*"I hear you,"* Sean said. *"We're in uncharted waters but we're ready. Watch and wait and do nothing unless we tell you."*

Quitus pointed at Cassie. "You're doing well. You may yet live to return to your Embran roots."

Cassie behaved as if she hadn't heard Quitus. David seemed frozen with fear.

"Bring that one here," Quitus said, indicating Elin. "I need to use her. Make sure she doesn't struggle."

Sean sprang in front of Quitus. "You fool, do you think I'll allow you to hurt Elin?"

Elin felt safer until Cliff, with Sally by an arm behind her back, edged into the bar. Sally showed no emotion but Cliff's face was creased with triumph. He held a hand aloft, brandishing a small cylindrical object. "I am the keeper of The Bloodstone for Quitus," he cried. "If you hounds and your people had stayed out of the way, my partners would not have had to confront you. But you had to interfere. Don't move until I tell you what to do."

He sneered around for the benefit of his audience. "Worms always turn. Didn't anyone tell you that? Did you think I would be happy as the invisible cook forever? Rose learned better, and Molly—and others who have died without you knowing anything about them."

Elin stared at Cliff. She had never seen any sign that the man was other than human. If that was true, he didn't have the advantage he believed he did.

Quitus gave a high shriek of pleasure. He looked sick and triumphant at the same time.

Still in her yellow silk outfit, Sally didn't struggle, even when Cliff shoved her head to one side and held The Bloodstone inches from her neck.

"Don't." Cassie threw herself toward Cliff. "Stop it now. We'll help you to get out of this, but stop what you're doing now."

Cliff tripped Cassie, and her brother after her, so they fell beside Sally. "You will all get your decorations, too," he said, his voice singsong and unhinged sounding.

The body of Quitus shuddered and faded, replaced by Aldo, who shook with rage. "That's enough. No more resistance from any of you. You are all dead and I am the leader here."

Elin held Leigh's hand and kept her eyes on Sean.

Quitus took Aldo's place again, even paler and more sunken this time.

"You never can trust a vampire," a familiar gravelly voice said, the instant Gabriel catapulted from his chair and took Cliff down with the kind of tackle he had probably used a thousand times on the football field. "You can't get me with that blood thing twice. Saul knows that. Elin saved me the first time." He held Cliff's hand and his deadly cylinder above his head. "It won't work on you either, Cassie."

"But Quitus made me his proxy," Cliff screamed. "The only way any of you will survive is if you do what I tell you. You're all going to grovel to me."

Sean and Niles moved as one and took hold of Quitus's arms. They held him down. "We're going to send you home," Sean said. "Wherever that is."

"Give her to me," Quitus gasped. "The dark-haired one. She can save me. I have to eat and I need the fae."

His face an expressionless mask, Sean took Quitus's scrawny neck in one hand and snapped it. Hauling the creature onto his back, Sean drove the stake into Quitus's heart.

"Leave the rest to me," Niles said. He dragged the corpse outside and slammed the doors behind him.

Pulling Leigh with her, Elin flew at Sean, who embraced them both but put them quickly aside. "We aren't done yet," he said, nodding toward the still writing Cliff.

"Surely you'll allow me some little part in this," a silvery voice said, echoing across the room. "After all,

I... well, I'm not at all to blame, of course, but I want to feel the love again."

If she hadn't been so shaken, Elin would have laughed at the sight of Tarhazian materializing, an almost repentant cast to her features.

"Sally," the Queen said. "Your friends miss you. I would like to take you back. I forgive you."

"Thanks a bunch," Sally said. "I don't want to leave my friends here, either."

Tarhazian sucked in her lips. She scarcely took her eyes from Elin. "I understand," she said with a lot of pained effort. "In that case, I give you my permission to pass back and forth between the worlds."

Sally's mouth fell open but she had the sense not to say anything else.

"I'm going to take you and Elin back with me now. It's time for you to be with your own people, both of you."

"Elin is with her people," Sean said. He hugged his mate to him. "But we may let you visit... if you behave yourself."

Tarhazian's eyes narrowed, but a grudging smile transformed her beautiful face. "We shall see," she said. "We shall see."

Taking an open space in the bar, she spread her arms and uttered words no mere mortal, or part mortal, understood.

Floating, Aldo appeared above them, dressed once more in the scarlet robes of mountain fame. He hovered, soundless.

"A gift," Tarhazian cried. "For those Embran who wait for justice in their world. These are the ones you're waiting for. They stole slaves who are no longer of use to you. You will decide how Aldo and his servant are to be dealt with."

Aldo's mouth opened and closed. Horror filmed his eyes, but they grew startled as Cliff was sucked from the ground and thrown into his arms.

They fragmented and dissolved from sight.

Cassie and David sat down suddenly, as if relief had left them weak.

Tarhazian grew farther away, smiling all the time, until she was gone. She left Sally behind.

"You are loved, Elin." The Queen's voice floated back but Elin decided she was the only one who heard it.

## chapter THIRTY-SIX

Does everything seem strange to you?" Elin said, holding Sean's right palm to her cheek.

"Because we're here in the cottage again and you thought we'd both be dead by now?"

He gave her a smile guaranteed to melt her bones but she wasn't ready to smile back yet.

Sean knew the signs of delayed panic and he saw them in Elin now. The hands that held his shook. "I never gave up hope," she told him, meeting his eyes. No one had eyes the violet color of Elin's. "But everything seemed stacked against us."

He could watch the expressions cross her face forever. "I promised to keep you safe."

She frowned. "And you believe in things being possible," she said, tilting her head. "I believe what you tell me but I still start to doubt when other people seem so sure of themselves. I don't want to be afraid anymore."

When Sean looked at her, he appeared fascinated and completely absorbed. She owed it to him to learn something about being confident. "I'm not afraid when I'm with you," she added in a small voice. "I don't want you to think that."

"When you stop telling me what you're thinking and feeling—that's when I'll worry." He brought his mouth to hers and she saw his eyes close.

The kiss was tender, gentle, and there came that word again—confident. Sean was confident of her.

"You know you've got all of me, don't you?" she blurted out and immediately rested her forehead on his chin. "That didn't sound right. You do have all of me and you know it."

Sean's laughter rumbled. She could feel it vibrate from deep in his chest and spread into her own body.

"Messed it up again," she said. "I'm just going to keep my mouth shut, then I won't embarrass myself."

"Promise?"

He expected the swat she landed on his shoulder. "I said I wanted to come here," she said. "Is that okay with you or would you rather go to your house?"

"That didn't last long," he said.

"What?"

"You. Keeping your mouth shut." He braced for another swat but she slid her arms around him and held on.

"My house is your house, Elin," he told her. "Remember?"

She nodded and seemed a little more relaxed. If she went to sleep now, he didn't think he could stand the disappointment.

"Everyone looked so tired when they left Gabriel's,"

she said. "Saul was funny, waiting outside against the wall as if nothing had gone on inside."

"Odd guy," Sean said. "I've got a feeling we know him as well as we're ever going to. But he's there for us, I believe that."

Elin's chin rose. "And we're there for him, right?" The flash in her eyes warned him she would only accept the affirmative.

"You're right about that."

"So are you okay about us being here while we rest up?" she said tentatively.

"Absolutely, but it's cold in here, I'd better get the fires going."

"I'm not cold," she told him, feeling a bit cheeky. "Why not let me keep you warm."

He bowed his head to look into her eyes. "Are you propositioning me?"

Taking hold of his sleeves, she swung back and forth. "Could be."

"My lucky night," he said and kissed her cheek. "How come you aren't cold?"

"That's all cleared up," she said, keeping her eyes down. "I think it's a gift from Tarhazian. When I feel like it, I'll check myself out for anything else she may have messed with. I don't feel like it now."

"Do you need to go to sleep for a while?"

Elin pursed her lips and studied him. "Let me consider that? If you want to go to sleep for a while, I'll absolutely understand."

The corners of his mouth quivered. "And if I don't want to sleep?"

"Why don't you come up to the loft and let me show you?" She led the way to the ladder. "Heat rises, doesn't it. Whatever warmth is left in the cottage will have gone to the loft. Makes sense to go up there. I can wrap you in our quilt and help you warm up even more."

She started up the steps and made it to the fourth one before Sean grabbed one of her ankles. "I never had you pegged for a tease, but I must have missed it earlier."

Elin tried to jerk her leg away, to no avail. And she squealed when he pushed his head between her legs and settled her on his shoulders. She hung on to his hair while he ran up to the loft.

"Are you trying to kill us both?" she said, out of breath from giggling.

"I'm a leader, not a follower, girl. Other people tried killing us tonight—no more of that stuff. Take off your clothes."

He stood her on the bed and moved away, his fists on his hips. Since he could tell that the sum of her clothing was the current pretty piece of clingy silk, he figured it wouldn't take much to get rid of it.

Elin crossed her arms. She was so excited her nerves jumped, her heart jumped, and she couldn't catch her breath. She ached in the best places to ache.

"Well?" Sean said. Free of its band again, his dark blond hair fell to his shoulders, and in the gloomy loft, his eyes turned into a golden warning.

She panted. "Don't look at me like that," she said.

"Like what?"

"As if you're planning to eat me." She slapped a hand

over her mouth and a muffled, "I didn't mean it that way," came out.

Sean stripped off his shirt, never looking away from her, and managed to get rid of the rest of his clothes, too. "I hope you did mean it that way because that's exactly what I aim to do. Eat you. Little piece by little piece."

"You have no shame," she said, studying him from head to foot. "There you stand, naked as the day you were born, and you aren't a bit ashamed."

Advancing, he slid his hands beneath her arms but spread his long fingers and settled the pads of his thumbs on her erect nipples. "Is there something I should be ashamed of?" He glanced down at himself. "Is there somewhere I come up short?"

Elin cut off her own little shriek of laughter and cleared her throat. "Not in a single place. There's nothing about you that could possibly be called short." She closed her eyes and her knees sagged. With only a touch—or two—he knew exactly how to arouse her until she hovered on the edge of climax.

"Off with this," Sean said, shimmying the dress over Elin's head.

She held his shoulder and stepped out of her panties.

Holding her to him, he massaged her spine and buttocks, the backs of her thighs, and she curled over his shoulder, rubbed her breasts against him, took little nips at his skin.

He straightened and her feet left the bed. The shin she ran across his pelvis connected with a solid erection. "I want you," she muttered.

One heft and she was over his shoulder in a fireman's lift.

"Hey," she cried. "What are you doing? That's not fair. I can't reach anything."

That brought laughter from Sean but it quickly faded and she was eased beneath the quilt and joined by her only love, the only man she had ever wanted or would ever want.

"Now you can reach anything that appeals to you," he said, pulling the quilt over them. "Would it be okay if I talked just a little bit? Right now? I know you're not supposed to talk too much at moments like this, but—"

"Moments like what?" She wrapped herself around him and held on.

"When all you really want—that means both of us—is to make love."

"Get on with it," she said. "Talk."

"Damn, I love you, Elin."

He heard her swallow and felt the way her body turned soft and pliable in his arms. "And I love you," she said. "I used to wonder what it would feel like to love. You know, to love a man this way. It makes me want to laugh and cry at once. I can't believe it. You make me into a whole person and I didn't even know I wasn't already."

"I was looking for you," he told her. "Not searching around, looking at every woman I saw with that in mind. But I was lonely. Deep inside lonely. After we met, I don't think I ever doubted we'd be together."

"I know." She sounded funny.

"What is it?"

"You let me know you'd choose me over anything or

anyone else. Even when I was a deceitful pain, you didn't want to give up on me."

Sean turned on his back and pulled her on top of him. He spread his legs and nestled their bodies together while Elin looped her arms around his neck.

"I didn't tell you everything. I was afraid to. But once I had, I knew how stupid I'd been to worry about it. Hey." He jiggled her until she raised her head. "Do you want me to build you a cottage like this? I think I could."

"This is a special place. It was our first place. There's nothing wrong with your house—our house. Or there won't be when I've finished with it."

Sean hardly had to move at all to take their minds off where they should live.

*epilogue*

Summer had come and gone. The days were short again but Elin still felt the urge to walk in the darkness along the pebble beach that stretched for miles on the Saratoga Passage side of Whidbey.

In the distance, on the other side of the Passage, a few lights winked on Camano Island.

In their heads and hearts, the island's paranormal communities waited, without discussion, for some other attack from malicious forces. But they only grew more determined to prevail.

Tonight the moon sat on a thin rim and the stars turned the sky into a black bowl of diamonds.

"Piggyback?" Sean said, breaking a long silence.

Elin chuckled and leaned against him. "What do you think?" She loved to ride on his back with her face against his neck and jaw.

Sean ducked, she grabbed his shoulders, and he hiked

her up, his big hands grasping the backs of her bare thighs beneath her dress.

His shoes scrunched over the tumble of rocks.

The surf rippled insistently at the shore and the scent of the water traveled on a breeze.

"You love it down here, don't you?" Sean said.

"Mmm."

"It's not just a habit for you, Elin, I can tell that. For the past week or so it's been as if you've been waiting for evening because that's when you most like to get down here."

She blew softly in his ear and felt him smile. "You understand me too well, my mate. I feel pulled here. At first I didn't know why, now I think I do. I think it's the chimney under the water. Inside myself I'm waiting for it to show me something." Her kiss on his neck had the predictable result—he shuddered as if she had tickled him. "Now I've said it out loud, nothing will happen. All your fault."

"Hah! No way, girl. What will be will be. If any two people should know that, it's you and me."

Rubbing her cheek against his hair where it fell free in the wind, she let the silence sink in again.

They crunched on around a small point to where the beach straightened a little. In the distance, the lights glowed at Niles and Leigh's place.

"Gabriel seems better," Sean said. "I don't think he'll be in a hurry to meet someone else after Molly, but he looks more peaceful."

"Yes...Sean!" She caught her breath. "You can see that, you have to."

He stopped walking and looked at the sky. "What was it, a shooting star?"

"No, *that*, the pink and gold arc. It's coming out of the water. See?" She pointed to where a streak of brilliance shot upward then began to arch over. "Where is it going?"

"Sweetheart," Sean said gently. "I can't see a thing like that. You'll just have to tell me about it. Any of that useful green stuff? We should stockpile some of that—even if you are the only one who can see and use it."

Elin almost stopped breathing. She wiggled down from Sean's back. "It's going into Leigh and Niles's house," she said, jumping along sideways, pulling him by the hand. "I never saw gold before. There's pink but there's a dark purple. I don't like the purple."

Sean's eyes were narrowed to glittering slits. "You think it means something bad."

"Not really bad. It just makes me edgy. Come on."

He laughed. "We can't just drop in on them when we feel like."

"Come on," Elin insisted. "I need to be with my Deseran sister."

She started to run, slipping and sliding as she went. Sean ran, too, but faster. He hauled her along behind him. "I believe you," he said, anxiety in his voice. "But I hope we're both wrong."

They scrambled up the steps to the top of the concrete bulkheads where the Latimers' house had been built.

At the door, they both stopped, panting.

"They're having a quiet night at home," Sean said but Elin could hear his uncertainty.

"The worst that could happen is they invite us in—or tell us to get lost."

Elin hammered on the door. "I don't care anymore." She glanced nervously at the ethereal arc coming from the sea and connecting with the roof of the house.

Seconds passed. Sean gave Elin's hand a pull to suggest they leave, when the door opened a crack.

Leigh, on her knees, had opened it for them, then she sank to sit, huddled over. "The baby," she whispered.

Without a word, Sean swept her up into his arms and headed into the house.

"Where's Niles?" Elin said.

When Leigh didn't answer, Sean said, "She's having a rush—a contraction. This is heavy. Let her get her breath. Hush, hush, hold on to me tight. Dig your fingers in. It'll help."

He headed toward the bedroom but Leigh said, "The bath. I can't lie down."

Sean changed course and Elin ran ahead to fill the tub with warm water. "Is that right?" she asked Sean.

"Yeah. Do you want to wear a nightie in there, Leigh?"

She shook her head. "No. Nothing."

She made ineffectual efforts to help them undress her.

"Sent Niles to get Sally," Leigh whispered. "She's not answering. I said I didn't want Saul."

Sean raised his brows at Elin.

"Niles . . . he's not comfortable with Saul and this is . . . I want it perfect for him. The baby won't come for a long time."

Sean lowered her carefully into the water and kept an

arm around her shoulders. "How long have you been in labor?" he asked quietly.

"Only a few hours. First babies take a long time."

Moved to tears, Elin kissed Leigh's belly, then her face, and Leigh turned blindly to kiss Elin's cheek.

"I had candles and things ready," Leigh panted, and clamped her teeth together. The water running on her face was a mix of bathwater and sweat.

"We'll use the candles soon," Elin said.

"How does the water feel?" Sean asked. With his free hand, he rubbed her back hard.

"Good," she said, but her face was contorted. "It feels right." She raised a hand and ran it through the air.

Elin smiled. "She's feeling our colors."

Another twenty minutes and they heard someone crashing into the house. "Leigh?" Niles yelled. "I'm home."

"In the bathroom," Sean called. "She's doing fine."

He made Elin want to hug him. How could anyone feel unsure or unsafe with a man like him? He would always do whatever he did well.

Niles entered the bathroom and took in the scene. "Thank you," he said. "Sally's gone to friends—that's what Gabriel says. I tried to call Saul but he isn't answering."

"We have everything we need," Leigh breathed. "I think I want to come out of the water."

Immediately, Sean stepped aside, and while Niles lifted his mate, Elin threw a huge white towel over her.

Niles took Leigh to the bedroom and this time she didn't complain, until he tried to lay her down.

"Let her sit on the end of the bed," Sean said. "Are you okay with me taking a look—both of you?"

Sliding behind Leigh on the bed, Niles said, "Of course we are." He leaned against her back and she pushed into him.

Sean took Elin with him to the floor.

"Is it burning?" Sean asked.

"I think I see the head," Elin said.

"Burning," Leigh moaned. "I want to push."

With Niles holding her, she pushed and the baby's head crowned fast. "It's coming," Elin said, scarcely able to take a breath.

"Push again," Sean said. "Niles, kiss your mate. Really kiss her."

For an instant Elin thought Niles might refuse but he looked into Leigh's upturned face and kissed her, gently at first, then with mounting passion.

And the baby's head was born.

Elin felt jumpy. "We have to catch him," she said, holding out her hands.

"We'll catch him," Sean said.

"How do you know all this?" she muttered.

"Son of a sawbones," he said shortly and grinned at her. "He taught me everything I know."

The infant moved down a little more then seemed to stop.

Leigh cried out and Sean squeezed her thighs hard. "Hold back just a minute."

His face showed nothing of what he was thinking. Elin saw the cord and it was loose with no sign of being caught up.

"Push," Sean said and his very good patient did as she was told.

But the baby didn't make any progress. "Sean?" Niles said but got only a quick shake of the head in response.

"Everything's great, Leigh. Elin and I will help this little soul the rest of the way."

Elin got the sensation that she'd moved away from herself. What she needed to do, what he quietly guided her to do, she would manage well. He let her know that her hands were smaller than his and with mind talk she would never forget, he indicated they would widen Leigh inside.

*"Ready? I will pull the bones farther apart. One shoulder is caught. Yes, the left one. Reach in and ease it out. Babies are strong, all they need is a welcoming committee. There. You have it. See it slip free? A miracle."*

"Quick, Niles," he said. "Your job now, get here."

With the four of them clinging together, tears streaming down their faces, Niles caught his tiny child and Sean moved Leigh to lie down so the little one could be placed on her chest.

"Listen," Niles said while Sean continued to work over Leigh. "Listen to her cry."

Elin watched Sean's face while he laughed and said, "Your daughter has good lungs." And Leigh could only keep on crying and laughing at the same time.

Niles is desperate to prove a man's heart beats within his predator's body. And Leigh—the mysterious beauty possessing powers she doesn't yet understand— may be the one woman who can help him.

Please turn this page for an excerpt from

*Darkness Bound.*

## *chapter* ONE

*W*e're going to highjack this woman, body and soul," Niles Latimer said. *"I feel like crap about it but we don't have a choice—unless we give up and wait to die, one by one."*

Standing in the bed of his truck beside a small stone cottage, he spoke telepathically to his second in command, Sean Black, who was several miles away, leaping through great, dark trees on agile feet. Sean was in his werehound form and at the speed he moved would arrive momentarily.

Niles paused, flexed his shoulders. From behind him he heard the familiar sounds of the powerful animal grazing past branches, using the dense forest as cover to allow him to move freely, hidden from any inconvenient and curious eyes. Even in his human form, Niles wasn't tempted to turn around when Sean arrived—werehounds recognized each other instinctively.

*"We appear to have no choice about the decision we've made,"* Sean mind-tracked. *"Unless, as you say, we scrap this plan completely and accept the inevitable. There's still time for you to leave before she gets here. She doesn't know you, doesn't expect you to be here, so if you pass her on the way out you can say you took a wrong turn."*

Niles understood reverse psychology when he heard it. *"Accept that our numbers will continue to shrink while we cling to the fringes of human society, never allowed to live among them openly, you mean? I'm not ready to do that."* Okay, so he had cold feet about the woman, but they wouldn't get the better of him.

*"We're living among them now,"* Sean said.

*"Carefully,"* Niles said. He looked over the waters of Saratoga Passage sweeping in beneath the bluff where the cottage stood. Wind spun dead leaves and grit into the cold air. He sighed, loving this place, hating that he and his kind could not find peace there. *"We consider every move we make. If they knew what we are we would be forced to leave."*

*"Or stand and fight."*

Niles swallowed a curse. *"Fight the human world we want to be part of? Back to reality, Sean. We are sworn never to harm a human unless they threaten us. Without them we have no hope of getting back our own humanity. We are not like the werewolves—they are animals and they like it that way. We're not the men we were meant to be either, dammit, but we're not giving up, not now. Not ever."*

*"They are too quiet,"* Sean said. *"The wolves. I keep*

*expecting them to interfere with our plans somehow."* On these occasions he wished hounds could hear wolves' thoughts, but they couldn't, just as the wolves couldn't hear them.

*"If they knew our plans, Brande and his pack would have every reason to stop us. We know too much about them. He knows we could make their lives hell."*

*"It's getting late,"* Sean said. *"Are you sure Gabriel gave you the right day for her arrival at Two Chimneys?"* Two Chimneys was the name of the cottage the woman had inherited from her dead husband. She was about to come back for the first time since that death.

Niles rarely noticed fading light. He preferred the darkness and had perfect dark-sight, but he glanced around and wondered if Sean might have a point. *"Gabriel ought to know. He's going to be her new boss. She's supposed to start in his office in the next couple of days and she'll need to settle in here first. Gabriel said she'd come today."*

*"This thing you're doing could blow everything apart,"* Sean said. *"It could totally backfire. What if she goes running for the nearest cop the minute she finds out what you are?"*

*"I'll feel my way. If she isn't receptive to me, we'll forget it—for now. We'd have to anyway."*

*"How will you know if she's receptive?"* There was laughter in Sean's thoughts. *"When she arrives, you say, 'Hi, I'm gonna be your new mate. All the females of my species have died giving birth. I need you—' "*

*"Knock it off, Sean."*

Sean wasn't done yet. *"I need you to have my off-*

*spring, and find more females to do the same thing with other members of my team. We want to restock our ranks. Oh, and we can't be sure you won't die the same way our own females did."*

*"Get back to the rest of the team and bring them up to date,"* Niles said sharply. *"They've got to be on edge. I'll check in later."*

Niles felt Sean close his mind, and heard him go on his way.

A flash of silver caught Niles's attention. A small car passing the cottage on the far side. Leigh Kelly had arrived. He stood absolutely still, his eyes narrowed.

He had waited a long time for this day, this meeting. If this woman knew his plans she wouldn't even get out of her car.

The thought of what lay ahead scared the hell out of him.

\* \* \*

Leigh left the front door of the cottage open to let in fresh air. The little house had been closed up for eighteen months since her husband, Chris, died, and a musty smell inside made her eyes sting.

Or she told herself it was the smell that caused the start of tears.

*Can I do this?* She had thought she could, thought she was ready.

She glanced at the open steps leading up to the sleeping loft and nearly lost it completely. A recollection shouldn't be so clear you could see it. But she could see

Chris climbing down those stairs early in the morning, his dark blond hair mussed, beard shadow clinging to the grooves in his cheeks and the sharp angle of his jaw—and that half-sleepy, half-sexy and all impish smile on his lips.

Leigh shivered and hunched her shoulders. No matter how hard this was at first, she would get past the waves of hurt, even disbelief. She had come too far not to make it all the way back to a full life.

For a few moments she leaned on the doorjamb and made herself take in the main room of the cottage, and the two fireplaces, one on either side. This would be a happy place again. Sure it would take time, but Chris would want her to make it and she would, for both of them.

They had almost two years of wonderful time together before their marriage—only days together after they had married. But she wouldn't wipe out a moment of that time, except for losing him.

Shaking away the memory, Leigh walked inside, dropped her bag, and had started shrugging out of her green down coat when a thud, followed by another, and another, froze her in place. Her dog, Jazzy, still sat on the edge of the cottage porch, unperturbed, even though his head was turned toward the noise. Nothing moved beyond the big front window.

The thudding continued.

Carrying her coat, her heart thundering, Leigh tiptoed into the kitchen to peer through the window over the sink, then the one in the door, covered by a piece of lace curtain held tight at the top and bottom of the glass by lengths of springy wire.

Her stomach made a great revolution. Late afternoon had turned the light muzzy but in front of a wall of firs that was acres deep in places stood a shiny gray truck with a long cab and a businesslike bed piled high with chunks of wood. In that truck bed stood a tall, muscular man in a red plaid shirt who tossed the logs to the ground beside the lean-to woodshed as easily as if they were matchsticks.

Leigh put her coat back on and crossed her arms tightly.

*What was he doing here?*

The door stuck and it took several wrenches to get it open. The ground was muddy from recent rainfall. Crossing her arms again, she kicked off her shoes and stuffed her feet into a pair of green rubber boots by the wall, where they were always kept—beside a larger pair.

Leigh glanced away from Chris's boots at once.

"Afternoon," the man called.

Leigh shaded her eyes with a cold hand and squinted to see him. He was very powerfully built, with dark wavy hair, long and a bit shaggy. The sleeves of the red wool shirt were rolled up. His Levis clung to strong legs, a dark T-shirt showed at the neck of his shirt. She couldn't make out much more.

"What are you doing here?" she said. And she felt vulnerable since he could probably throw her as easily as one of the chunks of wood.

"Well—"

"Are you planning to squat here?" she asked, keeping her voice steady and sharp. "Because if you are you can forget it. This is my place. Get on your way."

She wished she weren't alone and kept herself ready to rush back the way she had come if he threatened her somehow.

"Hey, sorry. I'm just delivering wood like I told Gabriel Jones I would. I meant to do all this before you got here." He had one of those male voices you don't forget. Low, quiet, and confident. And now that he had stopped moving wood an absolute stillness had come over him, a watchfulness. He was taking her measure. "I must have my days mixed up," he added.

That explained it, right? Gabriel had asked this man to bring the wood. "I see." She felt like an idiot, but she couldn't be sure he wasn't trouble and likely to turn on her.

"The shed was full when...the last time I was here." The day she and Chris had left, never to come back together.

"Apparently your stash got borrowed," the man said. He flipped up one corner of his mouth. "With the house empty for so long you probably hosted a few beach bonfires. It's starting to get cold. You'll need this yourself now."

She didn't care about how cold it might get. The man sounded reserved but sure of himself and he made her edgy. He was probably right about the beach fires. Kids from the quiet little town of Langley and the outlying areas needed a way to let off steam and there were worse ways than having beach parties around Chimney Rock Cove.

"I've already stacked some of this by the front door," the man said. "Easier to get it to the fireplaces that way."

She had been too busy forcing herself to go into the cottage at all to notice details.

The man didn't seem threatening—not really. Except for that stillness that didn't feel quite natural. "You sound as if you knew I was coming," she said. Of course he did. He had already said as much.

"You know how things are around here," he responded without looking at her. "Everyone knows everyone else's business, but your new boss, Gabriel, he said you took some sort of office job at the bar. He mentioned it to me when he got me to clean your gutters."

The blood that rushed to her face throbbed. It would look awful, splotchy and bright red around the freckled bits where her skin stayed pale. "Clean the gutters?" she said, and swallowed. "Gabriel thinks of everything."

"I was glad to do it. Niles Latimer—" he hopped down from the back of the truck and wiped his right hand on his jeans, and wiped and wiped, then hesitated and put the hand in his pocket. "I'm in the cabin by the beach." He hooked a thumb over his shoulder. "That way."

Leigh felt his stillness even more strongly. Something restrained by his own will. If he didn't want to hold it back, what then?

A rapid but stealthy current of energy invaded her, touched her in places and ways beyond understanding. She was responding to him. The most subtle yet definite change in light, an intensity, sharpened the lines and shadows of his features.

These things didn't really happen. Fancy had taken over because she was tired and anxious. Strange and fascinating men didn't set out to charm a woman they had only just met—or to possess her. *The presence of danger.* Leigh gave an involuntary shiver.

*Shape up!*

She advanced on him with wobbly determination, only she'd make certain he never knew she was not sure of herself. "I know the place," she told him, shooting out her own hand. "I'm Leigh Kelly." She used to be so confident, at least on the outside. To a fault, some said. The same people might have called her a "smart mouth" and she knew some had.

He glanced at her face with bright blue eyes, lowered that gaze quickly and yanked his hand out again. He wrapped very long, workman's fingers around hers and she winced when her bones ground together. Niles Latimer pulled back as if she had shocked him.

"Nice to meet you." There was no particular accent that she recognized. He cleared his throat. "I'm sorry you lost your husband."

"Are you?" She closed her eyes for an instant. "Forgive me—my social skills are a bit rusty sometimes. Thank you, but Chris has been gone quite a while now and I'm back in the swing of things." She surprised herself by adding, "Wonderful memories can't be so bad."

She followed his gaze to her left hand where her wedding ring still looked new and three embedded diamonds glinted.

Leigh had never considered taking the ring off.

Once more she felt his unwavering attention on her. That was it—he watched her as if she was the only other person in the world and he had to commit her to memory.

And that, she thought, was a ridiculous conclusion on her part. He paid attention when he talked to someone was all. That was polite and probably too rare.

Niles pushed his sleeves higher on the heavily muscled, weather-darkened forearms of a physical man. "Is it all right if I carry on unloading now?"

"Of course," Leigh said. "Thank you. But tell me how much I owe you for the gutters and the firewood." Whether she'd asked for them or not, both things were needed.

"Nothing," he said airily, sweeping wide an arm. "Housewarming present. Rewarming. This tree had to come down and I've already got enough wood for half a dozen winters. Anyway, neighbors look out for neighbors."

Refusing the kindness would sound churlish but it made her feel very uncomfortable to accept. "Um," was all she could think of to say. Leigh felt iron determination under Niles's calm manner, determination and control drawn as tight as a loaded crossbow. It didn't make her comfortable.

He laughed and it suited him—and made her smile. "I reckon I scared you. That was dumb. I should have thought of that possibility and come to the door to introduce myself," he said. "Sorry about that. But let me get back to unloading. Then I'll stack it."

"Oh, no." She shook her head. "No such thing. Leave it on the ground and I'll do it. I'm tougher than I look and I need the exercise."

"Stacking wood is a man's job," he said, showing no sign of realizing his own reminder that she was alone now. "You'll have plenty to do giving the house a good clean."

She dithered but said, "Well, thank you, then." At another time she would have told him a woman could stack wood perfectly well. Today she didn't mind having a man do something for her.

She only glanced over her shoulder once on her way back and he was already making the first layer of wood in the lean-to. Gabriel would never send anyone untrustworthy, and Leigh decided she liked having Niles there, doing ordinary things and making the place feel less empty.

# THE DISH

### *Where Authors Give You the Inside Scoop*

### *From the desk of Vicky Dreiling*

Dear Reader,

Some characters demand center stage. Like Andrew Carrington, the Earl of Bellingham, known as Bell to his friends. Bellingham first walked on stage as a minor character in my third historical romance *How to Ravish a Rake*. I had not planned him, but from the moment he spoke, I knew he would have his own book because of his incredible charisma. He also had the starring role in the e-novella *A Season for Sin*. As I began to write the e-novella, I realized that it was almost effortless. Frankly, I was and still am infatuated with him. That makes me laugh, because he is a figment of my imagination, but from the beginning, I could not ignore his strong presence.

After *A Season for Sin* was published, I started writing the full-length book WHAT A WICKED EARL WANTS so that Bell could have the happily ever after he richly deserved. A chance encounter brings Bellingham and the heroine, Laura, together. Bellingham is a rake who hopes to make a conquest of her, but despite their attraction, there are major obstacles. Laura is a respectable widow, mother, and daughter of a vicar. Bellingham only wants a temporary liaison, but he finds himself rescuing the lovely lady. His offer of help leads him down a path he never could have imagined.

I've dreamed about my characters previously, but my dreams about Bell and Laura were so vivid that I woke up repeatedly during the writing of WHAT A WICKED EARL WANTS. Usually when I dream about my books in progress, I only see the characters momentarily. But when I dreamed about Bell and Laura, entire scenes played themselves in my head, DVD style, and sometimes a few of them in a night. While I didn't get up in the middle of the night to write those scenes down, thankfully I remembered them the next morning and some of those dreams have made their way into the book. I'll give you a hint of one dream I used in a scene. It involves some funny "rules."

This couple surprised me repeatedly when I was awake and writing, too. I was enthralled with Bellingham and Laura. Yes, I know the ideas come from me, but sometimes, it almost feels as if the characters really do leap off the page. That was certainly the case for Bell and Laura.

As the writing progressed, I often felt as if I were peeling off another layer of Bellingham's character. He is a man with deep wounds and very determined not to stir up the past. Yet I realized that subconsciously his actions were informed by all that had happened to him as a young man. I knew it would take a very special heroine to help him reconcile his past. Laura knows what he needs, and though he doesn't make it easy for her, she never gives up.

I confess I still have a bit of a crush on Bellingham. ☺
I hope you will, too.

Enjoy!

*VickyDreiling.com*
*Facebook.com*
*Twitter @vickydreiling*

♥ ♥ ♥ ♥ ♥ ♥ ♥ ♥ ♥ ♥ ♥ ♥ ♥ ♥ ♥ ♥

# From the desk of Stella Cameron

Frog Crossing
Out West

Dear Reader,

My dog, Millie, doesn't like salt water, or bath water, or
rain—but it is the sight of all seven pounds of her trying
to drink Puget Sound that stays with me. Urged to walk
into about half an inch of ripples bubbling over pebbles
on a beach, she slurped madly as if she could get rid of
anything wet that might touch her feet.

That picture just popped into my head once more,
just as I thought about what I might write to you about

the Chimney Rock books and how stories shape up for me.

We were standing at the water's edge on Whidbey Island, looking across Saratoga Passage toward Camano Island. *Darkness Bound*, the first book in the series, was finished and now it was time for DARKNESS BRED, on sale now.

Elin and Sean were already my heroine and hero. I knew that much before I finished the previous story, but there were so many other questions hanging around. And so many unfinished and important parts of lives I had already shown you. When we write books there's a balancing act between telling/showing too much, and the opposite. Every character clamors to climb in but only those important to the current story can have a ticket to enter. The trick is to weed out the loudest and least interesting from the ones we *have* to know about.

The hidden world on Whidbey Island is busy, and gets busier. Once you are inside it's not just colorful and varied, sometimes endearing and often scary, it is also addictive. Magic and mystery rub shoulders with what sometimes seems…just simply irresistible. How can I not want to explore every character's tale?

That's what makes me feel a bit like Millie draining Puget Sound of water—I have to clear away what I don't want until I find the best stuff. Only I'm more fortunate than my dog because I do get to make all the difference.

Now you have your ticket to ride along with me again—enjoy every inch!

All the best,

Stella Cameron

♥     ♥     ♥     ♥

## *From the desk of Rochelle Alers*

Dear Reader,

How many of us had high school crushes, then years later come face-to-face with the boy who will always hold a special place in our hearts? This is what happens with Morgan Dane in HAVEN CREEK. At thirteen she'd believed herself in love with high school hunk, Nathaniel Shaw, but as a tall, skinny girl constantly teased for her prepubescent body, she can only worship him from afar.

I wanted HAVEN CREEK to become a modern-day fairy tale complete with a beautiful princess and a handsome prince, and, as in every fairy tale, there is something that will keep them apart before they're able to live happily ever after. The princess in HAVEN CREEK lives her life by a set of inflexible rules, while it is a family secret that makes it nearly impossible for the prince to trust anyone.

You will reunite with architect Morgan Dane, who has been commissioned to oversee the restoration of Angels Landing Plantation. As she begins the task of hiring local artisans for the project, she knows the perfect candidate to supervise the reconstruction of the slave village. He is master carpenter and prodigal son Nathaniel Shaw.

Although Nate has returned to his boyhood home, he has become a recluse while he concentrates on running his family's furniture-making business and keeping his younger brother out of trouble. But everything changes when Morgan asks him to become involved in her restoration project. It isn't what she's offering that presents a challenge to Nate, but it is Morgan herself. When he left the Creek she was a shy teenage girl. Now she is a confident, thirtysomething woman holding him completely enthralled with her brains *and* her beauty.

In HAVEN CREEK you will travel back to the Lowcountry with its magnificent sunsets; slow, meandering creeks and streams; primordial swamps teeming with indigenous wildlife; a pristine beach serving as a year-round recreational area; and the residents of the island with whom you've become familiar.

Church, community, and family—and not necessarily in that order—are an integral part of Lowcountry life, and never is that more apparent than on Cavanaugh Island. As soon as you read the first page of HAVEN CREEK you will be given an up-close and personal look into the Gullah culture with its island-wide celebrations, interactions at family Sunday dinners, and a quixotic young woman who has the gift of sight.

The gossipmongers are back along with the region's famous mouth-watering cuisine and a supporting cast of characters—young *and* old—who will keep you laughing throughout the novel.

Read, enjoy, and do let me hear from you!!!

*Rochelle Alers*

ralersbooks@aol.com
www.rochellealers.org

♥

*From the desk of Laura Drake*

Dear Readers,

Who can resist a cowboy?

Not me. Especially a bull rider, who has the courage to get on two thousand pounds of attitude that wants to throw him in the dirt and dance on his dangling parts. But you don't need to be familiar with rodeo to enjoy THE SWEET SPOT. It's an emotional story first, about two people dealing with real-life problems, and rediscovering love at the end of a long dirt road.

To introduce you to Charla Rae Denny, the heroine of THE SWEET SPOT, I thought I'd share with you her list of life lessons:

1. Before you throw your ex off your ranch, be sure you know how to run it.
2. A Goth-Dolly Parton lookalike *can* make a great friend. And Dumpster monkeys are helpful, too.
3. Next time, start a hardware store instead of a bucking bull business—the stock doesn't try to commit suicide every few minutes.
4. "Never trust a husband too far, nor a bachelor too near." —Helen Rowland
5. If you're the subject of the latest gossip-fest, stay away from the Clip-n-Curl.
6. Life is full of second chances, if you can get over yourself enough to grab them.

7.  "To forgive is to set a prisoner free, and discover that
    the prisoner is you." —Louis B. Smede

I hope you'll enjoy THE SWEET SPOT, and look for
JB and Charla in the next two books in the series!

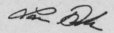

OKANAGAN REGIONAL LIBRARY
3 3132 03457 4006